CATCHING

SHADOWS

Ana Ban

Catching Shadows by Ana Ban

Glenda,
All the best!
Ana Bane

For Aunt Deb Boldt, who has had faith in my writing longer
than I've known.

CONTENTS

Part One

Infiltration

SHE'D FOUND DONOVAN. IT WAS no more than a flash, a brief glimpse of his profile in the shadows of a building, but there remained no doubt in her mind it was him. She would know him anywhere. Mia looked up as her partner leaned a hip against the desk.

"It's seven o'clock," Alec said. Her lack of response was not a surprise to him. "Go home."

"Sure."

"Mia," he said, waiting until her gaze met his. "Go home. It can wait."

Frustrated, she leaned back in her chair and linked her hands behind her head. "Eighteen months, Alec. Eighteen months we've been chasing a ghost, and this is all we've got. A couple of lucky shots from CCTV."

"And any more time here tonight will not change that. Go home. You have a date, remember?"

"Yeah, you're right. I shouldn't be late again."

With a satisfied nod, Alec pushed off the desk and studied her just a moment longer. "Promise me you'll get some sleep tonight, too."

"Trying to tell me I need beauty rest?" Mia said it as a tease, even knowing he was right. Standing, she gathered a few files to review before bed.

Alec shook his head but didn't bother to remind her it was supposed to be a night off. "No. I'm telling you that you need sleep. For once, listen to me, would you?"

She sent him a faint smile. "I'll do my best."

Jogging to the lot across the street, Mia threw the files on her passenger seat and started the engine. Glancing in the mirror, she frowned at her reflection, rubbing at the mascara smeared beneath her eye. With a sigh, she realized she wasn't wearing mascara.

Though Mia would never admit it to his face, Alec was right. She needed sleep; she just doubted that would happen until Selena and Donovan were caught.

Selena and Donovan weren't the only case Mia and Alec had worked in the last year and a half, but it was the most frustrating. The mystery of it consumed her. The lack of evidence infuriated her. Mia knew, *knew*, that the inexplicable quantities of art and artifacts showing up on the black market were the criminal duo's handiwork, but she had no proof. It bothered Alec, too, but not the way it ate at Mia. He could leave it at work, enjoy his downtime. Mia tried. She'd been seeing Cole for a few months, enjoyed the dinners and theater and even enjoyed the sex. But her brain never switched off. She never left the job on the job.

Cole was a great temporary distraction, a casual good time, but he wasn't—and would never be—more than that. Mia couldn't see herself getting seriously involved with him, with anyone. Not now. Maybe not ever.

Still, she hurried home, jumped in the shower and was out again in record time. Sweeping her hair up into a messy bun, Mia rubbed some concealer under her eyes, slipped on a slinky black dress, and was back out the door in twenty minutes.

She'd still be late, but luckily, Cole seemed to be understanding about her tardiness.

△ △ △

FIFTEEN MINUTES. COLE HAD BEEN sitting at a table, waiting, for fifteen minutes. He'd dressed in black slacks with a dark blue shirt that brought out his eyes, leaving the top buttons undone for that carefully disheveled look. He checked his watch yet again. No one made him wait. Things had to change with Mia, and they had to change tonight.

She arrived, planting a quick kiss on his cheek. When Mia slid into the opposite chair, Cole took the time to appreciate the ample amount of cleavage the little black number offered. "You look great."

"Thanks. And sorry I'm late."

"I'm used to it by now. Just glad you're here," Cole said, opening his menu. No reason to start with reprimands. There would be time for that later. "I've ordered some appetizers; thought you might be hungry."

"Starved."

She looked tired, Cole noted. A classic workaholic. That would change. He studied her dark hair secured on top of her head by several pins, thought about how it would look when he took each of those pins out later. He liked to watch her hair tumble down around her shoulders. Those auburn streaks that would catch the light and helped her look a bit less exotic.

Mia Gonzalez was the perfect arm-candy, the ideal supplement for his envisioned future. Her job would have to go, of course. She could spend her time devoted to the things other well-to-do wives dallied with, fundraising and luncheons and the like. He fingered the ring in his pocket. He'd picked the swanky oyster bar on the waterfront for the proposal. She'd never been here. Cole knew most of her meals were by delivery service to the central precinct. The waterfront was an odd mixture of upscale restaurants and warehouse buildings, interspersed with trendy nightclubs. Things Mia liked to avoid, but he would change that, too.

5

"My parents are hosting a party for the governor this weekend. It will be the next step in furthering my own career," he said as she perused the menu. Mia answered with a murmur of assent, so he continued. "I'll announce my bid for congress early next year. The campaign trail can be long and arduous, but I think you'll adjust winningly."

"Mmhmm."

Mia would be his perfect complement; she would pull in the minority vote without making any of his contributors uncomfortable. He caught sight of the waiter with the bottle of champagne, making his way toward their table. Cole palmed the ring and continued his speech. "Candidates traditionally do better when they're in a committed relationship. I'd like you to be with me, Mia. Not just as my girlfriend."

Folding the menu and setting it on the table, Mia struggled to focus. "I'm sorry, Cole, what were you saying?"

Cole sighed, leaning back in his chair and fidgeting with the ring, still hidden under the table. "You haven't heard a word I've said."

"No, I just..." Excuses came to mind, but they didn't seem adequate. "Please, I'm all yours. Talk to me."

"My parents are hosting a party for the governor," he began again.

Almost instantly, he lost her eye contact. He watched as she scanned the front of the building, her eyes snagging on something outside.

"It's the next step in my plan to run for congress," Cole continued. Mia nodded, but again, her eyes strayed. Cole had had enough. "Really, Mia, you can't even give me five minutes?"

"Cole, I'm sorry, I have to go—"

Before she could finish, Cole threw up his hands. "Why do I even bother? Is this work?"

"Yes," Mia said, already grabbing her small purse, feeling for the gun on a leg holster. "I thought you understood."

"Understood that your work takes precedence over everything? No, I don't get it. And let me say, if you walk out that door now, we're done." That caught her attention. She stared at him for a full five seconds before slowly shaking her head.

"I'm sorry you feel that way," she said, genuine sorrow in her tone.

With one last melancholy look, Mia turned to rush out the door. The waiter arrived with the champagne. Angry, jilted, Cole sent it back. "Bring me a bottle of whiskey instead."

△ △ △

ONCE OUTSIDE, MIA WHIPPED HER cell phone to her ear. "Alec. How fast can you get to Thames and South Ann Street?"

"Five minutes. What's up?"

"Make it two. I think I've found Donovan."

Before he could respond, Mia ended the call and slipped the phone back into the purse, simultaneously flipping the switch to silent. Though it was just a small clutch, she never would have purchased it without the long cord attached. Quickly slinging it over her head, Mia half ran down the street.

She'd seen a man walking in front of the restaurant—tall, lean, dressed in black. His dark hair cut close, his eyes on the ground. And though he seemed as if he wasn't paying attention, Mia knew he was well aware of every detail.

Continuing in the direction she'd seen what her gut told her was the criminal mastermind and right hand to Selena, she whipped her head back and forth, searching. Down a narrow side street, she saw a dark figure pause at a doorway and silently followed. Sticking close to the wall, gun now at the ready, Mia made the approach on her toes to keep her heels from clacking against the pavement.

He began to turn her way, and she immediately dropped into a crouch behind a dumpster. Heart hammering in her chest, she counted to five before risking a glance.

He was gone.

"Damnit," she said aloud, on her feet once again.

Running to the door, trying the knob even though she knew it would be locked, Mia reached into her tangle of hair for a pin that could jimmy the lock. A hand grabbed her wrist, and before she could respond, she was shoved against the wall in a small crevice beside the door.

An unyielding body and unbreakable grip left her immobile as a harsh voice whispered in her ear. "Don't move."

Years of training kicked into gear. Classics were classics for a reason. Mia shot her heel up toward her attacker's groin. Though a knee blocked the assault, she used the off-balance position to her advantage.

She pulled against the grip on her wrist, as an attacker's automatic response is to pull back. As he did, Mia went with the momentum and, in a move almost dancelike, twirled to become face to face with him.

Recognition hit at the same time her free fist made contact with the ribs. He released a small grunt of pain.

"Alec," she whispered in relief and annoyance. "What the hell?"

Not speaking, Alec simply put a finger to her lips.. Forgetting for a moment that her partner had slammed her against the wall and was still invading her personal space, Mia listened carefully. Within seconds the voices she heard became clear.

"...meeting tonight. Think we'll get the details ahead of time, or on the fly like normal?" the first voice said.

"Are you kidding? She would never trust anyone to know anything except Donovan. We knew that going in," the second voice answered.

"Yeah, I'd just like to know what's going on for a change."

"That's not what we're paid for."

There was a knock—two quick, one pause, three quick. A code?

The door opened and talking ceased. When it closed again with the two criminals on the opposite side, Alec released Mia from the wall. "Please tell me you were not about to go charging into a building, illegally, by yourself, while these two goons were coming up behind you."

Mia could see the anger in Alec's eyes and knew it came from fear. "If you want the truth, I can't tell you that."

"What were you thinking? You could have been killed. You think that's above these guys? Killing a cop? Killing a woman? It's not!"

"I'm sorry, Alec. You're right. I wasn't thinking," Mia said in an attempt to calm her partner down.

Approaching him, she could see every muscle was tense as if he prepared for a fight. Laying a hand gently on his arm, Mia waited for him to make eye contact. His eyes, usually a deep, calm green with specks of brown, were now on fire. Slowly, one muscle at a time, she felt him begin to relax. The flames eventually receded, leaving only a spark.

Alec took a deep breath before speaking. "I thought you had a date."

Grinning then, she knew she'd been forgiven. The smile disappeared just as quickly as it had appeared. "I did. When I saw Donovan, he was walking past the restaurant. I couldn't let the opportunity pass me by. Cole didn't agree."

"Oh," Alec said in understanding. "I'm sorry, Mia."

With a casual shrug, she began walking toward the street. "My work comes first."

"Well, since we're both free, how about a little dinner? I hear the Chinese place on this street delivers."

His car was parked at the end of the narrow street, in position to see anyone entering or exiting the alley. Mia opened the passenger door and slid inside, entirely at home. "Sounds perfect. I'm starving, and you're buying."

In the end, though they sat for several hours, the stakeout was a bust. Even Alec's assurances did nothing to boost her spirit.

Alec managed to convince Mia to go home and catch a few hours' sleep, but she arrived at the station bright and early. As she scanned through the street videos for the third time, she took a sip of the thick liquid that passed for coffee in the station. With eight years on the Baltimore PD, she had every CCTV camera and angle in her precinct memorized from thousands of hours watching them for a perp.

Selena had done such an excellent job of remaining a ghost that Mia had no idea what she looked like. No photos, no first-hand accounts. For that matter, Mia and Alec weren't even positive Selena was a female. They had a name, and only a name, to go off of.

Donovan was almost as good at avoiding cameras, but over the last four years that he'd been on police radar, they had gotten two clear shots of the mysterious man and several more partials. There were also numerous eyewitness reports by petty criminals they'd arrested, who'd squealed after mere hours in lock-up.

None of these had ever dealt with Selena directly. For a while, Mia had toyed with the theory that Selena didn't exist, and Donovan was the true leader. Something in her gut told her otherwise, and it seemed to be popular opinion that the elusive criminal was real.

"Anything?" came a voice from the doorway.

Mia glanced at Alec and shook her head. "He's good."

"We're better," Alec said with a grin, sinking into the chair beside her and placing a sandwich on the table.

"Thanks," she said, smiling appreciatively. Taking a bite, her eyes continued to follow the screens.

"Didn't sleep well, did you?"

"No. As usual." Alec slid a small piece of paper in front of her. Sparing it a glance, Mia scoffed. "Therapy? Really?"

"Sleeping disorders are a real thing. If you don't want to talk through your issues, you could at least get some drugs—"

"I don't take drugs," she interrupted him.

"I realize you're against medication, and for good reason, but if you could see what I see..." Alec trailed off, seeming nervous. Her eyes flicked to him, surprised. "I'm just concerned if you don't start getting proper sleep, it will affect your judgment, your health."

"You're worried about my decision last night to go after Donovan alone."

"Yes. Among other things."

Not wanting to argue, knowing she hadn't had a clear head the night before, Mia nodded. "I'll think about it."

"There's something I need to tell you." Mia looked at Alec again, hearing a strange note in his voice. "Cole Prior was brought in last night. DWI. He's sleeping it off in the tank."

"Shit." Mia closed her eyes a moment, allowing the guilt to wash over her. "It's my fault. I shouldn't have left him alone."

"There's more, Mia. Among his personal belongings, he had a ring—an engagement ring."

"An engagement—Christ, we've only been dating a few months. We hadn't even said the L-word."

"I just thought you would want to know."

"I'll go speak to him. Thanks, Alec." Stopping at intake on the way, Mia headed to the holding cells and found Cole sitting on one of the cots, his back against the wall and his eyes closed. "Cole?"

He opened his eyes, the bloodshot whites testament to his night. "Enjoying this, aren't you?"

"Why would you say that? Cole, I care about you. If I'd had any idea that you'd end up in here last night—"

He cocked his head to the side. "You'd have what? Stayed? Don't kid yourself, Mia."

An officer arrived to unlock the cell. Giving him a grim smile, Mia glanced over to Cole again. "You're free to go. I've brought your things."

For a moment, Cole's eyes widened before he slipped back into his carefully nonchalant demeanor. "I guess these last few months weren't a total waste."

His attitude hurt her but also helped her realize this parting was for the best. "Cole, about that ring..."

"It was a mistake. Don't worry, I won't be making it again. See you around, Detective Gonzalez."

Mia watched him leave with a strange mix of remorse and melancholy. Not exactly how she should be feeling after a break-up. No tears had come last night, and none came now. She only felt guilt and just a smidgen of relief.

Only one thing would take her mind off Cole Prior: throwing herself into work.

That night, Mia found herself parked outside the same building, trying her luck on a different entrance. The buildings were some of the oldest in the city, big brick affairs with undoubtedly twisting pathways and endless hallways inside. There were also several well-known tunnels from out-of-service trains, along with the theorists who believed there were hidden tunnels further below ground—existing from the days of prohibition, or the underground railroad, or some other wild story that had no proof.

Still, she'd often wondered if there were any truth to the seemingly outlandish claims. It would certainly explain their lack of ability to catch Selena on camera.

There was a tap on her window, and Mia jumped. It was unlike her to be caught off-guard—and that, if nothing else, told her she was running on fumes. The thought reminded her of the card tucked into her back pocket that Alec had given her earlier in the day.

Rolling the window down a few inches to the man himself, Mia accepted the small object he passed through even as he gave her a mild reprimand. "You didn't call me."

Knowing she was in trouble, Mia was contrite enough to look sheepish. Tucking the small earbud that he'd handed her into her ear, she said, "Thanks, partner."

"One of these days, you're going to give me a heart attack," he complained with a smile. "I'll take the east side of the building. Let's catch us a bad guy."

Grinning back, she gave him a thumbs-up and rolled up the window. He disappeared around the corner, and Mia settled in for a long night.

Several hours later, she spotted activity down one of the narrow alleys. Sitting up straight and squinting into the dark, she notified Alec. "Three bogeys. By the build looks like men. I'm going to get a closer look."

"Wait for me," Alec said through the earpiece.

Ignoring him and slipping out of the car, she ran to the edge of the building, risking a glance around the corner. Two men had disappeared through a doorway; the third stood in the alley, taking a slow look around him. Perhaps he had sensed her presence. Instinct had her ducking her head behind the wall.

13

"That's him," she said in a deep whisper of excitement. "I'm going after him."

"You will wait for me." Alec sounded sterner than she'd ever heard him, and it made her pause. But he could be minutes away, and Mia had only a moment to decide.

"I'm sorry." The words were merely a thread of sound. She took off down the alley as the door Donovan had walked through began to close. Slipping through the crack just before the door shut with a soft click, Mia found herself launched into the pitch dark.

Tentatively extending a hand, she brushed against something soft, like cloth. Exactly like cloth. Before she could react, her back got slammed against a wall so hard her breath escaped her lungs in one aching breath. The earbud slipped from her ear and bounced along the floor. Struggling just to breathe, her arms flailed about wildly.

"Who are you?" a deep voice growled in her ear.

Though her fists continuously made contact against the hard body pressed up against her, Mia made no impact whatsoever. Sagging against the wall, allowing the strong arm still pressed against her middle to support her weight, she made a conscious effort to speak.

"My name is Detective Gonzalez...and you're under arrest."

The deep, rough laugh that should have sent chills down her spine instead sent heat curling wildly, starting in the pit of her stomach and spiraling along each nerve ending. She caught her breath just enough to inhale a deep woodsy scent with subtle hints of citrus. Before she could analyze any of it, he spoke again. Without the snarl that accompanied his earlier words, his Irish brogue was prevalent. "The infamous Mia Gonzalez. So lovely to finally meet you. Unfortunately, we won't be able to chat as your partner is just outside the door. Another time, perhaps."

Mia felt a sharp prick in her upper arm. She collapsed, the darkness now complete.

Two

"MIA...OPEN YOUR EYES FOR me...that's a good girl."

The voice seemed familiar, yet not what she wanted to hear. What happened to the deep, musical lilt that moved through her like velvet against the skin? A hand squeezed hers gently, but it felt too soft. She moved away, searching for another's touch. She craved the rough fingertips of...

The thought shot Mia's eyes open, and she saw her partner sigh in relief.

"Alec." Mia tried to speak, but her voice felt coarse. She wondered what type of drug she'd been shot with. Alec moved a straw to her lips, and she took a few deep, grateful sips. "What happened?"

He put the straw in position again, and she sipped while Alec spoke. "You went after Donovan. Alone. After I told you to wait." The anger in his voice was still very much in evidence. He took a breath before continuing. "When I got to the alley, you'd already lost your earbud. I broke the door down and found you lying on a landing. There was no access to the main level, only stairs leading up or down. After I called for an ambulance and backup, I waited with you. Do you remember what happened?"

"He...drugged me," she managed. "I got in the door before it closed, but it was pitch black. He had me pinned against the wall...he said...something."

The interaction seemed shrouded in a hazy mist, a lovely side effect to being knocked out. The part she did remember, in vivid detail, was her response to his touch, the sound of his laugh...

Mia decided not to even try to explain her purely feminine reaction to Donovan's presence. How could she? It didn't even make sense to herself.

After speaking, she coughed to clear her throat, and Alec soothed her. "Shh, it's all right, you rest now. You've been out about an hour, and you need to sleep. We can talk more in the morning."

"Did they search the building?" Mia asked as a doctor came in. Alec must have pushed a button when she'd woken up.

After doing the routine checks, the doctor told her the bloodwork returned with positive traces of Ketamine. She was familiar with the name as an anesthesia, and it explained her fuzzy memory. They were doing more tests to be sure that was all that was in her system.

Once the doctor left, she stared at Alec, waiting for him to answer. "They found nothing."

"Nothing?" she asked, incredulous.

"They searched the entire building. It was all empty rooms."

"Obviously, there's a hidden passage or underground tunnel," she began but stopped at Alec's expression. "What is it?"

"We're off the case, Mia."

"What?" She began to sit up, enraged. "How could they do that?"

"You know perfectly well why. You acted emotionally, putting yourself and me at risk. You've not been thinking clearly."

Mia sank back into the pillow, fury rolling through her. "What else?"

He sighed heavily, knowing he couldn't hide the truth from her. They knew each other too well. "Therapy is no longer optional."

"Great. Desk job and a shrink. What are they having you do?"

Alec's eyes tightened; he was obviously unhappy with the next part. His next words hit like a blow to her chest. "I'm being reassigned."

"New partner."

"For now," he clarified, though it sounded more like wishful thinking.

She nodded, unable to look him in the eye. "I think I'll rest now."

He stood, and Mia felt his hand squeeze hers again. He pressed his lips against her forehead for a brief moment before he left. Curling into a ball, she felt a single tear roll down her cheek before giving in to her exhaustion.

△ △ △

THE DOCTOR'S OFFICE WAS IN the middle of a strip mall, sandwiched between a hairdresser and a psychic. Mia had a fleeting thought that she'd have better luck at the psychic.

A bell jangled as she pulled open the door, and the receptionist glanced up with a tight smile. "Can I help you?"

"I have an appointment at one-thirty."

"Have a seat. Dr. Engel will be right out."

Nodding, Mia slid into one of the plaid cloth chairs near the window. There were several magazines scattered on a low table, but she ignored them to gaze outside.

She'd been released from the hospital yesterday, and after taking the rest of the day off, had had a long meeting with the chief that morning. Oddly, he didn't seem upset, more concerned. That worried Mia more than if he had just yelled.

He had also wasted no time in setting her up with a therapist.

After a few minutes, the door opened, and a woman who looked to be in her forties walked out, her pale red hair pulled back into a ponytail. "Detective Gonzalez?"

Standing, Mia held out her hand to shake. "Mia, please."

Nodding, Dr. Engel gestured into the office. "Have a seat."

The inside of the office had been sparsely decorated with a single bookshelf behind a wooden desk. Four chairs were positioned in a loose circle in front of the desk. Mia chose one and sat.

Dr. Engel settled in beside her, perching a notebook on her lap. "So, Mia. Can you tell me about why you're here?"

"I was asked to do sessions after making a poor decision in the field."

Dr. Engel studied her. "Would you elaborate on that?"

Shifting in her chair, Mia explained, "I was on a stake-out with my partner. We were covering two different doors, and I spotted the perp at mine. We've been chasing this person for a year and a half. I went after him. My partner asked me to wait, but I didn't want to miss the opportunity."

"That doesn't seem like a big offense."

"It happened twice. In a row."

"Even still." Dr. Engel leaned forward, bracing one elbow on her knee. "Why else are you here?"

"I haven't been sleeping well.".

"Since when?"

Mia let out a short laugh. "Since forever."

"I see." Dr. Engel leaned back again, jotting a few notes down. "Has it become more severe? Do you believe it's affecting your judgment?"

"I was something of an insomniac before I joined the force. Most nights since, I just feel restless, never feeling refreshed after sleep. The last couple of years have been worse, and my partner seemed worried that my lack of sleep was impairing my decisions."

"But you don't."

Mia shrugged.

"When you deprive yourself of sleep, your physical state can become akin to being drunk, which, as I'm sure we both know, can absolutely affect your judgment. I can prescribe you a medication which will assist with keeping you asleep at night, but in our sessions together, I'd like to uncover the root of the problem."

"I don't like taking drugs," Mia said firmly.

"That is something I'm aware of, but it may be the only short-term solution we have. It's also why I would like to continue sessions with you, to solve your sleeping problem instead of just covering it up with drugs, as you said."

And, if she didn't follow Dr. Engel's advice, Mia would also be looking at more than just a desk job. Paid leave was not the vacation it sounded like.

Resolving to do whatever it took to get back in her chief's good graces, Mia nodded her consent.

Before she left, Mia set up weekly appointments with Dr. Engel. This seemed excessive to her, but she was willing to do whatever it took to get back to her real life.

When she arrived back at the station, Alec waited for her, eyebrows raised. "How did it go?"

"Fine," she said quietly. "I'll pick up a prescription tonight that's supposed to help me sleep. She promised me it wasn't a permanent solution."

Alec seemed relieved and squeezed her shoulder before returning to his desk. Sighing, Mia made herself comfortable and immersed herself in paperwork. By the end of the day, her back ached from lack of movement, and she glared at the chair as she stood to pack up her things.

Mia knew it wasn't the chair's fault. It was hers, but it was so much easier to be angry at an inanimate object.

After work, she stopped to pick up her prescription at the pharmacy. She stared at the bottle a long time that night before finally shaking out a pill and downing it with a glass of water.

Half an hour later, she was asleep.

△ △ △

It WAS A STRUGGLE TO open her eyes, but as a glaring noise penetrated into her brain, Mia realized her alarm was going off, as it had been for several minutes. Reaching out to feel for the snooze button without having to open her eyes, she cut off the noise before curling back up with a groan. Her eyes felt heavy, as if she were waking from sedation, and her whole body felt weak.

There were many reasons she stayed away from medication; this feeling was a major one.

On the upside, she had slept a solid seven hours. The downside of that is now her body craved more. Forcing herself to get up, Mia trudged to the kitchen to pour herself a steaming mug of coffee. She drank it down, black, scalding her throat in the process, but she didn't care. Immediately refilling the cup, she waited impatiently for the caffeine to kick in.

Dressing mechanically, Mia made her way to the precinct, lacking the motivation that had been her driving force for the last eight years. A demotion—which is not what the chief called it, but it was nonetheless—had left her as a shell of the person she had been just three days ago.

Instead of dwelling on that fact, she just did as she was asked, and soon the paperwork and therapy sessions became routine.

On her second session, she'd been using the sleeping medication for six nights. Though she'd been sleeping, Mia still felt groggy upon waking instead of refreshed. When she asked the doctor if that would change, her answer didn't give much encouragement.

"Your body will adjust, but you may always have that lingering feeling of grogginess in the morning. Once I feel confident that we're on the right track with your sessions, we can reduce your dosage to half a pill." Mia nodded, accepting that, for the foreseeable future, she wouldn't feel like herself. When she didn't offer up a topic of conversation, Dr. Engel prompted, "Tell me about your family."

With a sigh, Mia answered vaguely, "I don't have any family." Dr. Engel pursed her lips, waiting for her to go on. She did with reluctance. "My father died when I was thirteen. My mother died when I was sixteen. No brothers or sisters, and the little bit of extended family I know of doesn't speak to me."

"That must be a lonely life," the doctor commented.

It was irritating, the typical blame-the-parents for everything wrong in your adult life. "Not really. My work is fulfilling, and I have good friends."

"Mia," Dr. Engel said gently. "I've seen your file."

Mia's eyes dropped to her hands, clasped together in her lap. Of course the doctor had seen the file. "Then you know why I'd prefer not to talk about it."

Dr. Engel nodded. "All right, we'll leave it for today. Tell me about your romantic relationships."

Rolling her eyes, Mia felt herself getting snippy. Before answering with snark, she took a deep breath. "They're pretty much nonexistent."

"Do you blame your work for that?"

"No." Mia's voice hardened. "I blame myself."

"Why is that?"

"Because work is my priority, and I haven't met someone who made me feel differently."

"How often do you date?"

"Occasionally." Dr. Engel paused again, and Mia knew that meant she was waiting for her to open up. Though this was necessary to get her life back, it was still frustrating. "The last person I dated was Cole. We were together for about three months, dating casually. We'd go out to dinner, or the movies, when we both had time. I thought he was understanding about my work. Turned out, he wasn't."

"It can be difficult to forge a relationship with someone who doesn't fully understand your commitment to your work. It's a commendable trait, but I hope you realize that there is more to life than work?"

"Like I've said, I just haven't met someone more important to me than my job. When I do, it'll be different."

"Hmm," Dr. Engel murmured, writing notes on her pad. It was becoming difficult for Mia to reel in her annoyance. "Do you think it really will be different?"

"Why wouldn't it be?"

"Mia," the doctor said, pausing in her writing to make eye contact. "We all have a tendency to have the 'one-day' attitude. One day I'll eat healthier, one day I'll meet the man of my dreams, one day everything will just magically fall into place. I believe you have a good head on your shoulders, a realistic mindset. The truth is, we get what we put into things. Your work is fulfilling because you put everything into it. How do you think your relationships would be different if you gave them the same effort and attention?"

Mia opened her mouth to respond but shut it again. It wasn't that she couldn't see the truth to the words—she did and understood the concept. "What if I choose to date men who I know I have no future with on purpose? Knowing that I'm not ready for a bigger commitment yet?"

Dr. Engel seemed satisfied by the response, nodding and jotting down more notes. "That could very well be true. But I'll tell you a secret: none of us is truly ready for the things that matter the most."

Her words rang through Mia's head the rest of the day, and as she finished her shift, she saw Alec returning. His new partner was Detective Malone, who'd been on the force for about five years but had just made detective. Alec and Mia had made detective within a couple of months of each other, so she was sure he was enjoying passing all his knowledge on to the younger man.

Approaching them, Mia greeted them both by last name. "Woods. Malone."

"Hey, Detective Gonzalez," Malone said with an eager smile.

"Mia, please." Alec watched the exchange with a bemused expression.

"Yes, ma'am. Mia. And you can call me Adam. We were just going over a case, but I can give you a few minutes if you want to talk..." He gestured between Alec and her, and Mia smiled gratefully.

"I won't keep him long."

Alec raised an eyebrow at her once Adam was out of earshot. "He's like a lost puppy dog."

Letting out an appreciative laugh, she answered, "He's sweet. I hope he can stay that way with the things he'll see in this line of work."

Alec nodded. "That's always a difficult thing, watching good people become hardened over time." He studied her for a moment, and Mia wondered exactly what he saw. She felt a little raw after therapy. "How was your session today?"

One shoulder rose up before she let it drop. "Fine. The doctor's really good at digging."

"I'm sure that's hell for you," Alec said with a lopsided grin.

Offering him a small smile back, Mia squeezed her hands together nervously. "Here's the thing, Alec..."

Before she could finish her thought, they were interrupted, the urgency in Adam's voice undeniable. "Alec! We have to go, now!"

Alec reacted quickly, glancing at Mia for just a moment. "I'm sorry."

Waving him off, she backed away from his desk. "Go, it sounds important."

"We'll talk later," Alec called over his shoulder as he followed his new partner out the door.

Shoulders slumped, Mia walked back to her desk. She had finally been ready to admit to her feelings for her partner—but if his sudden departure wasn't a sign to keep her mouth shut, she didn't know what was.

Three

MIA SAT IN THE SAME chair of the therapist's office, picking at a stray thread sticking out of the fabric. She'd answered every question in each session but didn't feel like she was required to offer up details unprompted.

"How have you been sleeping?" the doctor asked, finally breaking the silence.

"Like a rock, thanks to the medication."

"Are you feeling more alert during the day?"

"Yes, and no. I'm still a bit groggy when I wake up, and it takes me a while for that feeling to dissipate. I don't really ever feel like I have a lot of energy, but I'm consistent."

"Did you have a lot of high and low energy before the medication?"

"I suppose you could say that. Doesn't everyone?"

Dr. Engel paused in her note-taking to meet Mia's eyes. "Our sessions aren't about everyone else; they're about you."

"Fine. Want to hear about my dreams next or something?"

"Have you been having dreams?"

"Not since I started taking the medication."

"Before that?"

Mia shifted in her chair once. Why had she opened her mouth? "Pretty much nightly."

"What were they about?"

"Nightmares, mostly. Disconnected realities, nothing that ever really made sense. There were a lot of times I'd wake up feeling like I'd run a marathon."

"Do you sleepwalk?"

"Not that I know of."

"Has anyone ever told you that you talk in your sleep or sleep fitfully?"

"I've lived alone since I was sixteen."

"None of your romantic partners ever spent the night?"

"No," Mia said, feeling uncomfortable again. Dr. Engel was very good at that. "Like I said before, I've never met anyone who I trusted that much."

"I think we can start cutting your pill in half. Give that a try for a week; let me know next week how that goes. If you're starting to not sleep again, you can always take the whole pill."

"That sounds good to me."

"Is there anything else you'd like to talk about today?" Dr. Engel asked after studying Mia for a moment.

"Not really. I've just been feeling a little useless lately."

"That's understandable, going from field work to office work. Is there anything else that's making you feel that way?"

Mia smiled ruefully. "I'm working regular hours now, which leaves me with more time at home than I had before. I spend my downtime working out, but paperwork just doesn't fulfill me the same way."

"That's a common issue for workaholics. I see it most often in retirees, who go from working seventy-hour weeks to suddenly having free time; they realize they have no outside interests or hobbies. Did you have any interests when you were younger that you could try again?"

Mia's life before her parents died had not exactly been conducive to hobbies, but she didn't want to bring that up right then. And since she'd been working from her fourteenth birthday, she hadn't had much time since to figure out what she liked to do for fun. "There might be something."

"If you're not sure what you're interested in, I can give you a copy of the local paper. There are always classes and group get-togethers; you never know what might strike your interest."

Mia agreed and took the paper. Sitting on her couch, feet curled beneath her, Mia examined the calendar of events. Arts and crafts? No thanks. Photography? Not her thing. Cooking classes? She laughed aloud.

Finally, toward the bottom of the page, she spotted a four-week class on Morse Code. She couldn't imagine there'd be much interest in learning such an outdated skill, but it grabbed her attention. It could be fun and possibly useful in her line of work. There was an online enrollment, so before she could chicken out, Mia pulled out her laptop and signed herself up.

Flipping through the rest of the paper, she spotted an ad for self-defense classes. Though she'd taken several classes with the force, it might be fun to enroll in a course outside of work. Since her laptop still sat beside her, Mia did a quick internet search and perused the many dojos available.

She ruled out the kickboxing classes, Taekwondo, and Jiu-Jitsu, along with any that were geared toward mixed martial arts fighting. While all those were a good workout, and she knew bits and pieces of them from the training she'd done, they weren't as practical for her.

Kickboxing was an excellent workout, but there really wasn't hand-to-hand combat, no sparring. Taekwondo was also a good workout and great for flexibility but impractical for real-life situations. Jiu-Jitsu focused on ground fighting, which was great to know how to get out of—but she'd learned, as a smaller female, that it was always better to stay on her feet. The same problem came up in mixed martial arts; while there were many talented people in those fights, they always took it to the ground.

That left her with a Krav Maga school, a Kenpo school, and a Muay Thai school. All three offered a free introductory lesson, and she noted the times of each class. Might as well try them all since she had nothing better to do with her time.

With a sigh, Mia stood and began her nightly cleaning ritual. Though she'd never been a messy person, she'd discovered a whole new level of OCD since being demoted.

Her apartment was on the top floor of a two-story brick building; there were four apartments on her level and four on the main. It was a quiet building on a quiet street, which suited her just fine. There were times she'd thought about buying a house, but the upkeep and maintenance was not something she'd ever had the time, or patience, for.

Her apartment had two bedrooms, two bathrooms, and a combination of living-dining-kitchen. The furniture was a hodgepodge of hand-me-downs and thrift store finds. Mia didn't care much for decorating, and as long as it was comfortable, she also didn't care what her furnishings looked like. Since she rarely had guests, and up until a few weeks ago, she'd barely spent time here, her little apartment worked just fine.

Dishes were done, coffee was prepped to begin brewing for the next morning, floors were swept, and pillows were fluffed. Pulling on rubber gloves, Mia began scrubbing down all the counters in the kitchen. The second bedroom, which she used as an office, was the most organized it had ever been due to the lack of paperwork she brought home nowadays.

Once she'd made her way through each room, Mia stopped in the doorway of her bathroom and stared at the tub. It had been a long time since she'd made up a bath and allowed herself to relax.

Inspired, Mia dug out a couple of candles and bubble bath she'd received in a Christmas gift basket. Once the water was running, she turned on some soothing music before slipping into the hot, soapy liquid.

Though it would have been nice to have a book to read, she decided instead to work on relaxation techniques. First, she focused on her breathing, bringing in air deep through her nose, pushing it down into her lower abdomen before releasing it out of her mouth. Once she'd taken several deep breaths, she picked a body part to relax one at a time until her whole body felt light and buoyant.

It wasn't an easy thing for Mia to shut off her brain, but between the rigorous cleaning and utter relaxation, she was soon fast asleep.

△ △ △

THE BED MIA LAY IN was soft and warm; she felt like she floated on a cloud. When her eyes opened, she expected there to be darkness, but there was a white-yellow glow, similar to the hour of sunrise. It was the soft light of a dream.

In her comfort, she had yet to notice the arm of steel wrapped around her waist or the hard length of a body beside her. Instead of feeling trapped, she felt secure.

"Stay with me," a voice whispered, flowing in gentle waves across her skin. "We belong together."

"I'm right here," Mia murmured back. Though her eyes were open, she couldn't make out the line of his face or the color of his eyes. He was as indistinct and fuzzy as the filtered light.

His hands began stroking along her skin, awakening in her feelings that had long since been buried. The rough pads of his fingers sent tingles down her spine. The smell of cedar and lemon sank deep into her lungs.

"Don't you want this? Don't you want me?" The voice was as familiar as a memory.

"Yes," Mia gave in. "I want you, Donovan."

△ △ △

SITTING UP WITH A START, cool water sluicing off her skin, Mia placed a hand over her racing heart. Where in the world had *that* come from?

Shaking her head to clear the haziness of the dream, Mia toweled off and drained the now cold water from the tub. Grabbing the bottle of pills from the medicine cabinet, she slipped one out and cut it in half, as Dr. Engel had instructed. If taking medication was the only way to sleep a dreamless sleep, the trade-off might be worth it.

After changing into comfortable pajamas, Mia slid into bed, unable to fully shake the vividly real feeling of being wrapped in Donovan's arms.

Mia needed more distractions. She had a trial martial arts class and the Morse Code session this week. It was a start.

Arriving early for her first Morse Code class, Mia parked in front of the community center and had a moment of doubt. She'd never been what one would call a 'joiner,' and starting something new like this, with people she didn't know, felt mildly terrifying.

Shaking herself out of the uncertainty, Mia forced herself to open the car door and walk inside. She'd only been to the community center one other time when one of the women on the force had had a baby shower there. The main room held display cases of items from Baltimore's history, like a mini-museum. Mia found a helpful clerk at an information desk, and she pointed Mia to the right room.

When she walked in, Mia found she was the first to arrive. She was surprised to see a telegraph sitting in the center of the main table. Walking closer to get a better look, she startled slightly when a voice interrupted her inspection.

"Beautiful, isn't it?" A man who looked to be in his eighties spoke in a powerful voice.

"It is," she said, then extended a hand. "I'm Mia."

"Nice to meet you." He returned the gesture. "I'm Max; I'll be the instructor for this class."

"How many people are you expecting?"

"Three, besides you. We've got a few minutes. Go ahead and make yourself comfortable."

She chose a chair and pulled out her notebook. Max wrote on the chalkboard and was just finishing when two more people came in, an older couple who introduced themselves as Jim and Patti. They were overly chatty, which worked well for Mia as long as she didn't have to talk back.

The last person arrived just as Max began to introduce himself, a quiet teenager named Ron. It was interesting to see someone so young take a class like this, and it didn't take long for Patti to ask him about it.

"I'm doing a class project on the telegraph," he told the room. "We had to pick a specific invention and how it shaped the era that it's from."

"Well, you came to the right place," Max said proudly. "I was a communications officer in World War II, so I have firsthand experience using such a fine machine."

Max gestured toward the telegraph sitting in the room and began to point out the different parts. He was extremely knowledgeable, and the four in the class were held at rapt attention.

"Did you know that the first telegraph message sent by Morse went from Washington DC to right here in Baltimore?" Max asked. Only Ron nodded. "In 1844, he sent the message, 'What hath God wrought?'"

Pulling papers from a stack on the table, Max handed each of them a copy of the Morse alphabet. Written out as it was on the paper, there was a pretty pattern to the dots and dashes.

"This is the alphabet and numeric system Morse came up with to transmit over his telegraph. On the machine, each dot is a tap, each dash is a tap that is held down for three times as long as a dot. Each dot or dash is followed by a silence equal to a dot, and each letter is separated by a silence the same length as a dash, while each word is separated by a silence the length of seven dots. That can be confusing until you hear it. Let me demonstrate with my name."

Max then tapped on the table to demonstrate, spelling out his full name, Max Hoyt.

"Do you all hear the pattern?" he asked. The class nodded, and he continued. "Great, take a few minutes to practice your own names, then we'll all have a listen."

Mia began to tap out patterns on the table.

Dash, dash. Dot, dot. Dot, Dash.

Mia.

33

She found herself having fun. Working on her last name next, it took a bit longer to get the hang of. Gonzalez sure had a lot of letters in it.

After several minutes of watching them, Max interrupted the practice. "All right, now, each of you will take a turn. For those just listening, your job is to figure out each other's last names. Any volunteers to go first?"

Ron volunteered, then began his tapping. It was a lot more difficult to interpret than Mia imagined it would be.

"Mia? What did you get for his last name?"

"I got Carey."

Patti and Jim put in their guesses, each coming up with something different than she had.

"You're all pretty close. It's Casey," Ron said.

Mia went next, and Jim was able to get her last name correct. When they had all gone—Patti using her maiden name to mix it up—they all had a new appreciation for the secretive language.

"I'd like you all to practice the alphabet for the next class, and we'll try it out on this beauty," Max said, resting a hand on the telegraph. "Thank you all for coming."

Shaking Max's hand before she left, Mia walked out as a loose group with Patti, Jim, and Ron. Patti and Jim chattered while they walked, and Mia found herself giving them a polite smile and a wave before escaping into her car.

Overall, she'd thoroughly enjoyed the class. She had two more martial arts trials set up later that week before she would make her decision on which to join. Mia looked forward to having something to devote her time to again.

None of it made going to therapy any easier. Dr. Engel smiled when Mia filled her in on her adventures of the week. "What an interesting class you chose. I'm happy to hear of your progress.

Speaking of, you've done well in your sessions so far. For your next two sessions, I'd like to go through some testing with you."

"What kind of testing?"

"Word association, ink dot, others of the same sort."

"Psych evals?" Mia raised an eyebrow. "Is that normal?"

"'Normal' is not a word I prefer to use," Dr. Engel hedged. "But yes, after eight sessions, I like to take my patient through these to see where their mental state is at."

"All right," Mia said, still skeptical. "If I pass, does that mean I can be done with therapy?"

Dr. Engel quirked a smile, the first sense of humor from the doctor that Mia had witnessed. "There is no pass or fail...but it's a good start."

"I'm game," Mia said, settling in for the first round of tests.

They went through a good twenty minutes of Dr. Engel holding up papers, murmuring over her answers, and jotting down notes. For her part, Mia attempted to keep her answers as dull as possible.

The last ten minutes were word associations. She never could quite figure out why doctors believed they could see into a person's psyche just based on the words they used, but she played along— most of her answers related to police work.

Until Dr. Engel said the word *bedroom* and Mia responded with *red*.

Dr. Engel didn't seem to think it strange, but then, she'd never seen Mia's baby blue quilt before. It threw Mia off, and she stumbled over her next answer. Dr. Engel paused to see what the holdup was for such a simple word as *tree*. Mia forced herself to focus and made it through the rest without a hitch.

"You've done well today," Dr. Engel congratulated her as they wrapped up.

Mia shrugged. "I didn't really do anything."

To that, the doctor only smiled, a bit condescendingly, Mia thought. Her life became an easy routine of work, therapy, martial arts classes, and cleaning. She would meet Alec for dinner once a week, but the conversation became difficult when they couldn't talk about his cases. It quickly dawned on Mia that, without work, she was a bit of a boring person.

After taking the three trial martial arts classes, she'd decided to go with the Krav Maga school. While she enjoyed all the classes she took, she'd been looking to focus on uneven pairings—three on one, or more than that, instead of just the classic one on one—and that instructor seemed the most accommodating.

On her last Morse Code class, Max had been able to get a hold of a second telegraph machine, and they split up into two groups, sitting in separate classrooms to send messages to each other.

Patti and Mia teamed up against Jim and Ron, a classic battle of the sexes. Though each team made a few mistakes, Mia felt pretty confident with the skills she'd learned.

"Is everything all right?" Max asked as she packed up to leave.

The question startled her, and Mia thought about her response before answering. "I've really enjoyed the class, Max. Thank you. I suppose I'm just a little sad it's over."

He grinned then, taking Mia's hand between both of his. "I'll be doing another course in the summer. You can always sign up again."

"I just might," she replied with a genuine smile.

△ △ △

"I NEED YOU TO FIND out what you can on this case," Chief Alvarez said as he dropped a thick file onto Mia's desk. "I'd like the results sent directly to me."

"Sure thing," she said, flipping it open to reveal the contents.

It had been five months since she'd begun desk duty, and though she didn't get the same charge by it as she did by fieldwork, Mia was proficient. As she immersed herself in the report, she became wholly engrossed in the mysterious circumstances surrounding a missing shipment. Pulling up the search engine on her computer, she typed in a few keywords and clicked through the results.

With a gut feeling that there was much more to the story than was in these papers, she grabbed the file—and, going against her direct orders—walked out to her car.

It was the first case to come across her desk that had really piqued Mia's interest. Though she'd been asked to strictly do research, it just wasn't in her to leave this alone. As she parked the car, she argued with herself over what she was doing—but whatever drive she'd always had to get to the bottom of a case was taking over now.

Brentwood Industries was a shell company for the DeLuca brothers. They owned a shipping yard adjacent to the Marina Terminal. It was out of the central precinct; but, then again, Mia wasn't there to make an arrest.

The shipping yard had a tall fence surrounding the facilities. Several low buildings sprawled across the landscape, looking completely benign with their dreary sidings. Parking near as she could without raising suspicion, Mia gazed out across the yard and waited for some kind of activity.

Pulling the thick file from the passenger seat into her lap, she read it while keeping one eye beyond the fences. Alec and Mia had had several run-ins with the DeLuca family, though they'd never chased them directly. She'd nicknamed them the crème-de-la-creeps.

Anthony DeLuca, who went by Tony, was the oldest brother of four. Down the line was Alfonso, who went by Al, Enrico, who went by Ricky, and the baby Marco. Tony was, for all intents and purposes, the leader of the group. Al was the enforcer, Ricky was the brains, and Marco was a womanizing wild card.

More often than not, it seemed the brothers were covering up a stunt pulled by the youngest of the family. They were the cruelest criminals Mia had come across in her time on the force. The DeLuca family was one of the longest-standing crime families in the area. They had direct ties going back to the days of prohibition, and in her time on the force, some of the most gruesome sights she'd seen had been directly related to the brothers.

It seemed that their business had expanded, and she was determined to find out what was going on behind those gates.

Scouting the perimeter for security cameras, Mia drew a crude map on a blank piece of paper and worked out an entry point. Her goal was the largest building on the property, which had several windows just above her sight level. Luckily, someone had been kind enough to leave some crates stacked against the wall, which would give her the height she needed to see inside.

The yard seemed unusually empty for the daytime, and though it was a welcoming sight, she knew it would be better to wait until night. Shifting her car into gear, Mia glanced at the clock. She'd be early to her therapy session if she left now. After, she'd go home to prep for her night's activities.

Mia sat in Dr. Engel's office, no longer feeling the same dread as had accompanied her in those first sessions. Perhaps talking about her life and problems had actually helped; perhaps it had just become routine.

Either way, Mia sat and waited without fidgeting for the doctor to begin.

"I'd like to revisit your childhood," Dr. Engel said as she leaned forward, watching Mia intently. It seemed Mia's confidence was premature. "I know you felt resistant before, but I believe it's important in order to understand your sleeping difficulties."

"You've read my file. There's not much more to tell."

"I'd still like to hear it from you."

Crossing her arms, Mia glared at the doctor. "What do you want to hear? That my dad was a bastard who liked his beer and cocaine? That he'd beat my mom and me whenever the mood struck? That he put me in the hospital four times before I was seven years old?"

Dr. Engel stayed quiet, waiting for her to continue. In a calmer voice, Mia did just that. "I went to school every day with bruises. Some of my teachers cared enough to ask, but I always came up with an excuse—which I'm sure now, looking back, that they saw right through. I was terrified of being at home, but when I stayed away, it was so much worse for me, my mom. There were many days where I thought he'd kill her, or me, or both."

The doctor didn't offer condolences or excuses, for which Mia was grateful. She'd heard them all, and they did nothing to ease the pain or the guilt.

"I used to pretend I was another person. Stronger, braver, someone who could stand up to him. A warrior who could save my mom. There were so many times I'd fantasize about what our life would be like without him if only I were bigger, older, smarter." Mia scoffed, all the bitterness directed inwards. "Other girls dreamed of being princesses. I dreamed of being his nightmare."

Squeezing her hands together, hating the doctor for forcing her to relive this, Mia barged on, knowing Dr. Engel wouldn't let it go until she spilled it all. "One night, I came home late from school; I was thirteen. There was an assignment I'd missed, and the teacher

39

asked me to stay and talk about it. My father was so angry, coked-up, beer cans scattered everywhere. When I walked in, my mom was huddled on the floor, against the wall in the living room. She looked so frail, so battered, so broken. When she looked up at me, it was like all the life in her eyes had been sucked away. I'm not even sure she recognized me through the blood trailing down her face."

Staring down at her lap, Mia stayed silent so long Dr. Engel finally spoke. "What happened then, Mia?"

Still staring at her hands, Mia continued. "Something came over me. He came at me, and instead of cowering, I fought back. My punches did nothing against his large frame, and he became enraged. He went back to my mom and slammed her head into the wall, over and over, screaming at me while he did. I ran to the kitchen, truly believing he'd killed her. I grabbed a knife, the biggest one I could find. Screaming like a banshee, I rushed back to the living room and stabbed him in the back. When he spun around, I just kept stabbing at him. That whole time, I felt like I was watching myself from far away, almost like it was a movie playing out before me. A horror movie." A single tear leaked down Mia's cheek, and she didn't bother to wipe it away.

"Our mind is a powerful thing," Dr. Engel said quietly. "Above all, it seeks to protect us."

"Twenty-three times," Mia said dully. "Twenty-three stab wounds. I don't remember doing that. At some point, I curled up next to my mom, cradling her head in my arms. There was so much blood. Then, the cops came. I'm not sure who called them, and the rest of that night is a blur. Somehow, my mom survived, but she was never the same. I spent some time in the juvenile system but pleaded self-defense and was released due to my mom's mental and physical decline. I took care of my mom for the next few years. She was practically catatonic. In some twisted,

40

sycophantic way, my dad was her reason for living. Not even I was enough."

Mia leaned forward, bracing her elbows against her knees as she rubbed at her temples with the palm of her hands. "She stopped responding, and eventually, she stopped eating. I couldn't afford medical care. Our house was paid off, thankfully, as it had been handed down from my grandma to my mom, but I still had to pay for taxes, utilities, food. I had to quit school and work. After she died, I earned my GED and got accepted into a community college, where I earned my bachelor's in criminal justice. The police academy came next, and, well, you know the rest."

"Thank you for sharing that, Mia. I know it wasn't easy." Mia nodded, too mentally exhausted to work up indignation for the fact that the doctor had forced it out of her. "That is something no child should ever have to deal with. But it seems you did become that strong, brave warrior you dreamed of."

If that was the consolation prize, Mia needed to find a new game show.

Four

INSTEAD OF GOING BACK TO the precinct, Mia went straight home from the therapy session. Besides feeling emotionally drained, she wanted to prepare for her night's excursion.

The first thing she did when she walked in was run a hot shower. When Mia stepped through the steam, she allowed the water to wash away the feeling of melancholy that had overtaken her. Dredging up the past never seemed to be as helpful as shrinks deemed it to be.

Locking away the horrors of her childhood once again, Mia turned her focus to her task that night. This would strictly be a reconnaissance mission since any evidence obtained would not be admissible in court. But, if she could find out what the DeLucas were up to, it would give the department a start.

Wrapping herself in a towel, Mia caught her reflection in the mirror. For the last few months, her eyes had had a dull shine to them. She knew it had everything to do with being demoted and starting the medication. The soft black spots beneath her eyes that were ever-present had shrunk just slightly, thanks to more consistent sleep, but they were still very much visible.

With a sigh, Mia dried her dark hair and wrapped it up in a bun to keep it out of her way. She dressed for the evening's activities in black leggings and a long-sleeved black shirt. The clothes were comfortable and gave her a better range of motion.

Without any pockets, Mia wrapped a utility belt around her hips and placed the few items she would need inside it: her cell phone— placed on mute—a pocket knife, and a pen camera. The camera had come in handy over the years; not only was it compact and excellent at low-light photos, but it also made no noise when releasing the shutter. Perfect for stakeouts and, on nights like this, when her actions bordered on illegal.

Mia's lock-picking set came next, along with a small but powerful flashlight. Feeling as prepared as she ever would, she drove toward the marina.

Parking several blocks away, she slipped on a jacket that would cover her utility belt in case she walked past any civilians and made her way by foot to the spot she would use to break into the shipping yard. Taking off the jacket, Mia left it on the ground near the fence.

Without giving it too much thought, she scaled the fence and dropped down, keeping a careful eye on the low buildings for any sign of movement.

After counting to ten in her head, Mia moved toward the building that was her target. There was a camera at the door, but she went directly to where the wooden crates were stacked, pausing with her back pressed to the wall to assess her surroundings once again. Still no activity.

A single light gave off a warm glow inside the building, but it was quiet otherwise. Gingerly climbing atop the crates, Mia slowly lifted her head until she could see through the window.

The room was empty of people but stacked full of wooden crates. Unlike the ones she stood on, these were still full of cargo.

None were open for her to get a glimpse inside, so Mia knew what would come next. Climbing down, she snuck a peek around the corner of the building, eyeing the camera. It was pointed directly at the door, so there was no way around it. The only way to get through one of the windows would be to break the glass, but she wasn't willing to make that kind of noise or mess.

Pulling out the small flashlight along with her lock picking set, Mia took a deep breath before shining the light directly at the camera. It wasn't perfect, but it would obscure the image long enough for her to get inside. She could only hope there was no one watching the cameras now.

The last obstacle was using the lock picking set. She needed two hands for that and one to keep the light steady. Before getting frustrated, Mia tried the handle.

It was unlocked. That seemed lucky.

Making sure she was out of sight of the camera before flicking off the light, Mia stepped fully inside the room and closed the door. Pausing again, she waited with bated breath for any sound; none came.

The first crate she crouched beside read *Fine Columbian Beans*. When she tried to lift the lid, it was wedged in nice and tight. Glancing around for some kind of crowbar to use for leverage, Mia spotted several lined up against the wall.

Grabbing the closest one, she returned to the crate and pried the lid off. There were, in fact, burlap bags of coffee beans placed neatly inside. Curious, she hefted one of the bags out and found a tarp lining. Setting the beans on the ground, Mia pulled out a pocket knife and carefully slit the tarp along the edge where it was attached to the crate. When she pulled back the fabric, she let out a gasp of astonishment.

Snapping pictures as quickly as she could, Mia carefully lay the tarp back before replacing the beans. Someone would notice the tarp had been taken out eventually, but she had to hope they blamed the people that initially packed them.

Satisfied with her night's work, Mia made her way out of the shipping yard the same way she'd come in, running into no trouble. After vaulting the fence, she picked up her jacket and hurried back to the car.

At home, Mia typed up a detailed report, transferring the pictures from the tiny camera to her computer, and sent it all to the chief. She'd hear about it tomorrow, she was sure, but still couldn't bring herself to regret what she'd found out.

△ △ △

WHEN MIA WALKED INTO WORK the next day, the chief gestured her toward his office, as expected. To her surprise, Alec and Adam were also waiting.

"Detective Gonzalez, it seems you've come across some interesting information," Chief Alvarez began. "Though it was acquired through means other than computer research, I'd like you to share your findings with Woods and Malone."

Mia had the grace to look contrite but quickly straightened her shoulders and delivered the report. "Brentwood Industries is a shell company for the DeLuca family. On the surface, it looks like an ordinary shipping company bringing in coffee beans from Columbia. However, I believe coffee is not the only thing they are importing."

The chief placed photos on the desk. Though she'd taken them, it still shocked Mia to see the sheer amount of weaponry uncovered in those crates. This one had been full of semi-automatic rifles.

"This is now the highest priority. Detective Gonzalez, you'll be teaming up with Detective Woods and Detective Malone on this."

"Sir?" Mia asked, heart in her throat.

"You've been cleared for field duty. Congratulations." Attempting to keep the happy dance that was threatening to reveal itself under wraps, Mia dipped her head in acknowledgment and mumbled a heartfelt 'thank you' instead. Alec and Adam left the office first, but the chief held Mia back. "You'll still see Dr. Engel

45

once a week for the foreseeable future and follow whatever directions she gives you."

Mia knew he implied the sleeping medication. With the half doses she'd been taking, she was still sleeping better but felt more like herself during the day. That was something she could agree to. "Yes, sir."

"And Mia?"

"Sir?"

"It's good to have you back."

Walking out of his office, feeling a buoyancy in her step that had been missing, Mia sought out her new—and one old—partners. Alec leaned against his desk, arms crossed, a broad smile on his face.

"Detective Gonzalez, I'm so excited to be able to work with you," Adam said first, and their smiles were contagious.

Sliding into a chair next to his desk, Mia relaxed back, allowing her own smile to blossom. "Me, too. So, what's the plan?"

"Here's what the chief didn't tell you," Alec began. "The reason we're on this case is that it ties to Selena and Donovan."

Adam pitched in eagerly. "We believe one of the shipping businesses is also a front for Selena. Even with inspections cracking down on international cargo, there is still way too much slipping through. Someone's turning a blind eye."

"So, that would mean the DeLucas and Selena are in direct competition?" Mia asked.

Alec nodded before continuing. "It would seem so, but they could also be working together."

"Why would you think that?"

Alec pulled a report out of a file, sliding it over to her. "This is why."

Reading over it quickly, she raised an eyebrow. "Donovan's been spotted working with Tony DeLuca?"

"Yes. We have an undercover who confirmed it."

Rubbing her chin, Mia ran through the report again. "In all the time we've chased Selena, we've never come across guns. It just doesn't seem like their M.O."

"They're criminals, Mia," Alec said. "This isn't above them."

Though it didn't feel right, she kept her mouth closed and nodded. Instead of arguing over opinion, they would investigate and get the facts. "What's our way in?"

"Marco," Adam answered. "He's known to hang out at The Lounge."

"All right," Mia said, sitting back. "Let's hit that tonight."

△ △ △

MIA DROVE SEPARATELY FROM ALEC and Adam, knowing it would be beneficial to cover more than one entrance. It was decided for Adam to sit inside to keep an eye on their mark but not make contact. Mia parked on the street two buildings down but still in sight of the front door. Alec covered the rear entrance.

The Lounge was an upscale bar, and Mia watched as Adam, dressed to the nines, slipped the bouncer a tip before being let in. They all had earbuds in so they could communicate, and as he stepped inside, the low throbbing of bass became unbearably loud.

"Try to find a quiet area," Mia said loud enough for Adam to hear over the noise.

He didn't answer, which was for the best since they didn't want anyone thinking he was loony. After a couple of minutes, the noise lessened as he found a spot in a far corner from the band.

It was eight o'clock, and it didn't take long for Mia to spot Marco, making his way to the entrance with his entourage. They were let in immediately. "Marco's on his way in. He's with three friends and two guards."

Muscle was always easy to pick out. It was in their stance, their clothes, and the way they saw everything without moving their heads.

From there, Mia settled in to wait, knowing it could be a long night. Adam gave periodic updates, but otherwise, it remained silent between the three of them.

Around ten o'clock, Alec spoke urgently. "Activity in the alley. It looks like Al DeLuca is joining the party."

"Who's letting him in? Does he have a key? Is anyone with him?" Mia asked in quick succession.

"He's alone; he knocked, and the door opened. I couldn't see by who."

"Adam, give us an update when you can."

After a few moments, Adam spoke quietly. "Al pulled Marco aside. It looks serious."

They all waited for more information. Minutes passed, which Mia spent scanning the front of the building. "They're leaving," Adam finally said. "Just Al and Marco."

"Back or front?" Alec asked.

"Back."

"Adam, get out now; I'll pick you up in front. Alec, follow them, and we'll follow you." Pulling into traffic, Mia paused the car long enough for Adam to emerge and slide seamlessly into the passenger seat. Hesitating at the next block, she waited for Alec's instructions.

"They're on foot," Alec said. "Can't move yet; they'll see me."

A car approached behind her, so Mia made the turn and eased into a parking spot too small for her car. "I see them. Coming out of the alley now."

Adam and Mia watched as the brothers approached a black SUV. Once they pulled away from the street, she put the car back in gear.

"Black SUV. Heading south on Broadway. I'm two cars behind. Turning left onto Fleet." Continuing to follow, she gave Alec directions as they happened. When they headed into the southeastern precinct and began to slow, Mia told Alec to make the call.

They were a few blocks from the DeLucas' shipping yard, at an office building she wasn't familiar with. It was a five-story glass-front building, with a small sign in front of the parking lot, which read *Brentwood Industries.* Mia drove past, parking at a side street until Alec could catch up with them. The black SUV parked in front of the building, and though the building was dark, there was a smattering of cars still in the lot.

"What's our way in?" Adam asked.

Mia shifted in her seat to look over the building just as Alec approached her window. Once she'd rolled the window down, he asked, "Any thoughts?"

"Adam, stay out front. Alec and I will approach the building. When back-up gets here, hold until we give the go-ahead." Adam and Mia exited the car, and they began to walk toward the building as a group. When they reached the parking lot, Adam hung back, and Mia looped an arm through Alec's as they walked toward the front doors.

"Do you have any sort of plan here?" he whispered.

"Not exactly," Mia hedged, sending him a sly smile.

Approaching the front doors, they could see into the deserted lobby. Mia scanned for cameras, not being able to pick any out. There was a chance there weren't any, but it seemed unlikely.

Pulling on the handle of the door, she found it unlocked and walked inside. There was a reception desk along one wall, with a few leather chairs gathered together opposite. Mia and Alec headed to the elevators beyond.

There was a helpful digital display to the side of the elevator, so Mia pushed the button and watched the floors light up. As she turned to the stairwell, she spoke aloud for Adam's benefit. "Third floor."

They hurried up the stairs after scouting for adversaries, pausing outside the third level. Alec and Mia were still in sync even after five months of not being partners, and they assumed their positions on one side of the door, guns out. He met her eyes and nodded once before opening the door a crack. He waited for ten seconds, listening for any noise beyond the door. When he was met with silence, he stuck his head out to take a look around.

After Alec emerged fully through the door, Mia followed, keeping their bodies back to back as they came to the only hallway in the building. Offices were in each direction, and the only light in the building came from the left. With an unspoken command, Alec and Mia moved slowly down the hall.

"They're here," Adam's voice came over the earbud.

Neither Alec nor Mia were able to acknowledge that and continued the slow approach. Once they were within a few feet of the open office, they could hear voices.

"Get your head out of your ass," Al said gruffly.

"Hey, man, this isn't my screw-up. Why don't you get Ricky to fix it?" Marco's lighter voice responded.

"Ricky's busy right now, you know that."

"What do you want me to do with these guns?"

Alec and Mia glanced at each other. Just loud enough for Adam to pick up through the earbud, she said, "Now."

Waiting only a beat longer, Alec and Mia burst through the door, guns drawn. "Baltimore PD. Hands up!"

They faced a very startled Al and Marco. Al immediately lunged for the crate of weapons sitting on the floor, but Alec was faster. While he tackled Al and restrained him, Mia kept her sights trained on Marco.

"Hands over your head," she told him calmly. "Kneel down, link your hands, and place them on the back of your head."

He did as he was instructed, though his eyes were spitting fire and promising vengeance. Just a minute later, four officers from the southeastern district came through the door, guns drawn and cuffs ready.

"Alfonso DeLuca, you're under arrest."

"Marco DeLuca, you're under arrest."

Alec and Mia backed away, allowing the officers to wrangle the brothers out of the building.

Five

THE PRECINCT WAS ABUZZ WHEN Mia walked in the next day, and when she glanced to the meeting room, she could see why. The Commissioner and Deputy Commissioner were both seated at the table, along with Chief Alvarez. Alec met her at her desk, a solemn look on his face.

"They need to see you," he said.

Even more curious now, Mia followed her partner and Malone to the windowed room, which held a long conference table. When she entered, they all looked up at her with the same solemn expression. Alec and Adam followed her in, closing the door behind.

"Gonzalez." The chief nodded in greeting. "We haven't released this yet, and don't plan on it. This needs to stay in this room, between the people in this room. Understand?"

"Yes, sir," Mia said. Laying a photograph on the table, he slid it in front of her. Mia looked down, did a double-take, and gasped.

It was a side shot, catching three-quarters of a woman's face as she glanced over her shoulder. Mia peered closer to scrutinize, but it was unmistakable.

It was her. "Where did you get a surveillance picture of me?"

The men exchanged glances, seeming satisfied by the question. Her confusion only grew.

"That's not you, Mia," the chief answered gently. "That's Selena."

Looking up in bewilderment, Mia studied each face in the room, waiting for one of them to yell, 'Just kidding!' But they didn't.

"We had a team undercover for a year acting as petty criminals before they were finally hired by Selena. They were able to get this shot the same night you spotted Donovan on Thames," Chief Alvarez continued.

"How is this possible?" Mia asked in a whisper, understanding now the hard faces of the men surrounding her.

"You don't have a sister or any family that looks like you?"

Shaking her head, Mia felt dumbfounded. "I'm an only child. I only have one girl cousin, but she's in high school."

"Perhaps your father had another child..." began the Deputy Commissioner before getting cut off by her chief.

Waving a hand to show she didn't take offense, Mia said, "None that I know of, but it's a possibility, I suppose, no matter how small." After a brief pause, she asked, "You've had this photograph for nearly six months. Why wait until now to show it to me?"

She looked directly at the chief, waiting for an explanation. "We wanted to keep it under wraps, didn't want this leaked to the public." He opened another file, slid it in front of her. The report of Marco's questioning dated the day before. "Marco DeLuca was more than happy to flip on Donovan when he was faced with life in prison. He claims he overheard Donovan saying Selena has been missing for four months. This is backed up only by the reduced activity on their front. Alfonso isn't talking."

Continuing to study the eerie photo of her doppelganger, Mia's mind spun out, analyzing every angle of the impossibility. There was a reason these men were in this room, why she'd been invited in. "You want me to go undercover."

"No," Alec said, taking an aggressive step forward. Malone placed a restraining hand on his arm.

Sparing him a glance before meeting the chief's eyes, Mia continued, "That's why you called me in. Why you don't want this photo getting out. You want me to go undercover."

"Yes," he answered briskly.

Taking another long look at the photo, Mia nodded her head. "I'll do it."

The chief let out a satisfactory breath. "I knew you would." Glancing at his superiors, he said, "Do you mind if I have a word with Detective Gonzalez alone?"

They nodded, gesturing for Alec and Adam to leave before them. Once it was clear, the chief turned back to Mia. They sat beside each other at the head of the table, hands folded and heads bent close.

"There're a few things I'd like you to know. The night you were drugged, I was going to take you off the case either way. Though I hated what happened to you, it did serve as a legitimate cover to reassign you."

"Sir?" Mia's head tilted, not sure she fully comprehended what he was saying.

"I'd gotten the photo that morning. Had I known you were staking Donovan out that night, I would have stopped you, realizing then that I would put you undercover at some point, and I didn't want Donovan to see you. The problem was, we didn't know when it would be, and I couldn't risk anyone with the knowledge that you are Selena's spitting image. Even you."

"The psych evals?"

"We don't know how long this case will last. This isn't a drug sting or catching hookers. You will become Selena. Live, breathe a hardened criminal. The FBI is sending in a specialist to help train you, and she asked that you undergo psych evals before placing you undercover. You passed."

"You understand I'm feeling deceived right now," Mia murmured, thinking the last five months over with new eyes.

"Rightly so. Just know, everything I've done is because I believe in you. I believe you're the one able to take Selena down."

"Thank you, sir," she said, not sure what else to say. "What is the plan?"

"You still have more training to do, now that you are able to know your assignment. Within the month, you'll begin life as Selena."

"How will I cover the fact that we know nothing about her?"

"Simple. Donovan will find you held hostage, tied up, and tortured. Memory loss is a common side effect."

This took her back. "Tortured?"

He smiled sadly. "Unfortunately, most of your injuries will have to be real. Are you going to be okay with that?"

She thought it through. What was ending the ring of terror worth? "Yes."

He leaned even closer, forcing her gaze on his. "Mia, I'm not going to lie and tell you undercover work is easy. It's not. In this case especially. You will be living another life, becoming another person. It's really not even the type of case we would typically handle, but given the special circumstances..." He trailed off, gesturing a hand toward the photograph. "The Commissioner decided this was the best course of action. The FBI specialist will prepare you. I need you to understand this will not only affect you physically but mentally and emotionally as well. This is also incredibly dangerous, and I will understand completely if you'd like to back out. You won't have support, and you won't be able to speak to anyone from your life right now for an indeterminate amount of time.

"I'd like you to take tonight and think through everything, really think about it. You can let me know your decision in the morning. If you do decide not to go through with this, you will still be back on the case. If your answer is yes—well, your final training begins tomorrow."

Sucking in a deep breath, Mia nodded. "I understand."

"Take the rest of the day off. It may be the last vacation you get for some time."

Shaking his hand, Mia stood up and left. Alec perched at his desk, staring at her with questions in his eyes. Stopping first for her purse, Mia went to Alec before leaving. "The chief has asked me to take the day to think about my answer."

He nodded, his jaw clenched. "Mia—"

"I'll talk to you later, okay?" Briefly placing a palm on his arm, conveying without words her need for discretion, Mia raised an eyebrow.

Alec snapped his mouth shut. She hated seeing him this way. With nothing more to say, she began to walk away. To her back, he said, "You better believe it."

At home, Mia stood in the middle of her living room and took a slow look around. She didn't need time to think about whether or not she would take the job; she already knew her answer. But what should she do about her stuff?

There was nothing here she cared about, Mia realized. There were no childhood mementos—she'd rather forget that entire portion of her life and move on—there were no valuable personal items, sentimental or monetary. Her best friend—fine, her only friend—was Alec.

Maybe it was better that they'd grown apart these last months. She still cared about him, as a partner, as a friend, even perhaps as more, but it wasn't enough to make her stay. It wasn't enough to take the coward's way and go back to her life of work and work and work.

She should feel sad or anxious about leaving this life and jumping into the unknown, a potentially highly dangerous situation, but she didn't. There was only excitement and anticipation to be found. And this strange sensation that this was the path that would lead her to where she was meant to be.

The knock on her door that night was no surprise. She'd been expecting it since she'd walked away from Alec. Checking the peephole as she always did, Mia confirmed it was her partner and opened the door.

He was fuming; she could tell he'd let this build up all day. Mia waited patiently, knowing it was best to let him get it off his chest.

"This is idiotic! I can't let you go undercover with absolutely no backup. I can't. How could you even think about doing something like this? Have you thought about it at all? We don't know where Selena is. What if she shows back up out of the blue? They'll kill you!"

"I have to do this," was all she could say before he began again.

"Donovan is a viper, and you're just waltzing into his nest! I won't be able to save you. No one will."

"I have to do this," Mia repeated firmly. "I need to do this."

Alec paced across the room and back, visibly agitated, but she knew the worst was over. "I don't like it, Mia. This is dangerous and stupid. By far the dumbest thing you've ever tried to do."

"It's not up to you, Alec. I'm asking you to support me, but if you can't, it won't stop me."

"Will anything stop you?" Pausing before her, Alec looked deep into her eyes. "Can I even get you to think twice?"

"Alec, I..."

Before she could even begin to argue, all words cut off as Alec's lips met her own. She gasped, which only gave him room to maneuver. The suddenness of the move was unexpected, but hadn't she thought of this before? Hadn't she been ready to tell Alec how she felt months ago? Hadn't she even thought of him today and wondered?

She prepared for the onslaught of electricity she thought surely would come.

There was none. This man, who knew her better than anyone, who she connected with on levels she never had with anyone else, sparked nothing inside her.

On the surface, Alec and Mia made sense. They should have been perfect for one another. They cared about each other, and the rare times that Mia allowed herself to contemplate what this moment would be like, she imagined so much more.

Yet even if there had been more, it wouldn't have been enough.

Still, in a desperate attempt to ignite some feeling, Mia reached up with both hands to grip his hair, pressing her body against his. She wanted that link, that primal connection between two people who cared for each other, who wanted each other. She craved that bond, felt it was inside her grasp.

Yet, there was nothing.

Pulling away to suck in a lungful of air, Mia stared at her partner, her closest friend for the last two years, and her heart broke.

He backed away slowly, looking immediately contrite. "I'm sorry, Mia. I shouldn't have kissed you."

"No, Alec, it's fine," she said in an attempt to reassure him, but it came out flat.

Brushing his hand across his mouth, he gave her a half-smile. "Not exactly what I expected."

"Me either." Letting out a shaky laugh, thankful for the little bit of levity he offered, Mia held out a hand. "Friends?"

58

His lips quirked up at one corner as he clasped his hand around hers. "Friends. I still don't like this."

"I know, but how could I say no?"

To this, he had no answer.

△ △ △

FIRST THING IN THE MORNING, Mia found the chief in his office to tell him her decision. He didn't seem surprised, but the concern remained prevalent in his expression. Giving her directions to an offsite training facility, he told her that her training would continue there.

"Good luck, Mia," he said, clasping her hand between both of his. There was an insane moment where she thought that would be the last that she ever saw of him.

Stopping at her desk to pack a few things to take with, knowing she would likely not be back to the precinct until this was over, Mia said goodbye to Alec before heading down to the address she'd been given on the docks.

Mia parked outside a long row of empty warehouses, wondering if she'd gotten the address wrong. For an FBI training facility, it didn't seem like much.

Stepping out and slamming the car door, she walked toward one of the doors and tried the knob. The room sat empty, and she hesitated before entering.

Shaking away the strange feeling, Mia stepped inside and scanned the room, noting each exit and the placement of each item, few as they were. Large, empty oil drums were grouped together to her right, and wooden crates were stacked near the center of the room. Above her, a walkway followed the perimeter of the building, with a loft area on each end.

"Hello?" Her voice echoed out into the room. From the walkway opposite, Mia's eyes caught an object glinting in the dim lights. While her focus caught on that spot, she heard the first explosion of gunfire.

Instinct took over, and she immediately dove for cover behind the oil drums, reaching for her holster simultaneously. Gun in hand, Mia peered around the corner as more shots fired off.

"Baltimore PD!" she shouted above the cacophony of bullets ricocheting off the walls. "Cease your fire!"

Her announcement did nothing. Training her sights on the same place where she'd spotted the glimmer of metal, Mia let out a breath and squeezed the trigger.

The barrage of bullets ended, and she wasted no time in slinking along the wall to the closest staircase, gun kept at the ready. Taking the stairs as quickly as she could while still being able to look around for her attacker, Mia reached the landing and stared in complete confusion.

The glimmer of metal was not just a gun; it was a machine that now had a curl of smoke sifting upward from the hole of her bullet.

"Well done," said a voice from behind.

Spinning at the sound with her gun automatically in position to shoot, Mia took in the woman who stood, arms crossed, with a bemused expression on her face.

She had a long and lean body, with a strength that was readily apparent even beneath the basic black pantsuit she wore. Her blonde hair had been pulled back into a no-nonsense bun, her eyes shrewd as she assessed Mia.

Realizing this had to be her trainer, Mia lowered her weapon though she didn't re-holster. "Who are you?"

"Agent McKenzie," the woman supplied, holding out a hand to shake.

Approaching her warily, Mia returned the gesture. "It was shooting blanks?"

"That it was. I wanted to see what I was working with. You have good instincts, a quick reaction time."

"Thank you?" Mia said though it came out as more of a question.

The corners of the agent's mouth tipped up, which Mia took to be a smile. "I'm here to give you a crash course in espionage. Normally, training for a case like this should take years. We've got less than a month. I don't agree with that, but I also realize this is an extreme circumstance." She began walking then, back down the stairs. Mia followed, still reeling from the little experiment. "I've been fully debriefed on the job and will do everything in my power to get you ready. Are you willing to do what it takes?"

"I am," Mia said with confidence.

Pausing, Agent McKenzie glanced back at her and quirked an eyebrow. "We shall see."

Six

AGENT MCKENZIE WAS A MADWOMAN.

She began by having Mia do sprints up and down the warehouse, dodging objects she threw at her. They were not all soft and squishy. After that, she pulled a punching bag from a storage area and had Mia doing rounds of thirty seconds each, with a ten-second pause between. Next came target practice—as it turned out, the warehouse had been equipped with soundproofing, so if someone happened to be around, they would be unable to hear the shots.

Instead of standing and shooting at the target, Mia went back to sprints. Starting at the end opposite the targets, she ran up and down the length of the warehouse before turning back to shoot. All the while, Agent McKenzie watched, passing a pipe between each hand, yelling out encouragements like 'faster!' and 'too slow, you're dead!'

After two hours, Mia dripped with sweat and found herself loving every minute of it. Agent McKenzie grinned—a bit evilly, Mia thought—and said, "Great. Now we can begin."

"Begin?" Mia asked, dumbfounded. "What has all this been?"

"Warm-ups," Agent McKenzie said, then lunged with the pipe aimed for Mia's head.

Acting on instinct, Mia dropped her stance, allowing the pipe to swing over her head while she moved in, executing a strike to

McKenzie's gut. The agent grunted, but it didn't slow her next attack. While Agent McKenzie arched the pipe back toward her, Mia brought up her hands, using her right to slow down the agent's attack and sliding down to grip her wrist while the left slammed against her arm, directly above the elbow. Mia was careful to use control; though Agent McKenzie didn't seem to be holding back, Mia didn't want to dislocate any joints.

Keeping hold of her wrist, Mia used McKenzie's momentum against her, bringing her to the ground in a face plant. With a flick of her wrist, the pipe went flying, and Mia held her in an armbar— but Agent McKenzie wasn't done.

Pulling her left arm through until she flipped onto her back, Mia lost her leverage, letting go instead of attempting to fight it. Agent McKenzie gained her feet while Mia put her guard up, waiting for the next move.

Agent McKenzie lunged again, her fists a flurry of motion. Deflecting them best she could, Mia waited for her opening and landed another punch, this time to the ribs. It didn't slow the agent down.

They continued to exchange attacks for several minutes, and Mia felt her body giving out, running on pure adrenaline. The smallest hesitation on her part and Agent McKenzie had her on the ground, arms in a lock around her throat.

Though Mia kept fighting, struggling to get out of her iron grip, black dots began to dance at the edges of her vision.

Against her better judgment, Mia tapped out.

Agent McKenzie released her immediately, springing to her feet effortlessly while Mia rolled to her hands and knees, gasping for breath. Mia knew the position was the worst for catching breath, but it was all she had energy for at the moment.

"You have decent technique and commendable control. But the fight lasted way too long," Agent McKenzie said, her voice annoyingly calm as she circled Mia's aching body. "How long should a fight last?"

Squeezing her eyes shut to steel herself for movement, Mia got clumsily to her feet. "A few minutes?"

"No," Agent McKenzie said, her tone hard and mocking. "Three seconds."

"Three seconds?" Mia asked incredulously, her eyebrows furrowed.

"Yes. You should be able to end any confrontation in three seconds or less. And you could have here. Why didn't you?"

Mia's brain attempted to wrap around her words. She finally blurted out, "The armbar. You wanted me to injure you?"

"I'm training you for undercover work, Detective Gonzalez. This is not sparring in your dojo. Do you think someone out there is going to appreciate that you spared them pain? They're not. They will use your weakness to their advantage."

Though her breath still came in short gasps, Mia fully stood and tamped down her temper. What the agent said made sense, but Mia didn't know if she could hurt someone who'd done nothing wrong.

Her thoughts must have been clear on her face, for Agent McKenzie's voice softened just the tiniest bit. "Mia, you'll be playing a part. You will have to play it convincingly, or it could have dire consequences. I don't just mean getting choked out"—she gestured toward the ground, where Mia'd almost been unconscious just moments ago—"it will constantly be life or death."

Turning away, Mia paced several lengths away before returning to where she stood. With a decisive nod, she finally answered. "I understand."

Agent McKenzie studied Mia carefully a moment longer. "All right. Let's take a break from the physical." Taking a seat at the only table in the building, she gestured for Mia to do the same.

Files were sitting closed atop the table, and Agent McKenzie quickly pulled open the top one. "Tell me about the target, Donovan."

"Right hand to Selena. From Ireland, though his records have been wiped clean."

"Handsome," McKenzie murmured, pulling out an 8x10 photo and laying it on the table. Mia's eyes flicked down briefly, that weird little rush instantaneously marring her senses. "You find him attractive."

Mia met her look with instant denial. "No, I don't."

The agent's lip quirked. "Yes, you do, and that's not a bad thing. It will certainly help convince him you're Selena." That was the last thing Mia had expected her to say. Seeing the hesitation, Agent McKenzie explained herself. "If I were a man, I would tell you to ignore your feelings. Since we're both women, we understand that emotions can be a tool. For example, if you were disgusted by Donovan, it would be very difficult for you to hide that fact from him. The fact that you find him attractive—use it. In this case, leading him on is a good thing. Just as long as you remember that it's a ploy, and you don't allow your feelings to become real."

"We don't know the relationship between Donovan and Selena," Mia said while digesting her words.

"True. But, if he looks like this, and she looks like you, and they've been working together for years—trust me, there's something there."

"Have you ever gone undercover, like this?"

"I'm not sure anyone has ever gone undercover quite like this. It's a very unique situation. Most undercover work is attempting to buy drugs from a dealer. Some of the more advanced cases require assuming a new identity and slowly working your way into a criminal's trust." She pursed her lips, thoughtful for a few beats, while Mia waited for her to circle back to the question. "I had one case like that. It's not often an agent will assume more than one identity in their career—too much of a risk of being recognized. My case lasted for three years. I've done and seen more than you could possibly imagine."

Three years. Mia knew this case could go on for a long time, but she hadn't really thought in terms of years.

"It isn't easy," Agent McKenzie continued. "But that's why I'm here to help you. You must learn to think like Selena, act like her, respond like her. And, if that wasn't difficult enough, we know nothing about her."

Mia allowed a small smile to grace her lips. "That's what the torture will be for."

"Yes. Feigning memory loss will be beneficial for you. During that phase, you will have injuries that will need to heal. It would be best for you to drag out your progress as long as possible. Use that time to study the people around you, find out what you can about who Selena is."

"It's a bit daunting."

"That's an understatement. But that's what this training is for. Your chief believes you can do it, and from what I've seen so far from you today, so do I."

The words meant more to her than she realized. "I believe I can, too. I'll do whatever it takes."

"All right, we're done for the day, but with a caveat. Take care of what you need to today, for starting tomorrow, you won't be going home."

This came as a shock. "What?"

"It's prudent no one sees you that could possibly know what Selena looks like. You'll train and sleep here going forward."

Glancing down at her arms, Mia realized several bruises were already starting to form. If the rest of the training was anything like today—and she knew, without a doubt, it would be—Mia could see the reasoning behind keeping her out of sight. It looked like her 'torture' would start now, with any cuts and bruises she received in training.

"All right. What time should I be here in the morning, and what should I bring with me?"

"Be here at eight o'clock. Bring clothes you can move in, and your badge and gun. Toiletry items. You won't need anything else."

Nodding her understanding, Mia made her way out to her car. It was an odd feeling driving through the streets of Baltimore, knowing she wouldn't see them again for at least several weeks.

Or, depending on how this went, years.

When Mia got home, she took a good look around her apartment, having a moment of melancholy. After that night, she had no idea when she'd see it again.

Thanks to her cleaning sprees, the apartment was the cleanest and most organized it had ever been. The chief had told her someone would look in on it and collect any mail. Her pay would also be held in a separate account until she completed her assignment. Her rent and few other bills would be paid out of that account. The only things she really had left to do were pack and clean out the food in her fridge and pantry.

She thought about calling Alec, but the truth was she didn't know what more to say to him. They'd had their major goodbye the night before, and it felt right to just leave it at that.

With nothing more to do, Mia lay down early and attempted to sleep. It would be her first night without taking medication, so she found herself lying awake longer than had become routine in the last months.

Without the medication, her subconscious wreaked havoc on her mind. Much like so many years of her life, there was no coherent thought or scene playing out, just snippets of movement, shadows of sound—a strange dream.

Running through the dark. Opening a door to reveal a shadowy figure. A warm embrace. The scent of cedar and lemon.

Mia woke early in the morning with her heart racing and the vague feeling that Donovan had been the shadowy figure in her dream. Shaking away the feeling, Mia showered quickly and finished packing, determination set on her face. She would get through training, she would put Donovan away, and then she would come home.

All her training would remain at the same warehouse as she'd begun in, with the addition of a small cot in the upstairs loft area that would be her bedroom. There was a bathroom with a shower, and that was it as far as luxuries went. It didn't bother Mia—she'd been through worse.

Agent McKenzie ran her hard, interspersing physical exhaustion with words of wisdom and practice interrogation in order to keep her in character. She even began calling her Selena, so Mia would get used to answering to the name.

It was surreal, to say the least. Mia had a sinking feeling it would get stranger yet.

On the second week, a man walked into the warehouse with Agent McKenzie. He was well over six feet tall and built like a brick wall.

"Agent Richards," he introduced himself. "You can call me Kenny."

"This is Selena," Agent McKenzie said. "Kenny is going to be your sparring partner this week. He's a teddy bear in real life, but he won't take it easy on you."

"The more bruises, the better, right?" Mia said flippantly.

Kenny showed no surprise to the statement. Mia was sure he'd been briefed with enough details to explain his job there, and no more. During her training at the Krav Maga studio, Mia had been pitted against men and women of all sizes, so though his sheer mass didn't have her as nervous as perhaps it should, she was sure his skill level ranked at extraordinary.

"Let's get started, shall we?" Agent McKenzie said, squaring them off in the middle of the warehouse.

Typically when Mia sparred with a new opponent, she preferred to scope them out and get a feel for their fighting style. In their training thus far, Agent McKenzie had made sure to drill it into her that being quick and being first, in real-life situations, was usually better.

As soon as Agent McKenzie shouted 'go!' Mia moved in, though not head-on. Executing three strikes as swiftly as possible, she moved out of Kenny's range and off to the side. When he retaliated, she managed to deflect his first two attacks before meeting the third with her face. He was quicker than he looked, and his punch packed a wallop. Since he hit Mia high on the cheekbone, her eye immediately began to water.

It didn't slow her down. She went in, distracting him up high while she took out his knee with a swift side kick. Kenny went down but used it to tackle her at the waist. Hitting the floor with a huff of breath, Mia fought until she could gain her feet.

The fight continued for several minutes, and though she held her own, she felt Kenny took it easy on her. Agent McKenzie broke them up eventually, giving tips on performance. Mia listened through ringing ears, wiping blood off her knuckles. Unfortunately, it was her own.

After she finished speaking, Agent McKenzie had them go several more rounds before dismissing Kenny for the day. Even though Mia was bleeding, bruised, and exhausted, she felt good.

"The rest of this week, we'll work on two-on-one scenarios," Agent McKenzie told Mia as they took a break for lunch. "How are you feeling?"

"Beat up," Mia said with a small, bloody grin.

The rest of the week continued with more of the same. Her body was on the point of collapse each day, but Mia knew each injury would make their story more credible. It was much easier to allow herself to get bruised in a fight than to stomach someone torturing her.

On the third week, Agent McKenzie made the announcement she'd been waiting for. "On Wednesday, you'll be moved to a cell, where you'll be chained up. You'll have no food and only a small amount of water. On Thursday, we'll let your location leak, letting the information work its way up to Donovan. I don't imagine it will be too long before he comes to get you."

Mia swallowed hard. "What else?"

"We will inject you with Scopolamine."

"Truth serum," Mia whispered, her stomach dropping.

"Not exactly," Agent McKenzie said. "There really is no such thing. Scopolamine is known to cause retrograde amnesia. Having a small amount in your system will give your memory lapse story the credence it needs."

"Will I forget my training?" Mia asked, nervous about this part of the plan.

"You shouldn't, though I can't answer that definitively. You won't receive a full dose. We just want enough in your system to be traceable. More than likely, the last couple of weeks will be a bit hazy."

"This seems like a big risk."

"One that has been deemed worth taking."

Mia nodded, knowing she had no further argument. Their last two days of training became even more intense, which was an impressive feat considering what she'd been through so far. When Wednesday morning arrived, Mia ate breakfast and waited for her transport to arrive.

Agent McKenzie pulled a windowless van directly into the warehouse, having her climb into the back before driving her out. Mia didn't know where the building was that they would be using as a cell, but she was sure it would be in a deserted area. Her nerves were kicking around, though the only outward sign she gave of that was an arm wrapped around her stomach. After twenty minutes, the road became rough, and she knew they would be close to their destination.

Once the van stopped, Agent McKenzie appeared at the back, pulling the door open. The room they'd pulled into was dark and musty, more than likely a basement. She led Mia silently down a hallway, where several cement cells were in a row, complete with iron bars. Stagnant water sat in corners, and flickering bulbs spaced several feet apart were the only source of light.

"Homey," Mia commented, attempting levity.

"Home sweet home," Agent McKenzie answered, pointing through the open gate of a cell. "Make yourself comfortable."

Mia sat on the ground. There was a bucket beside her which would be her toilet. Her nose wrinkled in disgust.

Agent McKenzie made quick work of the chains. After studying Mia for a moment, she began unlacing her shoes, removing them and the socks. Mia's bare feet hit the cold cement floor, and she instantly shivered. Agent McKenzie murmured an apology.

Scooping sand off the floor, Agent McKenzie rubbed it through Mia's hair and smudged it over any exposed skin. Mia understood the need to look like she'd been there for months, but it also felt a bit ridiculous. Finished with that, the agent left momentarily to retrieve a metal cup filled with water.

"This is all you'll have, so pace yourself, but make sure you drink it. I'll inject you now with the Scopolamine. Do you have any last questions before I do?"

"Will I be okay?" Mia asked in a small voice.

Agent McKenzie placed a hand on her forearm, showing more emotion than the entire time they'd trained together. "You're smart, with good reflexes and a likable face. You'll be fine."

"Thanks, Agent McKenzie."

She studied Mia for a moment. "Merissa."

"What?"

"My name is Merissa. I think you've earned it." They shared a smile of understanding, and Mia watched as Merissa readied the syringe and found the vein. "This has been mixed with a solution that should lessen the effects but will still test positive. I'll wait here for a while to see how you feel."

As the drug made its way through her system, Mia's eyes started to feel heavy, as if she'd been awake for more than a day straight. She had a hard time keeping them open or concentrating on performing the task of keeping them open. Her natural response was to fight against the feeling, but then she'd get distracted by a flutter of dust in the pale light.

"Mia? How do you feel?"

"Mm," she murmured. "Sleepy."

Her words came out slurred as if she were drunk, but there was nothing she could do to change that. From somewhere far away, she heard Agent McKenzie's voice, but it wouldn't mesh into a coherent thought. Allowing her head to drop, she settled in to wait.

All she could do now was wait.

Agent McKenzie stood, sighed. And then she set the scene for when Donovan would arrive.

Seven

TIME BECAME A BLUR. MIA only woke for minutes at a time. How long had she been there? It could have been days. It could have been hours or years.

Upon waking, she remembered there was something important for her to do, but before she could catch that thought, she'd fall unconscious again. Mia lost track of how many times she'd woken, only to be dragged back under.

Eventually, she woke for longer. Eventually, she remembered to drink water. With clumsy fingers, Mia picked up the water cup and sipped gingerly at the cool liquid.

To pass the time, she repeated facts back to herself. *My name is Mia Gonzalez. I'm an undercover detective for the Boston Police. Donovan is a criminal.*

Then she practiced her cover story. *I'm Selena. I was taken and tortured for information. Donovan is my partner. Possibly my lover.*

The Scopolamine hadn't erased her memory. As her eyes focused on her hands, she realized there were dried patches of blood, crisscrossed marks up and down her arms. Agent McKenzie must have done that after she'd been knocked out. Mia appreciated not being awake for that bit.

As she continued to drift in and out of consciousness, Mia listened for any sound of activity in the corridor. Her forehead rested against her knees, bare feet now numb to the cold. Continuing to wait, having faith she wouldn't be stuck there forever, her mind began to wander. Thoughts became intermixed with her dream world until she had no idea what was real and what was fantasy.

Needing more to occupy the time, she tapped out the Morse code alphabet against her leg. When Agent McKenzie and Mia had discussed how she would get a message back to the precinct if the opportunity arose, one of the options was to get in front of a CCTV camera and tap out a message. She'd have to make sure the camera got a full shot of her face, as the precinct would be running facial recognition software.

It wasn't perfect, but anything else they came up with seemed to be too risky.

An infinite amount of time later, a noise intruded on her thoughts. So faint that she thought at first she had made it up, she heard yelling. Minutes passed, and it grew louder. Mia knew it was almost time. No backing out now.

Something scraped against the door. More yelling. Finally, the door pushed open, grinding against the floor. Mia's head still rested against her knees, too heavy to hold up. Her body sagged with exhaustion. Complete silence fell, though she could feel another presence in the room.

She didn't move, terrified to give herself away. Finally, what she'd been waiting to hear. Just a whisper of sound, a voice almost as tortured as she felt. "Selena."

Slowly, tenderly, she raised her head and allowed the pain to show on her face, in her eyes. As her gaze met her rescuer's, Mia felt shocked by the expression he wore.

No hard mask of evil existed there. Just pure, unadulterated anguish. An intensity of which she'd never witnessed before and could only come from love.

Their eyes locked for several long moments. Even through the haze of drugs and exhaustion and dehydration, Mia felt that unfamiliar heat begin to unfurl. She'd only encountered this man once before, six months ago, yet he felt oddly familiar to her in that moment. A warm embrace. A safe haven.

Finally, he moved, kneeling before her and reaching for her cuffed wrists. Mia cringed away as if she were being struck. "Shh, it's all right, you're safe now. They will never have you again."

Donovan spoke in gentle tones, making quick work of the restraints. His eyes flicked between her injuries, and Mia could see the livid fury simmering just below the surface. Not bothering with asking permission, he scooped Mia into his arms and carried her out of her prison.

Mia tucked her head against his chest, keeping one eye on their surroundings as he took the hallways at a jog.

"Get a blanket. Meet me at the car." He barked the order at the first man they passed, who was quick to comply. To the man beside the first, Donovan continued, "Give the all-clear. Move out."

The man spoke into a radio, which Mia assumed went into the ears of all the men on the operation. The ones she saw moved fast, efficient. Military trained, she felt certain.

Once they broke into the clear air of night, Donovan slid into the back of a dark SUV, still cradling her in his arms. The first man hurried over with a blanket, which Donovan wrapped gently around her shivering form. The door shut, and they were on the move.

With the warmth of the blanket, the tremors became worse before they slowed. Donovan rubbed Mia's arms and legs through the material, whispering encouragement as they zipped through the night. The windows of the car had been darkly tinted so that no one could see inside. A separation window between the driver and the backseat gave Donovan a semblance of privacy.

Mia snuggled into his arms, and his warmth began to seep through. She realized he would probably be able to warm her quicker than any blanket. The thought terrified her, and she remained silent.

The car pulled into an underground garage. Donovan carried Mia into an elevator and punched the button for the top floor. Mia knew the building, though it was not one she'd ever suspected of being Selena's.

After Donovan submitted to an eye and hand scanner, he entered the penthouse and brought her straight to the bathroom. She was acutely aware that they were alone. He set her gently on a settee before turning to an oversized tub to run the water.

He knelt before her again, carefully removing the blanket. When her hands were free, he held them with such gentle fragility Mia felt tears gathering in her eyes.

"Do you know me?" he asked. Mia hesitated, then shook her head. This seemed to hurt him, but he continued. "My name is Donovan. I'm going to help you into a bath. It will warm you up and get you clean. After that, a doctor will examine you. You've been held for several months. Do you remember?"

Turning her head away, Mia allowed a tear to leak from the corner of her eye. His hand cupped her cheek, his tone growing even softer. "Please don't worry. You're safe now; I'll make sure of it. I'm going to help you out of your clothes. Please don't be afraid."

Taking a deep breath, Mia waited another moment before meeting his eyes. Slowly, she nodded her consent. He lifted the ragged, torn shirt over her head. She wore nothing beneath but dirt. Helping her to her feet, Donovan slid her pants to the floor. She shook again, but it had less to do with the cold and everything to do with the man before her.

Lifting her easily into his arms, Donovan brought Mia to the tub and began lowering her into the welcoming heat. As her toe first touched the water, she gasped and pulled her foot away.

"Take all the time you need," he said, watching her face.

Steeling herself, Mia nodded again and let him lower her all the way. The heat pricked her skin, and it took several minutes before it began to feel good. As it did, she relaxed back into the tub, closing her eyes. Donovan remained at her side, and she remained absurdly aware of him.

Once she managed to relax, he reached for a bottle of shampoo and worked it into her hair. His fingers massaged her scalp, working out the grime of the last few days. After rinsing her hair, he lathered soap onto a sponge and wiped it in small circles over her skin, being extremely careful with the many cuts and bruises.

Though Mia could tell he was attempting to be clinical, she felt every pass of his hands down to her core. He replaced the sponge and squeezed her hand. "Wait here for a moment."

Mia watched as he walked to the standup shower, turned on the spray, and tested the temperature. When he came back, he held out both hands. "Let me help you stand up, and we'll get rinsed off in the shower."

Nodding, Mia grasped his hands and pulled herself up. She felt unsteady on her feet, and Donovan took his cue and wrapped an arm around her waist to lift her over the edge of the tub, setting her down near the open shower. With one hand, she tested the spray; it felt much hotter than the tub had been. Though it felt good, as soon as it hit her open wounds, she let out a hiss of pain.

Donovan was there immediately, ignoring the deluge of water as it poured over his clothes. His body blocked hers from the spray, and she felt ridiculously protected. Taking a steeling breath, Mia put a hand on his chest and backed him away, letting the water once again pour over her. She couldn't believe the amount of dirt that washed down the drain. The pain receded to a dull ache.

Once she'd been rinsed clean, Donovan produced a large, soft, warm towel from a heated bar and wrapped her in it like one would a child. As was quickly becoming habit, he lifted her into his arms and carried her to the adjoining room, setting her in the center of a large bed.

"Relax," he said in a quiet voice. "The doctor will be right in. I'm going to put on some dry clothes, and I'll be right back."

When he disappeared down the hall, Mia scooted against the headboard, falling back into the plush linens. Taking her first look around, she was surprised by the décor. Most things in the room were soft whites and muted beiges, giving it an all-over clean feel. Perhaps she had expected black satin and blood-red accents.

She saw nothing personal in the room, though it managed to feel cozy. Her own apartment had just the barest furnishings and no sense of style due to her lack of time and interest. Though—and she was afraid to admit this even to herself—had she had either of those things, this was how she would have decorated.

A woman entered then, slight of stature but wearing a warm smile. At first glance, Mia would have placed her in her thirties, but the graying of hair around the edges and a few deep laugh lines had her pegging the woman as late forties to early fifties.

"Hello, dear," she said in a soothing voice. "I'm Dr. White. Let's get you patched up, shall we?"

While she spoke, Donovan reappeared, leaning against the wall with his arms crossed—just watching. Focusing on the doctor, Mia nodded her approval. Much like the rest of Selena's employees, she worked quickly and efficiently.

Her final act was to draw a syringe of blood. Mia knew this was a good thing; the doctor would test it and find evidence of the Scopolamine.

She glanced back at Donovan and asked for privacy. He seemed hesitant but acquiesced. When he disappeared from the room, the doctor looked back at Mia, her bandaging done. "What do you remember from the last few months?"

Mia tried to convey fear with her eyes, not wanting to talk.

"Are you able to speak?" the doctor asked next. Taking the out, Mia shook her head. Dr. White nodded, contemplating. "Do you feel safe here?"

Keeping her eyes steady on Dr. White's, Mia slowly nodded. The doctor seemed satisfied by this.

"You have quite a bit of physical healing to do, and I believe with proper rest and care, your memories will come back to you." Pulling a card from her pocket, she set it on the bedside table before continuing, "This is my number—if you need anything, day or night, please call. I will be back tomorrow to check in on you."

Mia nodded again. Donovan returned then, sporting a tray with tea and toast.

"You've read my mind," Dr. White said. "Take it slow with solid food. Wait a few minutes between bites to be sure it stays down."

Donovan placed the tray beside Mia on the bed. "Try to drink and eat. I'll be back after I walk the doctor out."

They left, and Mia knew they'd be discussing her. She really hoped she'd played the part right, and they both believed she was Selena.

So far, this was not how she expected being undercover to be. Perhaps that was due to her injuries. Or, she'd completely misjudged Selena and Donovan.

When he returned, Mia had taken two bites of the dry toast. The herbal tea was delicious and hot, warming her insides in a way the bath couldn't.

"Finish what you can," he encouraged. "Are you in pain? The doctor left medication if you need it."

Mia shook her head. The last thing she wanted was drugs affecting her coherence. Taking another bite, she met Donovan's gaze, wondering what was really going through his mind. His eyes stayed steady on hers until she felt as if she were sinking into him. Mia was the one to break contact, fiddling with the teacup.

"Tired?" he asked with the same gentleness he'd been exhibiting since he found her.

Nodding, Mia allowed him to take the tray before shifting down to lay her head against the pillows. Returning to her side, Donovan rested his palm against her upper arm.

"I'll be here if you need anything in the night," he said, gesturing toward the overstuffed lounge chair sitting beneath a set of windows. As he spoke, he seemed to remember she couldn't. Holding up a finger, he disappeared again, only to return with a bell. Setting it on the table, he explained, "To get my attention."

Instead of just nodding, Mia tried out a tentative smile. His answering one transformed his ordinarily hard, rugged face, and she nearly gasped at the difference.

"Sleep well," he whispered, placing a kiss on her forehead. "You're safe here."

When he turned out the light, Mia noticed a small glow coming from the bathroom. Thoughtful, she realized. She listened as he pulled a blanket from a drawer and settled into the chair.

A little thrill of excitement raced through her as she realized she'd done it. She was in the viper's nest, as Alec had put it. Turning on her side, she watched Donovan's silhouetted form against the chair.

Everything from the day ran through her mind. She recorded each as she would on paper, determined to remember every detail. Donovan's breathing changed. In the dim light, she studied his face as it softened in sleep. He'd been unfailingly kind and gentle with her, but she knew underneath lurked an evil criminal. She would have to be on constant alert. How was she ever going to sleep?

Surprisingly easy, it turned out. After staring at Donovan's dark form for just a few minutes, Mia remembered nothing until morning, feeling more rested than she had, even with medication, for a long time.

When her eyes opened, there was just a faint stream of light through the blackout curtains. For the moment, she was alone, and she also had to use the restroom.

Testing her muscles, she sat up gingerly. After pausing to assess her injuries, Mia decided she would give standing a go. Swinging her legs sideways, she shifted down until her toes touched the ground and slowly allowed her feet to hold her weight. There she stayed, gripping the side of the bed until she felt sure she could move.

Mia took a few steps toward the bathroom, using tables and walls as support. When she'd made it to the doorway, she heard a noise from behind. An instant later, two arms wrapped around her middle.

"I'm sorry I wasn't here," Donovan said. "Let me help you."

He guided her into the bathroom, though he allowed her to stay on her feet. When they reached the small room that housed the toilet, he left her to her business. She was quick, and as soon as she opened the door, he was there again to help her to the sink and then back to the bed.

Once Mia settled back under covers, she realized where he'd been. The tray was back, with more toast, tea, and some fruit.

"Dr. White said to add things slowly," Donovan said. "We'll try some vegetable soup for lunch."

Mia nodded and tried out a smile again before taking a sip of tea. It tasted of lavender and had pieces of fresh ginger floating in the liquid.

"The ginger will help settle your stomach," he explained when he saw where her attention had gone. She looked up at him again, surprised. This was certainly not what she'd expected from a man like Donovan.

After taking a bite of toast, she tried some berries. They were sweet and tasted fresher than she usually got from the grocery store.

"I have some work I need to do today, though I will be here the whole time. It would be best for you to rest as much as possible. I've brought some books if you'd like to read." He gestured toward the bedside table, where Mia was surprised to see a stack of books. "And the bell is still here if you need me for anything. If you want to get out of bed, please ring for me."

Mia nodded her understanding and ate more of the toast. He waited until she finished with the tray before taking it out of the room. Just a few minutes later, he returned with a glass of water, setting that next to the books.

"Drink when you can. Dr. White was concerned you might be dehydrated." With a smile, Mia selected a book from the pile and slipped further under the covers. Before leaving, he reminded her again, "I'll just be in the next room."

With nothing else to do, Mia opened the book and was amazed to find a title of a novel she'd been wanting to read. It had been drilled into her to take her recovery slow enough to be believable. Every part of her wanted to get started on her real work, but she knew she had to bide her time and earn Donovan's trust back. If that meant lying in bed and reading a good book, that is precisely what she would do.

Throughout the morning, Mia continued to read, well-rested enough to not even attempt sleep. Donovan checked on her about every hour, bringing her into the bathroom when she needed it. At lunchtime, he brought vegetable soup as promised, fresh chunks of vegetables in a clear broth that was clearly homemade. Toast was on the side, and to her astonishment, Mia ate all of it.

Just after lunch, Dr. White visited again, checking bandages and replacing them with a fresh batch. She asked more questions about Mia's condition and seemed encouraged by her appetite. That afternoon Mia read and napped the best she could, only drifting lightly. By the time dinner arrived, she'd gone stir crazy.

When Donovan brought in another tray, Mia had already sat up, feet dangling a few inches from the floor, waiting for him.

"Do you need to use the bathroom?" he asked, rushing to her side. She shook her head. He seemed to understand. "You'd like to get out of this bed." Her bright smile was all the answer he needed. "Dinner al fresco it is."

Grabbing a robe from a hook in the bathroom, Donovan wrapped it around her, tying it securely at her waist. Then, without waiting for consent, he scooped Mia up and carried her through the spacious loft. She only caught glimpses of the rooms as they went by, getting the impression of similar decorating as the bedroom before he stopped at a patio door. Swinging it open, he set her in a comfortable patio chair before going to fetch the tray.

The view was breathtaking. They were easily thirty stories up, one of the larger buildings in Baltimore. The height afforded them a beautiful view of downtown enveloping the bay, and further out, the ocean.

"Gorgeous, isn't it?" Donovan commented, setting the tray down. The look on her face was more than likely a sufficient answer, but she nodded anyway. "It's one of your favorite spots."

This took her attention away from the view and to his face. He smiled lightly and indicated the food. "You should eat."

The fresh air felt amazing, though the breeze at this height left her shivering. Donovan noticed immediately, retrieving a blanket from inside to wrap around her. He didn't speak much, watching the city with her, though Mia knew he didn't miss a single movement she made. As she finished the meal, Donovan began speaking again. "Dr. White suggested beginning some physical activity tomorrow. I've called in a PT to help you regain your strength. Will you be comfortable with that?"

Mia studied him carefully before nodding. The sooner she could be healthy, the better. She'd never laid around so much in her life.

The next several days fell into an easy pattern. Donovan brought her breakfast in the morning and stood in the bathroom while she showered. The PT would show up, and all of the exercises were done in her room. Lunch on the balcony followed by reading in bed until dinner when Donovan would join her again on the balcony.

He continued to sleep on the chair in the room, though she couldn't imagine it to be very comfortable with his lanky body. Mia still didn't speak, and that was getting difficult. After three days, she made it to the bathroom on her own. Donovan still hovered, clearly overprotective, but allowed her to use her own power.

When Mia had been there a week, she felt physically fit and healthier than usual, too, with Donovan's home cooking. In the past, the rare times she ate were hastily consumed from takeout containers, and it was a nice change.

The PT had mentioned a full gym on one of the levels of the building, and her body itched to use it. More than that, though, she was ready to fully begin her work.

As she went to sleep that night, she watched Donovan's figure for a long time. She could tell by his light breathing that he was already asleep. He had shown her nothing but concern, and she still had a difficult time connecting this Donovan with the rap sheet she knew so well.

It didn't help that his every touch still felt like electricity zipping through her body. That was something she had to shut down, but

84

her body had other ideas. Then, her biggest concern—what would happen if the real Selena showed up?

It was with these thoughts that she finally drifted to sleep, the outline of Donovan still behind her lids. She felt restless even in sleep, the way she always had before she'd started the sleep medication.

Images flitted through her mind, vivid dreams with no meaning, flashes of intuition that quickly disappeared. Suddenly she felt locked down as if a heavy weight pressed against her. Struggling to breathe, reaching for consciousness, her eyes shot open with a gasp.

His scent hit her first. Cedar and lemons. Donovan was there, his hands firmly holding her upper arms, his legs straddling her hips.

"Shh, Selena, breathe, you're safe," he whispered, over and over. When Mia calmed down enough to stop struggling, Donovan released her arms and shifted into a more conventional position beside her. With a tender caress, he wiped a tear from her cheek. "You were having nightmares, crying in your sleep."

He stayed by her side for a few more minutes, staring into her eyes. His scent settled deep into her lungs. His warmth enveloped her, even across the several inches of space between them. Though the nightmares had receded, her heartbeat quickened for a whole other reason.

"Will you be all right to sleep?" Donovan finally asked.

Sucking in a breath, she nodded. He stroked her face one more time, resting his palm briefly against her cheek before rising.

"Donovan." Her voice came out cracked, hoarse from no use. He spun in shock, staring at her. For the first time since she'd met him, he seemed hesitant. Vulnerable. Later, she would blame the nightmares. Reaching one hand toward him, she whispered, "Stay."

Approaching cautiously, the way one would a frightened deer, Donovan returned to the bed. When he stretched out beside her, Mia scooted down so that her head lay against his shoulder while his free arm wrapped around her waist. With no more distance between them, his warmth quickly enveloped her. Snuggling into his chest, Mia felt her heart slow to a normal pace. Something shifted inside her.

It was easy then to drift off to sleep. A final thought crossed her mind just as sleep took hold. It described exactly the way it felt to be in Donovan's arms.

Home.

Eight

MIA'S EYES SLID OPEN, AND she had a moment of complete disorientation. There were arms wrapped around her, and she was pressed against a hard body. It had been a long time since she'd been this close to another; even when she dated Cole, he had never slept over. And then she remembered—she'd invited him in.

"Good morning," Donovan said quietly. Carefully shifting out from his embrace, Mia put some distance between them so she could look at his face. He studied her right back. "How are you feeling?"

Mia swallowed once before using her voice. "Better," she said. Making the decision to forge on, she continued, "I...I remember you."

The smile that lit his face rivaled the view from the balcony.

Shaking her head in what she hoped conveyed frustration, Mia explained, "Not my memories, but you. I know that we...worked together, and that I have...feelings for you. But no more details." She'd been forced to pause several times to clear her throat.

"It's a start. Give me a minute, I'll make you some tea for your throat."

Nodding, Mia waited for him to leave before she rose to use the restroom. When she returned, Donovan hadn't, so she ventured out to find him.

It was the first time she'd really wandered on her own. The room immediately outside the bedroom was a sitting room, with two comfortable chairs set before a fireplace, which was double-sided into the bedroom. Shelves of books lined the walls and, in the corner, she found an old record player. The entire shelf surrounding it was filled with albums of every variety. It was a peaceful room, and Mia could imagine herself sitting there, listening to music while reading a book.

She continued on into the open plan of living room, dining room, and kitchen. Beyond that, another hallway where Mia assumed that she would find an office and perhaps Donovan's quarters. Given the relationship he and Selena obviously had, it wouldn't surprise her if they had shared a room, but there were no masculine touches to the suite. That led her to believe he had his own space.

Donovan worked in the kitchen. Mia knew he spotted her as soon as she stepped into the living room. Like the bedroom, the décor was basic and homey, yet there were no personal items. No photographs, trinkets, or trip souvenirs. Nothing to ascertain the personality of the owner.

Mia circled the room, running a hand along the shelves as she did. Behind her, Donovan set the tray on the coffee table and waited for her to turn.

"Is anything familiar?" he asked.

Shaking her head, Mia sat on the sofa and took a sip of the hot liquid. It helped soothe her hoarse throat. "I would like to look around today."

Donovan agreed. "I'll give you a tour of the building. As much as you're up to, anyway. I've called Dr. White to let her know some of your memory has returned. She'll be in after lunch."

"Okay." Mia took another sip. Finally, she could begin what she'd been sent here to do.

After she showered and Donovan canceled her therapy for the day, he began by taking her to the roof of the building. There was another patio set up, with several round tables and chairs and many pots interspersed, which would be overflowing with flowers in the spring. The other half of the roof had been set up as an enclosed greenhouse.

Donovan took her inside, and here she found vegetables, herbs, and berries all in different stages of growth. No wonder Donovan's cooking tasted so good—it used the freshest of ingredients.

"This is incredible."

"Your favorite spot is the balcony," Donovan said. "This is mine."

For a moment, Mia studied him, then asked the question that had been burning since he'd first rescued her. "What...what exactly...are we?" He tilted his head, and Mia realized how ambiguous her question had been. "Are we...married? Dating? Something else?"

Understanding, he smiled softly. "We've never really put a label on it. We are partners. In business, and in every other way," he added, watching her carefully for a reaction. "I can say that I have been faithful to you since the moment we met, six years ago."

The intense emotion and sheer honesty spilling out of Donovan made Mia feel overwhelmed. Having no words, she approached him slowly and slid her arms around his waist, allowing her head to rest against his chest. His heartbeat was strong and just a little quick, and it pleased her that she would be the cause.

"Would you like to see the rest of the building?" he eventually asked, pulling away. Nodding, Mia allowed him to take her hand as they left the roof. "The first ten floors are offices, with no access to this elevator. The elevator and the emergency stairs can only be operated by me or you. We'll have to reprogram you into the system," he explained, and Mia looked up at him, surprised at her turn of luck. He continued, misunderstanding her expression, "We have a security protocol in place if one of us is...taken."

Interesting, but good news. Not sure how she would have explained a new hand and eye print.

They went down one level, and the doors opened to the most well-equipped gym she'd ever seen. It housed every type of equipment imaginable, including several she'd never seen before. There was a wall of free weights, and two walls were mirrored. The other two were covered in windows with the same amazing views as the penthouse. One section sat empty but for floor mats ringed by punching bags. Mia itched to try them out.

"When you're feeling up to it, you can continue your therapy sessions in here until you feel comfortable without the PT." Donovan led her back to the elevator, and they continued the tour. He showed her their offices next, an ample space with two desks and advanced-looking computer equipment. After she'd looked around, Mia felt weaker than she was willing to admit. "Are you ready for lunch?"

Mia nodded, allowing him to steer her toward the elevator once again. His arm wrapped securely around her waist, and she relied more heavily on it than she would have liked.

"How is your throat feeling?"

Mia spoke without needing to clear it first. "Better. Mostly just out of practice."

"We've pushed you a lot today. After Dr. White's visit, you should rest."

Though it wasn't what she really wanted to do, she agreed. When they entered the loft, she sat on a bar stool that overlooked the kitchen island while Donovan prepped her meal. The more she got to know him, the harder time she had relating this person to the criminal she'd been assigned to take down.

"Donovan?" Mia asked softly.

His attention immediately turned to her. "Yes?"

"What kind of business are we in?"

Leaving the fruit that he'd been chopping on the cutting board, Donovan approached her and held both her hands in his. "Why do you ask?"

Looking around pointedly, she answered, "It seems we're pretty wealthy. I just...I just wish I could remember more."

Casting her eyes downward, Mia allowed all her frustration to show on her face. With gentle fingers, he tilted her face toward him. "It will come back soon. Please do not feel frustrated."

Nodding, Mia waited for him to answer her original question. Releasing his grasp, he looked her steady in the eye. "We run a mainly shipping business that has a variety of local and international dealings. Perhaps in the next couple of days, you could sit in with me on some client phone calls. It may help you remember something."

Not trusting her voice, Mia merely nodded again. Seeming satisfied by her compliance, he returned to fixing their lunch.

Instead of sitting on the patio, he placed two plates on the counter and joined her after pouring tea into cups. "What did you think of our building so far?"

"It's a lot to take in. How much more is there?"

"Like I told you earlier, the first ten floors are offices for our employees. I won't take you down there until you feel ready. You and I don't oversee the daily operations directly; we have an office manager for that."

"Do we have more than one office?"

"This is our main building," Donovan said. "We own other properties and, of course, our location on the docks, as well as similar sites internationally."

"Do we travel a lot, then?"

Donovan hesitated before answering, "As needed."

There was something Mia was missing, but she didn't want to force the issue now. It would only make Donovan suspicious. She finished her lunch without any more conversation, her thoughts on overdrive.

△ △ △

WHILE DR. WHITE EXAMINED MIA'S injuries, she saw her small smile of satisfaction at the progress. Once finished, the doctor met her eyes. "Donovan tells me something of your memory has returned."

"Kind of," Mia said. "Not memories, exactly, more...feelings."

Her eyebrows furrowed. "What do you mean?"

"I know how I feel about Donovan. The feelings are there, but the reasons behind the feelings are still missing. Is that normal?"

Pausing before answering, Dr. White crossed her arms, supporting her chin with her capable fingers. "The mind is still very much a mystery, even with our advanced sciences. Every person that has head trauma recovers in different ways. I'm not sure we can peg any of it as 'normal.' I will say, anything coming back to you is encouraging."

"Dr. White?" Mia asked as she turned away to pack her bag. When she faced her again, Mia fiddled idly with the blanket beneath her. "Were you...were you my doctor...before?"

"On occasion, yes."

"What was I like?"

The doctor approached Mia, laying a gentle hand on her arm. "I realize how frustrating it is to lose your memory, but I cannot tell you who you are. You will discover that in time."

"Please. Anything you can tell me would be helpful."

Sighing, Dr. White gave in. "You've always been extremely intelligent, headstrong, and decisive. Those can be good qualities, but they also have their negatives."

"I'm...I'm not a very nice person, am I?"

Pursing her lips, Dr. White studied her. "Not always. But there is good in you. Just remember that."

Mia nodded once, contemplating her words. Once the doctor left and she was supposed to be resting, Mia continuously turned the words over in her mind. If she kept playing this timid, sweet patient, would Donovan see right through her? Anyone could see how much he cared for Selena; it was in his eyes every time he looked at Mia. If she didn't start acting the way Dr. White had described, would this entire ruse be for naught?

Eventually, Mia slipped into a restless sleep. Now that her body had become accustomed to rest and good nutrition, she wasn't sleeping as deeply, which left room for dreams to maneuver.

△ △ △

THE BLACK LEATHER FELT STIFF and uncomfortable on her legs, but she walked with confidence through the loft rooms in the blood-red stiletto heels. Donovan was there, in his office, on a phone call. He looked up as Mia stopped, hip cocked, leaning against the wall, the unmistakable look of desire on his face. Her lips quirked up, knowing what was in his mind.

He finished the phone call and stood, approaching her slowly, assessing her from head to foot. There were no words, only an electricity in the air that seemed to arch between them.

"What would you like, mistress?" His voice came out husky, and the realization hit her that she was in control.

"Kneel," she commanded. He did so immediately. The rush of power was heady.

"What shall I do now?" he asked, his hooded eyes looking up at her.

"You know what," she said, her voice dropping an octave. "Be a good boy, and you will be rewarded."

△ △ △

MIA WOKE WITH A START, soaked in sweat, shooting into a sitting position. Thankfully, she was alone for the moment. After that dream, Mia didn't think she could face Donovan.

Feeling sticky and warm, she decided to take a cool shower. With any luck, the mundane act would help to calm her racing heart and bolster her ability to look Donovan in the eye.

Running the water in the shower, Mia took a moment to study herself in the mirror. The bruises under her eyes, which had been present for as long as she could remember, were completely diminished. Her amber eyes were bright, though wary. Even though she hadn't been in the direct sun since she'd been in training, Mia's skin had a healthy glow that had always been lacking from her fast-food diet. It was amazing the difference just a week had made; she barely recognized herself.

Stepping into the shower, Mia let the water cascade off her in waves. She watched, mesmerized, as it swirled down the drain. Closing her eyes, she let the last vestiges of the dream fall to the floor, imagining it draining away with the water.

Wrapping a towel around herself, Mia opened the closet doors for the first time and perused the wardrobe for an outfit to make her feel less helpless and more like Selena. It was a very different style than hers—the black leather of the dream wasn't too far off.

Picking out a pair of somewhat comfortable-looking black dress pants and a silky red blouse, Mia paused at the case of shoes and gave it a once-over. Most of the collection consisted of black heeled boots, but as her eyes drifted down, a splash of red caught her eye.

Gasping, she knelt on the closet floor and grabbed the pair of heels, staring at them in astonishment. They were the exact pair she'd worn in the dream.

It had to be a coincidence. Or she'd seen the pair when Donovan had the closet door open to select an outfit for her, and her subconscious simply used them in the dream.

That's all there was to it.

Shoving the heels back in their slot, Mia hastily grabbed a pair of flat boots and ventured out to find Donovan. He wasn't in the main living area or the kitchen, so she walked down the hall toward his office. There was an unwanted flashback to the dream as she found him behind a desk, on the phone. Standing in the doorway, Mia waited until he spotted her and motioned her inside before entering.

Quickly hanging up the phone, he gave her a once-over. "You look refreshed."

"I slept a little and took a quick shower. I thought, perhaps, regular clothes would make me feel more...human."

They shared a smile at that. "I hope you're feeling comfortable here. It is your home, after all, even though I realize it doesn't feel that way right now."

"I thought it would help if I got back into my normal routine," Mia said, watching for his reaction. "You never know what might trigger a memory."

"Absolutely. Because of the nature of our business, most of our deals are conducted at night. In fact, I have a meeting tonight you can sit in with me on. If at any point you get tired, I'll bring you straight back here."

"Sounds like a plan," Mia said with a smile.

After dinner, Donovan led her downstairs to their offices. Though she knew there must be other people around, she had yet to meet any and found herself wondering if that was typical or for her benefit while she healed.

Staying silent until they were in the office, Mia began to walk around, getting a feel for the space. Where upstairs, everything was soft, feminine, these were decorated in steel and black, more masculine and modern. Was this two sides to Selena's personality, or did Donovan choose the office décor?

Mia found both appealing for different reasons. In the loft, the French country feel was warm and inviting, and she felt surprisingly comfortable in it. The office, however, felt more conducive to work, and Dr. White's words rang in her head.

Intelligent, headstrong, decisive. That's the impression this color scheme gave off.

"What is it?" Donovan asked. He had been watching her analyze the office.

"I was wondering, did I decorate the office and the loft?"

"You did. Why do you ask?"

With a shrug, she tried not to sound crazy. "It's almost like two different personalities. But I suppose that makes sense. A person shouldn't act the same at home as they do in business."

When she glanced back at Donovan, it was difficult to decipher the look on his face. It was a combination of curiosity and fear. Finally, he settled on an easy smile. "That's a good philosophy," he said. Opening a drawer, he pulled out a large pair of dark sunglasses and offered them to her.

"What are these for?"

"We've always been cautious in our business. Few people have seen your face. With recent events, that caution seems justified."

"So, I do all my business interactions with sunglasses on?" she asked doubtfully, grasping them between two fingers.

"It was your idea."

Slipping them on, Mia pouted her lips and struck a pose. "Very Hollywood."

To her surprise, he laughed—a deep, husky sound that made the blood sing in her veins. She suddenly found herself thankful for the glasses; they hid the startled look she now portrayed.

Clearing her throat, Mia went behind what Donovan had told her was her desk during their tour and sat down, rifling through the drawers. There was very little there, and she wondered if Donovan had cleared it out until he thought she got her memory back.

The file drawers were empty, and the smaller drawers had just the very basics in them. Looking up at Donovan, who was watching her from across the room, Mia suddenly felt self-conscious.

"It doesn't seem like I do much work," she joked, sliding the glasses off and laying them atop the desk.

"I've been handling your clients while you've been away," he said, and the pain in his eyes at the latter part of his statement was unmistakable.

Swallowing, Mia nodded once before returning to his side of the room. Approaching him slowly, she steeled herself for the contact, telling her body firmly not to react. Her palms slid around his waist, though she kept a respectable distance between them.

"I'm here now," Mia said, looking him directly in the eye. Then, she added quietly, "I'm sorry I've caused you pain."

His breath came out quickly as if surprised by her guilt. Carefully, he raised one hand up to cup the side of her face before gently pulling her toward him. His hand pressed her face to his chest, where she could hear the steady beat of his heart.

This was about comfort, and though the electricity between them still hummed, it was only background noise for the moment.

When it was time for the conference call, Mia stood behind Donovan wearing her sunglasses. The man whose image flickered onto the screen was older, though handsome, and when he spoke, Mia picked up his Italian accent immediately.

"Donovan," he greeted.

"Buon giorno, Signor Moretti," Donovan replied. Since it was the middle of the night for them, it was early morning for Mr. Moretti.

"I will get right to the business," Mr. Moretti said in clipped tones. "We have a large shipment that needs to get into the States. Will you be able to handle this?"

"Of course, Signor Moretti. How large of a shipment is it, and when is your deadline?"

"It is thirteen hundred and fifty kilograms and needs to be in New York in two weeks."

Donovan pulled up a spreadsheet on his computer. "I have a ship in Monaco that can be in Rome in a day."

"That is acceptable."

"Our fee is the normal arrangement of twenty percent up front, the balance once it's delivered. As soon as the funds are in our account, I will give the order." Mr. Moretti nodded, and the call terminated.

Donovan tapped a few more keys, Mia watching over his shoulder. It looked like some kind of banking website, though not one she was familiar with. A funds transfer was already in progress, and, seeing that, Donovan made his next phone call to the ship captain that was currently docked in Monaco.

Mia found the process fascinating and decided not to ask too many questions yet. As Agent McKenzie had said, she'd learn more for the time being from just watching.

After staying up so late, Mia ended up sleeping in the next morning. Donovan prepared her breakfast as usual, and she asked if she could use the gym.

"Of course," he said. "I'll reprogram the security system so that you have free reign in the top levels. Right now, for your own protection, don't go below level eleven, all right?"

"Sure," Mia said, excited to get in a real workout.

That's how she spent the next several days—eating meals Donovan made, working out in the gym, and sitting in on more calls. Donovan was choosy about which calls she could sit in on, and Mia knew he kept the darker side of the business from her. She bided her time, knowing that, eventually, she would change that.

After that first night where Donovan slept beside her, he slept in his own room. She was strong enough to get to the bathroom on her own, and the reprieve of his masculine form was a relief. Spending so much time with him as it was, Mia found herself having moments of truly enjoying his company. The conversation with Agent McKenzie rang in her ears during this time about using her feelings for the good, but it felt like it would be too easy to cross a line.

Getting the physical activity helped to exhaust her enough to sleep at night, without medication and without dreams. The last thing she needed was her subconscious to dredge up more inappropriate thoughts of her caretaker.

With another week under her belt, Mia decided to speak to Donovan again about the business to wrangle more details out of him. Waiting until dinner time, she steeled herself for the conversation.

They were on the patio, the sun sinking below the horizon. As the colors morphed from brilliant orange to pink, purple, and finally a deep blue, she glanced over at Donovan.

"I'd like to become more involved in the business," Mia began.

He looked at her, surprised. "Do you think you're ready? You've been through such an ordeal, and without your memory..."

"I feel useless right now. It doesn't have to be anything big; I'd just like to do more with my time."

After pondering that for a moment, Donovan nodded. "All right, I'll see what I can come up with."

They were silent a few minutes before she decided to delve into the next part. "Donovan, I..." Before she could finish, there was a crash from inside the apartment.

Donovan jumped up, and Mia was quick to follow. The unmistakable sound of gunfire rang out, and she found herself shoved behind the couch in the living room. There was shouting, but she couldn't make out individual words over the ringing in her ears.

While she watched, Donovan pushed the couch forward, lifting the edge of the rug to reveal a trap door. Yanking it open, her eyes landed on a cache of weapons. He grabbed two guns, shoving them into her hands, before taking two for himself. They glanced at each other once before spinning around, aiming over the top of the couch.

For the first time since she'd been in Donovan's care, Mia felt proficient. The feel of a gun in her hand was natural, and they worked together as if they'd done it all their lives.

There were easily ten figures in the apartment, dressed in all black, semi-automatic weapons shooting wildly. It didn't seem they even knew where Donovan and Mia hid, but that wouldn't last long.

Setting her sights on the first, Mia calmly squeezed the trigger, aiming to maim rather than kill. They began dropping in screams of pain, clutching at their legs as she continued to fire. Donovan was shooting next to her and realizing quickly that they were wearing bulletproof vests, took her lead and aimed for their lower extremities.

Once the attackers were down, they exchanged clips before standing and heading for the exit. It seemed the attackers had come out of the elevator, even with their security in place, so Donovan and Mia aimed for the stairwell.

Before they could reach it, more of the dark figures piled out. Donovan yanked her down again, covering her with his own body.

This time they were behind one of the overstuffed chairs, which did not give them as much cover as the couch had. Somewhere in the recesses of her mind, Mia thought the furniture must be specially made to withstand bullets because not one had come through the fabric.

In perfect synchronization, Donovan and Mia spun around once again, aiming for whatever body parts they could get their sights on. From the first batch of intruders, Mia caught sight of movement from the corner of her eye, too precise to be just writhing in pain.

With wide eyes, she watched as the man pulled out an egg-shaped object from his pocket. He looked directly at Mia as he pulled the pin and threw it into the fray.

Nine

THERE WAS NO TIME TO lose. If they didn't move quickly, Donovan and Mia would be caught in the explosion of the live grenade.

"Go. Now." Though her ears were ringing, Donovan's tone brooked no argument.

Clasping her hand in his, Donovan leaped to the stairwell, dragging Mia down the first dozen steps with him and losing their guns in the process. Though he had to release his grip to give them both freedom of movement, Mia remained on his heels, feet moving quicker than they had since she'd been brought there.

On each level they passed, Mia could hear fists pounding on the doors. Three levels down, an explosion rocked the building.

Donovan grabbed her again, throwing her to the floor of the next landing, his body instantly becoming a shield. Debris shook its way down on top of them, and they wasted no time in finding their feet and continuing the race down the stairs.

Though Mia expected to exit at the ground floor, Donovan placed his hand on a hidden panel, and another door slid noiselessly open. Sparing her a glance before sealing the secret entrance, they continued down three more flights of stairs.

Even with her gym training, Mia felt winded by the time Donovan pushed open the remaining door. What they stepped into made her stop and stare.

The cavernous room was chilly and dark. She gazed around in amazement, but only for a moment. Without missing a beat, Donovan swung his leg over one of two motorcycles waiting for them, looking back at her expectantly.

In a moment of panic, Mia realized she'd never been on a motorcycle, but Selena surely had. Understanding dawned in Donovan's eyes, and he held out a hand patiently. Without hesitation, she accepted it, sliding onto the seat behind him. Her arms wrapped around his waist just as they took off, the jolt of speed taking her by surprise.

As they exited the initial room, insight blossomed. They were in tunnels, underground. The infamous tunnels that were constantly argued over and thought to be a myth. Somehow, Selena and Donovan had found them and used them for transportation.

Mia's theory had been correct. This was how they got around and never spotted on CCTV.

The wind whipped her hair in a long stream while Donovan applied steady pressure to the gas. The occasional light lit their way, and she took note of each offshoot from the main tunnel they seemed to be in. It was incredible, and she wished she had more time to document where they were, but she knew in time that would come. Right now, their safety had to be first priority.

Taking several turns, Donovan eventually slowed, stopping in another cavernous room that looked much the same as the one they'd started in. Waiting for her to dismount, Donovan followed suit and parked the bike.

"Where are we?" Mia ventured to ask, having to speak louder to beat out the temporary haze.

"A safe house," he said, once again grabbing her hand and leading her to the middle of the wall.

Much like the hidden door to the basement levels in the building they'd just evacuated, Donovan placed his hand systematically to reveal another door. Following him inside, he made sure the door was back in place before leading her up another three flights of stairs, through another hidden doorway, and to the top of the building.

This one was much shorter at just six stories, but her legs were burning by the end. Another scan led them inside. Gone were the light, feminine tones. What Mia assumed used to be windows were shuttered in metal. There was no artwork on the walls, and the sparse furnishings were more industrial than homey.

"We shouldn't have to stay long," Donovan promised on seeing her assessment of the room. "I know it's not what you're used to."

"It's safe?"

"It is."

There was a sitting area, a sleeping area, and a kitchen, and the only door on the inside led to a bathroom.

"It's very...open," Mia finished, and it brought out a chuckle from Donovan.

"That it is," he responded, taking a step toward the kitchen before collapsing to one knee.

"Donovan!" Mia cried out, kneeling beside him in an instant. "Were you hit?" With shaking fingers, she pulled back his jacket, where one of his hands had gripped in pain. When he pulled his fingers away, they were smeared with blood. "You were shot. You need to lie down."

Carefully wrapping an arm around his waist, Mia helped him to the bed, setting him on the edge before removing his jacket and shirt. "Lie back. Emergency medical?"

"Bathroom."

Rushing into the only enclosed space, Mia searched through the cabinets until she found a white case with medical supplies in it. It seemed they were well prepared for this type of emergency; the case was fully equipped, and she'd also spied a defibrillator.

Dragging the side table closer to where she could now see he'd been grazed with a bullet, Mia popped open the case and immediately pressed a cloth to the wound, instructing Donovan to hold it in place while she prepped the other tools.

"This is going to sting," she warned, wincing as she poured rubbing alcohol over the wound.

Besides a small grunt of pain, he took it manfully. They were lucky in that the bullet only grazed his side; she wouldn't have to perform major surgery, though he would need stitches. Thankfully, she'd taken a crash course in emergency field medicine, and she made quick work with the needle and thread.

Donovan watched her thoughtfully while she concentrated, and though it crossed her mind that she could be blowing her cover, making sure he was healed was more critical. After snipping the thread, Mia swabbed disinfectant gently over the wound once more before applying a bandage. "There now. All better."

Gathering all the supplies back together, Mia went to stand but was held back by a hand on her arm. Though she'd been studiously avoiding his gaze, she met it now, registering the awe in his eyes.

"Thank you," he said quietly. "You continuously amaze me."

Their eyes locked, and slowly, irrationally, Mia lowered toward him. Her brain screamed to stop, but she was past the point of no return. There was a gravity surrounding Donovan that pulled her in, inexorably closer, until their lips met.

The fire that immediately consumed her spread through her entire body, alighting a passion in her she never knew existed. Deepening the kiss, Mia let her hands sink into his thick hair as they'd been craving to do since the beginning. She felt his arms wrap around her waist, holding her closer still.

The kiss deepened, evoking a breathy moan from deep in her throat. There was a haze over her actions; her brain temporarily shut off while her body experienced sensations she'd only ever read about.

Wanting more, needing more, her hands began to trail down his chest—only to find his newly bandaged injury.

Yanking away from him with a gasp, Mia stumbled several feet away, one hand covering her mouth in shock. It seemed he was also having difficulty catching his breath, and though her ego wanted to believe that was because of her, Mia knew it was her careless control with his wound.

"I'm so sorry," she whispered through her palm.

"Selena," he said sternly, "you have nothing to apologize for. I have been waiting for that moment for longer than you know."

"But, still, your injury..."

"Is fine, I promise. You are very adept with a needle and thread."

"It's something else that just came to me," she hedged, attempting to play off her temporary lapse of judgment on her memory loss.

"I think you will be surprised by how much you know," Donovan replied cryptically.

Needing to busy herself and calm her racing heart, she picked up the box of supplies, along with the garbage, and brought it into the bathroom. As she turned to leave, Mia caught sight of herself in the mirror.

Her eyes were large, bright with excitement. Her lips were slightly swollen from his kiss. Touching her fingertips lightly to her mouth, Mia let herself relive the moment, savoring the feel of Donovan's body beneath her touch.

It couldn't happen again, she told herself. But now that she'd opened that can of worms, would it be more suspicious if she held him at bay?

Refocusing on her task, Mia exited the bathroom and took in his still form. His eyes were on her, and she ordered herself to think. "Would you like something to drink? You should have some fluids after the blood loss. Is there a laundry? I can try to get your clothes clean. How about something to eat?"

"Selena." Donovan held out a hand to her. She approached him but didn't make the contact she craved. "There are clothes here for both of us. I'd like to rest for a bit, but then I will clean off and change."

Nodding, Mia glanced at the kitchen. "I should at least get you a water." Without waiting for his response, she rummaged around until she found a glass and filled it. Setting it on the side table, she grabbed a small chair and pulled it alongside the bed. "Who were those people?"

"Our competitors."

Shaking her head, letting her frustration show, Mia ran her hands through her hair. "That doesn't make sense. Business competitors don't come into your home with guns blazing!" Attempting to calm down, she leaned forward and placed a hand on Donovan's wrist. "I think it's time you explain to me exactly what it is we do."

He shook his head, keeping his eyes steady on hers. "You're not ready."

"What does that even mean? I was attacked tonight, same as you!" Attempting to calm her raging temper, Mia quieted her voice. "I'm so tired of not knowing, not remembering who I am, my life. Please, Donovan, just tell me."

Instead of responding, he watched her a long time, looking for something in her face, her eyes. She hid nothing from him, her curiosity and frustration running rampant in her expression. Finally, his look softened, and he began to speak. "We run a completely legitimate shipping business. We also run an illegal one."

She processed this before nodding for him to continue. "We've delved into many different avenues, though we've both been clear from the beginning we wouldn't get involved in the drug or weapons trades. Our morals may be few, but we do have them." His mouth upturned into a self-deprecating half-smile.

She thought back to the last case she'd worked with Alec and Adam. They'd been sure Donovan had been working with the DeLuca brothers. It seemed Mia had been right that Donovan being involved in weapons didn't match his usual activity. "What, exactly, are we shipping?"

"Art, artifacts, jewels. That kind of thing."

"Tell me about the tunnels we just came through. I remember stories about them—people don't think they're real."

He smiled again, more genuine this time. "The tunnels are the real genius behind our business. When we first met, you were certain they existed. We began buying up property strategically, hiring out-of-state companies to come in and excavate beneath the basements. There's still more work to do on them, but over the years, we've connected the majority of our properties to the docks."

This was incredible, and Mia took a moment to soak it all in. Standing, she paced away and back again, thinking through the ramifications of the details he'd just revealed.

After several paces, she sat again, her focus on Donovan. "This is a lot to sift through."

"I understand."

"What's our next step?"

He seemed satisfied by the question. "I'll clear the building with our team of security. Then, we'll have to retaliate."

Her eyebrows furrowed. "Is that necessary?"

"We don't stay on top by being soft," Donovan said, his voice hardening.

Considering his expression for a long moment, Mia's mind raced a mile a minute. She had to be careful here, as balking at his suggestion might give her away. Then again, she was still a cop and couldn't condone unnecessary violence. "I'm not suggesting we let it go. But, perhaps there's another way."

Donovan finally agreed. "We both need some rest. We'll discuss this after."

As Donovan slept, Mia rested fitfully beside him. Not allowing herself to lay beside him, worried at her reaction to his close proximity, she sat slouched in a chair beside the bed. Concern over his injuries prevented her from fully falling into sleep, but exhaustion from the events of the last several hours finally won out. She must have drifted off because another vivid dream assaulted her subconscious.

$$\triangle \triangle \triangle$$

CLAD IN BLACK LEATHER ONCE again, she stood against the wall, peering through her dark lenses as Donovan discussed details with the construction manager. They were paying the crew in cash, and, well, they expected the best in return.

"We can run the conduits through this building, but it would raise your electric bill exponentially. That's fine if you want to pay it, but it might raise suspicions."

"An alternative?" Donovan asked.

"Solar power. We can punch cables through at the sites of your properties and attach a small solar panel on the roofs. They would be relatively unnoticeable."

Donovan glanced at her, and she simply nodded.

"Let's do it." Without any further comment, the contractor gave the order to his men. They were quick and proficient, a product of working for cash instead of hourly. When Donovan approached her, he spoke quietly. "I'll stay to keep an eye on them if you want to take care of the other matter."

With a smirk, she answered, "Gladly."

Not wasting any more time, she approached the sleek bike and swung a leg over. Revving the engine once, she kicked it into gear and spun away from Donovan, heading back toward home.

△ △ △

AFTER THEY'D BOTH SLEPT, MIA convinced Donovan to let himself rest for the remainder of the day. He had contact through a burner phone with the head of security, and they planned on meeting that night.

When Donovan left, Mia truly went stir-crazy. He was right; this safe house was not what she had become accustomed to. Being holed up in their loft with its wide-open spaces and breathtaking views was very different to this utilitarian prison. Though she felt like a caged tiger, above all, she worried for Donovan. She could rationalize her concern by believing if something happened to him, she would lose her case—but the truth was, she'd started to care for him.

Her fingers touched her lips briefly as she forced herself to see reason. She didn't just care for him; she lusted after him. Her undercover identity was quickly becoming intertwined with who she was on the inside, and while going down this path might help convince Donovan of who she was, it could only lead to heartache.

To take her mind off the impossible situation, Mia worked out. Though there was no fancy equipment like the gym in their building, she managed to work up a sweat with the basics. Push-ups, sit-ups, burpees, lunges. She even used the bathroom doorway as a pull-up bar by clinging to the edge with her fingertips. When she'd exhausted herself, she took a shower and allowed the water to soothe her jittery nerves.

The only clothes kept there looked to be combat-ready; black cargo pants and black t-shirts. The entire bed frame shifted to reveal a pull-out compartment, in which she found a stash of weapons. It seemed Donovan and Selena were prepared for any eventuality.

Strapping a belt around her waist, Mia loaded it with knives and two Glock .45s, as that was her sidearm with the force. Checking the sights before sliding them into compartments, she marveled at the quality of the weapon, wondering briefly where Donovan and Selena had acquired them. He'd told her specifically that they were not involved with drug or weapons trafficking, but that didn't mean they didn't have connections.

As she stood, Mia heard noises at the door. Assuming it was Donovan but taking no chances, she pulled one of the guns out and trained it on the entrance.

The security beeped, and Donovan entered, seeming surprised to find her standing at attention. "Selena? Are you going to shoot me?"

"No," she replied, dropping the weapon. "Just being cautious."

He nodded, taking in her attire before walking toward the kitchen, setting down the backpack he'd had slung over his shoulder. "I brought us a few supplies and met with our head of security. They went into lockdown and have already cleared our building. It would be better if we waited to go back until we discover where the leak came from."

Trying not to react to those words, knowing in her gut how a leak of this extreme would be handled, Mia picked up an apple off the counter and examined it. "Has this happened before?"

"Once," he said, muscles tensing. "When you were taken."

"How are the ribs?" she asked to distract him.

"They've slowed me down a little, but I'm not in pain."

"You need to let it heal properly. Or at least contact Dr. White."

"No. I'll be fine." Mia let it go, understanding the stubborn streak. He changed topics this time. "I have to leave again."

"I'm coming with you."

"Absolutely not. If something happened to you..."

"And you think I could let something happen to you?"

His lips pressed together, and Mia thought he would argue. To her surprise, he agreed. "We'll need to disguise your face and your hair."

Without hesitation, she opened the small cupboard where she'd found her outfit and pulled out a black scarf, along with another pair of sunglasses. There was also a military-style jacket that she slipped on, which covered the small arsenal on her hips.

Placing the scarf atop her head, she began braiding her hair quickly, including one side of the scarf into the braid. Once she got to the bottom, she looped the scarf one way and the braid the other around her head, securing the ends with a knot on the top of her head. Donovan watched without a word.

"I look like I'm trying to hide," she said, slipping on the sunglasses. "Isn't it better to wear normal clothes? Most people aren't paying enough attention to pick out an individual in the crowd. I stand out because I'm trying to hide."

"That is true, under normal circumstances," Donovan said. "But these are not normal circumstances. We've always been careful to keep your face hidden and will continue to do so."

Deciding not to press him further, Mia merely nodded and followed him out the door. They made their way back down to the underground levels, where the motorcycle waited. She climbed on behind Donovan without provocation, enjoying the feel of her arms around his body more than she should.

With a rev of the engine, they were off, heading in the opposite direction than the loft. They took a longer route with several turns before stopping in another, similar room. Now that Mia knew what to look for, she could see the tell-tale crack along the otherwise seamless wall where a door would slide open.

Donovan palmed open the door, and she followed on his heel, moving silently through the stairwell. At the next scanner, Donovan paused to check a small surveillance camera that seemed to be positioned just outside the door. Mia imagined this building must be open to the public, or at least held workers of some kind for Donovan to be displaying this kind of caution. Seeing that the way was clear, he activated the scanner, and they walked through the door, hand in hand.

The hallway they emerged into was unremarkable, with beige walls and gray carpet. As they rounded the corner to the lobby, Mia was surprised to realize it was daylight out. Being in the safe house had seriously messed with her internal clock.

At least her sunglass-clad face wouldn't seem quite so out of place. Her heartbeat sped as they approached the doors, realizing she would be going outside for the first time in weeks. It would also be her first chance to get a message to her precinct.

"Follow me exactly," Donovan said in a low aside.

From her experience, Mia knew Donovan had the location of each CCTV camera memorized as she did. He would be trying to avoid them; she just needed one to see her.

They walked quickly, though not overly hurried, to their destination. He had yet to tell her what that was, but it would soon become apparent.

Donovan paused just shy of an intersection, and from the location, Mia knew there was a camera at each corner, along with down the alley to her left. No matter which way they went, they'd hit a camera.

"I need you to stay right here," he said. "Exactly here. Do you understand?"

"Yes," she answered. He squeezed her hand gently before moving with his head down across the street. Once he disappeared into a building, she made her move.

Taking ten steps into the alley, Mia flipped her glasses down to stare directly into the camera. She tapped a finger nervously against her leg, keeping an eye on the corner.

Tap, tap, tap, hold, hold. Hold, tap, tap, tap, tap. Tap, hold, tap, tap. Tap. Hold, tap, tap, hold. Tap, Tap. Hold, tap. Hold, hold, tap. Hold. Hold, hold, hold. Hold, tap.

Thirty-six Lexington.

Tap, tap, tap, tap. Hold, hold, hold. Hold, hold. Tap.

Home.

Hold. Tap, tap, hold. Hold, tap. Hold, tap. Tap. Tap, hold, tap, tap. Tap, tap, tap, tap.

Tunnels.

Not wanting to risk more, she ran back to the exact spot Donovan had left her. Seconds later, he stepped out the door and headed back to her, relieved to see she remained where he'd left her.

Mia didn't risk a glance down the alley as they passed; she merely clasped his hand in hers and followed him to the next stop.

Ten

THEY WOUND THEIR WAY THROUGH the streets, cutting through alleys and buildings as needed to avoid the cameras lurking at most corners. They didn't speak, just kept their hands locked together, keeping an even pace. When they finally paused, it was in front of a drab brown building, two stories high. Mia was unimpressed by its exterior and even less so by the inside.

The stench hit her first, and she was careful not to gag. Donovan glanced down at her, judging her reaction to the piles of garbage and several sleeping bodies in the hallway, before leading her down a set of stairs.

"Sorry for the smell," he murmured. "These are not the most upstanding citizens. Stay close to me, stay silent. Understand?"

Nodding, Mia watched with trepidation as he pulled open a door at the bottom of the steps. It led into another small hallway, with a single door at the end, the smell infinitely better. Donovan strode up to it confidently, knocking loudly twice, pausing, rapidly three more times, one more pause, and a final knock.

The door opened, and a large man with dark skin and darker eyes filled the frame, his arms crossed. Neither Donovan nor Mia backed down, showing confidence she didn't necessarily feel in the moment. Her eyes tracked the weapons barely hidden beneath his black leather jacket, making a mental plan in case they ran into trouble.

"Donovan," the man said, his deep voice rumbling out, and Mia detected a note of admiration in his tone. That might prove to be useful.

"Leroy," Donovan acknowledged him with a bow of his head. "I'm here to see Reggie."

"Thought you might be." Stepping back, Leroy allowed them entrance. To her surprise, he tipped his head at Mia as she passed. "Good to see you, Selena."

Not wanting to speak, as Donovan requested, Mia merely nodded her head in greeting, letting her lips quirk up at one corner. Once they stepped through the doorway, it was a very different scene from the one above.

The room opened up into what was clearly a playroom. A couple of pool tables, dartboards, and other assorted games were scattered about the room, with a long bar against the back wall. Two scantily clad women stood behind it, looking bored, while a group of men sat on couches in a small gathering area. To the right, the entire wall was made up of dark, reflective glass—undoubtedly a two-way mirror.

Mia guessed there would be offices behind that wall, where a person could oversee the activities in this room. Sticking by Donovan, she paused as he did, waiting for someone in the group to acknowledge them. Leroy was just inside the door they'd come through, about fifteen paces from where Mia stood. Her eyes continuously swept the room from behind the dark lenses.

They were made to wait in some show of chauvinism that merely annoyed Mia, but Donovan remained expressionless. The men stood as a group, though the ring leader approached first.

"Hey, man." Reggie had a relaxed attitude that belied the weapons Mia spotted on each man.

His crew seemed overly confident, their posture both slumped and condescending simultaneously. As she scanned for weapons, Mia also assessed their weaknesses. There were many.

She immediately nicknamed them the three stooges.

"Reggie," Donovan greeted the man with dreadlocks and several gold earrings, which matched the chains around his neck. "It seems we have some things to discuss."

"Where'd you hear that from?"

"Anderson."

"You believe anything that snitch tells you?" Reggie asked, throwing an amused smile at his closest henchmen. The three stooges grinned at each other and nodded.

"In this case, I do," Donovan said, ignoring the asides. "So, what was your end game?"

"You accusing us of something, Donny?" Reggie flashed his weapon, stuck in the front of his pants. Typical.

To his credit, Donovan remained relaxed, not bothered in the slightest by the sight of the gun. "I am. And I would like an answer to my question."

The stooge to the right, closest to Mia, shifted slightly and positioned his hand for a quick grab. That was the wrong move.

In a single leap, Mia was in front of him, slamming her fist into his solar plexus. As he bent forward in pain, she uppercut under his chin with her left, spinning, whipping the gun from his side holster with her right and executing a chop with her left to his throat as she came full circle.

As he dropped, she'd already transferred his gun to her left, digging into the ribs with her right on the next stooge. Before either left standing could react, she'd grabbed the next gun, tossing both straight to Donovan. With another spin, she'd jammed her elbow into the third stooge, right in his gut, while the second came in for a grab. Her foot connected swiftly with his groin, and he was down for the count.

To finish off the third, still reeling from her elbow, Mia grabbed both sides of his head and brought it down to connect with her knee, slipping his gun out while he fell.

Only Reggie was left, and he'd yet to move. In one more graceful arc, Mia placed herself directly behind him, her right arm slipping around his waist to grip the gun still in his pants. Clicking the safety off, she pointed her left hand, with the third stooge's gun, straight at Leroy.

Donovan posed in front of her, one arm pointed each at Reggie and Leroy. Mere seconds had passed from the time she'd decided to move. Her thoughts flickered to Agent McKenzie, imagining the agent's approving nod.

Mia met Donovan's eyes to see the shock and slight awe. Besides that brief look, he gave no reaction to her actions. Leroy was the only one who'd been able to move. He had his gun aimed at her, but with Donovan and Mia both with arms steady, Reggie and his crew were outmanned.

Reggie attempted to move, and Mia merely cocked the gun in his pants as a reminder he did not currently have free will.

There were several more seconds of silence. Leroy had yet to lower his weapon though they clearly had the upper hand. Mia waited. To her surprise, Reggie began to laugh. "It's good to have you back, Selena."

Glancing at Donovan, Mia raised an eyebrow, asking the question without words. He nodded, and they relaxed their position. Releasing her grip on the gun in Reggie's pants, Mia stepped away and discharged the clip from the gun as Donovan did the same. They tossed them to the side as Leroy re-holstered and assumed his position at the door as if nothing had transpired.

The three stooges began to come to, except for the man Mia had kneed in the face. He'd recover, but it would take a little longer. Once the first two found their feet, they both glared at Mia, but her attention was no longer on them. Reggie gestured toward the couches, so Donovan and Mia—stepping gingerly over the stooge still in a prone position on the floor—accepted the invitation. Donovan sat, but she remained standing, feeling more at ease when she could see everything.

The two ladies behind the bar busied themselves wiping glasses, though they didn't seem surprised by the sudden outburst of violence or its quick end. Mia imagined it was just a casualty of the job.

Reggie leaned back, seemingly relaxed after the confrontation. His two stooges stood behind him, arms crossed, continuing to glare daggers.

"You know I want to stay on good terms with you," Reggie began, "but there were rumors, and I'm a businessman first and foremost."

"What rumors?" Donovan said in a clipped tone.

Reggie's eyes flicked to Mia, and she understood. The fact that she—or, more accurately, Selena—had been missing hadn't gone unnoticed. "We heard you were captured, Selena. Gone."

"And you were, what, just cashing in on an opportunity?" Reggie shrugged, which was confirmation. Donovan gestured toward Mia with a flourish. "Well, as you can see, she's very much free."

"Look, I'm not proud of what I did, and I've learned my lesson. Never underestimate the two of you." Reggie leaned forward, resting his elbows on his knees and clasping his hands together. "How can I help?"

"You can tell me who invaded our home," Donovan said in a light voice. Though he seemed friendly on the surface, Mia could sense the seething tension lying just below the surface.

Reggie glanced back at his stooges, trepidation on his face. It was plain to see he'd backed himself into a corner, and it came down to who he feared more; Donovan and Selena, or those who had put out a kill order on the couple.

"The DeLuca family," Reggie finally answered. Mia's stomach dropped, though she gave no sign of her sudden apprehension.

There were several beats of silence. She didn't move, knowing Donovan used the uncomfortableness in the room to his advantage. Finally, he spoke. "Here's what I would like from you."

Once on the street again, Mia took a deep breath of fresh air, glad to be out of that horrid house. When Donovan jolted to a stop, she did too, taking the lead from him.

He stepped close, his body crowding hers, but she didn't give ground. His eyes were aflame, but beneath the anger she could see the fear and knew whatever he was about to say came from love. "You didn't listen to me."

"I stayed by your side, and I didn't say a word. Those were your directions."

His mouth popped open, and Mia could see the rebuttal he wanted to argue battling with amusement. Eventually, his body relaxed, a small smile playing at his lips. "I'd forgotten how much fun it is to watch you in action."

Knowing she'd been forgiven, Mia looped her arm through his and began walking down the street. When she spoke, she watched carefully for a reaction. "Is that something I knew how to do? It felt...instinctual. That seems to be happening a lot lately."

"Muscle memory," Donovan said offhand. "You know more than you think you do."

Deciding to stay quiet, Mia allowed him to lead the way to their next destination. They would have a conversation about the DeLuca family, but she would wait until they were somewhere a bit more private.

They moved in silence until back at the safe house. Before they talked, Mia asked Donovan to lie down so she could re-dress his wound. She sat opposite him in the chair while he leaned back against the headboard.

"All right. Explain everything to me."

Donovan studied her a moment before coming to some internal decision. She needed to know what they were involved with. "The first stop we made was so I could speak with a man named Anderson. He's a weasel like Reggie claimed, but he's got a handle on all things that happen in this city. He told me Reggie ratted us out to the DeLuca family in exchange for getting his crew in the local drug trade."

Donovan paused here, seeming to work up his courage. "The DeLuca family is trouble, but they've always had a healthy respect for you and me. When you went missing, I went a little crazy. I approached the leader of the family, Tony, to see if I could sniff out information. In the past, when we've needed to work together, he's always kept his word. And even though I didn't tell him directly that you were gone, he must have put two and two together."

That would explain why the police department had seen Tony and Donovan together—they'd just mistaken the meeting for a business deal. Mia turned the information over before she asked, "You think this DeLuca family are the ones that took me?"

Since the real Selena was still out there, somewhere, Mia wondered if the DeLucas might have really had something to do with it. "Tony wasn't forthcoming with information, though I was able to link the building we found you at to their family. It's possible one of the brothers was working solo. It wouldn't be the first time." His fist had clenched while talking about the disappearance. Mia reached out to grasp it gently. Words didn't seem adequate considering this new information of their attack, so she remained silent. "We need to deal with this family, once and for all."

"You have a plan," Mia said, and it wasn't a question. When he'd given Reggie instructions, she knew he'd already pieced together something.

"There are four DeLuca brothers. Two were arrested recently but released due to lack of evidence." This hit Mia hard. Crates full of illegal weapons was a lack of evidence? "Reggie is going to set up a meet between the brothers and us. If we can't work out something like gentlemen, it's on to Plan B."

His tone sent chills down her spine. Before she could respond, the cell phone rang. Donovan lifted it to his ear. "Yeah?" After listening for several beats, Mia watched his eyes harden. "We'll be right there."

"What is it?"

"Our security caught an intruder."

Mia followed Donovan back toward the tunnels and swung onto the bike to head in the direction of their condo. Half a mile before reaching the ravaged building, Donovan pulled to a stop.

Mia looked around, not recognizing this offshoot. "Where are we?"

"Holding cells."

Swallowing back the sudden bad taste in her mouth, Mia slipped on her sunglasses at Donovan's request and followed him inside the building. On the basement level, they exited the stairwell, and the scene was very similar to the cell she had been held in while waiting for Donovan's rescue. It was not a welcome sight.

Feeling her tense, Donovan glanced down. "Are you all right?"

Not wanting to speak, she simply nodded. The head of security met them near the door. Donovan had told her his name was Bruce, and she dimly remembered him from her rescue. "We found him in your offices. He had no identification on him, and he hasn't said a word, so we're running facial recognition. Doesn't look like the same kind of muscle that attacked. In my opinion, he looks like a cop."

Mia's stomach tangled in knots at his last statement. Since she had gotten a message out, had Alec tried to be a hero? Was he now sitting in a cell because of her?

"Take us to him," Donovan said.

Filled with trepidation, Mia followed the two men down the dreary walkway. Near the end of the hall, a man sat slumped on a low cot. His wavy hair was familiar, and it took all her willpower not to speak.

Donovan stood with his arms crossed, staring at the prisoner. "What's your name?"

There was no reaction whatsoever.

"I said, what's your name?" Donovan said, his tone dropping from hard to lethal.

The man lifted his head, his eyes flickering from Donovan to Mia. Though the dark glasses hid her expression, Mia's eyes were wide with fear.

"I have nothing to say to you," Adam finally responded.

Donovan continued questioning Adam, but Mia was past hearing him. This was all her fault.

When Donovan gave up, he brought Mia with him back to the door. She had a feeling, had she not been there, the interrogation would have been a lot more physical.

"Let him sit," Donovan instructed Bruce. "I'll be back later to speak with him again."

They left, and Mia couldn't get Adam's face out of her mind. Sweet, enthusiastic Adam was in a cell because of her, and there was nothing she could do to help him.

"It's time to meet with the DeLucas," Donovan said before they got back on the bike. "I'll deal with him later."

Terrified to speak, Mia nodded and slid on behind Donovan. They exited from the same building as their excursion earlier that day when they had confronted Reggie. Mia followed Donovan soundlessly, and he did nothing to break the silence.

A black SUV, one she recognized from her rescue, was parked in a garage connected to the building. They slid into the front and, without a word between them, drove to the spot they were to meet with the DeLuca brothers.

When Donovan parked, Mia found she knew the area well. It was on the docks on the outside of the DeLucas' shipping yard. There was an SUV similar to theirs already waiting. Donovan hesitated before opening the door, looking over at her.

"Let me do the talking," he said. "They only need to see you, know that you're alive and well. Understand?"

"I understand," she said, her emotions still in a whirlwind from seeing Adam locked up.

After squeezing her hand once, Donovan stepped out of the driver's side while Mia followed suit, immediately meeting him in front of the car and staying just behind as he walked forward.

Once they reached the halfway point between the two cars, all four doors opened, and Tony, the leader, emerged along with Al, the muscle. Instead of the other two brothers, as she expected, two more large men stepped out with guns held loosely before them. They remained by the car, watching, while the brothers approached.

"Tony, Al," Donovan greeted.

"Donovan," Tony responded, then looked around him to give Mia a once over. With a raised eyebrow, he added, "Selena."

She didn't move or speak, just kept her eyes sweeping between the four and over the grounds behind the gates. Donovan's tone was less than friendly. "I'd like to know why you tried to kill us."

Tony held his hands up, palms out, in the classic innocent pose. In complete opposition, Al crossed his arms, clearly unhappy with Donovan's forwardness. "Whoa, Donovan, I think there's been a misunderstanding."

"I don't."

"Why would we go against you? We've been able to work together in the past, and we don't step on each other's toes. I wouldn't want to mess up a good thing."

Mia's eyes flicked over Al, watching his facial cues. An eye twitch gave him away. Placing a hand gently on Donovan's arm, she pulled him a few steps back.

"Give us a moment," Donovan requested, turning to her and bringing their heads close.

"Al knows something. Tony really is clueless."

Donovan met her gaze briefly, nodded his head, and returned to the conversation. "Tony, you and I have had good dealings in the past, but that doesn't change the fact that someone in your family ordered a hit on us. If you don't take care of it, I will."

Tony glanced over at Al, noticing the murderous expression on his face. He contemplated the situation a long time before turning back. "Let me investigate this. If I find out what you say is true, you have my word that I will handle it."

"Reggie knows how to get a hold of me," Donovan answered before spinning on his heel to walk away. Though Mia hated turning her back on the brothers, she wasted no time in following. Back in the SUV, Donovan spun out of the dirt lot, heading back to the garage. "I'll bring you to our other home. We'll stay there until we can rebuild. It's a bit more comfortable than the safe house."

"You're going back to interview the prisoner, aren't you?"

Donovan spared her a glance. "Yes."

"I want to come with you."

"It won't be...pleasant," Donovan said in an attempt to talk her out of it.

"You think that bothers me?" she asked with more bravado than she possessed. "After the last few days, you don't think I can handle it?"

Donovan studied her a moment. "Fine. Let's go."

When they arrived back in the long hallway, the head of security was once again waiting for them. Bruce passed papers to Donovan. "Facial recognition came through. You won't believe this." Reading through them, Donovan's hands suddenly clenched into fists, scrunching the paper as they tightened. Mia shot the head of security a quizzical look. He saw her gaze and answered her unspoken question. "I was right; he is a cop. But, there's more. Our software hit a match from a newspaper article. He was a football star in high school and was featured more than once in the Boston paper, where he grew up."

Mia took the crumpled papers from Donovan's hands. As she scanned the pages, her stomach dropped, and she felt bile threatening to rise.

Donovan was already down the hall, his fury a living, breathing thing. "You stupid son-of-a-bitch. You think you can get away with this?"

This was a different side to Donovan than Mia had experienced in his care; however, it didn't surprise her that it existed. Though truth be told, her own rage was at the same level.

To her astonishment, Adam lifted his face to look squarely at Donovan, an evil smile spreading across his lips. "So, you've found out my little secret. It was bound to happen sooner or later."

Mia stood behind Donovan now, hands shaking with anger. "Now we know why the DeLuca brothers got released so quickly. They had a man on the inside."

"It's true. I'm their favorite little cousin." Adam stood then, approaching the bars. "You may know my secret, but I also know one of yours."

With this, Adam Malone—scratch that, Adam DeLuca—focused his attention on Mia. A well of fear bubbled up, knowing he could blow her entire cover with just a few words.

Something snapped inside her. She couldn't allow this to happen. In an instant, Mia went from raging fury to utter calm. Her hands ceased to shake, and she stepped up next to Donovan. In a cool, clear voice, she gave her first command as Selena. The words rolled from her tongue like waves across the shore.

"Kill him."

Part Two
Split

Eleven

THE NIGHT WAS HER TIME. These streets were her domain.

As Selena walked toward her destination, she slipped past each camera, unnoticed. When you knew what you were looking for, it was easy to avoid detection.

Once inside the building, Selena nodded to the guard, Leroy, at the inner set of doors. He held them open for her politely before turning back to his post. Down the staircase, the raucous noise became clearer. The thundering beat of stomping feet ground into her system and made her hungry for blood.

The arena was a simple square platform, raised up for all to view. A cage of steel trapped the men inside, and depending on the opponent, could either help or hinder their intentions.

She stood alone above the melee, focus riveted on the man standing still and silent in the ring. The match had not yet begun, and while his opposition danced and waved, this man was stoic. His dark eyes missed nothing as they roved over the crowd, his bare chest, displaying each delicious muscle, gleamed in the light. His hands hung loosely by his sides, deceptively motionless.

This was not about fame for him. It was about survival.

Licking her lips, Selena leaned forward in anticipation of the battle about to ensue.

Standing in the center of the cage, an umpire held a wrapped hand of each man, dropping them suddenly in a signal to begin. The man with the dark eyes brought his hands up to guard his face, his raptor's gaze taking in each nuance of his opponent's form. When his opponent's shoulder dropped, screaming his move to a seasoned observer, the man flung his hand out, making contact with his opponent's jaw. As he hurled backward, the dark-eyed man followed, pummeling him like a jackhammer without pause.

The crowd went wild as the opponent dropped—out for the count. Less than five seconds, and the match was over.

Air moved quickly between Selena's lips in the presence of his raw power. Excitement coursed through her.

He was the one.

In the dark alley adjacent to the building that held the fighting matches, Selena leaned against the wall, waiting. Her heartbeat quickened as the door opened, the light from inside casting the figure into stark relief. He began moving up the street, directly toward her. Waiting until the last moment to step out, Selena had the pleasure of catching him off guard.

For a moment they stood, each judging the other. Though a hood covered her hair, Selena had no doubt he could tell she was a woman.

"Do I know you?" His voice still held the lilting cadence of Ireland.

"No."

"Excuse me, then." He made to walk around her, but Selena stepped into his trajectory once again. His eyes narrowed just slightly. "What is it that you want?"

"You," she said plainly. "To work for me, that is."

Crossing his arms, he studied her again, curiosity lighting the depths of his eyes. "And what type of work is it that you do?"

With a smile, Selena held her hands out to her sides. "First, you'll have to pass the interview."

He glanced around him once as if looking for a candid camera crew. With half a laugh, he spoke again. "Sure then, I'll play along. What's the interview?"

"Why, beating me, of course."

"Look, I'm not sure what your game is here, but it's been a long night for me. I think I'll just get on."

Still, she didn't move, arms extended in invitation. "Afraid to fight a woman?"

"Not if she attacks me first."

With a shrug, Selena leaped forward, her fist extending toward his stomach at the last moment. He barely evaded the strike, and she slipped under his arm, now behind him. Using her momentum to spin, Selena back-fisted with her left, making contact with his cheek. He stumbled back, stunned, and looked at her in a new light.

"That counts."

Fast as lightning, his hand snaked out, gripping her wrist in an unbreakable hold. Spinning her into him, he wrapped his arms of steel around her waist, her back pressed against his chest. For a moment, Selena enjoyed the feel of him but didn't let it deter her from her purpose.

Dropping her weight and lifting her elbows out simultaneously, Selena broke out of his hold, scissoring his legs with hers as she rolled on the ground. He fell back hard, not expecting the move. Following her momentum, Selena knelt above him, one leg on each side of his waist, forearm pressed to his throat.

"Good move," he managed through his choked-off windpipe. His right hand slammed into the bicep of the arm that was holding him down, his left hand reaching up to Selena's neck while his hips bucked. They flipped positions; his fingers now wrapped around her throat. He shifted his legs so that they were over her hips, pinning her hands against the ground.

Selena smiled. "Congratulations, Donovan. You've passed."

KILL HIM.

Those words had escaped Mia's mouth.

Her mouth.

What had she been thinking?

Snapping back to reality, the cold, calculating calm that had descended over her suddenly lifted, seeping away into her concrete surroundings. Backing away from the cell, Mia placed a bracing hand against the wall, looking between the men in the room in horror. Where had that come from? No matter what this man had done, he didn't deserve to die. That wasn't self-defense; that was murder.

Struggling to remain focused, to remain in character, Mia straightened, taking a deep breath in. Donovan was watching her, his eyes wide, though she couldn't read the emotion playing over his features. For the first time since Mia had discovered his real identity, Adam Malone, a man she had worked with and trusted, looked afraid.

Swallowing once, hard, Mia approached Donovan's side again, eyes on the man behind the bars of the cell. A man who had just threatened to reveal who she truly was.

"We obviously can't trust anything this man says," Mia said aloud. "His whole life is built on lies."

Donovan nodded, then gripped her arm lightly to lead her away. Once they were out of earshot of Adam, he paused to meet Mia's gaze. "We can kill him—or we can use him."

Relief flooded through her. Having a DeLuca under lock and key could prove to be beneficial. Taking the out without having to lose face, Mia asked, "What did you have in mind?"

"Let's get back to the safehouse," Donovan suggested.

At that, she nodded, following him through the long hallway. Upon leaving, Donovan spoke briefly with the security before leading the way out. Exiting into the dimly lit cavern, Donovan threw a leg over the waiting bike, pausing just long enough for Mia to join him. They sped off, her arms wrapped around his waist, down the tunnels that were slowly becoming familiar.

They rode in silence, Mia's own thoughts whirring through her mind like a vortex. It was difficult to come to terms with the fact that sweet little Adam Malone was actually Adam DeLuca, part of the notoriously criminal DeLuca family and, now, the enemy of Mia. Not only to her façade as Selena but to her true identity.

This situation had to be handled carefully. Donovan's trust in Mia would be put to the test.

The silence continued as they parked at the safe house building, making their way through security and up the stairs. Once inside, Mia leaned against the kitchen counter, staring despondently across the room.

So much had happened in the last twenty-four hours: being attacked in the penthouse, Donovan's injuries, their explosive kiss, chasing down Reggie, meeting with the DeLucas, and, of course, Adam. On top of that, a short doze in the chair had been her only sleep.

Now that they had a moment to pause, Mia felt all residual energy from the constant adrenaline escaping from her pores.

"You should get some rest," Donovan said quietly.

Shaking her head, Mia looked directly at him. "I'd like to know the plan first."

"All right." Donovan sank onto the edge of the bed. Though she wanted to join him, distance was best for now. "At least two of the DeLucas are plotting against us. From our meeting, we can assume it's Al and Marco. Tony won't be happy to find out his brothers went against his wishes, but they are still family. So is Adam. The DeLucas will do anything for family."

Letting out a breath, Mia connected the dots. "So, we make a trade."

"It's our best chance of getting through this unscathed." After a moment of silence, Donovan spoke again. "We'll still move into our other home for the time being. Our offices are temporarily shut down, but we'll get crews to work on them first before we begin to rebuild our home."

"Makes sense," Mia agreed, still refusing to move from her perch against the counter.

"Selena, please, come lay down. I know you didn't sleep well last night. Neither of us will make good decisions without proper rest."

She nodded but made no move to leave her spot. Donovan stood and walked slowly toward her. He stopped in front of her, a hand cupping her cheek, waiting patiently for her eyes to meet his. When they did, the well of emotion she was tamping down threatened to spill.

"Come on," Donovan said gently, taking her hand. He helped remove her jacket, then knelt to untie and slip off the combat boots. Next were her pants, leaving Mia in just her underwear and t-shirt.

There was nothing sexual in his touch, though she was very aware of him so close to her, his hair brushing against her thigh as he carefully lifted each foot out of the pants. Standing again, he led her to the bed, pulling back the covers for Mia to slide in. After removing his own clothes, leaving nothing but a pair of boxer briefs, she watched him settle in beside her.

Laying on her back, Mia stared at the ceiling. The only light was from the glow of the clock on the oven. Now, in the dark, she faced her demons.

"I tried to kill a man today," she whispered, barely loud enough for Donovan to hear. When Mia spoke again, her voice cracked. "Is that really who I am? Is that the kind of person I am?"

Donovan rolled to his side, bracing himself on an elbow, his eyes on her face though there wasn't much to see in the near darkness. "Selena." His voice was full of some unnamed emotion. "You didn't."

"But I wanted to," she said, tears leaking from the corners of her eyes. Mia repeated the words, barely louder than a breath. "I wanted to."

His hand brushed along her hair, pulling her to him. Mia went willingly, curling into his chest, and sobbed. When he wrapped both arms around her shaking form, she allowed him to console her, needing the contact more than she ever remembered needing anything.

He said nothing, just continued to stroke her hair, never loosening his grip. Cries racked her chest, her breath coming in gasps. Mia let it all out, even as a voice shoved into the dark recesses of her mind screamed at her to stop. It was beyond her control.

Eventually, her tears dried, and her breath evened out. Exhausted in every way possible, Mia drifted into sleep.

When she woke, Mia realized she hadn't moved from the position she'd fallen asleep in, and neither had Donovan. She remained trapped between his chest and his arms, their bodies pressed together in a way that was beyond familiar.

His breath was light, and she believed he was still asleep. Not wanting to disturb him, Mia allowed herself to enjoy the feel of each hard muscle that was now stamped into her memory. The heat from his body had seeped so deep into her, she felt it was lodged into her very soul.

Without any light able to come through the metal window coverings, Mia had no idea what time it could be. After her crying jag, she'd slept deeply, though it didn't feel as if it had been a long time. Even so, she was wide awake and knew that sleep would now elude her.

In the limited space she had, a fingertip lightly traced against the definition of Donovan's chest. The feel of him was so good, so familiar, Mia felt an ache down to her toes.

She'd begun this mission to find out the truth behind Selena and Donovan's business, but with each passing day, Donovan had shown her nothing but care and respect. Since the first time she'd met him, she'd felt this undeniable attraction to him, and it had only become stronger. In this business, there was every chance she wouldn't see tomorrow. So many things could go wrong—just two days ago, they'd been targeted by men with semi-automatic weapons and grenades. Adam could spill her secrets at any time. Donovan could find out who she really was.

With as much risk as there was in her job, why shouldn't she take the opportunity to find out what this craving would be like when finally quenched? Sure, Donovan loved Selena, not her, but right now, he thought she *was* Selena, so what did that matter? Mia wanted him more than she'd ever wanted anyone. Just once, she wanted to do something for herself. Just once, she wanted to feel.

His breathing had changed, and she sensed his eyes were open and on her, though neither of them could really see. Mia's finger continued to trace designs on his chest, even knowing he was awake and aware. A decision she knew she would come to regret had been made, and there was no going back now.

Her lips pressed against his neck, breathing in his scent. He let out a shocked breath, but he didn't pull away. If anything, he held her tighter.

Kissing her way to his ear, Mia's head was suddenly yanked back by her hair, and Donovan's lips were on hers. When she opened her mouth to pull in a breath, he used the opportunity to delve his tongue into her mouth, alighting each nerve ending as his fist tightened against her scalp.

One leg wrapped around his waist as his free hand slipped under her shirt. With a moan, she arched into him, all coherent thought escaping. He pulled his head back, and she whimpered, not wanting to lose the contact. Mia could just barely see his eyes glittering down at her in the darkness.

"Are you sure?" he asked gently.

There was no hesitation on her end. Using words that were faintly familiar, Mia whispered into the darkness. "Yes. I want you, Donovan."

He trapped her wrists in a vice grip above her head. Mia gasped quietly, but all sound cut off when Donovan captured her mouth with his. His fingertips trailed down her spine, his touch both gentle and rough, soothing and electrifying. He was a master at building tension, feeding it, fueling it until Mia felt she would burst with need.

Mia was completely under his control, her body his to do with as he pleased. His mouth moved down her throat and over her chest, leaving trails of fire in his wake.

Donovan wasn't just making love to her; he was claiming her. There was no turning back now, not for either of them. Mia felt desperate for his every touch, frantic with wanting him.

When neither could wait any longer, Donovan filled her, completed her. Mia hadn't realized what her life had been missing, but she now understood.

It was Donovan.

△ △ △

DONOVAN AND MIA LAY IN silence, their limbs tangled in the sheets. Her head rested against Donovan's chest, listening to the steady, reassuring beat of his heart. Neither moved or spoke. Mia knew, as soon as they did, the fantasy bubble she'd created would pop, and guilt would come crashing down.

Even with all the arguments against what she'd just done, she couldn't bring herself to regret it. Donovan's touch was pure bliss. If she could only have this one moment in time, if the rest of her life was spent alone, she would take the trade willingly.

It was a long time that they remained as they were. If not for the sudden piercing ring of the phone, they could very well have stayed there all day.

Donovan carefully extracted himself, rolling to his feet. Mia could see the silhouette of him in the strange blue glow and suddenly wished all the lights were on so she could enjoy the view. His wide shoulders tapered down to his trim waist, every inch of him wrapped in muscle. Though he obviously trained hard, she knew they were not all gained in the gym.

"Yeah," he answered the phone, listening for a few moments. "I understand. We'll be moving into our second residence today. Please make sure it's fully stocked." Another beat of silence. "That's fine. We'll meet with you then."

Hanging up, Donovan turned toward Mia. While he'd talked, she'd scooted up to a sitting position, her back against the headboard, hugging the sheet to her chest. She had no idea what to say or do and suddenly felt a crushing awkwardness.

"That was Bruce," Donovan said. "He's going to meet with us later today."

"Okay." It came out barely above a whisper.

Alerted by her tone, Donovan approached the bed, sinking down beside her. His hand rested lightly against her arm. "Are you all right?"

That felt like a loaded question. "Yes."

"You're not sorry for what happened between us, are you?"

Taking in a breath, Mia blew it out before answering. "No. That...that was amazing." His smile could have lit the room. "It's just...a lot has happened recently. I feel so lost, having people targeting me but not understanding why. Feeling things without the memories to back them up." As Mia said the words, she realized they were true both for herself and the role she was playing.

Donovan's hand moved from her arm to her cheek, leaning in to press his lips gently to hers. "It will come back. You're doing so well. You just need more time."

Nodding, Mia made to stand up. "I'll get ready to go."

Escaping into the bathroom, she paused a moment to study herself in the mirror. Her lips were swollen from his kisses, and she touched her lips lightly in awe. For a long time, Mia simply stared at her reflection, wondering who the stranger was staring back at her.

She was acting totally out of character. In her entire life, she didn't know that she'd ever broken down and cried like she had last night. Not when her father beat her, not when her mother died. The stress of training for the police academy, the sleepless nights or eighty-hour workweeks once she'd passed. All of the relationships she'd failed at. None of it had ever brought her to the bottom she'd hit last night.

Then this morning...that hadn't been a spur-of-the-moment act. She'd thought it out, reasoned it out, and given herself over to it based on feeling and pure need.

Blasting the water, Mia stepped into the shower, allowing the heat to soak through her sore muscles. Now that she'd had proper rest, Mia could feel each and every muscle she'd overused in the last two days. She washed quickly, knowing Donovan would want to be on their way.

Wrapping herself in a towel, Mia stepped out to find Donovan cooking breakfast, a mug of coffee already waiting for her on the counter.

"We've no tea here," Donovan explained, gesturing toward the caffeine fix. He was wearing a black t-shirt and a similar pair of cargo pants that they'd both donned yesterday. "Eggs will be ready in just a minute."

"Sounds great," she said, opening the drawers and pulling out her own matching outfit. Facing the wall, she dressed quickly, too chicken to find out if he was watching her.

Fully dressed, Mia perched on one of the stools at the counter, sipping the hot liquid Donovan had prepared for her in appreciation. When she looked up, Donovan's eyes were on her, a small smile on his face. Bewildered, she asked, "What?"

"You look much better," he said, scraping eggs onto two plates. Circling the counter to sit by her, he set down the dishes before speaking again. "I know you've been through a lot, and I can only imagine how overwhelming everything must be. Just remember, you have me to help you through it. I don't expect anything from you but to continue to heal."

Shifting her gaze to the food, Mia picked up a piece of toast and bit into it. "I don't feel like I'm the person you knew."

"You are. And you're not," Donovan answered, which only caused her to look back at him in confusion. "Memory loss is a tricky business. You may not make the same decisions as you would have before, but that's because you don't have your memories to rely on for advice. You won't make the same decisions, nor do I expect you to. But you, the person you are inside, the feelings you possess and the way you make me feel, that's all the same."

For a long time, Mia studied him, falling just a bit deeper than she already had, while also feeling relieved. Here, she'd been trying so hard to make the decisions Selena would make, to sound and act the same, when Donovan expected none of it.

"Thank you," she finally said quietly. "You have no idea what a relief that is."

Grasping her hand, Donovan brought it to his mouth to press a kiss in the exact center of her palm. Mia's heart fluttered uncontrollably in her chest. "Eat up. We've a long day ahead."

Twelve

SHOULDERS THROWN BACK, EXUDING A confidence born from skill, Donovan entered the abandoned building and searched his surroundings with a critical eye. Stepping out of the shadows, Selena kept the distance between them in order for him to feel comfortable. She'd given him no details the night before, only asking him to meet here, well after the time respectable people would be doing business.

"Hello again," he greeted warily. "Now that I'm here, can you tell me what it is you're wanting from me?"

"I'm looking for a partner"—she paused, sweeping her eyes from his feet back to his hard gaze—"in business."

"What kind of business?"

"Well, for one, I run the fights you've been competing in." He stilled, watching her even more carefully. "However, I'm looking to expand, and I believe you're the right person to assist me."

"What's your name?"

"I'm Selena."

"All right, Selena, I'm listening."

"Come with me."

Leading him through the main level of the empty building, Selena pushed open a door to a stairway. Taking the steps down at a leisurely pace, she remained silent while he followed diligently. At the basement level, she paused, casting a glance over her shoulder. Her eyes drifted over his muscular form as they walked into the empty space, reeking of mold. Against the wall lay a single sledgehammer; Selena raised a slim eyebrow at the silent man behind her.

"Go ahead, use it."

"You brought me down here for demolition?"

"To begin with. I believe there is something beyond these walls that will be useful to us."

With a shrug, willing to play along, Donovan scooped to retrieve the sledgehammer from its perch along the floor. With a mighty swing, he pulverized the wall, not stopping until there was a hole large enough to look through.

He paused, breath heavy, and gestured for her to have a look. As Selena peered through, a smile lit her face.

"It's exactly as I thought," she whispered, excitement coursing through her. Stepping back, she held out a hand for Donovan. "Have a look."

He stepped forward, sticking his head through the wall up to his shoulders. He let out a gasp of amazement.

Down below, there was empty space—the empty space of long-forgotten tunnels.

PRESENT DAY

MIA FINISHED HER BREAKFAST QUICKLY before picking up the small mess. When she went to make the bed, she brushed a hand against the soft sheets, the memory of this morning stirring her desire once again. She glanced over to Donovan, but he was shoving things into his pack.

Mia could no longer deny her attraction or desire for this man. If giving in only strengthened her cover, was the risk of losing her heart worth it?

Making the bed, she crouched beneath it and pulled out the hidden arsenal, strapping two guns and several knives to her belt. Donovan came over as she slipped on the same jacket she'd used the day before. "You know we're only going to our other home, not into combat."

Raising an eyebrow, she answered, "Aren't they one and the same nowadays?"

"Point taken." He frowned, selecting weapons for himself before sealing the drawer back under the bed. "Ready?"

"As I'll ever be." They left together, heading down the stairs and into the lower levels. Donovan worked his magic to slide open hidden doors. "What else is in this building?"

"It's empty," he said. "Condemned."

That made sense. They exited the building into the cavernous room which held Donovan's motorcycle, the only mode of transportation they used in the subterranean tunnels. He got on first, handing Mia his backpack. Slipping it on her own back, Mia took her seat, wrapping her arms around his chest.

The tension that ordinarily surrounded them was down to a pleasant hum. Pressing against his back, Mia watched their surroundings as they sped off through the main tunnel in an entirely new direction. After several minutes they pulled off, parking alongside a wall.

Donovan placed his hands against the nearly invisible crack in the wall, activating the mechanism to open the door. Before they went inside, Donovan took the backpack and slung it over one shoulder. Taking Mia's hand, he led her up the stairs.

As all the other buildings they used, they went up three flights of stairs before coming to another hidden door. Once through this door, they were on the basement level of the building. Any occupants besides the two of them would never know there was so much more to the structure.

Instead of continuing up the stairs, Donovan exited at the main floor, guiding Mia through a tiled lobby to a set of elevators. There were security guards behind a desk who simply nodded to the couple. The large space spoke of money and privilege.

Donovan surpassed two main elevators and stopped in front of a third, offset in its own alcove. When he pushed the call button, a red light blinked several times, and Mia realized it was reading his thumbprint.

The elevator dinged and opened, and they stepped inside. Here, there were no buttons, and Donovan spoke. "Penthouse."

The doors slid closed, and they began their ascent to the top floor.

"The top two floors are ours," Donovan said. "We own the building, but the rest are upscale condos. The very top floor is our second home. The floor below that holds our personal secondary offices."

Mia nodded, waiting for the elevator to pause. "It's safe here?"

He gave her a sidelong look. "Fewer people are aware of this location. It's as safe as we can be without just staying in the safe house."

The elevator came to a stop, and they stepped out into a short hallway. A reinforced door stood before them. Donovan placed his hand on a screen beside the door, then bent forward to allow an eye scan. When the door opened, he pulled Mia inside.

The setup inside was very similar to the first penthouse she'd stayed in, with wide-open spaces and soft colors. Running a hand along the peach couch, she looked at Donovan. "Is this bulletproof?"

He smiled. "Yes. We had it specially made."

That cleared up one thing about the raid. It wasn't simply luck that no bullets had found their way through the fabric of the couch.

Dropping the bag on the counter, Donovan walked to a sliding door, watching the scene below. "It's not as nice a view as our other place, but it's nothing to sneeze at."

Stepping beside him, Mia looked out at the view of the docks. They were near to the opposite side of Baltimore from the penthouse that had been destroyed, but the easy access to the docks must help in their business.

"Is there a rooftop garden?" she asked.

"No," he answered sadly. "But I did ask Bruce to stock the fridge."

Bruce arrived exactly on time. From what Donovan told Mia, only the three of them had access to this home. He trusted Bruce implicitly, and it made Mia wonder how their relationship had formed.

They stood at the counter of the kitchen island as Bruce laid out plans for Donovan and Mia to peruse—blueprints to rebuild their offices. While Donovan studied them, Mia began to ask Bruce questions. "How do you think the DeLucas were able to bypass our security?"

He sighed heavily, and she could see that he blamed himself. "Our system was nearly un-hackable, but not impossible. They must have had a computer genius working for them."

Pondering that information, her thoughts drifted to Adam. He had access to police files, and her prints were in the system. She wondered if he'd been able to somehow use her prints to override the security. "Were there any casualties in the offices?"

"Thankfully, no. We had several people in the hospital, but they are recovering."

"We're covering all their costs?"

"Of course, ma'am." Bruce glanced to Donovan and back again. "We've asked everyone to stay home for two weeks. They'll receive pay as normal. Your top people are continuing operations from the secondary offices."

Mia nodded, then looked to Donovan. He was done studying the plans, and she waited for his directions. "These look fine. Let's get this started immediately. I've some new ideas for the penthouse when we get to that point."

"I'm on it," Bruce said.

"We met with Tony DeLuca," Donovan said. "He assures me he will handle things on his end."

"You don't trust him," Bruce stated, no question in his tone.

"No. They always take care of their family. Which is why we're going to be using their cousin to our advantage."

Bruce nodded. "What should I do with him until then?"

"Leave him," Donovan said. "Bring him one meal a day, but otherwise no communication. We can't trust anything he says, so we won't listen. Then, when we're ready, we'll release him to his family. Notify the Baltimore PD on his true identity—we want to cut any ties he has, and that will also explain his disappearance."

"Consider it done," Bruce said, gathering the prints from the counter before turning to go. "I'll keep you apprised of the progress."

"Thank you, Bruce." Once he left, Donovan turned to Mia. "Hungry?"

"Sure." She smiled, perching on one of the stools. Watching Donovan in the kitchen had turned into a guilty pleasure.

They ate at the counter and didn't speak much throughout the rest of the day. Mia wandered the penthouse, finding a small exercise room which she made use of in her downtime. It felt as if they were perched on a precipice, secure for the moment, but one more step in any direction could potentially lead them off the edge.

After she'd gotten herself cleaned up, Donovan and Mia shared a late dinner on the patio.

"Why don't you get some sleep?" Donovan suggested once they were finished eating. "I should contact our clients, let them know we're still in business."

Not wanting to argue, she simply nodded her assent. As he was leaving, he pulled her close, pressing his lips to hers. The fire ignited instantaneously, leaving her weak and needy in a matter of moments.

Donovan pulled his head back to look Mia deep in the eyes. She was able to feel his own need with their bodies pressed so tightly together, and it left her breathless. There was a single moment of clarity, urging her to stop, but that was quickly squashed. Since she was already on a slippery slope, she might as well steer into the skid.

His head dipped down again, meeting her lips with a passion she'd only ever read about. Wrapping his arms around her, he pushed her back against the wall. The jacket she still wore fell to the floor, followed quickly by both their shirts. He made quick work of the button on her pants. As they slipped to the ground, he lifted Mia off her feet. With nothing to do but hang on for dear life, she wrapped her legs around his waist.

His mouth was at her neck, feathering kisses over any exposed skin he could reach. Without breaking contact, he was suddenly inside her, her body adjusting to his delicious invasion. Mia moaned for more, but pressed against the wall, she could gain no leverage. She was completely under his control.

One of his hands wrapped around both her wrists, holding them above her head. She was utterly helpless against his will, but every touch, each long stroke built in her a need that she feared would never be sated.

All coherent thought left her until all that remained was Donovan. His free hand wrapped around her waist, effectively locking her in place. Giving over to the sensation, Mia felt the pressure building deep in her core, spiraling out through each limb. When Donovan finally allowed her to fall, she screamed with release, taking him over the edge with her.

△ △ △

ONCE DONOVAN LEFT FOR THE offices, Mia wrapped herself in a robe and found her way back to the patio. She stood at the railing, gazing over the docks by the light of the moon. She was so close to earning his complete trust, but Mia feared it was at her own peril. Each touch, every taste was seared into her brain. A thumb brushed gently across her wrist, sore from his restraint. The combination of rough, dominant male and gentle, loving man had awoken in her things she hadn't even known existed. Dark needs that, given a lifetime with Donovan, might never be satisfied.

Would she be strong enough to take him down?

Mia's ultimate target was Selena, but she seemed to be gone for good. Would she—could she turn Donovan in when all this was said and done?

As Mia lay down that night, her thoughts were restless. Amazingly, wrapped in Donovan's arms the night before, she'd slept deeply and well. Now, with so many thoughts circling her brain and Donovan's absence, the dreams encroached.

△ △ △

THOUGH IT WAS THE MIDDLE of the night, two figures stood in the room where Mia slept. They discussed her. One, a woman, sounded like Mia, even with a hard edge to her tone that Mia didn't possess.

"It's time to move on to the next part of our plan."

"She's not ready," said a man's voice this time, and Mia would have recognized the beautiful cadence anywhere. Donovan. He was silenced with a single look.

"You're falling for her." The tone was flat yet conveyed disgust, and Mia immediately took offense though she couldn't be sure why.

"She's a good person, Selena," Donovan defended quietly.

Selena? This *must* be a dream.

"She's weak," Selena's voice snapped.

"Compassion isn't a weakness, it's a strength." Something lifted in Mia's heart at hearing Donovan's defense.

"What does that make me?" Selena's voice had dropped, turned...seductive. She practically purred the next questions. "Do you think of me when you're with her? Does she please you the same way I do?"

"There's no one else like you." Donovan's voice came out husky. Any glow Mia had received from his earlier words was crushed. "If you feel we're ready for our next step, I will see it done."

"Good." Satisfied, Selena took a step back. "Remember, she's only here because I allow it, and I can take her away any time I choose."

Mia's heart rate picked up, terror seizing through her. What did this mean?

Donovan only nodded, staring at the floor, the perfect picture of obedience. Selena seemed amused by his complete submission when she knew with anyone else that he was the one in control. When Selena spoke again, it was as much a threat as a command. Her voice was cold as ice. "I'll check back in a few days. Until then, I suggest you put your focus on the plan and forget about *Mia*."

△ △ △

MIA CAME AWAKE WITH A gasp, struggling blindly against the ghosts of dreams.

"Shh, it's all right. You're safe." A velvet voice broke through the haze, snapping her back to reality.

Heaving in deep breaths, Mia turned to Donovan, on his knees beside her. Her gaze shot toward the window, where Selena had been in her dream. Nothing but shadows.

Donovan's hands grasped her shoulders, his eyes boring into Mia's with an intensity she could barely comprehend. His voice was gentle, a direct opposition to his gaze. "What's wrong?"

Shaking her head in an attempt to clear it, Mia finally answered him in a whisper. "Just a dream."

It was just a dream.

Thirteen

DONOVAN JOINED SELENA ABOVE THE crowd, watching the fighters in the cage as they crashed together. He was the only other person allowed in this area, and Selena found herself relishing his company.

"Sanchez is doing well," Donovan commented, his gaze on the ring. She let out a sound of agreement, eyes sweeping the stands. "I've been collecting new talent. They'll be ready within the month."

"Good," Selena answered. Though the fights were lucrative, she had her sights set on something bigger. "I'd like you to take a look at the property by the docks tomorrow."

"Sure thing. What are your plans for it?"

She met his eyes before answering. "Luxury condos. It will be a nice revenue stream."

"That'll be a good location for it."

"Close the deal quickly. The top two levels will be yours to live and work out of. We'll need security."

"I have contacts from my military days. Men I trust with my life."

Cocking her head, Selena asked, "But do you trust them with my life?"

"I do."

Looking back to the crowd below, Selena tapped a nail against the railing. "Gather them by week's end. Once the building is ours, I'd like them to work up security for it."

"Will do. What more do you have planned?"

Stretching out the silence between them, Selena weighed her answer. "This building will be a trial run for our main offices. Once we've worked out the kinks, I have my eyes on a property uptown. That is where we will build our empire."

"What else will we need to build this empire?"

With a half-smile, she said, "Ships. Lots of ships."

PRESENT DAY

MIA WOKE SLOWLY, NOT QUITE ready to face reality. Donovan lay curled around her back, his arm securely around her waist. Mia took a moment to marvel at how much easier she slept in his arms.

Easing out from under his embrace, Mia left him sleeping and ventured to the bathroom. After the nightmare last night, she couldn't quite shake the feeling that something was amiss.

Throwing on workout clothes, Mia headed to the small space with exercise equipment, determined to burn off the last dredges of the dream. Choosing the treadmill, she ran at top speed for half an hour before Donovan popped his head in. Slowing to a walk, Ma smiled in greeting.

"Good morning," he said, his voice still rough with sleep. "How are you feeling?"

"Pretty good now," Mia said, gesturing to the machine beneath her feet. "Running always helps to clear my head."

"That it does." He watched her with hooded eyes before adding, "I'll fix some breakfast, join me when you're ready."

Nodding, Mia dismounted and went through a round of stretches. After getting dressed, she walked through the main room. The smell wafting from the oven made her stomach growl. Finding Donovan on the patio with a platter of fresh fruit and a carafe of coffee waiting to be poured, she joined him.

"Breakfast should be ready in a few minutes," he said, handing her a small plate to load up with fruit.

She did so without hesitation and fixed herself a mug of coffee. Donovan went inside and returned with a piping hot quiche. "That looks amazing. Everything you've made me has been. What got you into cooking?"

Donovan relaxed into his chair, picking at a bunch of grapes while the pie cooled. "I joined the military when I was eighteen. It was during a time of peace, thankfully, but it left us a lot of downtime. To pass the time, I cooked. Of course, cooking for a full garrison of men is very different than an intimate meal for two, but I enjoy it just the same."

Shock ran through Mia. This was the first truly personal detail she'd learned of the mysterious Donovan. Pressing her luck, she ventured for more. "Were you in the American military or Irish?"

"American. I never knew my father, and my mother passed away when I was sixteen. The only family I had—my mom's sister—lived in the States, and she took me in. When I joined the military, I never looked back."

"What about my family?"

He paused, studying Mia. "I think one of the things that drew us together is the similarity in our stories. You also lost your parents as a child, but, unlike me, you survived on your own."

There was an involuntary wince as Mia realized just how similar Selena's story was to her own. A new emotion welled up, one that Mia fought against because she never wanted to feel it toward Selena.

Compassion.

Desperate to change the subject, Mia asked the next question that came to mind. "This might sound ridiculous after so much time together, but what is your last name? And, also, what's my last name?"

He laughed, the first genuine laugh she'd ever heard from him. It kicked her already raging hormones into overdrive. "We don't really deal in last names."

Something Mia had always assumed was about to be confirmed. "Donovan isn't your real name, is it? Just as Selena isn't mine."

Sobering, Donovan leaned forward to take her hand, forcing her gaze to his. "No. They're not the names we were born with. But they are our names now, and that's all that matters."

"It's still strange, though, not having a last name. I feel like Madonna."

He laughed again, settling back into his chair. Forking a piece of the quiche, he popped it into his mouth before talking. "We could come up with a new one if you'd like."

"Maybe one day. Not today."

Donovan cleared his throat before bringing up a new topic. "I'm going to make a trip abroad; I'd like you to come with me."

"All right," Mia said. It was her job to stick to him like glue. "What will we be doing?"

"Business meetings. You've not come with me in the past, but with as volatile a situation as we have here and your memory loss, I think it would be best to stay together."

"I agree." Excitement began pumping through her veins. She'd never traveled abroad and had always wanted to. Even if it was all business, Mia had a feeling Donovan would still create a memorable experience. "When do we leave?"

"Tonight. I'll have our plane prepared, and we'll fly overnight to arrive in London in the morning."

"What should I pack?"

He smiled cryptically. "I'll help you with that."

They left for the airport in the evening. Donovan pulled the tinted SUV into the smaller, private airport northeast of the city. "This is our hangar. We have several planes to use personally and for our shipping, though the majority of what we do is through actual ships."

Nodding, Mia followed his lead, stepping out into the cool, clean space. Until they were in the air, her hair was wrapped up in a scarf, sunglasses donning her face. Adding in the long, red trench coat that covered the small arsenal at her hips, Mia felt like a movie star from the 1940s.

Boarding, she took in the splendor of the sleek plane. She'd only traveled by plane once before, and she'd been stuck in a middle seat of an uncomfortable commercial airliner. Her childhood had not been conducive to travel, and as an adult, she'd been so work-oriented that vacations had never been in her purview. Now, Mia realized, if she could travel like this, she would never stop.

There were four luxury seats clad in black leather, which fully reclined and swiveled to face a small round table. A large screen set into the wall was visible from each chair. The door to the cockpit was closed, and there was another area in the back that held a bathroom and a fully-stocked service area.

Donovan gestured to one of the chairs, taking a seat himself. "Make yourself comfortable."

Mia sat beside him and, once the door was secure, let down her hair and removed the glasses. Shaking out the long dark tresses, she glanced over at Donovan. He was staring right back at her, a small smile playing on his lips.

"What is it?" she asked, patting her hair self-consciously. "Do I have scarf hair?"

"You're beautiful," he said, and her heart gave one hard pounding beat. "I'm excited to show you my favorite places abroad."

"I'm excited, too."

After her weeks of training and remaining hidden from public view to being locked in a cell waiting for Donovan to find her and then staying indoors to recuperate, Mia was itching to feel true freedom.

The pilot's voice came over the speakers. "Prepare for take-off."

Donovan and Mia both snapped their seatbelts into place and swiveled their chairs forward. "We'll be stopping in London first."

"First?"

"We'll be visiting two more cities after that." Mia couldn't help but wonder what those stops would entail, but Donovan didn't seem open to revealing much more about the trip.

When they'd leveled off, Donovan unbuckled and stood, retrieving bottles of water and a bowl of fresh fruit from the back. Mia unbuckled her belt as well but remained seated.

"I'm going to speak with the pilot. I'll be right back," Donovan said, dropping a kiss on her temple.

Mia watched him disappear through the divider, her eye spying a handle beneath the television. Standing, she went to investigate and found a pullout filled with books. Shuffling through, she found one that looked interesting and brought it back to her seat.

When Donovan returned, Mia was nibbling on cheese, crackers, grapes, and walnuts and well into the first chapter of the book.

He smiled but didn't interrupt, instead pulling out a laptop from one of the bags he'd brought on the plane. As he tapped away, Mia snuggled into the comfortable chair, reading until her eyes drooped and she fell asleep to the soft sound of the engines rumbling.

When they landed at one of several private airports in London, Donovan handed Mia a passport to use as they went through customs.

"Audrey Anderson?"

Donovan flashed open his own passport. "Donald Anderson."

Her nose scrunched up. "You don't look like a Donald."

"Donny, then?" Donovan chuckled.

"All right, Donny." Mia rolled her eyes. "At least we have last names now."

"That we do." Dipping his hand in his pocket, he pulled out two gold bands, studying them briefly before slipping one on Mia's left hand. "For appearance's sake."

Glancing down at the glittering ring, Mia swallowed once, hard. Nodding, she hefted her suitcase and led the way off the plane.

Her hair was wrapped back into a scarf, sunglasses perched on her nose. The sun was just making itself known, fighting against the fog that seemed to be ever-present in England. Once they touched pavement, Mia allowed Donovan to take the lead, following him through a low archway into a square building.

There was a security checkpoint that they walked to first. Since there was no one else in line, Donovan placed his luggage onto the belt and greeted the man collecting passports. "Traveling for business or pleasure, sir?"

"My wife and I are here for vacation," Donovan lied smoothly.

When the security looked at her, Mia smiled politely, handing over her own passport. While she trusted that Donovan had good forgeries, she was still nervous at the deception.

Placing her bag on the belt, Mia carefully unwrapped her hair and slipped off the glasses, knowing the look wouldn't pass scrutiny. After a few more questions, the security passed them through. Before picking up her belongings, Mia donned her disguise once again, knowing London had even more CCTV than Baltimore.

In fact, Baltimore's system was modeled after London's. Avoiding the cameras would prove to be difficult, even for someone like Donovan. Near impossible without the use of underground tunnels.

A town car waited just outside the airport. The driver quickly took over her bag, loading their luggage into the trunk. Donovan opened the back door for Mia before sliding into the opposite side.

This was a lifestyle she'd never thought she'd be privy to and yet found she slid into the role effortlessly. Just like Donovan, who seemed at ease barefoot in his own kitchen or being chauffeured from private airport to a luxury hotel. The combination only served to add to his appeal.

They pulled up in front of the Dorchester, and her heart began to pound in excitement. Besides being a famous landmark, it was a renowned luxury hotel. Donovan opened the door while the driver transferred the bags to an attendant. Slipping a tip discreetly into the man's hand, Donovan then turned to lead Mia inside. Once checked in, Donovan led her to a set of elevators and straight to the Terrace Penthouse.

Waiting until the attendant left to take off her disguise, Mia did so immediately and took a good look around. There was a living room, dining room, and master bedroom with accents of white marble and leather. Through the bedroom, Mia came upon the bathroom, just stopping to stare. White-streaked black marble donned the counters while there was a river bath tub that she couldn't wait to sink into.

The terrace, which the suite had been named for, overlooked Hyde Park and had a stunning water feature. She could picture Donovan and herself drinking the bottle of champagne, which was sitting chilled next to a gorgeous bouquet of flowers in the dining room, while watching the sunset.

"Do you like it?" Donovan wrapped his arms around her waist, his mouth pressed against her ear.

"It's amazing. Do you always stay at places like this?"

"Yes. I've found it useful in business."

Relaxing back into him, Mia took a few moments just to enjoy the sensation of being here with Donovan. "So, what's on the agenda?"

"We have a few meetings this morning," Donovan answered. "Would you like to freshen up before we head out?"

Nodding, Mia stepped away from the embrace, turning to face him as she did. "Thank you for bringing me here," she said, kissing him lightly on the lips.

"My pleasure."

Deciding to take a quick shower, Mia did so before dressing in a tailored black pantsuit. Instead of the scarf, she chose to wear a wide-brimmed black hat with her sunglasses after wrapping her hair into a low chignon. The last touch was a pair of thin black gloves so that anything she touched would not leave fingerprints.

It had been Donovan's idea and one that she wholeheartedly agreed with. Not only did she not know, or trust, the people they would be meeting with, but if one of them did happen to run her prints—well, the only record they would find would be from the Baltimore PD.

Donovan lounged in one of the chairs in the living room when she emerged, reading a file in his hand. He gave her a once-over followed by a slow, sexy smile.

"We'll be doing a business lunch today," Donovan said, standing to take her hand. "But I'd like to take you out for dinner tonight."

"That sounds fun," Mia said with a smile. And very romantic. In this setting, she would have to keep herself in constant check. "What will we be doing this afternoon?"

"I'll be catching up with our office in the States," he said, leading her back to the lobby. "You have a surprise."

Giving him a sidelong glance, Mia didn't speak again as the same car pulled up, slipping into the back and waiting for Donovan to slide in beside her.

He took her hand, resting it lightly on his thigh but remaining silent. Since she didn't know who this driver was, Mia thought it best to leave conversation to a minimum. Their first stop was a towering building in the heart of the theater district. Donovan led her inside, checking in at the front desk before making their way to a bank of elevators.

"We're meeting with Michael Powers III," Donovan said quietly. "He took over the family shipping business at the ripe age of nineteen and has since exploded it into a multi-billion-dollar company. And that's only what's on the books. He also has a very lucrative side business, which is where we come in."

She'd heard of Michael Powers, as had anyone breathing in the world over the last decade. He was constantly in the news, whether it was Forbes or the tabloids. The billionaire prodigy was also a playboy, his preference of scantily clad supermodels common knowledge.

When one runs a successful company as Michael did, the question becomes, why would he delve into the dark underbelly of crime? What possible gain could he achieve?

Remaining silent, Mia kept her eyes open and her hands loose. Though Donovan had assured her that she wouldn't need a weapon on their travels today, it was reassuring to feel them at her hips.

At the top floor, the elevator doors opened to reveal a long desk. A prim-looking woman greeted them with a tight smile. "Mr. Powers will be available in a few minutes."

Donovan led Mia to the side, though they didn't sit in one of the ornate leather chairs. It was less than a minute before the door to the office opened, and Michael appeared.

"Donovan!" he called out, gripping Donovan's hand and slapping him heartily over the shoulder with his other hand. Turning to Mia, he gave her a once-over before a grin lit his face. "Is this the elusive Selena?"

"Selena, Michael Powers III," Donovan said in introduction.

Mia held out her hand to shake, but Michael scooped it into a kiss. "A pleasure. Please, come inside. Would either of you like something to drink? Marcia, bring in coffee, would you?"

Following the men back into the office, Mia let out a breath at the unnecessary splendor. This was less an office and more of an apartment. A full kitchen lined one wall, with an impressively sized dining table situated beside it. A gathering area that could easily sit twenty people was filled with round leather couches. An opulent desk offered views out of the floor-to-ceiling windows.

The artwork on the walls were originals, but they paled in comparison to the larger-than-life sculpture of a fully nude man and woman intertwined that sat between the desk and the wall.

Swallowing once, Mia turned her attention to the man who lounged comfortably on one of the sofas. Donovan followed suit, sitting across from him. Mia stood to Donovan's back, keeping her disguise in place. Though he seemed friendly and easy-going, she didn't trust Michael as far as she could throw him.

He raised an eyebrow at her decision to hover behind Donovan but said nothing. Marcia arrived then with a carafe of coffee and a tray of milk and sugar before silently leaving the room. Pouring a cup for each of them, Michael leaned back, studying Donovan's face. "So, my friend, what is it that you want from me?"

Fourteen

THE CONSTRUCTION WAS COMING ALONG. Donovan had found contractors who worked fast, efficiently, and without questioning orders. Watching the smooth run operation, Selena was impressed with the progress.

Though it was night, Donovan had crews running both shifts to complete the building as quickly as possible. They walked together to the top floor, currently empty of workers. The entire top two floors had been gutted, and aside from a few walls that had been framed up, it was bare.

Donovan began pointing out the layout, explaining his ideas for both safety and convenience. Selena nodded along, intrigued by the way his mind worked.

"Bruce is an expert in security," Donovan said. She'd met the man briefly and was impressed by his professionalism and efficiency reticent of the military. "Together, we've come up with a system that will be near impossible to bypass."

"Good work."

Donovan led her to the next level down, which would be their offices for now. Selena had grander plans, but they had to begin somewhere.

"These are our offices," Donovan said, gesturing toward one end of the large room. "They will be completely sound and blast-proof. Each of these cubicles will be surrounded by shatter-proof glass."

The layout of those offices was in a U-shape, with a common area in the center to be used for breaks. The elevators opened in a small lobby between where their offices would be and where the U-shape began.

"There will be eleven offices?"

"That's right," Donovan said. "You're good with that for now?"

"For now," Selena murmured. Walking back to the elevator, she pushed the button for the car and waited for it to open. When it dinged, she glanced to Donovan. "What do you plan to do with—"

Her question was cut off as she took a step and hit air.

"Selena!"

Two arms of steel wrapped around her waist, hauling her back into the room. Letting out a gasp, Selena stared at the opening where the elevator should have been.

Realizing she was still in Donovan's embrace, Selena felt his chest heaving in fear. Slowly, she turned, though she didn't back away. His arms loosened only enough to allow her to face him.

Her wide eyes met his as she tentatively reached up to stroke his jaw. "Thank you," she whispered fervently. "You saved me."

Donovan didn't respond. There were no words to fill the magnitude of this moment.

Selena had observed Donovan for months before choosing him to become her business partner. There was a deep, primal part of her that had known their partnership would lead to more. No one had ever made her feel the way Donovan did. It was terrifying for someone in her position. Everything she'd built had been on her own, without trusting anyone to know the real her.

But there was no denying the strength in their partnership and the spark of desire between them. Selena knew, without a doubt, that she could trust him with her deepest, darkest secrets. She could trust him with her body, with her life. She could trust him with her very soul.

Acceptance of this passed between them with a look. She was still in his arms, her lips parted, eyes dark with longing.

"Selena." Donovan said her name softly, with an ache she understood. She felt butterflies wing across her stomach. Their lips were just a hairsbreadth apart. All it would take to touch his would be for her to lift onto her toes.

Selena didn't have to. Donovan's mouth came down on hers with an unstoppable urgency. One of his hands snaked into her hair, holding her still for his assault while the other pressed against her lower back.

Something wild unleashed itself inside her at the contact. She wanted him, every single piece of him. In a quick move, Selena spun them away from the empty shaft and shoved him to the floor. Donovan landed with a surprised huff, blinking up at her. Her body raging to take what was hers, Selena followed him down, legs straddling his hips, and wrapped his hands in hers, holding him in place. He allowed her control, entrusting in her as she did him. She yanked off Donovan's shirt and her own before fusing their mouths back together.

Until this moment, she'd given up ever having someone for herself. Selena felt content with the life she'd built and taken her pleasure in her success instead of flesh. Now, she took, and the more she took, the more Donovan gave. The rest of their clothes fell to the floor, and as she lowered herself onto him, Selena looked deep into his eyes.

"You're mine now," she said, waiting for an acknowledgment of the statement to flicker in his eyes.

Without reservation or hesitation, she took all of him and gave him herself in return.

PRESENT DAY

MICHAEL POWERS WAS AS ASTUTE as the media gave him credit for, if not more so. Though he sent Mia flirty smiles, when it came down to business, his attention immediately riveted on Donovan.

"I'm just doing a friendly checkup, Michael," Donovan replied to the man's question.

Michael leaned back, crossing one foot over a knee. "It's never so simple with you."

Donovan gave him a grin. "Perhaps not. We're expanding, and I wanted to deliver the news in person."

This gave Mia a start. He hadn't discussed expansion plans with her. It made her wonder why Donovan would wait to announce it in front of a client. Remaining still, she watched both men for reactions. Michael laid a hand over his ankle. "Expanding in what way?"

"Four new routes between Europe, Asia, and America. We wanted to give our top clients first grabs."

"I see." Michael pondered this new information, then glanced at Mia. "Selena, what do you have to add?"

"Oh, I'm not the brains behind this operation," she answered flippantly.

The corners of Michael's eyes creased. "Then why, may I ask, are you here?"

Mia looked him dead in the eye. "I'm the muscle."

He let out a whooping laugh, directing his next comment to Donovan. "You weren't kidding about her."

"I don't often jest," Donovan deadpanned.

Mia scrambled for something to add to give credence to her presence. When she spoke again, Michael's attention swung back to her. "Opening new lines will alleviate some of the pressure the recent changes in shipping laws have created."

Michael looked between them once again. "Are you ever going to tell me how, exactly, you get around inspections?"

"No." Donovan allowed himself a small grin. "Sorry, trade secret."

"Not even as a professional courtesy?"

"We wouldn't continue to be good at what we do if we gave away all our tricks, now, would we?"

"Touché." Michael rubbed his chin between two fingers and a thumb, a twinkle lighting his eye. "Count me in."

Donovan nodded, stood, and held out his hand. Michael shook it, glancing at Mia. Not wanting to give him another opportunity to kiss her hand, she shot him a finger gun and clicked her tongue, an action that earned a chuckle.

"Always good to see you, friends," Michael said as he escorted them out the door.

Following Donovan out of the building and into the waiting town car, Mia remained silent, waiting for him to speak first. "You did well."

"You didn't mention the expansion before." Taking a chance, Mia gazed up at him quizzically as the car pulled away on some unspoken command.

He understood the question she merely alluded to. "It's something we were working on...before. I apologize for not giving you a head's up."

Nodding, Mia stared down at her gloved hands, twisting her fingers together on her lap. There were too many things running around in her mind to make polite conversation.

"We have one more meeting this morning before lunch."

"Who is it with?"

"Olivia Munich." Another well-known name. It made Mia wonder just how many famously rich people were involved in schemes like this. "Olivia made her wealth with no help from her family. At fifteen, she went from living on the streets to scrubbing dishes in a restaurant in the same building as Anderson Financial. She was young and quiet, so no one noticed her, and she used the knowledge gained in overheard lunch conversations to secure herself an internship at the company. The partners were so impressed by her that they hired her on full-time, even without a degree. From there, she rose straight to the top, eventually taking over Anderson."

Donovan's whispered words played havoc with Mia's senses. "And where do we come in?"

"We began by investing with her, and as our relationship grew, we discovered other opportunities to work together. Finances are her calling, but archeology is her passion. Between interning and taking over the company, Olivia earned a double major in both. In her downtime, she can be found on digs most anywhere in the world."

"And not all her finds end up in museums?"

"Correct," Donovan said.

They rode the rest of the way in silence as Mia prepared to meet the highly intimidating Olivia Munich.

The woman with blonde hair in a perfectly coiffed bun, sharp, intense blue eyes, and a flawlessly smooth face had just celebrated her fifty-second birthday. Had Mia not known that fact from the tabloids, she never would have guessed. Olivia's impeccably pressed pantsuit showed no sign of wear, even in the late morning of the meeting. Making a quick assessment of both Donovan and Mia, Olivia gestured toward two industrial chairs.

"This is Selena," she said in quick, clipped tones. "I was wondering when I would meet you. Sit down. Would you like tea, coffee?"

"No, thank you Olivia." Donovan did as she asked and sat before her desk.

Her office was less lavish than Michael's had been but still spoke of wealth. Decoration leaned toward modern with clean lines and no clutter, save the few artifacts on display. Everything in the office had a purpose, and that purpose was running a multi-billion-dollar company.

Taking up her usual place behind Donovan, Mia watched Olivia carefully. She was not a woman to tamper with or to underestimate. Mia hoped her demeanor gave off the same impressions.

Olivia ignored Mia and turned her attention to Donovan. "I assume all is well?"

Donovan nodded. "Of course. We have, however, decided to expand and wanted to share the news in person."

Olivia crossed a leg over her knee and leaned slightly forward. Mia knew enough of body language to read her interest. "What type of expansion?"

"Four new routes between the Americas, Europe, and Asia. Specifically, one out of Egypt."

"Aren't you accommodating," Olivia said with a small smile. "I'll have a shipment ready in one week. Will you be prepared by then?"

"Absolutely," Donovan said. "I'll have my man in Egypt contact yours for the details."

"Lovely. Were you here for finances today, also?"

"We were. I'd like Selena to look over our portfolio."

With a swift turn, Olivia pulled open one of the few drawers in her office and presented a file, leaving it open on the desk. Donovan stood, offering Mia his chair, though an open one sat beside him. It was an action to put Mia at ease, to let her know he had her back.

As they switched spots, Mia lightly squeezed his arm in gratitude, an action hidden from the woman waiting patiently across the desk. Sitting, Mia pulled the file closer and just managed to control her reaction when she saw the numbers on the page.

Mia had survived an impoverished childhood and had always been comfortable on a police officer's salary. Hence, it was difficult to wrap her head around just how many commas she saw on the page. Behind her dark glasses, Mia's eyes grew wide at the nearly unfathomable numbers.

"This is just an overview," Olivia explained in the silence. Mia had to focus on the words through the slight ringing in her ears.

Though she felt Donovan's presence at her back, Mia was glad he'd kept his distance, so he couldn't feel the tension running through her. "This is all from investing?"

"Correct," Olivia said. "I'm very good at what I do."

Glancing up at her half-smile, Mia appreciated that the older woman wasn't boasting, just simply stating a fact. Staring back down at the page, Mia forced herself to ignore the numbers and look at the investments. Everything she learned here today would benefit the case she built. "I see here we're heavy on a company called NoCorp. Why is that?"

Donovan answered for Olivia. "That's a company called Nautical Origins. They build our ships."

Blinking up at Donovan for a moment, Mia nodded before continuing. Flipping through the subsequent pages, she continued to peruse the information while Olivia and Donovan watched in silence. Finally, Mia looked up, a few thoughts occurring to her.

There was quite a bit of money in an airline that had recently gotten bad press and subsequently dropped their prices. There was another small company, called MBJ Tech, a name that Mia recognized because of her partner, Alec.

His mother had suffered from an extreme degenerative bone disease and had finally traveled to Europe in search of a cure. She underwent a groundbreaking procedure, being injected with tissue that actually rebuilt the brittle parts of her skeleton.

MBJ Tech was in control of the research and development of the treatment.

"We should cut all ties with this," Mia said, pointing toward the failing airline, "and throw more into MBJ Tech."

"Interesting." Donovan leaned over her shoulder to get a closer look. "But you're correct. Olivia?"

She nodded briskly. "I'll see it done."

Closing the file, Mia slid it back across the desk, though she itched to take it with. Standing, she stepped behind Donovan once again to allow him to wrap up the meeting. "Thank you for your time, Olivia. We'll be in touch."

He shook her hand, and when Olivia turned to Mia, Mia offered her own. Mia didn't think the finger gun would go over as well on her as it had with Michael. "A pleasure, Selena. Please, come visit again."

Mia answered with a single nod as she led the way out the door.

Back in the car, Donovan remained silent, simply taking her hand again, sliding off the glove to run his fingers lightly along Mia's palm. The action sparked a response in her, and she had to concentrate to control her desire.

"You had some amazing insight in there," Donovan murmured.

Mia shrugged. "Fresh eyes."

Using one hand to gently remove her glasses, Donovan's eyes met Mia's for a long moment, soft and searching. "Beautiful eyes."

Swallowing once, Mia felt ensnared by his gaze—much like a deer in headlights, unable to look away.

His face moved closer, his gaze remaining steady. As his lips brushed against hers, their eyes remained open, reading each other's innermost thoughts as his touch shot sparks through every nerve ending, a swirling mass that eventually pooled low in her stomach. Mia could actually feel her heartbeat in her chest, reaching toward him while her body froze in place.

Donovan pulled away as the car began to slow, carefully replacing her glasses and slipping the glove back on her hand. Another beat later, he spoke. "We're here."

Breaking away from his intensity, Mia glanced out the window at the restaurant they'd be having lunch at. Through the onslaught of emotions pouring over and through her, she managed to ask a question. "Who are we meeting with?" Her voice came out husky, a result of the desire pulsing through her.

That fact did not escape Donovan's notice. He brushed the pad of his thumb across her lips, causing her mouth to pop open with a swift intake of air. The car had stopped, but they had yet to move. Mia waited for the answer to her question while attempting to get her body under control.

"Andres McMillan." Donovan straightened as he spoke, squeezing her hand once before reaching for the door. "Are you ready?"

Not trusting her voice, Mia merely nodded.

Fifteen

THE RENOVATION FOR THE BUILDING was complete. Though Selena hadn't spent every night watching the progress, she began to find herself craving Donovan. Not just his touch, though she assuaged that need often enough. She craved his conversation, his opinion, and most oddly, his approval.

When she'd first watched him in the ring, he'd been so intense and focused. Though his eyes never strayed from his target, it was plain to see he missed nothing. His physical prowess still left her breathless.

Those skills transitioned so smoothly into business that, even though she'd hand-picked him, it still amazed Selena. He was intelligent and ruthless yet had an easy way with people that she severely lacked. He was the details man to her overall vision. Their partnership was a good match.

The night he'd caught her as she was about to fall, something substantial and irreversible passed between Selena and Donovan. Their connection went beyond the physical, beyond anything she could have imagined. In time, she would learn all his secrets—and he, hers.

With the penthouse completed, Selena wandered the main room, running a finger across the specially made furniture that could double as protection in the case of an attack. She knew where each secret compartment lay, the strengths and few weaknesses of the whole design.

"What do you think?" Donovan asked.

"The building is exactly how I envisioned it," Selena said.

"We make a good team."

"Yes," she murmured. "It seems we do."

Donovan approached her, but Selena moved away. She wanted him like a drowning man wanted air, but they had things to discuss. "I want to begin transitioning away from the fights."

"Now? They are our main source of income."

"I don't want to spread ourselves too thin. Our future is in the shipping side of things; we need to focus there."

"I agree, but we still need a revenue stream."

"Hand the fights over to Leroy. Take a cut, but not a big one. He's earned it."

"Consider it done." Donovan approached again, and this time Selena didn't back away. Rubbing at the spot on her shoulders that always knotted with tension, Donovan kissed her just under the jaw. "You're tense. What is it?"

"There's something I need to tell you."

He continued to kiss her neck, her shoulder. "You can tell me anything."

"You may never look at me the same. You may never come back."

"There's nothing you can say that would change the way I feel about you." Moving to stand in front of her, Donovan took Selena's hands gently in his. "You need to feel in control."

Selena nodded. Donovan led her down the hall. "Come with me."

Pushing open the door to the small library, Donovan went to the bookshelf and selected *Mastering Your Inner Self*.

Tipping the book toward him, the entire bookcase shifted. The hidden room was revealed to show a four-poster bed sitting in the center of the room, the red sheets a warning of things to come. The walls were lined with black leather objects in an astounding number. Donovan stripped off his clothes and moved to the bed, lying in the middle, his dark gaze on Selena.

She secured his wrists at each post, leaving his legs free. She went to the wall and selected a soft flog. It fit her hand like it had been made especially for her. The instant she knelt over Donovan, she felt bold, confident. He always knew exactly what she needed.

Selena was in control, a dominant. She didn't consider herself a sadist, for she didn't necessarily enjoy giving pain. No, what she and Donovan shared was all about pleasure.

"Tell me your safe word, my love."

"I won't need it."

"Say it," Selena ordered.

"Dagger, mistress."

Flicking the cords of leather against his thighs, Selena didn't stop until Donovan was fully aroused and begging for her to give him release. She didn't hesitate. Taking him, filling herself with him, Selena released his wrists so she could feel his hands on her heated skin. He teased and pinched and brought her to a fever pitch, holding her tight as her orgasm ripped through her, as his own climax left him breathless.

He kept holding her as she told him her deepest secrets, and long after her tears dried against his chest.

DONOVAN STEPPED OUT OF THE car, coming around to open Mia's door before leading her into the restaurant. The ground level was a wine bar; to her surprise, they continued down a flight of steps to the basement, dimly lit with maroon booths and gold walls. Though fairly busy, the maître d' led them to a roped-off area which had been reserved for their party, leaving several tables as a buffer between their meeting and the rest of the restaurant.

A man waited, standing to greet the couple as they approached. He had dark features, with closely cut hair and a neatly trimmed beard that ran along the edge of his jaw. His gaze reminded Mia of Donovan—focused and intense, missing nothing.

Donovan extended his hand in greeting before gesturing toward Mia. "I'd like to introduce you to Selena."

Instead of offering her his hand, Andres bowed respectfully. Sitting in the chair that Donovan pulled out for her, making sure her back was against the wall with a clear view of the restaurant and entrance, Mia removed her hat but left the dark glasses on. The lenses made it difficult to see clearly, but she was nervous about removing them.

"I trust you've had pleasant travels." Andres' deep voice held a hint of an accent Mia couldn't quite place.

"That we have."

Donovan hadn't given Mia any background information on Andres, as he had with Michael or Olivia. Of course, their prolonged, intense moment in the car may have had something to do with that. The other difference between the three clients they'd met today was that Mia had heard of both Michael and Olivia, whereas Andres McMillan rang no bells.

The men waited to speak until the drinks had been delivered. With the waitress out of earshot, Andres began the conversation. "Am I able to speak freely?"

"Please do," Donovan encouraged.

"There are new players in the management here in Britain. One has been resistant to our approach."

"Every man has a price." Donovan arched an eyebrow at Andres. "You have only to find it."

"I was hoping you could help me with that while you're in town," Andres said, holding his hands out, palms up. "I've tried everything I know."

"Of course. Set up a meet this afternoon."

"Done. As for your other routes, everything is running smoothly."

"Good." Donovan leaned forward, folding his hands together on top of the table. "We've already set a load for our new route in Egypt. Selena and I will oversee it personally."

Mia tried not to show her surprise at the statement. Egypt must be one of the stops on this trip. From what she'd gathered, Andres was not so much a client as a palm greaser. That begged the question, how did Donovan and Andres come to meet?

As lunch wrapped up, Donovan asked Andres for the name of the person they would be meeting later that afternoon before shaking the man's hand and leading Mia back to street level. Once in the relative privacy of the car, Mia asked the question that had been burning through the meeting. "How do you know Andres?"

Before answering, Donovan glanced over, reading her expression. She kept her face neutral, waiting for his reply. "We were in the military together. Myself, Bruce, and Andres were nearly inseparable. They saved my life several times, and vice versa. They are the only two people in this world who have my ultimate trust, aside from you."

Nodding, Mia turned her head to watch out the window as they made their way back to the hotel. The fact that the three of them were in the military together meant that Bruce and Andres were also fake names.

Donovan and Mia didn't speak again until they were back in the hotel room. He'd received a message from Andres to meet with their trouble official at three o'clock, which meant they had some time alone.

"I was going to make some calls to our offices," Donovan said. "Your surprise will be here before I leave."

"What, exactly, is this surprise?"

With a smirk, Donovan evaded the question, popping open his laptop instead of answering. "Stay close if you'd like to listen in."

Shaking her head at his coyness, Mia took a seat in the chair beside the couch so she could listen but not be seen. As the call connected, she heard Bruce's voice come through the speakers.

"Just checking in on our visitor," Donovan began after greeting his old friend.

"We've done as you instructed, one meal a day and no other contact. He hasn't spoken."

Considering this, Donovan continued after a moment. "You've tipped off the police?"

"Yes," Bruce said. "They've kept it quiet for now. An infiltration on this level reflects poorly on them."

"It may never become public knowledge, and that's fine. It may be time to contact Tony."

"Would you like me to, or would you prefer we wait until you're back?"

Donovan's gaze met Mia's. Her face remained neutral, though her heart rate had picked up. "I'll have you make the initial contact, but let's wait. We'll speak again from our next destination. Anything else?"

"The main offices have re-opened. Most of the damage was in the top levels, and the crews have begun work there now."

"That was quick. Excellent work, Bruce." There was no verbal response, and Mia imagined Bruce acknowledging the compliment with a dip of his head. "I've a name; if you could have Mason run it through the system, find out everything he can in the next hour, and send it directly to me. Henry Windham, London. Approximately forty years old. Works for the city."

"I'll send it right over," Bruce promised.

"We'll speak soon."

Though she hadn't heard the name Mason before, it made sense that Donovan had some kind of computer expert on his payroll. Henry Windham was the name of the man Donovan and Andres would be meeting with later today.

Before he placed his next call, Mia raised a question. "What's your plan with the DeLuca?"

Turning to face her fully, Donovan answered, "The DeLucas have some information we need. I'll have Bruce inform them of the situation, and when we return, we'll make the trade ourselves."

Mia cocked her head. "Have we done a lot of business with them in the past?"

So subtle she almost missed it, Donovan's eyes tightened. "Not exactly."

"When we met with them, Tony had mentioned we've worked together."

"That's true." Donovan sighed, running a hand through his short, dark hair. "A few years ago, we approached them with a proposition. At that time, they were our biggest competition, and we had come up with a plan to benefit both of our businesses. Shortly after, they got involved in weapons trades, so we kept our distance but kept out of each other's ways. Our business boomed while theirs slowly began going downhill, along with becoming dangerous. They got in deep with the cartels in Mexico, which at first was highly profitable but quickly became not worth the trouble."

"So, at least two of the brothers became jealous of us, hence the hit," Mia said, piecing together the little bit that she knew.

"Far as I can tell. Tony truly didn't seem to know much of what was going on in his own home, but turning a blind eye can be just as dangerous as knowingly allowing it to happen."

"Can I ask something about our business?"

"Of course." Donovan leaned forward, his focus solely on her.

"How do we get around customs? Obviously, there are bribes involved—but there must be more."

With a smile, Donovan reached out to take her hand. He spoke three words which made Mia's mouth fall open. "Unmanned Submarine Drones."

For a moment, her jaw worked, but no words would form. "Submarines? We have submarines?"

"Yes. Our ships, along with the subs, are a unique design that you and I came up with and approached NoCorp to build for us. In the bottom of our ships, there is an airlock container that will hold two of the drones if needed. Depending on the port the ship is departing or arriving, they will remain in the airlock or deliver directly to the warehouse."

"That opens up a whole bunch more questions."

"Questions I will happily answer, but I think it would be easier to show you. I promise you a tour of our facilities in Egypt, along with our dock when we fly home."

Though her head spun, Mia agreed, allowing him to continue with his phone calls.

For the next hour, she listened in while he caught up with the office manager, a woman named Felicity she had yet to meet, and the Baltimore Dock manager. It was an odd combination of legitimate business and code words that left her with even more questions.

Questions that would have to wait. As Donovan prepared to leave for his meeting, a knock sounded on the door. Donovan opened it to reveal a slight woman with a French accent, dressed in all black with her hair pulled back into a tight bun. She immediately began pinching, tugging, and pulling on Mia, jabbering away in French while she gestured for someone in the hall.

A bellhop entered, and Mia carefully turned her face away. He rolled a luggage rack inside the room in front of him while pulling another along behind him. Each rack was stuffed full of clothing covered by cloth bags.

The bellhop immediately left, with Donovan being shooed out the door directly after. He gave Mia a wink as she stood in the middle of a maelstrom, and her name was Sophia.

She turned Mia this way and that, eyeing up every aspect of her body before pulling several concealed garments off the racks and shoving the rest aside. Pulling Mia into the dressing room, Sophia found a place to hang her selections in the roomy closet. With one hand on her shoulder, Sophia pushed Mia onto a vanity stool. Completely bewildered by the turn of events today, Mia sat, blinking up at her.

"I will be doing a full spa treatment," Sophia said in heavily accented English. "Take a shower and wear only a robe after. Then, we will begin."

After handing Mia a small towel to wrap around her hair, Sophia directed her toward the shower, placing a lavender scented scrub inside to use on her skin. While Mia turned on the spray, Sophia hurried to the other room to retrieve the bags she'd unceremoniously dropped upon entering.

Stepping into the shower, Mia used the few minutes of privacy to relax, breathing in the calming scent of lavender mixed with jasmine. Too soon, she was done and found a short, silk robe waiting for her.

Sophia was ready as Mia emerged. The next hour was filled with waxing and tweezing while her face was covered in goop Sophia assured her was a face mask. Every inch of Mia's skin felt raw by the time Sophia was done with her.

Once Mia was able to apply moisturizer to soothe her aching skin, Sophia sat her back on the vanity stool to begin a makeover. Mia never spent any time on beauty—she was lucky to remember to throw on some mascara in the morning—but she couldn't deny, after the pain of waxing, the spa day was kind of fun.

After makeup was done, Mia felt more tugging and pulling, this time on her scalp, as Sophia swept her hair up. Since she wasn't allowed to look in a mirror yet, Mia had no idea what her face, or her hair, looked like.

Finally, Sophia dragged her unwitting Barbie into the closet. Unzipping the first dress, Mia's eyes widened at the elegant cuts as one after another Sophia held them up, made a face, and returned them to the rack. When there were only a few choices left, Sophia paused, her eyes meeting Mia's. Mia glanced down at the sheath of silk and back up.

They spoke simultaneously. "This is the one."

Sixteen

DONOVAN AND SELENA WERE IN their shared office, going over numbers from their first year of business. Though they still had a hand in the fights, most of their attention was now on the shipping business.

They currently owned six vessels, and Selena hoped to double that by the end of the second year. The business was still in the red, but Selena knew that would change quickly.

"We were approached by a group in Mexico," Donovan began.

Immediately Selena shook her head. "Love the food, as I'm sure I would love the beaches, but anyone looking to work with us from Mexico is going to inevitably be connected to the cartels."

"It would be a very lucrative—"

"No."

He sighed, running a hand through his hair. The action distracted Selena momentarily. Though they'd been sleeping together for a year and partners longer than that, her mouth still went dry whenever she looked at Donovan. Especially now, when his fingers left his hair disheveled.

"I know, I know we agreed to that. It's just, we're short on cash flow right now, and it would boost us over..."

"Cash flow is a momentary problem. Anyone who gets involved in weapons or drugs can never truly get out. They live in constant fear. I won't do that to us."

On this point, Selena remained firm. While they had the connections to acquire firearms when necessary, getting involved in that business would be the worst decision they could make, personally and professionally.

"You're right, of course. Forgive me."

Waving a hand, Selena dismissed the matter. "You look at the numbers, the details. I look at the overall. That's why we work."

Clicking through sites on her computer, Selena paused as an article caught her eye. "The building on Lexington is going up for sale."

Donovan's interest piqued. He moved around the desks to stand behind her, leaning forward to read the same information. His fingers found the back of her neck, rubbing in small circles subconsciously. Even as she felt the tension release, Selena turned to him with excitement bright in her eyes. "That's the perfect spot. We must have it."

Donovan nodded. "Leave it to me."

In six months, the Lexington building was not only theirs but well underway. As Selena walked the floorplan, she could see the few improvements Donovan had made on the original from the building by the docks. It wouldn't be much longer until this would be their new home, and the place downtown would serve as backup.

"Are you ready to go underground?" Donovan asked.

He'd been watching her quietly while Selena inspected the work being done, but she turned to him now and nodded. They went down the stairs together, not needing words. They always had a tendency to be on the same page in both personal and business matters. They'd shared everything with each other, and there were many times words were unnecessary and only seemed frivolous.

Upon reaching the bottom levels, Donovan placed his hand on the pad to reveal the remaining underground steps, which Selena descended without hesitation.

The small crew they'd hired worked in a different part of the subterranean paths, so after swinging a leg over one of the BMW sport bikes they'd acquired for speeding through the tunnels, Selena fell in behind Donovan. The dark glasses she wore were a necessary evil—not only to mitigate the effects of the wind the bikes created but also to hide her identity. Working in close quarters to so many people was new to her, and it was of the utmost importance to remain anonymous.

When they reached the crew, Selena dismounted and set the kickstand before walking to Donovan's side. He explained what the crew had been working on—a way to light the tunnels.

Donovan approached the man in charge while Selena hung back to observe. As they discussed the benefit and technicalities of running solar power over electricity, she leaned against the wall with her arms crossed. Once the man had laid out his points, Donovan glanced at her, and Selena simply nodded.

"Let's do it," Donovan said, relaying the unspoken command.

Without any further comment, the contractor gave the order to his men. They were quick and proficient, a product of working for cash instead of hourly. When Donovan approached Selena, he spoke quietly. "I'll stay to keep an eye on them if you want to take care of the other matter."

Selena smirked. "Gladly."

Not wasting any more time, she approached the sleek bike, swinging her leg over. Revving the engine once, Selena kicked it into gear and spun away from Donovan, heading back toward their new home.

Though she knew it was essential to split up from Donovan, Selena hated spending any of their time apart. The task tonight was a necessary evil, and one that she planned to enjoy thoroughly.

While Donovan dealt with the contractors in the tunnels, Selena had a meeting to attend.

Stopping a block away from their Lexington home, Selena made sure her disguise was in place—black scarf, dark glasses, black leather gloves to match the pants and jacket—before making her way to the ground level. Exiting the building, Selena walked at a steady pace to her destination, using a roundabout way to avoid anyone who might be following.

For Donovan and Selena both, their way of life consisted of more paranoia than might be considered healthy, but it had kept them alive and secret for this long. No need to fix something that wasn't broken.

Turning one more corner, Selena immediately began climbing up a fire escape until she reached the third floor. Swinging through an open window, Selena pulled out a heat sensor from a loop on her belt. With no activity, she headed up to the fourth floor, sweeping the rooms before heading back to the fire escape to access the roof.

Tony DeLuca would be waiting, and if he had set a trap, it would be on the inside staircase, which he would expect Selena to use. Instead, she crouched on the ledge, spotting Tony immediately but searching for others. He'd promised to come alone, but people so rarely held their word.

Satisfied there would be no surprises, Selena approached Tony silently from behind. She'd earned a reputation as a ghost and enjoyed startling her prey.

"Tony DeLuca, I presume," Selena said, pitching her voice low. He spun, his eyes wide and a hand resting over his heart. She allowed herself a small smile. "So nice to meet you."

"You scared the daylights out of me," Tony complained before visibly composing himself. "You must be the infamous Selena. You have a business proposition for me?"

"That I do." Her eyes swept the roof and surrounding area. The plan was to keep this as brief as possible before disappearing into the night. "We seem to be in the same business and thought that working together could be beneficial to both of us."

"That sounds agreeable, depending on your terms."

"We'd like access to your channels. In return, certain city officials who have been giving you trouble will look the other way."

Tony hesitated, surely thinking through the simple terms for some hidden benefit. Finally, he nodded.

"We have a deal?" Selena asked, wanting to hear it aloud.

He dipped his head in acceptance. "That we do. When will your first shipment need to come through?"

"Tomorrow morning, six o'clock. Once we know we can trust you, we'll redirect your trouble officials." The statement was both given and taken as a threat.

"Agreed," Tony said.

Acknowledging him with a flicker of a smile, Selena stepped backward off the ledge. The cable attached around her waist swung her forward and through an open window, leaving a gawking Tony alone on the roof.

PRESENT DAY

WITH NERVES RATTLING AROUND HER stomach, Mia took a deep breath and turned to look at herself in the full-length mirror. The bloodred dress offered a high neckline and scooped back, fitted down to her hips before flaring out just slightly, allowing easier movement. Gently tugging up the hemline, Mia stared at the shoes and had immediate doubts as to her walking capabilities while wearing them.

Donovan had returned just before Sophia left, with strict instructions not to intrude until Mia made her appearance.

Sophia had done her hair up in some kind of complicated bun that managed to look soft and romantic, a clip glittering with crystals snapped securely in the midst of all the pins it took to hold it all together. Releasing the dress to let it sweep gently to the ground, Mia rubbed a hand down the soft silk before looking herself directly in the eyes.

Sophia had done Mia's makeup to accentuate her eyes, applying heavy smudge that left them looking large and sultry. Mia hardly recognized the woman reflected back. She looked...sexy. Beautiful. Words Mia had never applied to herself before.

She was Selena.

Before she could talk herself out of it, Mia teetered to the door, making a concentrated effort to balance on the balls of her feet. Doing so helped her walk become steady, more confident. As she stepped into the living area, Mia looked up and straight into Donovan's heady gaze.

He let out a visible gasp as his eyes trailed down her body and back again, his expression filled with an emotion she was afraid to name. Just as he studied her, Mia swept her gaze across his lean form, taking in the sharp black suit he wore. He stayed monochromatic with a black shirt, glossy black tie, and even a black vest visible beneath the fitted jacket.

The look left her mouth dry.

"You look stunning," Donovan finally said, approaching Mia with a small box in his hand.

Peering down at it, Mia's eyebrows drew together as he popped open the tiny lid to reveal a pair of diamond earrings, twinkling even in the dim light. "Donovan, you didn't have to…"

He silenced her with a look, removing the earrings himself and slipping them in her ears. Mia swallowed back any more protest when he stepped back and smiled.

"Now, you're perfect." He seemed satisfied. Holding out his elbow like a gentleman, he lifted an eyebrow. "Ready?"

Nodding, Mia slipped her hand through the crook of his arm, pausing at the door to add an elbow-length pair of white gloves and, of course, sunglasses. The lenses were large, round affairs with glittering jewels along the edges. Mia felt like a movie star.

Donovan led her to the lobby, and she could swear numerous people stopped to stare as they glided by. It made her nerves extra jumpy, but Donovan placed his other hand over hers, the contact more reassuring than mere words.

Their car waited at the curb. Donovan deposited her into the seat before moving around to join her. The lights of the city passed by in a blur. Mia's attention was torn between Donovan in his dark suit and the unfamiliar sights.

They made their way toward the River Thames, and though she brimmed with curiosity at what their night would entail, Mia didn't ask. Donovan seemed content to just sit beside her, his hand keeping hers captive. Whenever she looked his way, Mia found his gaze solely on her, and they shared several long looks. A warm sensation swirled in her belly. Not just lust, though she felt a healthy amount of that. This was something different. Deeper.

The car stopped in one of the most popular tourist spots—just outside the entrance for the London Eye, the giant Ferris Wheel London was famous for. Waiting for Donovan to open her door, Mia accepted his hand and stepped as gracefully from the car as she was capable.

With her hand back in the crook of his arm, they walked at a sedate pace to the entrance. Mia could feel Donovan's eyes on her, waiting for a reaction, so she smiled at him. "We're going in a pod?"

"That we are," Donovan said, pulling open the door. The building seemed oddly quiet, with only several workers lingering around but no crowds of people waiting to board.

"Where is everyone?"

Donovan remained silent, so she looked at him. The small smile playing at his lips had her eyes narrowing. "I purchased all the rides for this evening. The Ferris Wheel is ours."

"You..." Mia found herself speechless. Her mouth had dropped open, but as someone approached, she quickly snapped it shut.

"You must be Mr. and Mrs. Anderson," the woman said with a bright smile. "We're so happy to have you. Please, follow me."

They followed and loaded into a waiting pod. A bottle of champagne sat ready in a bucket of ice in the center of the long bench, a waiter at rapt attention. Mia sat to one side, careful not to disturb the bucket of champagne, while Donovan settled in beside her. A tray of hors d'oeuvres was brought in and placed on the bench.

"Will there be anything else, sir?" the waiter asked.

"No, thank you," Donovan said in dismissal. With a bow, the waiter left. They were alone. The doors closed, and they began to move, slowly lifting into the sky. "The waiter normally stays on and doubles as a tour guide, but I thought you might like to be alone," Donovan explained, grabbing the bottle of champagne and popping the cork. He poured it into two glasses, handing one to Mia. "To us."

Slipping off her sunglasses, Mia clinked her champagne against his. "To us."

As they gained height, Mia stood and watched the skyline of London come into view. Donovan rose to stand beside her, softly whispering in her ear as he pointed out the main attractions. Big Ben, St. Paul's Cathedral, Paddington Station, Westminster Abbey, the Houses of Parliament—Donovan seemed to be knowledgeable on all of them.

Once they reached the top of the wheel, the pod stopped. At her quizzical look, Donovan explained as he lifted the tray and offered the appetizers to her. "Since I've bought out the rest of the night, I've asked them to stop us at the top."

Accepting a chocolate truffle, Mia took a bite and sipped on her champagne, the sweet bubbles going instantly to her head. Mia didn't drink much before taking this job, and since she'd been in Donovan's care, she hadn't seen any evidence of alcohol in any of the homes they'd stayed in. In fact, everything he'd fed her had been so healthy, Mia suspected she was probably in the best shape of her life.

Donovan stepped close, wrapping an arm around her waist, pressing her against his hard body. Mia felt the jolt of electricity and savored the feeling.

"You mean everything to me," Donovan said with a quiet intensity. "You deserve all of this and more. Our life is not what we've been dealing with back home, being attacked and hiding in safe houses. It's this, and I plan to show you just what exactly we have together."

"Donovan," Mia began, her words coming out breathy. "As long as I'm with you, that's all that matters. Crawling through sewers or wearing diamonds, it doesn't matter to me. Only you do."

With a shock, she realized that she wasn't just acting. Those words rang true, and they came from her, not the personification of Selena.

Closing her eyes against the wash of guilt, Mia leaned her forehead gently against Donovan's chest, breathing in his scent. When this ended, she would have moments like this to look back on. She wanted to make the most of it.

Lifting her head again, Mia pressed her lips to his, pushing against his body to be as close as possible. He met her hunger with his own but, too soon, pulled gently away. "We could get carried away rather easily."

"I would enjoy that even more than these amazing views," she said with such honesty it was nearly his undoing.

With a groan, his lips met hers again, but without the firestorm that had nearly consumed them the first time. Leaning close to her ear, Donovan whispered the words that allowed her to separate from him. "We have all night."

Eventually, the wheel began to move once again, and by the time they'd made it back to the ground level, the bottle of champagne was empty, and Mia's cheeks were flushed. Before reaching ground level, she slipped her glasses back on and held onto Donovan's arm, though this time it was more for balance than him being a gentleman.

The same group that had greeted them now bid them goodbye as Mia allowed Donovan to lead her back to the waiting car.

Their next stop was the Ritz Hotel, another famous spot she'd never envisioned herself stepping into. Donovan led the way, ushering her to the Ritz Restaurant, where music already flowed through the majestic room. They were immediately shown to a semi-private corner table, affording views of Green Park. A waiter, dressed to the nines in full livery, was ready to assist with another bottle of champagne.

Behind the dark glasses, Mia's eyes took in the tall marble columns, silk draperies, and gorgeous chandeliers. All the waiters bustled about like some forgotten era, and she immediately had a

196

flash to a scene from *Hello, Dolly!* If the staff spontaneously broke into song and dance, Mia didn't think she would bat an eye.

"A couple of nights a week, they offer dinner and dancing," Donovan said, leaning close to whisper in her ear. "I hope you're hungry."

"Starved. Do you think it'd be all right to take my glasses off?"

Glancing around first, Donovan nodded his approval. Setting them gently on the table, Mia met his gaze without interference. "This place is incredible."

"I'm glad you like it. London certainly has a lot to offer."

Deciding to share her earlier thought of musicals, she asked, "Do you think our waiters will break into a choreographed dance?"

His low chuckle sent waves of pleasure dancing through her bloodstream. "Let me guess. *Hello, Dolly!* flashbacks?"

Mia's eyes widened. "It surprises me that you've seen that."

"It surprises me that *you've* seen that," he retorted.

Giving him a cheeky grin, Mia realized the waiter approached with appetizers. She turned her face down and away so he wouldn't get a full look at her. It felt extreme to take these measures, especially here, in London, in a restaurant, but it was the way Donovan and Selena lived.

Once the waiter had gone, and Mia took a bite of something delicious and unpronounceable, she pressed her luck with Donovan. "Tell me something about yourself that you've never told anyone."

He placed a finger against his mouth, thinking through the question. "There are no secrets between us. At one time, you knew all my deepest, darkest secrets. I will happily share them again, but perhaps not tonight."

Swallowing hard, Mia switched directions. "All right, something not so deep and dark, then."

"My second favorite color is red," he said as his eyes dipped down, taking in the skintight dress sheathing her body.

197

Though the comment made her throat go dry, Mia managed to ask, "And your first favorite color?"

His eyes met hers again, brushing a stray piece of hair gently away from her face. "Amber."

The color of her eyes. With only a few inches between them, Mia closed the distance, pressing her lips to his. Her head spun with the contact, coupled with the champagne and the pounding beat of the music pulsing through her chest.

For a moment, Mia forgot who she was, where she was. All that mattered was the man before her. Donovan deepened the kiss, and though she wanted to wrap herself around him, Mia allowed the sensation to flow through their lips and wash over the rest of her body. When they parted, her eyelids lifted slowly to look at him.

"I love you," Donovan said, his husky whisper sinking into her very core.

And for a moment, Mia's vision went black.

Another scene superimposed itself upon the one before her. Donovan was still there, standing in front of her as close as he was now. The restaurant was no longer there, but they were surrounded by large, empty spaces and brick walls. Underground spaces.

The tunnels.

Donovan, saying those same three words. "I love you."

It was just a flash, gone in a moment. Reality snapped back, and Mia shook her head in an attempt to clear it. "Sorry. Must be the champagne."

Focusing back on Donovan's facial expression, Mia realized he had just said something very important, and she'd handled it poorly. There was an unreadable mask over his handsome features. She reached out to stroke a thumb along a line his slight frown had created.

"You are the most important person in my life," Mia said, once again with the unmistakable ring of truth.

His face immediately cleared, and he brought her hand to his chest. "Dance with me."

Bewildered, Mia glanced around before responding, "What? Here?"

He shrugged. "Why not?"

Then, without waiting for further argument, he simply stood and pulled her up and into his arms. The band played a slow number, and they swayed on their feet. Donovan kept an arm wrapped tightly around her waist, her body snug against his.

"Donovan?" Mia asked quietly, pulling her head back to look directly at him.

"Yes?"

"Tell me something about me that no one else knew."

He was silent so long she wasn't sure he was going to answer. Dr. White had directed them both not to push memories, and she thought he would argue against her question based on the doctor's recommendation. She hoped he wouldn't; Mia really wanted to know something about Selena from someone that cared about her. She had to have some redeeming qualities to deserve a man like Donovan.

Donovan continued to study her, and Mia wasn't sure what he looked for or if he found it. She kept her expression open and relaxed, begging with her eyes alone.

Finally, he spoke. "The day we met, you challenged me and proceeded to kick my ass. Looking back, that was the moment I fell in love with you."

Mia didn't know how to respond to that but felt a smile blooming at his words. "Why would I challenge you?"

"It was my job interview," he said. "Eventually, I got the upper hand, though I always had a sneaking suspicion you let me win."

"How long was it before we..." Mia trailed off, knowing he would understand the question.

"We'd been working together for several months. There was a connection between us that became more and more difficult to deny. We've never looked back."

At this, Donovan grasped her hand and led her back to her seat. As they finished the first appetizer and were presented with the next course, so many questions were swirling around Mia's mind that she didn't know what to ask next. "Can you tell me more about me? From before you and I met? What did I do? Did I have a job?"

Donovan smiled indulgently. "When we first met, I was fighting in underground matches. I was fresh out of the military and had something to prove, I suppose. Unbeknownst to me, you were the one running the show."

"I was running illegal fights?" Her eyes went wide at the news.

"It's how you got your start. The money you—and later, we—made from those fights is what we used to establish our current business. You had plans and needed someone to help you with running the operation. You had been searching for someone to trust for a year and eventually set your sights on me." His mouth tipped up in amusement at this remark. "You told me you watched me for another six months before approaching."

Mia's brain worked a mile a minute. "I must have had help establishing the fights. That's not something I could have done on my own."

"True, though the only person you ever contacted or saw face to face was Leroy."

"Leroy?" The man that had been security for Reggie? Reggie, the snake that had ratted them out and gotten their penthouse attacked?

"The same one," Donovan said. That, at least, explained why Leroy seemed to know Selena the day they'd entered Reggie's lair. "He took over the fights when we moved on to the shipping business."

"How did he end up being muscle for Reggie?"

"A story for another day." Donovan leaned forward, taking Mia's hands in his. "There's one more thing."

His mouth brushed against her ear, tickling the tendrils of nerves there. All of Mia's attention was on him, knowing this was important. Her words came out nearly breathless. "What's that?"

"There's a dark need that exists in both of us. Later tonight, I'm going to show you exactly what that entails."

Seventeen

THREE AND A HALF YEARS AGO

THE OFFICE WAS CERTAINLY A lonely place without Donovan's presence. With business booming, it was imperative that he travel abroad and meet face to face with the clients. Though Selena understood that and encouraged his trips, it didn't help to alleviate the melancholy of his absence.

Bruce knocked and entered the office, standing at attention until she acknowledged him. Donovan trusted Bruce with both their lives and Selena had a respect for the man that bordered on affection.

"I've just spoken with Donovan," Bruce announced when she gestured him forward. He sat opposite Selena, his back ramrod straight. "There's some good news from NoCorp."

"What is it?"

"They are ahead of schedule. They'll have both subs completed before the end of the month."

"That is good news," Selena said, surprised. People rarely over-exceeded. "Is he placing an order for more?"

With a dip of his head, Bruce answered. "Yes, two more in six months."

"Perfect," Selena murmured, taking out a map and placing it atop the other paperwork on the desk. Each of the routes was highlighted, with future plans penciled in. "When does the expansion at the docks begin?"

"Tomorrow," Bruce said. "Your vision is almost complete."

△ △ △

ZIPPING THROUGH THE TUNNELS, SELENA glanced back to see Donovan on her tail. With a determined grin, she hit the gas and took off, leaving him in her dust. It didn't take him long to catch up, and as she slid sideways to a halt, he was right beside her. Dismounting, Selena waited for him to join her, the smile still very much in evidence.

"I'll get you one of these times," Donovan said.

"Wouldn't count on it." Selena gripped his biceps as his arms slipped around her waist.

His eyes went soft, a look reserved for Selena alone. "I love you, you know."

"This is where you first told me that." She smiled at the memory. "Anyone else might think underground tunnels are creepy and gross."

"But not you. Such a romantic."

With a roll of her eyes, Selena stepped from the embrace and spun toward the exit. "No time for romance. We have work to do."

Ever the gentleman, Donovan palmed open both doors they came across, allowing Selena to go first. When they emerged into the cool night air, Selena took the lead, going straight outside and to the docks.

Tony DeLuca waited patiently with Ricky. Donovan and Selena had done plenty of research on this family before and after making the initial contact and knew all decisions went through Ricky before being approved by Tony. That meant they might actually get something accomplished tonight.

"Good evening, Donovan, Selena," Tony said. "This is my brother, Ricky."

Donovan nodded his head in greeting but allowed Selena to take point. "Thanks for meeting with us. We've come to warn you about your new business partners."

"What do you know of it?" Ricky asked.

Selena shrugged, not one to play games but not willing to give away her sources. "We hear things. We've enjoyed our mutually beneficial agreement, but I'm afraid if you continue down this course, we'll have no choice but to distance ourselves from your business."

Ricky and Tony shared a look until Ricky slowly shook his head. It was Tony who answered. "I'm sorry you feel that way."

"Don't say we didn't warn you," Selena muttered, turning to leave.

Donovan followed as they quickly wound their way back to the tunnel entrance. Once inside the enclosed space, Selena slammed a palm against the wall. "Idiots."

"They'll learn," Donovan said, a dark promise in his tone.

PRESENT DAY

THE DIM LIGHTS OF THE club set the mood for the talented jazz musicians to display their art. Donovan secured a private table in a dark corner of the large venue. The soulful strains resonated with a part of Mia that she hadn't known existed.

His earlier words had piqued not only an interest but a bizarre kind of pleasurable torture in anticipation of what else tonight would hold.

"This is incredible." Mia leaned close to speak to Donovan above the cacophony of sounds. Yet more champagne filled her cup, and the lightheadedness seemed to be here for the duration of the night. "I've been meaning to ask; how did the meeting go with the official?"

"It went well," he said into her ear. "Mason was able to find the information I needed. Henry has a daughter with severe autism. He's been trying to get her into a private school, but with no luck. It wasn't money he was after. I helped his daughter, and now he'll help us."

Taking in that information, Mia kept quiet since it was difficult to hold a conversation anyway. Instead, they both sat back to enjoy the music, and she continued to sip on her drink.

After a few hours, Donovan took Mia's hand and helped her stand, leading her back to the car. He held her steady on the steps and maneuvered her into the back seat with little effort. When he slid in beside her, Mia immediately leaned into him, breathing the scent that was wholly Donovan deep into her lungs.

He ran his fingertips lightly over her exposed skin, setting already overactive nerve endings on fire.

They entered the hotel room, and Mia suddenly felt nervous. It was an inane emotion, after everything they'd been through, and she fiddled with the fresh flowers left in a vase to distract herself.

Feeling Donovan's presence behind her, Mia closed her eyes, waiting for him to make contact. He didn't.

"Turn around," came his husky demand. She did so, slowly. He remained some distance away, watching her with hooded eyes. "Do you trust me?" he asked in the same low, rough tone.

Pausing only momentarily, Mia replied barely above a whisper. "Yes."

"I want to show you a pleasure, unlike anything we've done before. Everything I do is for your enjoyment. Do you know what a safe word is?" Mia swallowed hard and nodded. Donovan stepped closer but still didn't make contact. "I want you to pick a word that will be your safe word."

The word left her lips before she'd even thought it through. "Dagger."

Donovan's whole body stilled in shock. He stared at her for several moments before finally nodding. "Dagger it is. If at any point you feel uncomfortable, say the word dagger, and I will immediately stop. Do you understand?"

Mia had a difficult time speaking, so she merely nodded her head.

Mia knew, in her deepest core, that Donovan would never truly hurt her. That's not where the fear came from that left her mouth dry and limbs shaking. It was a fear of wanting what he was offering, even though she didn't fully comprehend what it entailed. Something in the look in his eye, the tone of his voice, left her body humming, answering a need buried deep.

He stepped closer still, pulling the dress from her shoulders with delicate fingers. He kept his contact light, slowly sliding the dress down and over her hips, kneeling to allow her to step out of its confines. After laying it delicately over the back of a chair, he turned his raptor's gaze back to his prey.

Mia stood in a matching red, lacy ensemble that Sophia had picked out. The bodice allowed for the low back of the dress while still supporting her breasts, while the scrap of underwear hooked to garters which held up the thigh-high nylons. With the heels still on, Mia had never felt so exposed—or so sexy.

Donovan continued to watch her, not touching, simply drinking her in. The anticipation was killing her, his earlier words still resonating deep. Based on his actions so far, Mia now believed she understood what he meant about dark needs.

Finally, he approached her, placing his palm over the corset against her stomach, still looking deep into her eyes. Leaning his head close, his lips hovered over hers, tantalizingly close.

"Don't move unless I instruct you to," he whispered over her mouth. Mia didn't move, didn't speak. Not even to nod her understanding. Donovan smiled. "Good girl."

Mia's breath came out in quick bursts, aching for the pressure of his mouth against hers. Abruptly, he pulled away. She immediately felt bereft.

"Come to the bedroom," he said in the same low, husky voice. Walking on shaky legs, Mia stopped just inside the room. Donovan entered after her, walking to the edge of the bed. There were black leather pieces attached to two of the posts, and Donovan paused beside one. "Come here."

Taking a deep breath, Mia moved toward him. He wrapped a piece around her wrist, securing it with Velcro. As he worked to secure her other wrist, he spoke. "I'm using Velcro, so you know, if you need to, you can escape. I want you to feel comfortable."

When his eyes met hers, Mia nodded.

Donovan stood before her, slowly removing his jacket and tossing it aside. Mia was splayed out before him, standing on already unsteady feet. He took his time, removing his belt and folding it in two, studying it.

"Pain and pleasure are highly connected," he said, keeping his gaze on the belt. "I'm going to touch on highly concentrated nerves, which will bring a flair of pain followed immediately by pleasure. Are you ready?"

Helpless in her need, Mia nodded. He rapped the belt lightly against her thigh. The shock of it brought out a gasp. Donovan watched her face carefully as he experimented in different areas, using varying amounts of pressure. The intense pleasure shooting through her core was unbelievable, and as he continued, occasionally brushing a gentle hand along areas he'd applied the belt, Mia felt herself winding tighter than she'd ever been. Just one touch, in the right spot, and she would explode.

Whimpers found their way past her lips, her body reaching toward Donovan with a mindless need. When he pulled feathers from his bag, every nerve ending was already on fire. He teased her with soft brushes over every exposed piece of skin until she could take it no more.

"Please," Mia pleaded.

It did nothing to relieve the pressure. He merely changed tactics, leaning in close to kiss her neck, along her arms. His lips brushed over the curve of her neck, pressed against her rapidly beating pulse. "Please, what?"

"Please, Donovan..."

His hands slipped around her, undoing the few snaps holding the bodice in place. As the cool air touched her newly exposed skin, she let out another gasp. Donovan stood before her, taking his time undoing each of his own buttons before finally sliding his shirt over his broad shoulders and revealing his toned stomach beneath. Retrieving the belt, he remained still, his eyes on hers.

Flames licked along her skin. Her body wound tight, aching for Donovan to alleviate the throbbing pressure. She'd never been so aroused or needy in her life.

Just when Mia thought he would fulfill her wishes, he spoke instead. "Now, we can begin."

She'd thought she was at the end of her control, but Donovan led her to new heights. He seemed to be an expert at bringing her to the edge, walking that thin, thin line between steady ground and freefall. She begged, she pleaded. She whimpered. Her body felt alive.

Donovan delivered punishment and reward like a tennis match, back and forth, back and forth. Finally, shaking, dripping with need, Donovan nudged her over that ledge once, twice, a third time. He filled her and completed her, giving Mia everything she never knew she needed.

It felt like a dream when Donovan released her wrists from the posts and carried her to bed. She snuggled against him, her body loose and limp and utterly satisfied.

Waking the next morning left Mia in a dull state of shock.

Since she could tell she was alone in the large bed, Mia allowed her muscles to stretch, feeling each delicious ache as she tested her limbs.

Opening her eyes, Mia glanced down at her bare skin, running fingers lightly over her raw wrists and the scattering of bruises along her upper arm. Though she didn't recall the exact moment those had appeared, the memory of begging Donovan to hold her tighter was very clear.

She had *begged* him.

Donovan had shown her things last night she never would have imagined in her wildest dreams—or, perhaps more accurately, her wildest fantasies.

For a moment, Mia's mind went over each teasing touch, every sharp snap of his belt, how many times her body had spiraled out of control. There was a pleasant haze of sub-reality as she lay in tangled sheets, wondering how her life had led her to this moment.

Feeling another presence in the room, Mia turned her head to see Donovan, clad only in a pair of pants, approaching the bed with a tray in his hands. His smile settled the anxiety that had immediately crept up.

"Good morning," he said softly, setting the tray near her before sitting on the edge of the bed.

Scooting herself up, Mia smiled shyly back at him. "Good morning."

"How are you feeling?"

That was a loaded question. Amazing, fulfilled, sore, embarrassed, horrified at her utter disregard of her morals, blissful.

"A little achy, but otherwise pretty amazing," she decided to go with.

He brushed his thumb across Mia's cheek, frowning as he glanced at her arm. Just as gently, he brushed his thumb against the scattering of purple dots there. "I'm sorry for that. I didn't want to mark you."

For the ridiculousness of the statement, Mia felt a laugh bubble up. It startled him. "I don't remember complaining."

He smiled, looking up at her from under his lashes. It seemed almost timid, which was another laughable moment compared to last night. To fight her awkwardness, Mia lifted a mug of coffee from the tray, sweetened with milk and sugar as she preferred it. Needing desperately to change the subject, she asked the first thing that came to mind. "What's on our schedule for today?"

"After breakfast, we'll be going back to the airport and heading to Paris."

"Paris?" Mia asked excitedly. It had always been on her short list of places to visit. "Chocolate croissants and the Eiffel Tower?"

"Of course." Donovan grinned, picking up his own mug of coffee. "Among other things."

"I'm sure you'll find many ways to amaze me."

Donovan ordered room service for breakfast, and they sat out on the balcony in the warming sunshine. It felt familiar, as eating on the balcony had become a habit for them in Baltimore, and Mia began to feel more at ease as last night's adventures morphed into a hazy, dream-like memory.

The flight to France was smooth and quick, her nerves slightly less jumpy as they walked through customs than the first time. They took a car service from the airport toward the hotel, Mia's eyes glued on the sights outside the window.

The streets were filled with people walking, sitting at outside cafés, and seeming to just enjoy life. The vibe was so different than any American city she'd been in that it felt surreal, almost as if she were watching a movie scene playing out around her.

As they passed the majestic Louvre and came to a stop in front of the Hotel Regina, Mia soaked in as much of the sights as was possible behind her dark lenses and floppy hat. While this hotel didn't have the same splendor as the one in London, it was gorgeous and had a charm all its own. The architecture included many archways, intricate carvings, and small details, like hand-painted walls and stunning windows. After being led to the Eiffel Tower suite, Mia itched to find out if the name of the room meant what she hoped.

The immaculate room felt fresh with its light colors and classic design. The bed fit into its own nook in the wall, separated by the rest of the room with drapes. As Donovan directed the bellhop, Mia wandered to the window, her heartbeat picking up pace.

Standing before the window, her eyes swept across the landscape, seeking out the one thing that had always beckoned her to Paris. Standing firm, towering above the gardens surrounding it, sat the Eiffel Tower.

Placing a hand over her chest, Mia felt a tear form in her eye and didn't bother to wipe it away. Donovan approached, placing a hand on the small of her back, his eyes on the same scene. "Beautiful, isn't it?"

Mia nodded, not ready to turn away yet. "I don't know what it is about the Eiffel Tower."

"It's a strong symbol," Donovan answered. "It has stood the test of time. Originally it was only meant to be a temporary display, but managed to survive not only its original intent but also through wars and sieges."

Though Mia could feel his eyes on her, she still wasn't ready to look away.

"The tower is proof that something which seems fragile and temporary has the ability to become permanent." Swallowing once, Mia remained silent on that point. "We're also above the gardens of the Louvre, and another section of the hotel has wonderful views of the grounds."

Grateful for the change of subject, Mia responded this time. "I don't think I've ever really liked art," she said carefully, not wanting to reveal too much in case Selena was an art connoisseur, "but I would love to see the Louvre."

"It's in the plan."

Mia turned to him, resting her palms against his chest. "Do we have meetings today or tomorrow?"

"Tomorrow. Today is all ours."

"All right," Mia said, pushing away from him to dig into her bag for a change of clothes. "What's first?"

"We'll be doing quite a bit of walking."

Knowing he wouldn't give her any more detail than that, Mia made use of the prettily antique bathroom. After freshening her makeup, Mia changed into a sundress—which felt like neither her nor Selena's personality but would help her blend in on this warm day. Braiding her hair over one shoulder, Mia secured the hat and gave herself a final once-over before emerging.

Donovan had also changed into lighter clothes; khakis and a loose, button-down white shirt with the first few buttons casually undone.

Mia had never seen him dress so informally, and it gave a whole new air to his personality. For the first time, as they walked through the lobby and onto the streets of Paris, it felt as if they were any other normal couple on holiday.

A small voice in the back of Mia's mind insisted on reminding her of the truth, no matter how much she'd inadvertently silenced it over the last several days.

She was a cop. Donovan was a criminal. And she was here to take him down.

Eighteen

As Selena stood staring out over the operation, she found herself missing Donovan. It was impossible for her to go with him while he traveled abroad, and he made those trips more and more often.

Inside their warehouse at the docks, one of the submarines had surfaced an hour ago, ready to be unloaded. The water was deep enough at the Baltimore dock for the submarines to come in on their own, slipping under the foundation and rising inside the building constructed around them. With their quiet propulsion and advanced technology, they were virtually undetectable.

This drone carried artifacts from Egypt, and as Selena watched the men carefully unload the crates, an idea came to her.

Perhaps there was a way for her to join Donovan when he traveled. To be with him full time, instead of simply living her life in the shadows.

From her back pocket, Selena pulled out a heavily folded photo, spreading it out flat to gaze at it as she had so many times before. A woman, in broad daylight, smiling at the camera for her first official police officer photo. Her dark auburn hair, amber eyes, and heart-shaped face were like looking in a mirror. The only true difference between the two was the softness in the cop's eyes. Selena had never had the ability to be truly happy. Even in her time with Donovan, there was still something lacking.

Mia Gonzalez could be the answer to all Selena's problems. It would take an incredible amount of planning and patience. Donovan and Selena had the intelligence and power to pull this off, and time was the one luxury she could afford.

Waves of anxious nerves born of anticipation raced through Selena as pieces of a plan began to take shape.

When Donovan returned several days later, Selena had been staring intently at her computer for hours. He watched her from the doorway, warmth spreading across his chest. When she looked up, and a slow smile spread across her lips, that feeling shot straight to his groin.

He'd been away for two weeks, longer than he'd anticipated and longer than he liked to be away from her. Donovan knew Selena had something important she wanted to discuss that couldn't be said over the phone, but some things took precedence.

Before she could stand, Donovan marched over and hauled her into an embrace. The moment their lips touched, Donovan lost all sense. Breathless, Selena pulled away to cup his face. "Welcome home."

"How has everything been here?" Donovan asked, his arms still wrapped around her waist.

"Fine. The new subs have been running seamlessly. We just unloaded a shipment a few days ago."

Something in her tone alerted Donovan to her inner turmoil. "What is it? What's wrong?"

"There's something I wanted to discuss with you," she said, visibly nervous for the first time since...as a matter of fact, Donovan didn't remember Selena ever being nervous.

Shifting away, Selena slid the crumpled photo from her back pocket. Donovan's gaze narrowed in on it immediately, knowing exactly what it was. They had no secrets between them. "I was thinking, while you were away, about how much I missed you and how much I'd like to be with you. There's only one way we could truly make that happen."

Donovan sucked in a breath. Selena could see the gears grinding away as he quickly sifted through each possibility. "Are you certain? This could be dangerous for both of you."

"I don't care," Selena said coldly. "I want to be free. I want to be with you. I want to see Paris."

PRESENT DAY

DONOVAN BEGAN THEIR ADVENTURE BY dipping into Le Grenier a Pain bakery and picking up a bag of pain au chocolats. Soon after, they wound their way through the Tuileries Gardens and sat at the outside café, where they ordered fresh-roasted coffee and enjoyed the chocolatey treats.

Since they'd had a rather large breakfast, Donovan and Mia both stuck to the snack while enjoying the view of the gardens. Though they were on the Louvre property, Mia had a feeling they wouldn't be stopping there quite yet.

When they continued walking, Donovan guided Mia toward Notre-Dame, circling around to visit the Pantheon and back along La Seine Riverwalk until crossing over to the hotel.

Donovan seemed content to go with the flow, stopping at small boutiques and watching street musicians share their craft. Each new sight had Mia wanting to explore. She felt as if she could never get enough of Paris.

While the amount of walking they'd done helped Mia to feel like she'd worked off the meal from the night before, she was still certain Donovan had something extravagant planned for this evening, as well.

In one of the boutiques they'd stopped in, Mia had found a slinky black dress that Donovan had delivered to the hotel so that she could wear it for dinner. After picking up the package at the front desk, they returned to the room to get ready.

The first thing Mia did was get into the shower, sweaty from the day and wanting a few minutes to relax under the hot spray. When she emerged, Mia wrapped herself in a robe that waited on a rack by the door. There were fuzzy little slippers along with it, so she slid those on to walk into the main room.

Donovan sat at the small table near the window, typing on his laptop. He looked up and, with a slow smile, stood to wrap his arms around Mia. His head dipped into the crook of her neck as he inhaled her clean scent.

"I was just catching up on some work," he said, releasing her and returning to the seat. A bottle of white wine, delivered while Mia showered, sat chilled in a bucket. "I'll be calling Bruce shortly; I wanted to wait for you to speak with him."

Sitting opposite, Mia selected a piece of fruit from a platter and took a bite. Reaching over to uncork the wine, Donovan poured two glasses, handing one to Mia and clinking the rims before taking a sip. She followed suit, letting the flavors roll over her tongue before swallowing.

Studying the label, Mia realized it was in French, and she was hopeless to understand it. "Wow. That's good."

"I've come to the conclusion everything tastes better in France." Donovan winked as he pulled up the application for making video calls.

While he connected, Mia stood with her wine and a cracker with cheese spread to watch out the window. Remembering a famous quote about America being my country, and Paris being my hometown, she could completely understand the sentiment.

Hearing Bruce's voice over the speaker, Mia sat back down to pay attention. He gave a quick update on the construction—which wasn't much different since they'd spoken only a day ago—before Donovan got down to the crux of the matter. "Contact Tony DeLuca tomorrow, give him our demand. Tell him he has a week to comply, and Selena and I will handle the trade."

"Consider it done," came Bruce's brisk reply.

Once they disconnected, Mia leaned forward, elbows resting on the table with her hands clasped beneath her chin. "Is everything else running smoothly?"

"It is," Donovan said, closing his laptop. "We've good people in place. Our operation can handle us being away."

"How often do you travel abroad?"

"About every two months, I'll spend a week or two traveling to meet with clients or as needed."

"Do you spend a lot of time playing tourist?"

Donovan shook his head. "Not nearly as much as I would like. Perhaps one day, we'll be able to travel without business obligations."

"I've enjoyed it all so far," Mia said noncommittally.

Checking the time, Donovan suggested she finish dressing since their car would be arriving in half an hour. Keeping her makeup to the bare minimum, unlike what Sophia had done to her the night before, Mia quickly donned the new dress that dipped low in the front and had a large bow on the left hip. It was semi-fitted and felt like a modernized version of a flapper dress. For tonight, she left her hair down and ran the curling iron through it for a few curls. Securing the earrings that Donovan had given her the night before, Mia clasped more modest heels on her ankles. Heels that wouldn't make her feel like she was about to tip over at any moment.

Mia found Donovan dressed in black suit pants, a crisp white shirt, and a full black vest. He'd forgone the jacket tonight, but the result was still drool-worthy, if not more so.

"You are so beautiful," he said through hooded eyes.

"Thank you," Mia whispered, not sure if she would ever get used to his attentions.

Offering Mia his arm, Donovan led her out of the hotel and into the same car they'd had from the airport. It was a short drive to their first stop—the Eiffel Tower.

Excitement coursing through her, Mia walked with Donovan toward the main square, stopping to gaze up at the tower now lit against the night sky. She gripped Donovan's forearm with excitement. "It's so incredible."

Once she'd had her fill, they followed the path to enter the structure. Mia stepped into the elevator after Donovan, exiting at Le Jules Verne restaurant. They were seated immediately with a stunning view of the city. A tinge of orange spread low across the sky, the lights of the city winking from below.

Donovan had pre-ordered the six-course meal, and as Mia nibbled on one delicious course after another, sipping wine a bit more sedately than she had the champagne last night, she barely spoke, preferring to take in the views from their amazing vantage point.

"You seem to really connect with this city," Donovan commented, breaking the comfortable silence.

"How could you not?"

He only smiled at that and returned to watching her watch the city below.

After the final course, and Mia felt once again stuffed to the max, they walked around the surrounding gardens, though her attention constantly returned to the tower. "I wonder if the people living here ever get used to it. Think it commonplace."

"I imagine they do, much as there are days in Baltimore I don't see the ocean. And then a dark storm rolls in, or a stunning sunset turns the waves orange and red, and it catches me by surprise once again."

Mia stopped and stared at Donovan for a moment. "There's so much more to you than meets the eye."

When they returned to the car, Donovan told Mia he had a big surprise for her. With the things he'd pulled off thus far, she couldn't even imagine what the surprise would be.

Driving back toward the direction of the hotel, they passed it and pulled into the Louvre. The lot was empty of cars, as the museum had been closed for hours, and excitement built again as Mia realized they were going inside, at night, with no one else around.

"The museum is closed," Mia reminded Donovan unnecessarily.

"I know." Donovan's lips tipped up in amusement.

Just outside the entrance, a man in a security guard uniform gestured them inside. Helpless to do anything but shake her head at Donovan's magic, Mia watched as he smoothly passed off an envelope to the guard before they were left to their own devices.

"You really need to explain that." Mia stared up at him, wide-eyed.

"He's a business connection. He's told the other security guards that we're foreign dignitaries on a private tour. They've all been well compensated."

Mia's jaw dropped. The amount of power Donovan possessed was indeed astounding.

Though Mia had never considered herself an avid art lover, she could easily spend days in the Louvre. As it was, she wasn't positive one night would be enough.

They wandered the halls, pausing at some exhibits longer than others but enjoying each one. When they came upon impressionist paintings, Mia found herself lingering by each Monet, moved by some emotion he managed to portray in each of his works.

"This makes me want to visit Monet's Gardens," Mia said to Donovan.

At this, he lifted her hand to his lips. "Whatever you want, we will make happen."

Her heart fluttered at his words, and she forced herself to move on. Sometime in the night, they met with the same security guard, who led them into the basement of the museum.

"This used to be a fortress, and the walls down here are dating back to the 1100s." The man, who introduced himself as Michel, gave them a history lesson as they descended.

The dark brick layers were still in remarkable condition, and Mia paused to place her palm against the cool stone. Occasionally along the winding walk, neon letters spelling out sayings in French lit the way. Donovan translated for her at each they passed as they continued to follow Michel back topside.

There was so much beauty in this one place, and when Donovan asked if Mia would like to continue looking, she gave him an unequivocal yes.

Mia would have stayed until the museum opened the next day, but by the wee hours of the morning, they decided to leave, not wanting Michel to get into trouble. As they made the short drive back to the hotel, Mia fell asleep against Donovan's shoulder. There was a fuzzy memory of being led up to their suite, but at some point, Donovan must have simply scooped her up and carried her to bed because she was out for the count.

After sleeping for only a few short hours, Donovan and Mia headed to the first meeting of the day.

"We only have two clients to meet with today," Donovan said in the car. "The first is with Pierre St. John."

Mia nodded, blinking back the tiredness still plaguing her. They'd ordered a quick breakfast of omelets and espressos, and she hoped the caffeine kicked in soon.

The old, white-washed brick building that housed St. John and Son was understated in its elegance. Immediately, Mia could tell the St. John's were old money but had not heard of Pierre. Apparently, American tabloids didn't pick up stories on rich French people as often as rich British ones.

Pierre St. John was in his fifties, his brown hair streaked with grey in a way that only served to make him more distinguished. His piercing blue eyes were intelligent, and his lean build told Mia he didn't spend all his time in these offices.

After shaking Donovan's hand, Pierre offered Mia his hand. With her gloves still on, Mia accepted it but didn't speak.

"Please." Pierre gestured with open arms to the comfortable leather seats. His accent was very slight, which told Mia he did a lot of business with English speakers. Donovan sat while Mia stood, as had become routine for meetings. "I heard there might be some trouble in Britain."

"What trouble is that?" Donovan asked.

"New laws since they've annexed themselves from the EU. Has this affected your routes?"

"No," Donovan said. "We've no problems there. All the officials have been friendly and understanding."

Amusement welled up at his statement, knowing that was Donovan's way of saying he'd found a way to bribe the officials. Pierre understood that as well and nodded briskly. "So, what have you come to discuss today?"

After Donovan explained the new routes, they left for the second meeting. Both client meetings went as smoothly as they had in London, for which Mia was grateful since she was still not on top of her game and constantly blinking back sleep. Donovan took pity on her, bringing her back to the hotel and leaving her to nap while he worked from his laptop.

As she slept, she dreamed.

△ △ △

THE ROOM WAS DARK, SAVE for several candles showcasing the sharp lines of the man's physique in their flickering light. He waited for her on a bed, lying on dark red sheets. His wrists were secured, his eyes glued to hers.

Approaching him slowly, Mia glanced down at feeling an unfamiliar object in her hand. The long, smooth handle gave way to a flat, two-inch-wide leather piece. Staring at it, an understanding dawned. This was what Donovan had shown her. The ultimate mixture of pain and pleasure. For Mia, this was about control over her environment, but never over the man himself. Between them, there was nothing but trust.

Between them, Mia was the dominant one, ensuring his pleasure.

Stepping forward, Mia flicked her wrist up, anticipation alighting her nerve endings. She could feel his hooded gaze as it rested on each part of her, sizzling as if he'd made physical contact. When she brought her hand up to use the device resting in it, suddenly, she felt restrained.

Incomprehensible pleasure coursed through her veins, and she arched back, her mouth widening in a gasp, her body beginning to spiral out of control.

△ △ △

As Mia's eyes shot open, the dream morphed into reality as she realized she was being restrained, much as Donovan had been in the dark room. Her fingers wrapped around the thick leather securing her wrists while his hands, his mouth were everywhere, overwhelming her senses until she could no longer differentiate between wake and sleep.

There was no time to adjust to the sensations flowing over and through her. Donovan pushed Mia to the edge again and again with no time to recover. She had no solid ground to cling to, her hands squeezing into fists around their restraints in an effort to anchor herself to this world, this reality.

When Donovan finally joined them together, her hips bucked as a scream ripped through her lips. Had she use of her limbs, Mia would have held him to her; instead, her body shuddered uncontrollably, with nothing to ground her.

Though her world was spiraling out of control, Donovan didn't hesitate, building the need in her yet again. Mia squeezed her eyes shut as her head arched back, ripples starting in her core and traveling along her skin.

Dazed and riding yet another wave, Mia screamed again, and this time, Donovan joined her.

After Donovan gently released her wrists, Mia's arms collapsed to the bed, refusing to move. Her limbs shook intermittently, her vision blurry and a wonderful haze resting over her thoughts. She felt Donovan at her side, his head pillowed against her chest, and doubted her physical ability to move.

They stayed like that for a long time, the only sounds at first their heavy breathing, lighter as they both came down from the high.

Speaking seemed unnecessary and an intrusion on the moment, so Mia remained silent. There were no words for what they had just shared.

Sometime later, Donovan lifted his head lazily, his hooded gaze meeting hers. Pushing himself up until they were even, his lips met hers in the softest, sweetest kiss. Then they trailed along Mia's jaw, down to her neck and collarbone before he placed a lingering kiss against her forehead. The action left her feeling helplessly cherished.

"You must be hungry." He spoke for the first time, softly. "Let's get ready for dinner."

Apparently impatient for her to stand, Donovan scooped Mia into his arms, eliciting a laugh from her. Standing her in the shower, he adjusted the heat and carefully, gently ran body wash along her skin. As he stood staring down into her eyes, she spoke for the first time since she'd woken to his ministrations.

"This is the first real memory I have of you," Mia said before explaining further. "Standing in the shower just after you rescued me. You stepped in front of me, fully clothed, because the heat hurt my injuries."

"That was, at once, the worst and best day of my life," Donovan said, voice choked with emotion.

Wrapping her arms around his neck, Mia leaned close, placing her lips against his pulse. "Mine, too," she whispered.

Nineteen

"MIA IS ALREADY ON OUR case," Donovan said, looking over the rough plan he and Selena had pieced together over the last few weeks. "She's seen me once. Perhaps we should give them a glimpse now and then to keep them interested."

Nodding, Selena added, "There are always undercovers looking to infiltrate our business. We find one or two, make them work for it, but slowly let them in. They will be vital in our plan."

"I've two in mind. They're from Mia's precinct; they've been sniffing around our operations for a while."

"Perfect," Selena murmured, seeing the plan come into focus.

"Selena," Donovan said her name gently, waiting for her to face him. "You're sure about this? Once we put this plan in motion, it will be unstoppable."

"Yes, Donovan." She gripped his biceps, looking straight into his eyes. "I've thought through the risks, and I accept them. I'm ready."

THE FIRST THING MIA NOTICED about Egypt was the mind-boggling amount of open space.

Watching out the plane window, she took in the grand majesty of endless golden sand and bright blue sky, hazy lines of heat meeting at the horizon to trick the eye. Landing outside of Cairo, she felt mesmerized by the squat dwellings interspersed with towering structures that looked like palaces of old.

The pyramids poking above the skyline were like mountains rising above the mists. It was unlike anywhere she'd ever been or anything she'd ever seen.

A transport took Mia and Donovan straight from the airport to a hotel near the pyramids in what was technically Giza. The huge circular pool with a swim-up bar was stunning but still paled in comparison to the closer view of the pyramids.

"I thought you would enjoy being a little outside the city," Donovan said as they were led to a deluxe suite. "The pyramids are really something, aren't they?"

"I don't know that you could ever get used to them."

Excited to see the view from the room, Mia was not disappointed. The suite offered a panoramic view of the outskirts of the city, with the pyramids in plain sight. Evening fell to night, and the golden light of sunset washed over the entire place. Much like Paris had, Egypt felt surreal.

Donovan and Mia both changed into loose-fitting linen clothing, for the temperature, even as the sun fell, was sweltering. He led her back outside and along the street, passing by vendors selling shawarma and a collection of other delectable foods, the aromas wafting in the air and stirring her appetite.

As the sun sank beyond the horizon, the couple came upon a night market on a street filled with cafés where tables had been set up right in the road. Donovan selected one and ordered a variety of dishes from the menu. Wonderful plates of shawarma, falafel, and koshari soon graced the table, along with a dip called dukkah, which Mia had never heard of but finished more than her fair share of.

"It doesn't seem like there are many tourists here," Mia said, taking a break from chowing down on the delicious food.

"Most of Cairo is tourist-oriented, but I've found the outskirts to be less congested and more local," Donovan answered, watching her eat with a small smile playing on his lips. "I prefer it."

"Since I haven't been downtown yet, I can't completely say I agree, but I have a feeling I will."

Egyptian coffee was delivered with dessert, which was a sweet couscous and surprisingly good. As they made their way back to the hotel, they stopped at several shops, and Mia picked out a few hijabs to wear if need be. Since she was already hiding her identity, the covering for her hair and neck both helped her fit in and served her purposes.

Before dawn the next morning, Mia and Donovan dressed for a day in the sun. They both donned hijabs and ventured to a camel-renting office. Letting Donovan negotiate, Mia waited outside the small building, watching the little bit of activity as the city came awake.

When Donovan emerged, they were led to the stables to pick out their camels. The giant creatures were surprisingly gentle, and after Donovan helped Mia into the saddle, he mounted his own. They typically would have been accompanied by a guide, but

Donovan had worked with this gentleman in the past and had negotiated for them to go alone.

The covering came in handy as the dust kicked up, and Mia kept her sunglasses secure on her face as they rode toward arguably the most famous landmark in the world.

They explored for half the day, and, thankfully, Donovan had thought ahead and brought picnic food to eat for lunch. After they returned the camels, Donovan brought Mia into downtown Cairo to visit the outdoor markets and the Cairo Museum.

Though they didn't have private access as they had at the Louvre, it was still worth facing the crowds.

After dinner in another traditional café, Donovan brought Mia down to the Nile, renting a Felucca to cruise the river while the sun dipped below the horizon. Mia had never seen anything quite like a desert sunset. The whole sky seemed to explode in various colors of pink, orange, and purple. The contrast of the water against the golden sand was an artist's dream.

While they sailed, they were regaled with music and stories of the ancient lands. Leaning against Donovan, breathing in the heavy desert air, Mia never wanted the evening to end.

The next morning, Mia and Donovan took a short flight to Alexandria, where their current dock was located. During the flight, Donovan explained that business was booming, and a second dock was built north of Alexandria, in Abu Qir.

As they made the trek to the new line, Mia watched the relatively modern city pass by. She already missed the view of the pyramids from their hotel room, and she felt herself longing for the type of lifestyle that would allow her to travel at the drop of a hat.

Glancing over at Donovan, she studied him while he watched out the window. There was so much more Mia wanted to know about the man, and she found herself wishing he could know the real her.

At that thought, tears sprung to her eyes, and Mia turned away, back to her own side of the car.

Cairo had been a small side trip, and one she was glad Donovan had included. It would be insane to travel to Egypt and not see the pyramids, after all.

As promised, Donovan brought her to the new docks for a tour. The facilities, while new, didn't stand out in their design. They fit seamlessly with the rest of the city's layout, with subdued colors and a boxy style.

Inside, however, was a different story. Everything was sleek metal and modern design, with the newest technology available running the operation. The most prominent building, upon entering, was like walking into a swimming pool, with a large rectangle of water cut into the middle and a wide pathway for workers to walk around.

"The floor drops into the water, allowing the subs to come in under the building undetected. Once they are in position, the floor rises and allows us to load or unload," Donovan explained.

They walked around the site, busy with men who took their jobs seriously. They all acknowledged Donovan while also giving him a wide berth. Donovan steered Mia into an enclosed office space with a plain view of operations.

One man was in front of a computer and immediately stood as they entered. "Donovan, good to see you," he said, shaking Donovan's hand.

"Amun, this is Selena."

The man's eyes widened before gripping her hand and pumping it enthusiastically. "So nice to meet you."

Giving him a small smile, Mia carefully extracted her hand before turning toward the window. Donovan stepped up next to her. "The sub should arrive in the next few minutes."

Mia nodded, excited at the prospect of seeing this in action. As promised, a few minutes later, lights began flashing all around the warehouse, warning of the incoming vessel. Another man came into the room, working the computers with Amun. It was a slow process, but eventually, she saw the top of the gunmetal gray machine breaking through the surface of the water.

With a gasp, Mia leaned forward, practically pressing her nose to the glass. The sub was easily fifty feet long and an incredible sight to behold. As the floor locked into place, the men who had been standing off to the side immediately began running to connect cables from the ground to hooks along the edge of the machine to hold it in place. A door slid open to reveal ample space inside.

There was a truck backed into the warehouse in a loading area, in which the workers quickly began transferring wooden crates out of and into the sub.

"This is Olivia's?" Mia asked quietly.

"It is."

Mia watched, fascinated, as the full truck loaded effortlessly into the modern marvel that was the basis of Selena and Donovan's business. An uneasy feeling churned in her gut as she realized this was exactly what the police needed to bring down their criminal empire, and Mia was at the helm.

Flying back to Baltimore was more depressing than relieving, and Mia stayed quiet throughout most of the flight. Donovan seemed to sense her need to be left alone with her thoughts, and she appreciated the fact that he left her to them.

Once they were back, Mia would need to find a way to get a message to her precinct, to Alec. If she knew her partner, he would be worried sick—between the revelation that Adam was a DeLuca and Mia's continued silence, he was probably going insane.

Donovan and Mia would also be making the trade with the DeLucas, which she was not exactly looking forward to. Nothing about that family was trustworthy.

When he slept, Mia spent the rest of her time studying Donovan, attempting to evaluate her feelings for him. Mia's training with Agent McKenzie came to mind, the conversation they'd had about using her attraction to gain his trust. She was all for it, but Mia thought even the agent would say she'd gone too far.

Everything inside Mia was torn, her cop instincts fighting against everything she'd learned and seen about Donovan. He wasn't the horrible person she always believed him to be. Yes, he did bad things, but he didn't hurt anyone. People didn't work with him, or for him, out of fear, but out of respect. That had to count for something.

Mia knew she was justifying her actions. She knew that she was in too deep. There would be no easy way out of this, no matter what good qualities she gave to Donovan.

Donovan and Mia didn't speak again until they were in the SUV that had been left in the hangar. Staring down at her hands, Mia fiddled with the delicate gold ring still gracing her finger. Twisting it off, she looked at it with melancholy before handing it to Donovan. "I suppose I won't be needing this."

Donovan took it, glancing sidelong at her. "Are you all right?"

"Fine." Mia shrugged, not meeting his eyes.

"I know you better than that," Donovan said softly, his eyes back on the road. "I've given you time for your thoughts, but now I'd like to know what they are."

"Coming back here...it makes me feel like it's ending," Mia said, barely above a whisper.

His gaze switched back to her, and Mia could feel the worry emanating from him. "What do you mean?"

"I don't know." Mia shook her head, frustrated at herself and the situation. "Just...whatever happens, I want you to know that this has been the most incredible time in my life."

"Selena, you're scaring me." Donovan pulled the car over, grasping her chin with his fingers and forcing eye contact. "What is going on?"

Tears sat on the brim, threatening to overflow. If Mia didn't get a handle on her emotions, everything would come crashing apart. Struggling to swallow back the tears, Mia reached over and placed a hand against Donovan's rough jawline, scruffy from travel. The words that she wouldn't be able to take back came tumbling out. "I love you."

His expression softened, and he leaned close to press his lips to hers. Mia's hands slipped into his hair, gripping him tight and pulling him close. She poured all her emotions into that kiss, every doubt, every fear, and, most importantly, the love that should not exist.

When they parted, Donovan lifted a trembling hand to cup her cheek. Mia leaned into it, savoring the protected feeling Donovan exuded.

"We're going directly to meet with the DeLucas," Donovan said. "Are you feeling up for that?"

Taking a deep breath, Mia closed her eyes briefly to center herself before nodding. It was time to focus. It was time to be Selena.

They drove to the same place they'd met with Tony before. The dark SUV was already waiting there, and Mia glanced around for Bruce. He'd be transporting Adam.

Donning her usual disguise, Mia stepped out of the vehicle simultaneously with Donovan and approached the middle ground. Behind them, a white van pulled up, and she presumed it was Bruce. He would wait for Donovan's signal to release the prisoner.

There was a feeling of familiarity as the doors on the other vehicle opened, revealing Tony, Al, and two of their goons. Al looked livid while Tony forced a calm façade, but Mia could see the underlying tension.

"Donovan." Tony's voice was clipped with annoyance. "I hear you have something of ours."

"We're willing to trade for the information we asked for," Donovan said with quiet authority.

Tony glanced back to one of his goons and snapped his fingers. The goon walked forward and paused just a couple of feet from Donovan. In response, Donovan gestured with his hand without looking away, signaling Bruce to come forward.

Keeping her eyes on the group before them, Mia heard doors opening and shuffling feet. Adam passed by, his hands tied and a bag over his head, followed closely by Bruce, who prodded him along. When the two were close to Donovan, Bruce halted their movement and waited for further instruction.

"We have an agreement to avoid any more unpleasantness between us?" Donovan called out to Tony.

With a dip of his head, Tony answered, "That we do."

Mia's vision went black, as it had done before. Instantaneously, another scene superimposed itself upon this one.

Tony, standing across from her much like he was now, except the ground beneath their feet was, instead, a rooftop.

"We have a deal?" She heard her own voice ask.

Tony dipped his head. "That we do."

Just as quickly as it arrived, it was gone, leaving Mia wincing in pain. Donovan gave her a quick side glance, noticing her sudden movement, but she gave him a small hand signal to let him know she was all right.

The DeLuca goon handed Donovan a small flash drive while Bruce simultaneously pushed Adam forward. He stumbled until Al caught him, ripping off his head covering and discovering duct tape over his mouth. Adam looked worse for the wear, his body gaunt, his eyes sunken in.

It was difficult for Mia to feel any pity for him.

When Donovan began backing away, Mia followed. Bruce remained where he was, watching the DeLucas as they returned to their vehicle.

Feeling Adam's glare on her, Mia looked back as Al ripped off the tape that prevented him from speaking.

"She's not—!"

Whatever he was about to say was cut off as Al pushed him into the back of the SUV. Shooting Donovan a quick look, Mia realized his eyes were on Tony, and he didn't seem to react to Adam's shout in the least.

Once Tony was back in the car, Donovan murmured just loud enough for Mia to hear. "Let's go."

Slipping into the car, Mia watched Bruce walk quickly back to the van, and, as he pulled away, they followed. After a few blocks, Bruce veered off while Donovan and Mia took a circuitous route to the penthouse by the docks.

For now, that was home.

Mia glanced toward Donovan's shirt pocket, where he'd slipped the flash drive. He hadn't told her yet what information was on it, and she didn't ask now. Her mind was occupied with what, exactly, had happened to her during the exchange.

The thing that had her worried was that it wasn't the first time. In London, when Donovan had told her he loved her, she'd had a moment that felt like a blackout and some strange, fuzzy scene like a memory that appeared from nowhere. An extreme case of déja-vu? Or her subconscious mixing together the present with stories she'd heard about Selena?

Or something else altogether?

The thought was terrifying.

Twenty

MONTHS OF PLANNING HAVE LED them to this moment. Selena stood at the desk, hands spread over the visual representation of the plan. Pointing to two mugshots taped to the left-hand side of the board, she began to speak.

"These two have recently come into our employ. They don't know that we know their true identity. We'll let them in on small assignments for the next few months, let them believe they are in our good graces. When the time is right, we'll let them see me."

"The first-ever Selena sighting." Donovan pursed his lips, moving his hand to the next clipping attached to the board. "Mia is already on the case. We've given her snippets of me, and when we're ready, we'll stage a meeting between myself and her."

"That will be easy enough. She actually gets out now that she's dating that weakling," Selena said with a sneer.

"Cole." Donovan's voice came out as a growl. "Are we certain it will last long enough for our purposes?"

Selena shrugged. "If not, we'll come up with another way."

"Once the photo of you gets back to Mia's precinct, she'll be taken off the case. We wait a few months before letting the rumors spread of your disappearance."

"It won't take long before they put her in my place. As if she could replace me."

"Then, the real work begins," Donovan said quietly.

Turning to him, Selena placed both hands on his chest. "Getting her to fall for you will be the easy part, my love. Trust me in that."

"And getting her to turn against her own morals?"

"Morals are fleeting. And the second phase of her time with you will ease that transition. Showing her the lavish lifestyle she could have with you should do the trick."

"And the third phase?" Donovan asked hesitantly.

"Leave that to me."

SIX MONTHS AGO

"IT'S TIME," SELENA SAID, GLANCING over at Donovan. "Mia has found one of our entrances. Those two cops have been in our employ long enough. We'll let them get a clear side shot of me, no more. It will be enough."

"I still don't like putting you at risk like this."

Selena smoothed Donovan's worried brow. "The risk isn't for me. It's for Mia."

"It's for you both."

"We have put a lot of thought into this plan. Are you backing out?"

"No," Donovan replied, his answer firm. "We made this decision together. We'll follow through."

Looking out into the night, Selena composed her face. "Have them in the right spot at midnight. Let my name slip. I'll enter and lead you away somewhere private to speak. That should give them enough time to get their photo."

Donovan nodded, then remained silent, allowing her time with her private thoughts. Selena was tired of hiding in the shadows. Soon, she would emerge, and Mia Gonzalez was the only thing standing in her way.

After her appearance, Selena waited for Donovan in the office. She had to organize her files, knowing her disappearance was imminent.

"They got the photo," Selena said as she sensed Donovan enter.

"You know about my run-in with Mia," Donovan said, waiting for her to turn.

Though Mia's name made Selena cringe, she was vital to the plan. Selena met his eyes with a hard look. "Did you give yourself away?"

"Almost." Donovan sighed, leaning a hip against his desk. "I spoke her name and immediately realized my mistake. She can't know I know her name. I was forced to inject her with Ketamine."

Nodding briskly, Selena waved away his concern. "It will leave no harmful effects but will give her a fuzzy memory of last night."

"She'll be taken off our case now and probably put into therapy. You know what that means."

Gesturing toward her organized files, Selena shrugged off his not-so-subtle hints. "I'm ready."

"Selena." Donovan approached her, gentle in his movements. His concern was nearly her undoing. His hands cupped her face as if it were the most precious thing in the world. "Stay safe for me, and I will remain strong for you."

Nodding, Selena pressed her mouth to his and whispered against his lips. "Make love to me, Donovan."

He backed away, taking her hands and leading her into the apartment on the top floor. When he began walking toward the room with the red sheets, Selena halted their progress and shook her head. "No, not there. I don't want to be in charge tonight. This might be our last night together for a long time; I want it memorable."

Donovan's expression changed, a lethal combination of love, lust, and need. Without further encouragement, he lifted Selena into his arms and didn't set her down again until it was to press her into the soft mattress of their bed.

PRESENT DAY

DONOVAN AND MIA SETTLED INTO their home with few words exchanged between them. Telling Donovan that she wanted to get a workout in, Mia quickly changed into comfortable clothes and made use of the treadmill in the small gym. She wanted to run until she couldn't think anymore.

Starting off at a steady pace, Mia didn't wait long to bump up the speed until she was running full out. Focusing on her breathing, she forced all thoughts away, aiming for a clear mind to assist with making decisions. Over the last few weeks, she'd made a lot of bad choices, though she couldn't come to regret any of them.

Donovan awoke in her things she never knew she wanted. Never knew she needed. He was the most incredible man she'd ever met, and she knew, in her heart of hearts, that she could never turn him in.

Faltering in her step, Mia gasped in alarm, bracing herself with a foot on either side of the track and slowing the machine. One shaking hand rose to cover her mouth as her eyes grew wide.

She couldn't turn Donovan in. It was her job, her reason for being here, and Mia was absolutely certain she wouldn't be able to do it.

Crumpling to the ground, Mia felt her heart breaking in two at the impossibility of the situation. She allowed herself several ragged breaths before forcing herself to calm.

Struggling to her feet, Mia stepped out of the room, listening for Donovan. He was in his office, not too far from where she was. Not wanting to make contact with him just yet, Mia continued down the hall. The bedroom was on the left, and another door led into a small sitting and reading room.

Stepping into the room she'd made little use of, Mia stood in the center and stared. The collection of books ranged from fiction to nonfiction, cookbooks interspersed with religion, health to mental disorders.

There seemed to be no rhyme or reason behind the sorting, and she wondered who used the room more, Donovan or Selena. One title drew her eye, and she stepped closer, curious. It was an average-sized book, with a plain blue cover with only the title printed on the spine.

Mastering Your Inner Self.

Tipping the book toward her to pull it out, unsure why she felt so drawn to it, the entire bookcase shifted.

Of course they had a hidden room behind a bookshelf. Stepping back with a gasp, Mia's vision suddenly flickered to black. As the room was revealed, another vision superimposed itself, just as it had before.

The four-poster bed sat in the center of the room, the red sheets a warning of things to come. The walls were lined with black leather objects in an astounding number. The room remained the same, but Mia's vision flickered to show Donovan, lying on the bed, his dark gaze on her. He was secured by his wrists.

Another flash of memory intruded, and she glanced down at her hand, surprised to find it empty.

Wincing in pain, Mia grasped both sides of her head and collapsed to the floor. Through the haze of pain, she could hear Donovan's panicked voice calling her back to him. Forcing her eyes to open, Mia blinked up at him, realizing she had somehow been shifted to her back. She lay on the floor, her head in his lap, his eyes desperately searching her face.

"Donovan?" Her throat felt raw. "What is this place?"

"It's our special room," Donovan answered, adjusting her into a sitting position. "How did you find it?"

"I'm not sure." She looked around, still dazed. "I pulled on a book..."

The look on his face was inscrutable. Something was nudging the edge of Mia's mind. Something huge and vital.

Something she'd been repressing for a long time.

Mia stood suddenly, backing away from the man who overwhelmed her every sense. Her eyes darted around the room wildly, yet seeing nothing. Donovan approached her, concern marring his features, but she shuffled away.

"Stay...stay over there," Mia stammered, terror seizing her ability to think, to process. Turning abruptly, she darted back into the sitting room but halted again as her eyes snagged on something.

There was a painting on the wall which would have made for an obvious safe. Instead, her eyes dropped to the record player on the shelf below it, much like the one from the first penthouse. Lifting the cover, Mia reached along the side and flipped a switch. A compartment beneath the player popped open, and a single object lay inside.

With trembling fingers, she lifted the creased photo and stared at it in shock.

Raising her eyes to meet Donovan's, Mia could see the same fear and confusion she felt reflecting back at her through his gaze. Turning the photo around, she held it up to him. "What is this?"

"Please..." Donovan begged, his whole demeanor slackening.

"What. Is. This." She separated each word, her voice hardening in a way that frightened her.

"Just let me explain..."

"I'm asking you to explain! What is this!"

Donovan shrank back at her explosion, and suddenly she saw a very different side of him. He was no longer the strong, dominant man Mia had come to know. He was a man being scolded by his mistress.

More flashes of memory crashed over her. A dream from her first week in Donovan's care, in which she'd been clad in black leather, and Donovan had dropped to his knees before her.

The red heels.

Squeezing her eyes shut against the sudden assault, Mia cried out in pain. Donovan's arms wrapped around her waist, holding her up, murmuring to her. At once, Mia felt instantly comforted and absolutely repulsed.

Snapping her eyes open, Mia shoved him away with as much strength as she could muster. He stumbled back, shocked at her actions.

"Donovan...I'm sorry." Mia's voice came out as a strangled whisper. Shutting her eyes, she spoke again, firmer. "No, I'm not. I don't understand what's going on here, but you're behind it."

Her fight or flight instinct had kicked into high gear, and now that she no longer felt threatened, the flight mode took over. Mia ran from the room, Donovan close behind her. With the front door in sight, she yanked on the handle.

"Wait, please..." Donovan's plea was almost her undoing, but she continued on, determined to leave. Yet when he spoke again, she stopped cold. "Mia."

Turning slowly, standing dead still in the doorway, Mia stared at him in shock. "You knew," she said quietly. Holding up the photo of herself in her officer's uniform as evidence, she continued, "This whole time, you knew. Why? To what purpose?"

"Mia, please, you can't go out there alone. You don't fully understand what's going on. I can protect you." Shaking her head in denial, Mia crushed the photo in her palm and turned away. "Mia, wait. I love you. You, Mia, I love *you*."

The pain coursing through her at his words took her very breath away. Shaking her head once more, Mia said her final words to Donovan. "I don't believe you."

With that, she ran.

SIX MONTHS AGO

THERE WAS NO TIME LEFT. Selena only had tonight, but the night was hers.

Though she'd been in hiding for six months, she was hoping to have one more opportunity to see Donovan before Mia became a permanent part of their lives. Mia would be transferred to a cell soon, and so far, their plan had worked to a T.

Making her way through the underground tunnels, Selena found the correct building and slid open the door, racing up the stairs and into the private elevator. Donovan would be alerted of her presence the moment she scanned her palm, and excitement coursed through her at seeing him again.

As the door opened, she was greeted by her favorite sight in the world—Donovan's face.

Before she could speak or even breathe, his arms were wrapped around her, squeezing her tight. They both murmured incoherently, and after several minutes, Donovan pulled away to inspect her.

"You're all right?" he asked, concern marring his ordinarily smooth voice. His fingers brushed against the bruises left along her face and the ones visible on her arms.

"Of course. This was my last chance to see you. Mia will be locked in training starting tomorrow. Everything we've planned for has come to fruition. Within a few days, you should hear rumors of Selena being locked up, and then you can come get us."

"It's all really happening," Donovan said quietly, still soaking in every inch of Selena.

Nodding, she embraced him once again before forcing herself to pull away. "I can't stay."

Though it was the only thing that she wanted to do. In time, she reminded herself. They'd been patient this long.

"I know," Donovan said before yanking her against him for one last, lingering kiss.

When they stepped apart, Selena turned abruptly and stepped into the elevator, not looking back. Knowing, if she did, she would never leave.

IT HAD BEEN A LONG, hard day. The only thing Alec wanted was to crack open a cold beer, throw a frozen pizza in the oven, and veg out in front of the TV.

Though it had only been a week since the news of Adam Malone's true identity had come to light, it felt as if he'd been running himself ragged for months. Between Adam's betrayal and no word from Mia, Alec's stress levels were at an all-time high.

Mia had managed to get one message to the precinct: an address and a single word; tunnels. Of course, having been her partner for so long, Alec knew what that meant.

The tunnels were real, and that's how Selena and Donovan had gotten around for so many years unnoticed.

When he'd gone to investigate the home address Mia had given them, Alec had found rubble. It had been attacked the day before her message, which only left more questions than it answered. They now had constant surveillance on the place and had seen construction crews in and out of there, but no sign of Mia. Or Donovan.

Worry was a constant companion, and Alec was sure he'd developed an ulcer. The beer in his hand was probably the worst thing for it, but he didn't care.

Midway through the pizza, there was a knock at the door. No one ever came over unannounced, and he almost ignored it, wanting to pretend he wasn't home. When another knock came, Alec sighed and stood to look out the peephole.

No one was there.

Another knock sounded, but it came from low on the door. Confused, Alec unbolted the lock and pulled open the door.

It took his eyes a long time to adjust what he was seeing and send the image to his brain. The woman was curled into a ball. While she looked physically fine, she had a look about her that reminded him of women that had escaped an abusive relationship.

When her eyes met his, all Alec could register was the sheer terror stamped there.

"Alec." Mia's voice came out cracked, her next words leaving him baffled. "It's me. You have to arrest me."

Part Three
Wakening

Twenty-One

WAKING WITH A CRICK IN his neck, Alec sat up with a jolt as the previous night came rushing back. His couch was probably the least comfortable piece of furniture in existence, but he didn't have time to think about that now.

Standing, he approached the closed door of his bedroom with no small amount of trepidation. "Mia?" he called out first. Pushing open the door, he asked, "Are you awake?"

As his eyes landed on the rumpled—and empty—bed, Alec let out a string of curses. Before assuming the worst, he did a quick check of the bathroom and the rest of the small apartment, but it was no use.

Mia was gone.

Alec immediately dressed and headed to the central precinct to report what had happened to the chief. Finding him in his office, Alec asked for a private word and shut the door. Too agitated to sit, he paced the room. "Mia showed up on my doorstep last night."

"She what?" Chief Alvarez thundered before visibly calming himself. "Where is she now?"

"I don't know!" Dragging his fingertips through his hair, Alec paused in his mad pacing to face his boss. "She was in shock, barely functioning. She needed to rest. But when I woke up this morning, she was gone."

"Alec. Sit down and report."

Dropping heavily into the chair, Alec took a deep, steadying breath before explaining the last twelve hours. "At roughly seven-thirty, there was a knock on my door. When I answered, I found Mia slumped on the ground. She was covered in dirt and barefoot.

She…she said the words, 'It's me. You have to arrest me.' But then she broke down in tears, and I carried her inside.

"When I asked what she meant, she started rambling on—mostly nonsense. She said things like 'She had my picture on the sub,' and just kept repeating, 'It's me, arrest me.' Like I said, I believed she was in shock, and she was also freezing—nothing could stop her chills. When I mentioned taking her to the hospital, she started flailing wildly and nearly knocked me out. So, instead, I had her take a hot shower and put her in my bed to rest. Eventually, I fell asleep on the couch, but when I woke up…"

Alec trailed off, unable to repeat the words again.

The chief sat back, contemplating the situation. "We've had no contact with her besides the one video sighting. She looked like she was in good shape then, that she had been treated well. What happened in the week since?"

"When I find that bastard, I'll be sure to ask him," Alec said with an uncharacteristic growl, allowing his temper and fear to overpower him.

"Calm down, Alec," the chief said, his tone gentle. "We need to find Mia, pull her out, but we can't do that if you're too emotional."

"I want in," Alec said fervently. "I deserve the chance to help."

"You'll have it. I'll call in the FBI, Agent McKenzie—the woman who helped train Mia—and notify the other precincts. If she or Donovan is spotted, we'll bring them in." Alec nodded once, the fire sparking in his eyes. The chief studied him a moment longer before letting out a heavy sigh. "Alec, before we begin—there's something you need to know. It's about Donovan."

△ △ △

COLD WAS BECOMING A PERMANENT part of Mia's world. Aching, bitter cold, teeth-chattering cold. It seeped up through the concrete floor her bare feet rested upon while she huddled against herself, too dazed to move.

Hugging her knees closer to her chest, Mia closed her eyes and murmured to herself. Truths to keep her sanity.

She had to remember.

"My name is Mia Gonzalez. I'm a detective for the central precinct. I went undercover as Selena. Donovan is her partner—a criminal. My feelings for him aren't real." She said the last with a quiver in her voice.

You know that's not true, came a voice from deep inside.

Squeezing her eyes tighter, Mia ignored the words and continued. "My name is Mia Gonzalez."

Not just Mia.

"I'm a detective for the central precinct."

In the daytime, maybe.

"I went undercover as Selena."

A pretense.

"Donovan is her partner—a criminal."

More than my partner.

"My feelings for him aren't real."

Stop kidding yourself, Mia.

Shaking her head, holding her hands against her temples in tight fists, Mia denied any claim *she* made. "No, no, no. This can't be real. You're not real."

I'm as real as you are.

Tears leaked from the corner of Mia's eye, dripping off her chin and landing with a large splat. "You took me away from Alec."

I was taking us back to Donovan. It's where we both want to be.

Sucking in a breath, Mia opened her eyes and stared blankly. The dark interior of the underground tunnels was the perfect backdrop for her breakdown. Empty and cold—exactly the way she felt after finding out the truth.

"I can't go back there."

There came no response this time, and Mia hated herself for expecting one. What was happening?

Yesterday morning, she'd found the secret room she shouldn't have known was in Donovan's loft. And the photograph that shouldn't have been there—a picture of Mia, having just graduated the academy.

Here she was, undercover in an attempt to take down two criminal masterminds when it had been their plan all along to place her into their lives.

Our plan.

"Shut up! Just shut up and leave me alone!"

You know I can't do that. You know who I am now; there's no more denying it. Accept me, and we can be with Donovan.

"Just leave me alone," Mia whispered desperately.

I can't do that. You need me.

"No, I don't."

You've always needed me. Just accept it.

Shaking her head again, Mia briefly wondered if it was in answer or denial. "There's nothing to accept. I'm going to go back to Alec and get back to my life."

Your life is no longer with Alec or the PD. Do you think they'd even want you back after you reveal the truth? They'll throw you in jail.

"Maybe that's where I should be," Mia answered bitterly.

You don't truly believe that.

"I'll go back to Dr. Engel. Tell her the truth. It's what she's trained for."

You want to hand me over to a shrink? The distaste in her words was palpable.

"I have to do something." Mia's voice broke, and she gave in to the tears once again.

Weak. You've always been weak. That's why you need me. I give you your strength. Accept me, and I'll get us out of here.

There was the Selena Mia had come to know. Mean, arrogant—the worst parts of Mia.

Yes. I may be the worst parts, but I'm still part of you. Accept it.

Startled with her own thoughts, Mia went back to squeezing her eyes together, shaking her head, and allowing the tears to fall freely.

"Go away," Mia murmured. "Just go away."

You know that's not going to happen.

Opening her eyes to stare vacantly at her feet, Mia began her mantra again. Truths that she held onto with an iron fist. "My name is Mia Gonzalez."

A pause, no response.

"I'm a detective with the central precinct."

△ △ △

EYES HEAVY WITH LACK OF sleep, Mia found herself staring at the ground. The cold had seeped so deeply into her bones she wasn't sure anything would ever warm her again. It was difficult to tell time in this cavernous underground room, so she had no idea how long it had been since she'd last slept or eaten. How long it had been since she'd left Alec's—how long it had been since she'd left Donovan.

Their last encounter made her wince whenever she thought of it. The terrified, miserable, betrayed look on Donovan's face as she'd verbally—and physically—put him down. The worst of her had come out in that moment, and Mia regretted it.

But then again, he was a criminal she'd been undercover to arrest, not fall for. This was his own doing, not hers.

Not hers.

An annoying laugh spread across Mia's mind, mocking her. Selena wasn't gone. She was never truly gone.

We're hungry, we're cold, and we're exhausted. Let's just go home. Donovan will forgive you, and we can go back to living our lives.

"Criminal lives?"

Better than sitting here any longer.

Pressing her lips into a thin line, Mia realized her options were limited, and she needed to make a decision. It was either that or die here.

For a brief moment, Mia allowed that thought to wash over and through her. Maybe the world was better off without her. Alec...Donovan. Maybe they were, too.

Then again, if she allowed herself to become weak from starvation, it would enable Selena to take over. Perhaps even permanently.

As far gone as Mia felt, she couldn't allow that to happen.

Pushing herself off the ground, Mia stood on unsteady feet, a wash of dizziness holding her in place. She'd been unmoving for far too long.

"I know, I know," Mia muttered, taking a shaky step forward. "It was stupid."

Though Selena remained silent, Mia felt a smugness emanating from inside that put her on edge.

One slow step after another, Mia made her way out of the dark room and into the main tunnel, but she paused in contemplation. Was she going back to Alec...or Donovan?

Glancing down at herself, Mia realized if she stepped foot outside, she would be thought a homeless beggar. Better to not draw attention to herself until she made a decision.

"The safe house," Mia murmured. "Clothes, food, a hot shower. Weapons."

Selena remained silent, so Mia took that to be agreement on her end.

It was a slow and steady walk as she made her way down the familiar tunnel toward the building that was considered condemned but actually held a safe house in the top level. Donovan and Mia had stayed there briefly after their loft had been attacked.

"His loft," Mia reprimanded herself.

It was difficult to tell how much time passed, but Mia trudged on, knowing she would make it there eventually. When she found the correct offshoot, she came to a stop in front of a deceptively seamless wall.

Though she'd never done it herself, Mia had watched Donovan enough times. Spreading her hands out along the wall, she felt for two indents, fumbling with her fingers for the buttons. Pressing one and then the other in rapid succession, the secret door slid open to reveal a set of stairs.

Making sure the door closed before making her way up, Mia was forced to pause and rest several times up the three flights of stairs. Sucking in one lungful of air after another, she placed her hand against the scanner at the top and waited for the next door to open.

Donovan hadn't removed her handprint from the system. The door opened silently. The next set of stairs was revealed, and Mia began the long trek up.

Though it took her ten times longer than it should have, Mia eventually made it to the fifth floor and the final set of security. With a deep breath, she pressed her hand to the pad and opened her eyes wide for the scanner to verify her identity.

The door opened, and Mia collapsed against the back of the sparse furnishings, relief rushing from her in waves. She forced herself forward, stumbling to the sink and drinking water from her palm. Once the worst of her thirst had been quenched, she scrounged for something to eat. She looked forward to a hot shower and a nap.

Perhaps then she could make a decision about what to do with her life.

Several hours later—or perhaps only minutes—Mia came to consciousness slowly. Her brain felt heavy with fog, her eyelids glued shut. There had to be a reason she'd woken; her body obviously needed more rest.

Listening hard, Mia tried to pick up on something out of place. In the silence, she caught the lightest sound of breathing. What hit her next was a scent that wasn't easily forgotten.

Donovan.

Forcing her eyes to open, they went unerringly to the man she'd been trying to avoid. He sat on a chair beside the bed, his eyes open and on her. When she attempted to decipher the look on his face, Mia couldn't decide if it was anger, relief, or a combination of the two.

"Are you all right?" he asked softly, his slightly accented voice skittering across her skin and awakening every nerve ending.

That was also a loaded question. "I have no idea how to answer that."

He nodded, allowing the smallest smile to tip his lips up at the corner. "Why don't we start with physically?"

"Cold," she answered, sitting up and scooting back to rest against the bedframe. "But otherwise fine. How did you know I was here?" He didn't speak, just watched her carefully. The answer revealed itself almost as soon as she'd asked it. "The security system notified you." No wonder she hadn't gotten an argument from Selena. "Of course."

"Mia, I—I'm so sorry for everything. And—if you don't want to see me again, I'll understand. You're not a prisoner with me. I just wanted...I just needed to know you're okay."

Searching his face, Mia took a moment before answering. "I need some time to myself."

His face fell, but he nodded. "I understand."

Pulling off the covers, Mia slid her feet to the floor. She'd dressed in the only clothes available—black cargo pants and a t-shirt—and pulled on the combat boots that were next to the bed.

Donovan stood as she did, watching silently as she placed a utility belt around her hips and loaded it with weapons. He moved to the kitchen, lifting a bag from the counter and offering it to her. "There are some provisions in here you might need. Please, at least take this."

A wealth of emotion passed between them as Mia hesitated. Swallowing hard, she nodded and accepted the bag. Without another word, she turned to the door. Leaving him was more difficult than she had thought it would be, even with the anger and resentment still rushing through her. Even though it had been Selena's plan—Mia's plan—she still felt betrayed by Donovan, but it didn't stop the flow of feelings that he had woken in her.

Pulling open the door, Mia started down the steps, stronger than she had been on her way up but still not in top form. Her body weak, her mind on Donovan, Mia wasn't paying as much attention as usual.

Too late, she heard the distinct pop of a gun; simultaneously, she felt a pinch against her chest and Donovan's strangled voice calling out her name.

Unable to fight, Mia sank to the ground, Donovan's name on her lips as her vision turned to black.

Twenty-Two

CONSCIOUSNESS RETURNED SLOWLY FOR THE second time that day. Mia's head pounded with the after-effects of the drug she'd been hit with, and she remained perfectly still in order to get a feel for her surroundings before alerting her kidnappers that she was awake.

The thin pad beneath her didn't quite mask the cold, hard ground it sat upon. Besides feeling sluggish, Mia felt relatively unharmed. There were sure to be bruises where she'd fallen, but nothing felt broken. The only noise she could hear was a low whistle, like wind through a crack in the wall. The scent of must surrounded her, but no other distinctive smells.

Cracking her eyes open, Mia found herself in a concrete cell. It was all too reminiscent of where the FBI had left her while she'd waited for Donovan to come to her rescue.

Alone for the moment, Mia rolled to her side before sitting up, bracing against the floor with a palm. Her mind began racing through the possibilities of who could have done this. Donovan?

Of course not, came the incredulous voice. *If we had just stayed with him, none of this would have happened.*

"We still would have left the safe house," Mia reminded the voice inside her head.

Silence was her answer, so Mia continued her list of suspects. The police department? Maybe. She couldn't even imagine what

Alec was thinking after she'd shown up on his doorstep in tatters, babbling nonsense and then disappearing into the night.

But they would have brought her to the station—or, at worst, locked her up in jail. This definitely wasn't jail.

The DeLucas? A strong possibility, and most likely. This whole thing had begun the night she'd helped Alec and Adam arrest two of the DeLuca brothers. Adam Malone—a traitor, a double agent within the police department. A DeLuca by birth.

He knew her secret—he knew Mia was undercover as Selena. When Donovan traded him for information from Tony DeLuca, the eldest of the four brothers, Mia was certain he'd spilled the truth.

They would know of the tunnels, even if they didn't have access to them. It wouldn't take much to find and keep an eye on the properties Donovan and Selena used.

Yes, the DeLucas were where Mia was putting her money. Now she just had to figure out the why—and a way to escape.

Taking stock of her situation, Mia realized she was still wearing the same clothes—minus the utility belt and the bag Donovan had given her. Though she hadn't looked inside, Mia had assumed it contained cash and maybe identification.

There's a hairpin in the left boot, Selena informed Mia.

Checking for herself, Mia found a hidden switch that, once compressed, shot out a long, thin piece of metal.

Grasping it in her hand, Mia stood and stumbled to the bars preventing her escape. A single lock held the doors together, and she quickly inserted the pin. It took some maneuvering, but she finally lined it up properly and heard the satisfying click.

The lock popped open, and she removed it quickly. Sliding the door open, Mia took a look both ways, finding a long hallway with more cells.

Donovan could be down here, Selena said.

Mia had already thought of that and planned to check cells as she went. There were three cells to the left, ending abruptly at a cement wall. Checking that direction first, Mia found nothing but empty concrete slabs and instantly reversed direction.

Doing her best to remain silent, she hurried along the hall, eyes searching both the cells for Donovan and the hall for cameras. It would do her no good to escape, only to be caught again.

There were no other prisoners, which either meant Donovan hadn't been captured—or that they'd done worse to him.

He's alive.

"I hope so," Mia said, approaching the end of the hall. Pausing at the edge of an archway, she peered around the corner to find a staircase leading up. Though eerily empty, moving forward was better than going back to her cell.

Taking the steps one at a time, still feeling the effects of the last couple of days, Mia paused at the top and listened carefully. The door in front of her was locked, so she inserted the same hairpin into the mechanism and fiddled carefully.

It opened easily—almost too easily. Shaking away the paranoia, Mia pushed open the door less than an inch in order to listen for activity beyond.

Hearing nothing, she continued opening until her head could fit through the crack. This door led into a basement—large and empty, with more cement on the floors and walls. Slipping into the deserted room, Mia searched the darkness for a way out. There were no windows, but on the far side, she spotted another set of stairs. Moving quickly, Mia paused at the next doorway. Trying the knob, she found it unlocked. Nudging it open, she pressed her ear to the crack to listen.

Though it was still quiet, a wash of warm air blew over her and made her shiver. There was also light on the other side—the soft light of lamps and fire.

Pushing open the door fully, she stepped into what could only be a man's study. A low fire burned in a fireplace, the walls were lined with books, and an ornate desk sat opposite the fire.

Staring around her, Mia was unable to put two and two together. Where was she?

Her need to run warred with her need to know. With her detective side taking over, she crept toward the desk and began looking through papers, searching for some kind of clue as to who had taken her. Nothing she found on top of the desk was helping to put the pieces together. Growing increasingly curious, Mia began pulling open drawers, taking in the scant files that did nothing to illuminate her predicament.

"If you have a question, you need only to ask," said a voice from the doorway. "No need to be sneaky about it."

Standing and spinning toward the voice with a gasp, Mia met the dark eyes of a man who was as recognizable as he was frightening. Though she'd never dealt with him directly or seen him in person, Mia knew exactly who he was.

Mia hadn't, at least. Selena had.

"Enrico DeLuca."

His smile grew, slow and calculating. "I see my reputation precedes me."

"What do you want with me?" Mia asked, surprised at the strength in her voice.

He stepped toward her, relaxed and careful with his movements. He thought he had the upper hand here, as he'd taken her weapons. And though she was in a weakened state, Mia knew that wasn't necessarily true.

Besides her fighting ability, which she had faith she could call upon if needed, he obviously wanted her alive for some reason. She didn't have that restriction.

"No need to be afraid, Selena," he said, raising his hands in a peaceful demeanor. Then, with a quirk of his lips, he added, "Or shall I call you Mia?"

They held a staring contest for a long while as Mia's brain tried to work out the implications of her current predicament. Ricky DeLuca had drugged her and held her hostage in a secret basement prison in what looked like his own home. He knew who she really was and didn't seem at all surprised that she had escaped.

"You may as well just call me your prisoner," Mia spat at him in answer. "What do you want from me?"

"I believe we can help each other," he said with careful nonchalance, moving to a bar cart and lifting a decanter in question. When she shook her head, he shrugged and poured himself a glass. "I don't want you to think of yourself as a prisoner here."

"Am I free to leave?"

"Not currently."

"Then I'm a prisoner."

"Suit yourself," he said, moving to his desk and motioning for her to sit. Mia remained standing, arms crossed and a glare on her face. "As I said, I believe we can help each other. You are in a unique position right now, between having Donovan convinced you're his partner and your own connection to the police. If you assist me, then I'll make sure you are free to live your life."

A threat lurked somewhere in his polite speech, and Mia wasn't impressed. "You'll kill me if I don't work for you?"

"I wouldn't put it so crassly, but yes."

"No thanks."

"Your choice," he said, taking a sip—the very picture of insouciance. "But I wouldn't make it so quickly. You'll have three days to decide. Carlos will show you to your room."

He waved someone forward, a man who had been hovering in the hallway. Automatically, Mia tensed for a fight. Carlos flashed a gun, an infuriating smirk crossing his lips.

"Please, follow Carlos. You are my guest, after all." Glaring but seeing no other option at the moment, Mia turned to follow when Ricky spoke again. "Oh, and—I have Donovan. Perhaps I should have mentioned that earlier. If you don't cooperate, I'll kill him."

Mia's heart stilled in her chest. Right now, the only thing she had working for her was the fact that Ricky knew she was Mia Gonzalez, a cop intent on taking Donovan down. She had to use that.

"Why would I care if you killed Donovan?" Mia asked flippantly. "He's a criminal."

Ricky smiled, his eyes studying her carefully. "I think we both know he's more than that to you. Whatever your intentions at the beginning, it's rather obvious you care for the man. I won't argue with you now—just be a good little cop, and no one will be hurt."

For the moment, there was nothing more Mia could do. Spinning on her heel again, she marched out of the room even though she had no idea where to go. Carlos was quick to grip her arm just above the elbow, leading her away from the front of the house and up a flight of stairs.

The room he shoved her into was well furnished with an attached bathroom. The windows were barred, and the door locked from the outside. Mia was sure there would be guards outside the door, so for the time being, she played the good hostage.

The first thing she did was go through the room, looking for anything that could be used as a weapon. In the closet, she found clothes that would fit—which she found very creepy, considering— and anything heavy seemed to be nailed down.

Short of squirting some shampoo in a guard's eye, it looked like she'd have to fight her way out the old-fashioned way.

With her fists.

It wasn't long before a knock sounded on the door, and Carlos entered with a bottle of water and a bowl of soup. He set it down on a small table and stood, waiting for Mia to eat.

"You're just going to watch me?" she asked. He didn't answer. She supposed he wanted to make sure she didn't pocket the spoon or shatter the bowl for a shiv. "That's not creepy at all. You do you, man."

Though his eyes tightened just slightly, Carlos otherwise remained perfectly still. Needing the nourishment, Mia sat obediently and ate every last drop of the meal. He left her directly after, leaving the water bottle—he must not have thought the plastic was dangerous.

For a while, she paced the room, then decided to do some basic calisthenics to work on regaining her strength. Selena was unusually quiet as she worked, probably listening to the swirling tangle of thoughts Mia found impossible to escape.

Point one; she couldn't let anything happen to Donovan. No matter how betrayed she felt, she still loved him. Point two; she couldn't let Ricky know how she felt. Her only leverage right now was in that he thought she was Mia, though he'd worked out she cared somewhat for Donovan. He didn't know—or need to know—the full extent.

It was impossible to tell how many guards Ricky employed or even where this house was located. All the windows she'd come across had had their shades drawn, and her own window was blocked from view. Mia had to assume they were in or around Baltimore since Ricky himself was present. He was too involved in his business to leave for any amount of time.

Judging by the size and architecture, however, she was inclined to believe they were well outside the city, on a sizable piece of property to keep nosy neighbors at bay.

Done with her measly workout, Mia took a long, hot shower to slough away the dirt and grime of the prison cell she'd woken in and rummaged through the closet. Inside, she found stretchy pants and a t-shirt that were comfortable and gave her a decent range of motion in case she needed to fight.

With nothing else to occupy her, Mia sat against the headboard with a pillow at her back. Closing her eyes, she took deep breaths, focusing on filling the lower part of her belly on each intake, tightening it as she exhaled. The repetitive action helped to clear her mind and expand her senses. Outside the door, Mia heard the guard sigh and shift his weight. Further away, the sound of low, masculine voices reverberated through the wall. Outside, through the blocked window, a branch brushed gently against the siding.

With nothing more to hear for the moment, Mia opened her eyes and studied the room again. Against the far wall, a shelf lined with several books caught her eye. Sliding off the bed, she pulled out one after another, searching for something to keep her interest.

At about the tenth one, her eyes snagged on the title, grunting a little in the back of her throat.

"This might come in handy," she said aloud. Settling back into the bed, Mia opened *An Introduction to French* and prepared herself for a long night.

For three days, Ricky left Mia to her own devices. The only human contact she had was with Carlos, who delivered her meals. She ate because she needed her strength. The thought that the food might be poisoned crossed her mind but was almost instantly dismissed.

If Ricky had wanted to kill her, he would have done so by now. He'd had ample opportunity from the moment he kidnapped her until now. Carlos didn't look above putting a knife to her throat or a gun to her head, even. No, food was the last thing to be concerned about.

Selena remained mostly silent but always there, hovering just on the edges of Mia's consciousness. A strange thing, to say the least, this sharing of mind. Knowing another resided there, even though that other person was still a part of her. They were as different as night and day, good and evil. Each dependent on the other, unable to exist without the opposite—yet still separate entities.

Finally, the night of the third day, Carlos opened the door wide and gestured for Mia to exit the room. Feeling more like herself with the consistent meals and daily exercises, Mia kept her arms loose and ready at her sides with her other senses open. It felt good to move outside the confines of her room, and it seemed she was fully healed from her bout of near starvation and hypothermia.

"Where are we going? Are you taking me on a date?" Mia asked the silent Carlos. He remained stoic, mute, but that didn't mean she couldn't have some fun. "You are, aren't you? I bet you're quite the romantic. Flowers, walks in the moonlight. Just a warning, though. I don't put out on the first date. You'll have to wait at least for the third."

The muscles across his back tensed, and Mia thought she saw a twitch in his left eye. It gave her no small amount of satisfaction.

He opened the door to a dining room and all but shoved her through. A fire burned low in the fireplace, more flame for the candles on the table. Fresh flowers in a riot of colors graced the center, and covered dishes gave off delectable aromas of spice.

Ricky stood by the mantel, a snifter of brandy swirling in his palm. He watched Mia with hooded eyes, so she straightened and waited for him to speak. "Good evening, Mia. Won't you join me for dinner?"

"Do I have a choice on it?"

He shrugged indifferently. "There's always a choice."

Since her options were limited to eating with Ricky or being thrown back in the room—or worse—she chose the former.

Approaching a chair, Mia leaned against it casually, resting her forearms along the carved backrest.

"Dinner it is. It looks awfully romantic. Don't you have a wife, girlfriend? Won't she mind?"

"As a matter of fact, I have both," he answered with another lazy swirl of his drink. "Brandy?"

"No, I think I'll stick to water."

"Your choice," he said with another lift of his shoulders. Gesturing with a hand toward the chair she leaned against, he added, "Please, sit."

She settled into the seat, and he took up position opposite. He took a long pull of his drink before setting it down with precise movements and arranging the cloth napkin in his lap. "Please, help yourself to cheese and antipasto. My chef has prepared a wonderful braised beef cacciatore."

A salad waited before her, a platter of cheese between them. Freshly-baked bread had been sliced thin—some for the soft cheese, some covered in sauce and mozzarella and broiled to perfection.

Taking a few pieces of each, Mia nibbled on it while studying Ricky. He seemed perfectly at ease, dining with a cop who was pretending to be a criminal. Little did he know, she claimed both titles. Mia decided to break the ice. "What is it you want to discuss?"

Ricky traced over the lines of her face with his dark eyes. "It is rather remarkable."

"What is?"

"How much you look like Selena. I only came into contact with her a couple of times, but the resemblance is uncanny. I'd never have known if it weren't for Adam."

"Oh, yes. How is the little rat?"

Ricky's lip pulled back in what was part smile, part sneer. "What he did is no different from what you did."

"I was catching criminals. He was helping them. That makes all the difference in the world."

"Does Donovan know?" he asked, toying with his glass again. "Does he know who you really are? That Selena is probably dead in a ditch somewhere, rotting away while you take over her life?"

Deep inside, Mia felt Selena stir, her hatred spilling over into Mia's words. "Of course not. You think I would still be around if he knew?"

"Some men are easily swayed by the wiles of women," Ricky answered. When Mia stiffened, his smile grew. "Don't be embarrassed. The fact that you're sleeping with him is quite obvious in your body language."

Willing herself to calm, Mia tried to be as flippant as he. With a one-shoulder shrug, she answered, "It was the best way to get him to trust me. It meant nothing."

"Be careful how much you protest, dear Mia."

Silence met his statement. Picking up another piece of bread, Mia spread some cheese atop before taking a slow, careful bite. Chewed without losing eye contact. The time for niceties was done. "Why don't you tell me what you want? In explicit detail, no more pretty words dancing around the point."

Leaning back, Ricky rested one elbow in his opposite palm, tapping a finger against his chin as he watched her. He had an excellent poker face; nothing seemed to ruffle his feathers. Luckily, Mia's was better—or, at least, on par with his.

"When I release you from my home, you will go back to the precinct having failed in bringing Donovan in, but you will have succeeded in tearing down his business. With no Selena—and now, no Donovan—their industry will crumble. Congratulations."

This was said so dryly Mia could only blink in response. "What will you do with Donovan?"

"Oh, he'll remain my guest. I'll need him for collateral, you see. For when you return triumphant to your department, you will take the place of our cousin, Adam. You'll be our inside woman, our informant."

"And if I don't?"

Ricky leaned back, still casual. "On your first offense, I'll kill Donovan. Your second offense—you."

His words hung heavy in the air. Ricky had just threatened Donovan's life and her own. His face was a mask of indifference as if appetizers and murder were on the same level of conversation. Though Mia felt as if the wind had been knocked from her chest, she remained as still and stoic as he.

"Isn't it three strikes, and you're out?"

The corner of his mouth twitched in what could be the beginnings of a smile. "This isn't a game, Ms. Gonzalez."

"And if I refuse your conditions?"

"Well, that would be your first offense."

He sure knew how to play hardball. Though she wanted to remain aloof and uncaring, Mia also needed to see Donovan. Needed to. Had to know he was alive and as well as he could be, given the situation. Whether it was her need or Selena's, she couldn't tell. Perhaps it didn't matter anymore. "And how do I know you've not killed Donovan already?"

Ricky sat forward, nodded toward the still-covered dish before her. "Let's eat, shall we? And then we'll take a walk."

Though eager to be on her way, Mia forced herself to slow, to act as if she hadn't a care in the world. As if seeing Donovan wasn't a priority.

The braised beef tasted delectable, but it may as well have been ash in her mouth. Mia tasted nothing, just chewed and swallowed automatically. For the sustenance, for the energy. Storing up until she had an opportunity to act.

"Tell me about yourself, Mia," Ricky said after a long silence.

"Not much to tell."

"What of your childhood? Your family?"

"Don't have one. My parents are both dead." If he could be stark and casual about death, so could she. "And you, Ricky? Are your parents proud of what you've become?"

He smiled, a little twinkle of firelight caught in his eye. "Why, of course. It's my father's business I've helped thrive. My mother might bury her head in the sand, but she enjoys the privileges this lifestyle can grant her."

"And your wife? Does she do the same?"

"My wife tends the children, as she should."

"How many children do you have?"

"Two. Both boys. The older will do well with the business one day. The younger—well, he has focus issues. I'm hoping he grows out of it. The doctors nowadays, all they want to do is push drugs and therapy."

"He has ADD?" Mia asked.

"So they say. My wife falls for that nonsense, hook, line, and sinker. Back in my day, our father would have beat any one of us and told us not to be a pussy. Times have changed."

"They certainly have. And what of your girlfriend? Does she know what you do?"

He waved a hand dismissively. "She's for the more carnal pleasures in life. Since she's well compensated, she asks no questions."

"A kept woman. The saddest kind of person."

"She gets on well enough. She has most days free to do as she wishes, apart from keeping in shape to please me. Lunches with friends, salon appointment every week. All I ask is she be available to me as I wish. The rest is for her to do with as she pleases."

"Whatever gets you through," Mia replied, setting down her fork. Disgust settled low in her stomach, preventing her from eating anything more.

Ricky stood, approached a buffet with a carafe of coffee and plates of dessert. Taking it upon himself to pour her a cup, he returned to the table and set the coffee and tiramisu down after she cleared her plate.

He leaned close, and she got a good whiff of his aftershave. Heavy on sandalwood and spice. She nearly gagged in her mouth.

"Cream, sugar?"

"Yes."

He moved away and back again, leaving the small silver canisters for Mia to use. After adding two sugar cubes and a dollop of cream, Mia drank the cup down full without breath. His eyes widened in what could be surprise, and she congratulated herself on finally breaking through his toughened exterior. Rising, Mia helped herself to a refill before sitting again.

Adding the same amount of sweetness, she took a dainty sip before trying a bite of the rum cake. Though not her favorite dessert, the chef had done a good job with it.

"How was your meal?" Ricky asked as if reading her mind.

"You have an excellent chef."

He seemed to take the compliment to heart, and she watched as he finished his own dessert. Mia only got through half of hers. Standing, Ricky pushed the chair back and set his napkin on the table. "You'll join me for a walk?"

Trying not to look too excited, Mia simply inclined her head and pushed back as he'd done. With quiet settling between them, they exited the dining room and made their way down a long hallway before beginning to ascend a separate staircase to the second floor.

They were in a section of the house she'd not seen yet, and it gave Mia a better understanding of its size and layout.

Ricky led her to a door and opened it with a key at his belt. After pushing it open, he allowed her entrance. The small room left little breathing space apart from the single bed, where Donovan lay. His eyes were closed, his breath light and even. Two rails ran the length of the bed, where his wrists and ankles were secured by chains.

To Ricky's credit, Donovan looked relatively unharmed.

"You have him drugged." It wasn't so much a question as a statement.

"For our safety, as much as his. It won't be forever, just for now."

"What life is this, to be a prisoner? To be drugged, near death?"

"You'd rather him dead?"

Catching herself, Mia squared her shoulders and made sure her eyes were dry as she turned to face Ricky. "No. That's not the way of cops. Brought to justice, perhaps, but not outright murder."

"Is that what happened with your father, Mia? Justice?" He asked so gently, yet it stunned her as if she'd been slapped.

Her spine stiffened, and she cringed, giving away more than she meant. Damn him, damn him to hell. "That was self-defense," Mia replied rigidly. "And it's not for you to bring up."

"Forgive me, as I see I've touched a sore spot. Well, now you've seen Donovan is alive and well. Come with me, and I'll give you another day to think over our agreement."

Mia took one last look at Donovan's still figure, soaking in his sharp features that had softened in sleep.

Not sleep. Anesthesia.

I know, Mia replied silently. *I swear we'll get him out of here.*

Twenty-Three

RICKY LED MIA TO THE door of her room, making sure the bolt was secured himself before leaving for the night. A guard she didn't recognize remained in the hall, and she'd spotted several more on the walk back from Donovan's room.

Sitting heavily on the bed, Mia closed her eyes and drew in one deep breath after another, forcing herself to calm. Seeing Donovan there, helpless, made her want to rip and tear the house apart just to get him out.

We need to go back now.

"We can't. If we went now, we'd fail."

How dare you! The man we love lies helpless, and you do nothing! Selena clawed against the restraints Mia held in check, though it proved more difficult than she'd counted on.

"Selena, stop!" Mia practically yelled into her own head. "We're going to get him, I promise. But we're going in with a real plan, not some half-cocked scheme that will get us all killed."

The clawing stopped, but the pain—Selena's pain, Mia's—remained.

"We'll get him out," Mia said again, quieter but with more conviction. For Selena, for herself. "We'll get him out."

From the waist band of her pants, Mia slipped out the butter knife and fork she'd managed to nab during dinner. It wasn't much, but it was a start.

Sleep didn't come that night. The two cups of coffee she'd downed in a matter of minutes probably had something to do with it, but their predicament is what kept her on her feet. She paced; she worried. Selena hovered there, her anguish a living, breathing thing. Between the two of them, they had to work out a plan. They had to escape, get Donovan clear.

And then what?

"Go to the police station. Get them to help."

A disgusted grunt was the response. *Help? I'm a criminal. Donovan's a criminal. They won't help.*

"We need to get rid of the DeLucas, once and for all."

Agreed. But your precious police won't be the ones to do that.

"They need justice."

Needing to think, Mia pressed the palms of her hands against her temples, pressing hard against her skull. One problem at a time.

Even if she got to Donovan in one piece, he was heavily sedated. General anesthesia, which would need to be administered about every four hours. Even if they caught him just as he was about to wake, he would be groggy for a time yet and nearly useless to them.

They needed a stimulant, something to yank him out of sleep.

Adrenaline to the heart? Mia could all but see the sneer in the words.

"It works in the movies," Mia muttered. But even if she'd be able to find a shot of it, Mia doubted her ability to shove it through Donovan's chest. "There are other stimulants."

They were both quiet as they thought through their options. Rummaging through medicine cabinets might be a necessary risk.

And if we can't find something to wake him?

276

"Then we carry him out," Mia answered with a release of breath. "We'll find a way."

Looking down at her small cache of weapons, Mia wondered what kind of damage she could do with a fork, a butter knife, and the hairpin still tucked safely in her boot. If she managed to get to Donovan in one piece, the hairpin could release him from his restraints. The problem lay in arriving at his room with enough time to work the locks.

Dropping to the edge of the bed, Mia ran both hands through her hair, forced herself to think. The best bet would be to wait until tomorrow when someone came for her.

Why wait? The tendrils of a plan flitted through Mia's mind. It would be risky—but then again, so would agreeing to Ricky's proposal.

"All right. I can do that."

Are you sure? There was no censure in the question, just pure curiosity.

"I've killed before."

No, you haven't.

"Of course I have," Mia insisted.

In self-defense, maybe. I've *killed.* I've *murdered.*

"What about Dad?" Mia asked softly. When silence met her statement, she gasped quietly. "That was you."

Yes. Selena's voice was so small, Mia felt a surge of empathy toward her.

"I created you," Mia whispered to herself. "You appeared when I needed you. When I couldn't do what needed to be done."

More silence, but it wasn't angry now. Selena felt despondent.

"You were the worst parts of me. You never even had a chance."

Yes.

So much became clear in that moment—a new understanding of the part of herself that had a name.

Selena.

"You were the worst parts," Mia said gently. "But you didn't remain the worst parts."

What do you mean? Mia could hear the tiniest spark of hope in the question.

"You found Donovan. You found true love. I never did that. And he loved you so much that he not only created the empire you imagined but went along with the crazy plan to get me with him full time."

I love him.

"I know. I love him, too. And it's time to get him back."

The small spark of hope suddenly burst forth, lighting Mia's insides like the brightest star. *You'll let me out?*

"Yes. I trust you to get Donovan back."

△ △ △

IT FELT SO GOOD FOR Selena to have control over her limbs again. Different, too. Before, she could only emerge while Mia slept, when her conscience was ripe for the taking. But now, Mia had given herself over to Selena willingly. Now, Selena could feel her hovering there. Fully aware of what was happening but unable to control the outcome.

How it had always been for Selena.

Suddenly Selena felt faint, dizzy. Stumbling, she slammed into the door, bounced off, and landed on the floor with a groan. Her right arm landed in an unnatural position beneath her prone body as she struggled to keep her eyes open. A key turned in the lock; the door opened.

Rough hands gripped Selena's shoulder, and a voice called out for her attention. The man who'd stood outside rolled her to her back.

And got an eyeful of shampoo when she brought out her hidden right arm.

He screamed and fell back, fingers scrubbing at the stinging liquid. In a lithe move, Selena straddled him and stabbed the fork into his neck with enough force to pierce deeply into his carotid artery. Blood gushed out like a geyser; his cries gurgled to a halt.

Selena's knees held his arms at bay as his body twitched, fought the inevitable. She held him down as the life drained out of him.

When his eyes went glassy with death, Selena stood and relieved him of his weapon and keys. Snatching his wallet and other items from his pockets before standing, she approached the doorway with caution. His shouts could have been heard if anyone had been close enough. Caution was her best route.

Sneaking a glance around the door frame, Selena found the hallway empty. Small blessings.

Closing the door to delay anyone who might come investigate, she tracked back the same way they'd walked earlier, streaking like an arrow through the long halls back to Donovan. At the first bathroom, Selena stopped and stepped inside, searching through the cabinets and drawers for an upper.

Finding nothing, she continued, turning in the hall. A guard had his back to her. Without slowing, she slid the knife she'd acquired from the first guard into her palm and crept closer on the balls of her feet. She slipped the blade into the man's kidney, effectively cutting off all sound.

As he crumpled to the floor, Selena retrieved the weapon, wiping it clean of blood on the man's shirt, and continued on her way.

Approaching a new hall, she glanced down and found it empty. The way to Donovan was straight, but Selena felt Mia hesitate.

We need to find medication. Maybe it's in a part of the house that's inhabited by Ricky or the guards.

Watching, listening, Selena balanced her words with the need to get to Donovan as quickly as possible. Deciding to take the risk, Selena started down the hall.

Pausing at the first closed door, she heard nothing. Opening the door a crack, Selena peered into the darkness and found a boy's room. Sports and Legos crowded the small space, from the neat soccer trim along the wall to the equipment in the corner. Shelves painted a cheery red held painfully put-together Lego sets.

When Selena began to turn away, dismiss the space, Mia held her back. *His son. The younger one has ADD.*

Which meant he could very well be on Ritalin. While it was prescribed as a way to help wayward children focus, it was also a stimulant and had a surprising side effect.

It helped snap people out of anesthesia, enabled them to be more alert in those first minutes of cloudiness.

With renewed hope, Selena marched into the room and into the adjoining bath. And there, in the medicine cabinet, was a bottle of the small white pills. And luckily for them, the medicine came in chewable form.

Next to the sink, Selena found a cup with cartoon cars zipping around the outside and filled it from the sink. The only way to get Donovan to ingest the pills, chewable or not, was to trigger his automatic swallowing.

Pushing the pill bottle into her back pocket, Selena slipped from the room once again.

Hurrying down the halls now, she found one more unsuspecting guard. Setting down the cup of water, Selena quickly dispatched him with the blade. Reaching Donovan's door, she ejected the hairpin from her boot and finagled the lock.

When she stepped inside the room, her heart jumped into her throat.

Donovan lay on the bed, so still, so cold. Rushing over to him, Selena contemplated whether to free him first or force-feed him the medication. She had no idea how long it would take to work—or even if it would. Deciding to free his hands first, Selena set to work and got the cuffs removed in record time. Taking out the pills, she shook several into her hand.

Ten milligrams is a typical adult dose, Mia offered.

Each pill was five milligrams. Starting with six of the little squares, Selena crushed the pills and mixed them in with the cup of water. Taking just a moment to brush back the lock of hair hanging in his eye, she lifted Donovan's head and tilted his mouth open, pouring half the liquid down.

"Come on, baby. Swallow the water." He gurgled before swallowing reflexively. Relief shot through Selena as she poured the rest of the drink into his mouth. "That's it. Just a little more."

Once he'd finished the cup, Selena laid his head back gently and got to work on his ankle cuffs. As the second lock clicked open, she heard him stir.

A low moan escaped his throat as he thrashed against the lingering effects of anesthesia. Letting the cuff collapse to the ground, Selena moved back to his head and clasped his hand. "Donovan? Can you hear me? You need to wake up. Come on, baby, open your eyes."

They blinked rapidly, those long lashes lifting to reveal his beautiful dark eyes. "Mia?" he slurred. As he focused, his eyebrows furrowed. "Selena?"

"Hi, baby," Selena said and, giving in, laid her lips to his. Just a touch, a promise of things to come. "Come on, we have to go. Can you stand?"

Slipping an arm under his back, Selena helped lift Donovan into a sitting position. His feet touched the floor as he steadied himself against the edge of the bed. Giving him a boost, he stood. Letting out a hiss of a breath, he said, "Legs are numb. Give me a minute."

"Okay. All right. We don't really have a minute."

Steeling himself against the pain, he nodded and, leaning heavily against Selena, began to walk. When they reached the door, she peeked out and saw no one. The fact that no one had come across any of the dead guards was sheer luck.

They eased into the hallway, pulling the door shut behind. Earlier, when Ricky had taken them from the dining room to Donovan's room, they'd passed the kitchen—and if their luck stuck, the back door.

Donovan had a difficult time with the stairs, but they made it to the ground level without incident. The house remained eerily dark and quiet, even for the late hour. They rounded the corner into the kitchen, and Selena let out a breath at seeing their escape.

Flipping the lock, she grabbed the handle of the back door and pushed. And felt her heart drop to her toes when an alarm sounded.

The raucous noise did more for Donovan than the Ritalin had. They bolted through the door and across the wide expanse of lawn. Mia had been right—they were well outside Baltimore, on a sizable piece of property. They were fenced in, a high, stone enclosure that kept the thick woods at bay.

With her arm still around Donovan's waist, Selena made a beeline for the edge of the property even as shouts sounded at their backs. She felt more than saw Donovan begin to sag—that initial jolt of adrenaline had quickly dispersed.

They struggled forward for several feet before he spoke. "Go," he managed on a breath. "Just go. Leave me."

"Absolutely not," Selena said firmly. Risking a glance back, she found four men on their tail. Couldn't tell if one of them was Ricky or not. "I'm getting you out of here."

He stopped talking, either because he knew when not to argue with her or because speaking had become a struggle. Either way, she dug in her heels and spurred them forward. When they reached the wall, they only had seconds before the guards were on them.

Yanking out the downed guards' wallets, Selena shoved what she could into Donovan's pockets, wanting him to have some cash once he cleared the woods. Before Selena could stop to think, she cupped her hands and braced herself in a squat. Donovan understood immediately—after she boosted him up, he could reach down to pull her over. His foot connected to her palms—a bare foot, which made her cringe, knowing the treacherous journey ahead of him— and he launched himself up, gripping the wall with shaking arms. The few days he'd lain immobile had undoubtedly taken its toll.

Grabbing his feet, Selena gave him an extra push. He cleared the wall just as the guards reached them. Looking up at Donovan, soaking in his beloved face, Selena smiled and mouthed, "Activate Exodus."

His eyebrows drew together as the reality of the situation dawned on him. Though she'd been expecting this, Selena could plainly see he thought they'd escape together. His face crumpled as he struggled with the truth, with the dire situation they'd been forced into. His thoughts were as clear to her as if he'd spoken them aloud; there was serious consideration at the idea of remaining to fight his way by her side.

Shaking her head, attempting to convey her own thoughts with her eyes, Selena called out, 'Go!' before the guards wrestled her to the ground.

When one swung a gun toward the still hesitating Donovan, he spurred into action, disappearing from view after one last tortured glance her way.

He had to live to fight another day. He had to live to rescue her—for real this time.

Wanting to give Donovan time to put as much distance between himself and this place, Selena struggled against the guard holding her down, gaining leverage and flipping positions. Her sudden freedom gained the attention of all four men—exactly as she'd planned.

As she punched and spun, kicked and disabled, Selena spotted Ricky approaching with a gun at his side, his face red with rage. Gripping the fourth and only guard to remain standing in a sleeper hold, Selena applied just enough pressure for him to know she meant business without knocking him unconscious.

"Hi, Ricky. Good of you to join us."

"You'll die for this, bitch."

"I don't think so." To prove his point, Ricky brought the gun up, aimed for Selena's chest. In his state of mind, she knew he would shoot his own man just to get to her. She had to talk fast, get him distracted.

"You see, this was my audition." The man struggled, so she tightened her grip for a brief moment. When he stilled again, Selena looked up to see interest flicker in the dark depths of Ricky's gaze. "I've decided I'll work for you, but I'll do it under my terms."

Now she had his full attention. His eyes flicked over his disabled guards, and Selena felt certain his thoughts went to the ones she'd incapacitated, lying dead in the house to his back. "You'll work for me," he said with disbelief, "after all this?"

Shrugging, which was no easy feat while still controlling the two-hundred-pound man, Selena replied, "Sure. But I have conditions." He waved the gun in a go-ahead motion, obviously curious enough to hear her out. "One, you won't hurt Donovan. Ever. Two, you'll send your dipshit little cousin far, far away to start a new life. And three"—here she paused, met his gaze with fire—"if you ever threaten me or Donovan again, I will do this, and worse, to your family."

With that, Selena applied pressure and dropped the unconscious guard to the ground. They squared off, his gun still loosely pointed in her direction while she stood with her hands spread. Inviting him to do as he wished. Willing him. Her utter confidence held him back.

"You ask a lot."

"I offer a lot," she shot back.

"Tell me one reason I shouldn't shoot you now."

Smirking, Selena told him the one thing that could save her— and the one thing that could be her downfall.

"Because I'm Mia Gonzalez. A damn good detective." Stepping forward until the barrel of the gun dug into her stomach, Selena brought her hands back to her sides and leaned close to Ricky, baring her teeth in a snarl. "But I'm also Selena."

Ricky stared with his mouth agape. After the bombshell she'd dropped, it would take him a while to form a coherent thought. "You—yeah, right. I'm supposed to believe that you're Mia Gonzalez *and* Selena?"

Denial worked, too. If nothing else, their conversation provided Donovan the time he needed to get away. "Why not? It makes perfect sense. Why do you think Donovan and I were able to evade the law so easily? Why do you think Mia and I look so much alike? *Because we're the same person.*"

The wheels were turning in his mind, all right. Selena let him think about it a bit longer, dragging their time out. "Do you remember our first meeting? I mean, the first time you met Selena?"

"Of course I do."

"I warned you about your new business partners. I told you that if you continued down that course, we'd have to distance ourselves from you. You didn't care. And I was right, wasn't I? You got in over your head."

His eyes grew wide as the truth dawned on him. "You're really Selena?"

"That's right, Sparky. So, you see, you don't need to corrupt me. I'm already corrupt."

Ricky had lost total control, and it was a new look for him. He still stared, his mouth moving without sound while he tried to catch up on everything Selena had told him. To her left, one of his guards groaned and started to come to, which seemed to snap Ricky back to his confident self.

He glanced down at the guards strewn about the lawn and back to her. "It seems we have a deal. Shall we discuss details in private?"

Inclining her head, Selena stepped over the last guard to hit the ground and sauntered back to the house.

Ricky led her into his office, and they watched each other across his desk. He stood behind it, afraid to sit down, while she stood with her arms crossed, daring him to do something about it.

"Who else do you have in the police?" Selena asked casually.

"You think I'm really going to give you that information?"

"Just thought we could do lunch or have a pajama party. Don't pretend you don't have more moles. Adam couldn't have been your only one."

"No. But if I need something from you, you'll know it. I don't trust you enough with more information than that."

"Understandable. How will I contact you if I need to?"

He considered her for a while before answering. "I'll give you a drop box location. If you have something urgent, you can leave me a note."

"Works for me," Selena said with a shrug. After they shored up the details, she backed toward the door. "All right, I'm leaving now. I'm going back to the precinct to tell them I brought down Donovan's business and get back to work."

Ricky's fingers twitched as if he wanted to stop her from leaving. He wouldn't get the chance, but if she could prevent another fight, that would be best.

Selena really did plan on going back to the police department. But first things first—she had to find Donovan.

The safe house had been compromised, so she knew Donovan wouldn't have headed back there. Her best bet was their first condo, which had yet to be found by the DeLucas. They had other property, only known to the two of them, but he would need time to get them stocked.

Injured and drugged, he would go where he knew he could rest.

Ricky insisted on driving her out of his property. With a blindfold. After being dropped off on a dark side street, Selena took a good look around and oriented herself quickly. Heading down the alley, she cut across at the next street and continued to make fast, random turns in case she had a tail. Once she felt secure that she'd lost anyone that would have been following, Selena ducked into one of their buildings and made her way to the secret door.

Getting into the tunnels and upping her pace to a jog, Selena wound her way to their first loft, pausing at a cache of clothes and weapons first. In it, she found a device that she waved over her body, searching for a bug or tracker that Ricky might have placed without her knowledge. Finding nothing, she pocketed the scanner and replaced the rest before continuing on her way.

Reaching the correct building, Selena walked through the lobby, nodding a greeting at the guard there, and slipped into the private elevator. As the door opened, Selena stepped out and stared at the keypad waiting for her print.

"You need to take over."

Mia hesitated at the request, trying to ascertain the thoughts behind that decision. *Are you sure?*

Sighing, Selena nodded decisively. "It will mean more coming from you."

Twenty-Four

PLACING HER HAND AGAINST THE pad, Mia waited for the door to unlock before pushing inside the apartment. Donovan had left a trail of dirty prints, some blood, and upended furniture in his wake. At least he was there, though Mia worried about what state she would find him in.

Following the mess back toward the bedroom, she found Donovan passed out in an awkward position. She moved him into a more comfortable spot before stepping into the bathroom. Finding a washcloth, she soaked it under the sink and returned to Donovan's side.

Running the cool cloth over Donovan's forehead, Mia studied his drawn face with a mixture of relief and longing. What they were about to enact would be the most dangerous thing they'd ever considered doing. The truth—nearly, if not all of it—would come out. For better or worse, they were now at the point of no return.

Making herself comfortable in the chair by his bedside, Mia covered his hand with her own. All adrenaline had already drained from her system, leaving her weak and exhausted. It had been a long day.

As she sat, she dozed. Her mind continued to be too full for a restful sleep, but she took what she could get.

Donovan stirred, a grunt followed by a sharp intake of breath. Mia's eyes shot open as she watched his eyebrows furrow in concentration. Agony and terror were a living, breathing thing, squeezing her insides as she watched him struggle for consciousness, for reality.

"Shh, there now, it's all right," Mia said, keeping her voice low and even so as not to frighten him more. "You're safe now; we're together."

"Mia..."

In the throes of his half-dream state, Donovan gasped her name. *Her* name. Mia's heart let loose a pounding thud before taking off at a sprint.

"I'm here, Donovan. It's all right. Open your eyes for me."

They flew open as he shot up in bed, a palm coming automatically to rest against his forehead as the action was too much, too soon. Squeezing his eyes shut against the wave of dizziness and the little bit of light from the hall, he took deep, even breaths before trying again.

Those dark, soulful eyes opened, landed on Mia's face. Stared in disbelief, then tentative hope. Finally, a smile spread across his lips, lighting his inner fire.

Without a word, he cupped her face and pulled her in for a kiss. The onslaught of passion directed straight to her low stomach, stirring a need she'd all but forgotten in the past days. Though her brain wanted to shut down and just feel, she had to be mindful of his condition.

Pulling away just enough to soak in his beautiful face, Mia whispered, "Welcome back."

"Mia, how..." he trailed off as a wash of memories crowded in. "Oh. I remember now."

"We'll have a lot to deal with, but we need you at full strength first. I know you just woke, but you'll need more rest."

"No." He shook his head and steadied himself against the edge of the bed, spinning his legs until they dangled off the side. "No, I've had enough laying down."

"Donovan, please—"

"How did you escape?"

The question cut off any protest she'd had on the tip of her tongue. "I agreed to work with Ricky."

"And?" he prompted.

"And...I told him who I really am."

"You did what!" He stood abruptly, then immediately fell back again. Mia grabbed his arms before he lost all balance, holding him upright. "Why would you do that?"

"It was the only way. The only way to ensure your safety."

His hand reached out, cupped her cheek. "And who will ensure yours?"

"Selena. And you," Mia said with a smirk.

"I can see we have a lot to talk about." He breathed out a sigh. "Help me into the shower, would you? I think it will go far toward making me feel human again."

Though she wanted to argue, Mia nodded in understanding and shifted to take his weight. He stood on shaky legs, but he stood. One slow step at a time, they made it into the bathroom.

Blasting the water of the shower, Mia helped Donovan out of his remaining clothes. Testing the spray, she nodded and wrapped her arm around him once again so he could step inside.

"Mia, you're getting soaked," he said with worry and humor in his tone.

Glancing down, she let out half a laugh. Meeting his questioning look, she explained, "It's like the night we first met. When you saved me from the hot spray on my open wounds. You were soaked that night, as I am now."

His lips tipped up, but his gaze remained steady, serious. One hand slid up her arm and framed her face. Pressing his lips to hers once, softly, Mia let out a moan and sank into him. With gentle hands, he removed her clothes and yanked her against his hard frame. His mouth trailed down her neck, nipping over the racing pulse there.

"Donovan, wait." She tried to be the voice of reason, but his tongue and clever fingers were having none of it.

"I can't," he breathed against her ear. "I need you. Right now."

Without waiting for protest, he gripped her hips, dragging her off her feet. With her back pressed against the cool tile, he joined them together in one long stroke. Mia's head fell back with a gasp, all protests done. He moved fast, frantic. She met his pace with an equal amount of desperation.

He was at turns rough and gentle, passionate and loving. And relentless. Always relentless. He pushed and pushed, leaving no time to think, no time to breathe. Mia wound up so tight and fast the explosion rocked out of her, surprising them both.

The endless waves of pleasure wrapped him up, forced him over the edge with her. Mia's head rolled back against the wall as her feet found purchase on the ground. He was no longer the only unsteady one.

Collapsing against her, his mouth found the crevice between shoulder and neck, and he breathed deep, taking her scent into his lungs. Mia's own arms wrapped around his waist, not only needing the contact but also ensuring he remained on his feet.

"That wasn't a good idea," she finally murmured.

Pulling away, he looked down with hurt in his eyes. "I'm sorry. So sorry for everything. For not telling you the truth when you were with me, for..."

"Donovan." Mia said his name sternly, forcing him to stop apologizing. "First of all, I only meant that you're still healing, and

I should have stopped this before you were more injured. Second, it's all right—all of it. I'm not upset with you. Honestly, I don't think I ever was."

"You're...not?"

"No," she answered truthfully. "I was in shock and terrified. That lasted several days, in fact. But...now that I know Selena's there, we...we can talk. We worked together to save you. She saved you."

"You both did. You are her, as she is you. And I love you, I love you both, I love all of you. Always have, always will."

The racing beat of her heart stumbled and fell before rising, so bright and full it nearly burst. Unable to match his words, Mia simply met his mouth with hers and poured everything she felt in that moment into a kiss.

When they finally parted for breath, Mia said the words she'd been dreading. "What now?"

"I've a few ideas." Donovan grinned wickedly.

Laughing, Mia slapped his hand away before lathering shampoo in her hands. "I mean about the DeLucas. And me, the police."

"You've already begun a plan."

Blowing out a breath, Mia massaged her fingers against his scalp. "I did. We did, Selena and I. And I don't think you're going to like the rest of it."

Mia waited until they'd dressed to spell out the plan. Donovan paced the distance between kitchen and living room, clearly unhappy. Reaching the wall, he'd turn and continue, muttering to himself as Mia watched. Needless to say, he wasn't thrilled with the plan.

"It's too dangerous." He finally stopped the manic pace and spoke directly to her. "I can't risk losing you again."

"Donovan." One word, his name, was enough to have him stilling completely. Standing, Mia approached him, placing her hands against his crossed forearms. "It's the only way. We have to. We need to rid the world of the DeLucas."

The rest, she left unsaid. Anguish poured from him like water from a cliff. Understanding, Mia took a step closer, and then another. Wrapped her arms around his waist, pressed her head against his chest until, with a sigh, he loosened his arms to mimic her gesture. "I can't lose you. Not when I've just gotten you."

"You won't."

"How can you promise that?"

Tipping her head back, Mia smiled. "Because I've got you, watching my back."

"We've a lot to plan."

"We've got a week. I'd prefer to do it sooner, but I'm afraid we'll need a week. And we're going to need some help."

"I'll do my part," Donovan assured her, as much as he assured himself. "You'll have the more difficult tasks."

Nodding, Mia stepped back, silently mourning the loss of warmth. There was time for that later. Now, they needed to move. "I need to turn myself in at the station. You need to remain hidden. I'll come find you tomorrow night."

"Mia." Donovan stopped her with a hand on her arm as she turned to leave. "I love you. Be safe."

Giving in, Mia collapsed into his embrace and met his mouth with hers. "I love you, too."

Before her body betrayed her and forced her to stay, Mia turned and opened the door. This time, she remained on guard, gun out and trained on anyone lurking in the shadows. At this point, she didn't think Ricky would turn on her, but their partnership could be considered tenuous at best.

Making it down to ground level, Mia opened access to the underground tunnels and made the long walk toward downtown. Their bikes would be somewhere down there, and she knew

Donovan would take care of them when he was able. For now, he had plenty to keep him occupied.

Though her nerves were jumping like crazy, Mia also felt oddly excited to see her precinct again. Alec, the chief, the rest of the crew who had once been her friends. Of course, she now knew that Ricky had one or more moles in the department. She couldn't trust anyone—save Alec.

Alec was the only one she was sure about. She just prayed he'd help.

Reaching the building she'd been aiming for, Mia quickly released her weapons belt and stashed it near the entrance. The last thing she needed was a standoff with the police department.

Taking a deep, steadying breath, Mia opened the secret entrance and made her way up the stairs. She wore all black and carried nothing in her pockets. No money, no identification. No weapons. Her goal was to make it to the station without being spotted. And once there—she only prayed the rest would work.

At the main level, she checked video surveillance of the hallway beyond and found it empty. Slipping into the cool interior of professional offices, Mia walked down the hall not slow, not fast. Purposely. Reaching the front doors, she pushed them open without sparing the lobby guard a glance.

The bright sunlight of morning hit her eyes, blinding her for a moment. She'd forgone even her dark sunglasses and found herself regretting that move. Straightening her shoulders, Mia continued her steady pace down the street and around the corner, stopping on the sidewalk leading into the central precinct.

A few uniformed officers wandered around, paying her no mind. Sucking in one more breath, she strode right through the front doors.

As she passed the front desk, the officer on duty glanced up, eyes widening as recognition clicked in. Without pause, she rounded the area and called the elevator. When the doors slid open, Mia began to pass the collection of desks where uniforms and detectives sat, hard at work.

Across the room, her eyes landed on Alec, and she nearly faltered in her resolve. Behind and all around her, the whispers began: her name, Selena's, Donovan's. After watching Alec for a beat, Mia turned her attention to the chief's office.

He stood in the doorway with his mouth agape. Silence settled over the room as his jaw worked, trying to find the words. Marching right up to him, Mia said, "Chief."

"Mia," he breathed out. "Detective Gonzalez."

Seeming to snap out of his stupor, the chief glanced around the room before motioning her inside his office. From the corner of her eye, she saw Alec approaching but waved him off.

"Give us a few minutes, all right?" Mia said quietly, trying to convey the need for stealth with her eyes alone.

Something in her expression had him nodding, agreeing. With a grateful smile, Mia stepped inside the chief's office and closed the door.

"Mia," the chief said again with palpable relief. In a move that surprised them both, he wrapped his arms around her back. When he pulled away again, tears lined the edges of his eyes. "It's so good to have you back."

Either the chief was an excellent actor, or he truly meant what he said. Mia didn't suspect him of being on the DeLucas' payroll, but she couldn't be positive about that, either. Even if he wasn't, Mia was relatively certain his office was bugged, so she acted accordingly.

"Sir," Mia replied with an appreciative nod. "It's good to be back."

"We'll need to do a full debrief with the FBI, but please, tell me what's happened."

"Donovan's business is shutting down as we speak. I've collected enough evidence to put him away for a long time."

The chief nodded and asked a few more questions. Mia lied through her teeth. For now, that was how it had to be. Until she knew she could trust Chief Alvarez, until she knew if his office was bugged, she couldn't say anything she didn't want Ricky to hear.

When he finally released her, Mia went out and met the questioning looks from everyone in the room. Not caring about anyone but Alec, she walked over to his desk and gave him a hug. "The chief cleared me for research. Anything you need help with?"

Her tone and the strange way she acted alerted Alec to the need for discretion. His eyes bore into hers, seeking answers, but he casually lifted a file and handed it to her. "This just came in."

"I'll take a look. Thanks."

After Mia worked for a few hours, she went over to Alec and handed him back the file. Under the file, she'd left him a note.

Say nothing out loud. Meet me at this address at midnight. Don't take your car. Watch your back. I'll explain everything then.

Twenty-Five

AT MIDNIGHT, MIA PACED THE lobby of her meeting spot with Alec. When he arrived, she would be trusting him with so much more than the truth.

Dressed in dark clothes, Alec arrived just after midnight, taking a good look around as he walked through the door.

"Mia," he said with relief on spotting her. "What the hell is going on?"

Placing a finger against her lips to indicate silence, she quickly ran the device over his clothes to check for a tracker or bug. Finding him clean, she gestured for him to follow.

They made their way down the hall, pausing at the small scanner at a locked door. Making sure they were alone, Mia pressed her hand against the pad and waited for the mechanism to read her print. Once the door opened, she pulled Alec through into the dark stairwell, making sure the door closed securely before moving down the steps.

He seemed to understand the need for silence, though his curiosity had to be on overdrive. When they reached a seemingly smooth wall, Mia paused, spreading her hands to find the little niche that would allow them access.

When the wall shifted and revealed what lay beyond, Alec's wide eyes stared in shock. "Holy shit."

They stepped into the cavernous room connected to the longer tunnel. Sliding the door closed again, Mia finally spoke. "It's so good to see you."

They embraced, even as he continued to gaze around. When she pulled away again, Mia studied his face, the dark smudges under his eyes, the weary lines around his mouth. "I've gotta tell you, you've looked better."

He smirked and gave her a little shove on her shoulder. "I blame you."

"And I'm sorry for that. Truly. I—I don't even know where to begin."

"The beginning is usually a good place."

Pacing away, she ran her hands through her dark hair and let out a sigh. "First off, I don't know who to trust at the precinct. Apart from you. The DeLucas have informants."

"Besides Adam?" he asked, eyebrows pressing together. "That rat bastard."

"Tell me about it. Though, he won't be a problem anymore."

"What do you mean?"

"It's part of the story." She launched into what had actually happened since she'd gone undercover. Mia decided to gloss over the training with Agent McKenzie and the mock-torture she'd executed before leaving Mia in a cell for Donovan to find. "Donovan isn't what I'd expected. He cared for me, brought me back to health. I started sitting in on some business deals, was gaining his trust, when we were attacked."

"The explosion," Alec murmured, his voice shaky. "Jesus, Mia, I thought you were dead."

"There was a minute there I thought I would be. I don't know how they found us—and believe me, it was the DeLucas—but they did."

"Adam. Even before you got on CCTV, we'd narrowed in on your location from when Donovan picked you up."

"You followed us. Of course. I don't know why I didn't piece that together."

"There were a few other things for you to worry about. So, what happened after that?"

"We stayed at a safe house, questioned some people about who put the hit out. Then Adam was caught sneaking around the explosion site, and Donovan's men held him. The first time I saw him, I was so worried. I thought it was my fault for getting that report out with the address. I thought he'd shown up on his own to, I don't know, prove something to the department. Turns out, he was behind it all."

"How did you find that out?" Alec asked.

"Donovan's got a pretty good team. They did a visual search, ran his face through whatever program they had, got a match from a newspaper article back when Adam was in high school. Before he changed his name. Donovan leaked the information to the police."

For a moment, Mia remembered wanting to kill Adam, to silence him. The horrible guilt that ensued. And the way she'd turned to Donovan for comfort.

Alec didn't seem to notice her momentary distraction. "I'd wondered if that was you."

"After that, we went out of the country." Pausing here, Mia thought over their trip fondly and knew she needed to skip quite a few details of her time in Europe, too. "Donovan had to meet with clients, didn't want to leave me alone with threats hanging over our heads. When we got back, we exchanged Adam for information from the DeLucas."

"What information?"

Pulling a flash drive from her pocket, Mia handed it over. "This. I think you'll find it very interesting."

300

"I'll take a look."

"You have a safe computer to use?"

He nodded. "I started doing sweeps of my apartment after I found out about Adam, made sure I wasn't being watched. Found two bugs. Took my personal computer in, had it checked out."

"That's good. Smart."

"So, what's the plan?"

"First things first, we need to figure out who the informants are."

"Have you talked to the chief about this?" When she remained silent, Alec pieced this part together himself. "You're not sure you can trust him."

"I think I can," Mia said to soothe any ruffled feathers. "I just can't be sure. I need to be sure. When we take the DeLucas down, I want no one around who can help them."

"What about Agent McKenzie?"

"You've met her?" Mia asked with no small amount of surprise.

"The chief called her in after you showed up on my doorstep. By the way, can you explain that? What the hell happened to you?"

For a while, Mia remained silent, observing her partner. Yes, she trusted him. But not with this. "For now, I can't explain that night. Please believe me when I say I'll tell you everything as soon as I can, okay? As for Agent McKenzie—yes, we can trust her. And we're going to need her for our plan to work."

Letting out his own breath, Alec eventually nodded. "What do you need me to do?"

After explaining the plan to Alec, Mia led him down the tunnel to another building in case he'd been followed. Mia said her good-byes and continued on her way. She'd promised Donovan she'd meet with him this night, and they had much to discuss.

Knowing he'd still be at the original loft, Mia set out at a jog until she reached the correct tunnel offshoot. Making her way up from the bottom level, she moved through the lobby and to their private elevator, waving at the security as she passed.

As soon as the elevator began to rise, she knew Donovan would be alerted. He'd be waiting for her.

When she stepped out and approached the thick door, it opened before she could place her hand on the pad. Donovan's eyes traced her form, settling back on her steady gaze. Without a word, Mia moved into his arms, met his waiting lips with hers.

He maneuvered them inside, pushing her against the door as it closed. When he pulled away, spreading teasing kisses along her throat, he spoke softly. "Hello."

"Hi," Mia returned with a light laugh. Before they could get too lost in each other, she moved away and asked, "How did everything go today?"

"It's all under control. Mason is waiting on our call."

Nodding, Mia said, "Let's do that now. We've only a few hours before I have to be at the station."

His dark eyes deepened with desire. "Quickly, then. There are much more pleasant things I'd rather spend our time doing."

Flames licked along her skin at his tone, his hooded gaze. Unable to speak, Mia simply nodded and waited for him to make the call. Minutes later, they headed back down into the tunnels. Donovan led the way to their meeting spot, their loosely connected hands their only contact.

"Where are the bikes?" Mia asked.

"We'll retrieve them after the meeting. I meant to earlier today but didn't have time."

That, and he was still recovering. "Tell me about your day."

While he talked about the calls he'd made, Mia continuously ran through the plan in her mind. Tomorrow, she would be fully debriefed with Agent McKenzie and Chief Alvarez. Part of the truth would come out then—would have to come out.

They made their way to yet another building, abandoned, condemned, much as the safe house had been.

Mason—whom Mia had only met as Selena—waited in the dark space, a messenger bag slung over his shoulder. His tall, lanky frame held confidence even in this dangerous situation. By agreeing to help, he'd also be putting himself, his career, on the line. For that alone, he'd earned her respect.

"Donovan, Selena," he said by way of greeting. "Let me set up and show you what I've got."

Flipping on a lamp on the only piece of furniture in the room, Mason unpacked his computer from the bag and set himself up on the table. Donovan and Mia huddled behind him, watching as his nimble fingers worked the keys.

"This is all I can gather on my own. The identifications you gave me earlier helped make some connections." Donovan had given Mason the wallets that Selena had stolen off the guards during their escape. "The police will have a wider data selection to pull from."

"What, exactly, are we looking at here?" Mia asked.

"It's a program similar to what the police have been using in recent years. It pulls data from phone calls, social media, and e-mails. Basically, any online presence."

That information was slightly terrifying. "What happens after it pulls the data?"

"Connections are made. Once I have the full roster from the police department, I can start cross-referencing them with known members of the DeLuca family and their...associates. Smartphones especially help with this—phone locations are constantly pinged. If they're meeting in person, my system will track when and where and how often."

"Holy shit," Mia said. "It works well for us now, but I may never carry a cell phone again."

Mason grinned over his shoulder at her. "That's just the tip of the iceberg."

"What do you have for us so far?" Donovan asked.

Pulling a flash drive from a zippered pocket of his bag, Mason handed it over. "This is a list of all known DeLuca members. I'll add to it as more information comes in. Chief Alvarez has been cleared. I checked into him specifically, as you asked. If he is working for the DeLucas, then he's the best I've ever seen at hiding it."

Relief washed through Mia, though she kept a poker face. Mason handed over another device, small enough to slip into her pocket. "The other thing you asked for."

Giving him an appreciative smile, Mia looked over to Donovan as he spoke.

"Good work, Mason," Donovan said, clapping the younger man on the shoulder. "If all goes well, we'll meet tomorrow night with someone from the department. His name is Ronnie Caldwell if you wouldn't mind checking into him first. I'm guessing Ronnie is short for Ronald."

"You've got it. And might I add, it's a bit strange working with the police for once."

Donovan and Mia shared a smile before he responded. "You have no idea."

"Anything else?"

"Just continue with your search. We'll be in touch."

They left, retrieving the bikes before heading back to the loft. Once parked, Mia dismounted and glanced over at Donovan. He seemed to be contemplating something, and she felt a little uneasy under his watchful gaze. "What is it?"

"You remember how to ride. Do you remember everything?"

"Yes and no. My time as Selena is there, but it didn't come back in a big rush. She's there, in my mind. She talks to me. It's more like when I need to remember something about her time, she tells me. Does that make sense?"

"It does."

"It's so strange." Suddenly unsure, Mia crossed her arms over her stomach, cupping each elbow in opposite palms. "How can you still want to be with me?"

No longer able to stand the distance between them, Donovan approached and placed his hands against her rigid biceps. "I love you—all of you. Once Selena and I were together, we held nothing back. I know you better than anyone. I know all of you. As you know me better than anyone. That information is inside you, somewhere. When you're ready, you'll remember that, too."

"You think she's still protecting me? I know about our dad," Mia added when his eyebrows creased together.

"I think she'll always protect you. That's why she was made. But she won't hide anything from you, not anymore."

That's true, Selena added silently. *You have only to ask.*

Sucking in a breath, Mia nodded for both of them and followed Donovan inside.

△ △ △

GETTING BACK INTO THE ROUTINE of detective work proved more difficult than Mia ever thought possible. The chief wanted to ease her back in, though she assured him she was ready and willing to work. He'd convinced her to take a few days, a week, to be sure. Alec would still be her partner, but she would be doing paperwork and research for the time being.

Doing that kind of work allowed her to watch and listen. Every person around her had become a suspect of being in the DeLucas' pocket. While she trusted Mason—and Ronnie, once the two of them began working together—to weed out the perpetrators, she'd always trusted her own gut instinct more.

When Agent McKenzie arrived late morning, Alec and Mia were pulled into a closed-door meeting with the chief.

In her pocket, Mia carried the small device given to her by Mason before they'd left the night before. It would block any surveillance equipment in a fifty-foot radius. Clicking it on, Mia nodded discreetly at Alec as he closed the door.

"Mia," Agent McKenzie said with a handshake. "Good to see you made it out alive."

"Thanks to you," Mia returned, feeling an odd sort of kinship with the older woman.

"I'm here for a debrief," she said, relaxing against the edge of the desk. "I know you've gone over everything with Chief Alvarez, but I'd like to hear it again."

Sitting, waiting for Alec to do the same, Mia took a deep breath before she began. "What I told you the other day was the truth. But it wasn't the whole story."

The chief's eyebrows furrowed together. "What do you mean?"

"I was approached by Ricky DeLuca. He knew, from Adam Malone—aka Adam DeLuca—that I was Mia Gonzalez, undercover as Selena. He held me for nearly a week, trying to convince me to work for him."

"Why are you telling us this now, and not before?" Agent McKenzie asked.

"I didn't know who I could trust." Looking directly at the chief, Mia gave him a helpless look. "I thought I could, I felt I could, but I had to be sure. I hope you understand."

His eyes had gone hard but softened as she explained. He let out a sigh. "You think we have informants in the department."

"Not think. I know. Alec and I have been working at weeding out the traitors."

"Is it safe to speak in here?" Agent McKenzie asked.

"It is right now. I have a suppressing device."

Her eyebrows rose at that information. "Where did you get that?"

"A contact from my time as Selena. Here's the thing: my cover was blown with the DeLucas, but not with Donovan. He shut down the business at my word and went underground."

"He still needs to be brought in," the agent replied.

"He will be. After we take down the DeLucas. If we move on Donovan now, we'll lose any leverage we have on the DeLucas."

"How so?"

The question hung out there while Mia battled internally at the next piece of information. If done right, it would convince Agent McKenzie and the chief to leave Donovan alone for the time being. They only needed to buy time.

"Because I convinced Ricky DeLuca that I was Selena."

"You what?" Alec burst out, speaking for the first time.

"I was in a tight spot," Mia answered evenly. "He held me at one of his properties outside of town. He was holding Donovan, too. Had me under constant guard. The place was crawling with his henchmen. When the opportunity arose, I escaped with Donovan. He made it out. I didn't. Instead, I convinced Ricky that I was already a dirty cop, playing both sides."

Silence descended upon the office. Mia waited, knowing there would be follow-up questions. It was imperative that she persuade the three in this room to believe her story.

"How did you convince him?" Agent McKenzie asked.

"Donovan had told me details about Selena's life to help me remember. One of those details included her first meeting with Ricky, so I played it back for him word for word. I think between that and the fact that what I was claiming was so outlandish that it had to be true convinced him."

Keeping her gaze and breathing level, Mia waited for one of them to poke holes in her cover story. With it being so close to the truth, Mia mentally crossed her fingers they would believe it.

"That was quick thinking," Agent McKenzie finally replied. "And since Ricky knows about Selena's feelings for Donovan, if you moved on him now, Ricky would realize the ruse."

"Exactly," Mia answered.

"Jesus, Mia," Alec muttered, rubbing at an ache over his brow. "You should have told me."

Glancing over at him, she shrugged. "I'm telling you now. Look, there's more. I've had someone running algorithms to try to determine who the moles are in the department. I've got a short list of suspects, but I'd like Ronnie to work with this person. He'll need full access."

"You're talking a full-scale investigation into everyone in the department," the chief said with a heavy sigh. "In secret. Using who I'm assuming is a criminal."

"He'll also need complete anonymity and immunity."

"Done," Agent McKenzie said decisively before the chief could argue. He opened his mouth to do just that when she straightened, crossed her arms, and faced him full on. "Chief Alvarez, you've got a shitshow on your hands. The DeLucas have plagued this city long enough. It's time to go at them, full bore. We have something we've never had before—an inside person. This investigation needs to remain between the four of us. Mia, you have the full backing of the FBI. Tell me what you need."

This was more than Mia could have hoped for. Though she could tell that the chief felt off-kilter, blown away by the amount of information she'd just laid at his feet, under that he seethed with rage at the thought of rats under his nose.

"There are four people in the department we're ninety-nine percent positive are moles. Roger Williams, Sonya Mitchells, Samuel Nicolson, and James Healy."

"Christ," the chief muttered, rubbing a hand over his face. "I've golfed with Healy. Went to Sonya's wedding."

"I know, Chief. So did I. We trusted all of them. We trusted Adam."

He sucked in a breath and nodded. "What do we do about them?"

"For now, we do nothing. Let them believe I'm sticking to my story and helping the DeLucas. I'll also need to prove my loyalty for the time being."

"How do you suggest you do that?" the chief asked.

"Have someone connected to them get arrested. I'm sure we've got warrants or reasonable enough suspicion to book one of their underlings. Once they're in, I'll get them out. It'll satisfy Ricky for the time being while we work to take his family down once and for all."

"I'll put Miller and Weaver on it."

"Great." Mia stood, extending her hand to Agent McKenzie for anyone watching. "Tomorrow night at midnight, go to the Woodworth Building, wait inside the lobby. Chief, go to the Empire Building at quarter after. I'll find you both. We'll be able to speak freely."

"And me?" Alec asked.

"Same place as last time," Mia said with a wink. "Tonight, bring Ronnie. Tomorrow, the four of us will meet again."

Twenty-Six

THE REST OF THE DAY, Mia busied herself with paperwork, research for Alec's ongoing cases, and a few other light things the chief gave her. Around three o'clock, Miller and Weaver walked in with two of the DeLucas' flunkies in tow.

Though Mia looked up, she feigned disinterest in the commotion they made. From the research she'd done on the family before going undercover as Selena, she recognized the two young men as Jessie and Emilio Moreno, second cousins to Ricky. They were drug pushers, low in rank, and quintessential scum bags.

Miller and Weaver made a show of pushing them back toward the cells for booking, but Mia continued with her research as if it were all just another day.

At half-past, she stood, stretched, and made her way to the bathroom. When she returned, Mia found a note placed carefully under her coffee cup.

Take care of it.

One guess as to what that meant. More curious would be to find out who went lurking when she'd left the area.

Luckily, she'd asked Mason to tap into the precinct's security feeds. Not only would he be able to tell her who dropped off the little note, but he'd also replaced the missing audio file from her meeting with Agent McKenzie, Alec, and the chief with a dubbed-over version of what her recount should have been. Hopefully, with anyone listening none the wiser.

She'd left out that particular detail with the others. Allowing a criminal hacker into their system went against every ingrained training as police officers. Taking the note and slipping it surreptitiously into an empty file, Mia went back to work. Though she'd 'take care of it,' doing so now would raise too much suspicion. Better to wait until early morning.

Instead, she packed up for the day and made her way to the car. This would be the first time she'd be going back to her apartment since before she'd gone undercover. Mia found it strange, to say the least. Though the worn stairs were familiar, it no longer felt like hers. Once she opened the door, Mia took a good look around, waiting to feel the relief of arriving home. The place had been kept clean and orderly, nothing out of place. Still, it didn't feel like home. Something was missing.

Donovan. From now and going forward, he was the only home she needed.

Wandering through the small space, Mia ran a hand over countertops and along furniture, reacquainting herself with each item. When she reached the bedroom, Mia looked at the pale-yellow comforter and wondered how she'd ever thought she'd been happy here. Living a half-life. Living a lie.

Sensing more than hearing an intruder, Mia spun with a gun in her hands and approached the doorway with caution. Her sights trained at chest level, she inched forward until she could see clearly into the living area.

Though she couldn't see anyone, Mia still felt a presence. As she moved forward to check outside the door, a dark form blocked her view.

Before she could react, the man placed his finger against her lips, asking for silence. Unable to disobey those dark, pleading eyes, Mia nodded her understanding and slipped the gun back into its holster.

Donovan lifted a device from his pocket, slowly moving about each room. He unveiled a bug under a lamp, another in each bedroom. He left them alone but motioned for Mia to turn on the suppressing device she'd used earlier.

"What are you doing here?" Mia asked as soon as she flipped the switch.

"I needed to see you," he replied.

"Is everything all righ—" Before she could finish, his lips crushed hers in a desperate, passionate kiss. His hands slid around her hips, lifting her straight off the ground. Helpless to do anything but hang on, he moved until Mia pressed against that pale-yellow blanket.

Though his kiss remained frantic, his hands moved slow, gentle. The juxtaposition of the two left her weak, needy. And instantly on fire.

Then his hands gripped hers above her head, leaving her immobile and helpless under his ruthless attack. His mouth dipped, teased along her jaw and neck. He moved ruthlessly down her body, exploring and kissing as one hand held hers tight. Mia struggled but not in protest. She wanted to get her hands on him. Needed to.

He moved relentlessly lower, kissing and nipping along the most sensitive parts of her skin. Breath short, Mia struggled to protest, to beg for more. But when he used his tongue, all thought flew out the door.

Crying out, writhing beneath his firm grasp, Mia shook and trembled with the force of it. His hands released hers, but all she could do was grip the blanket, struggling to remain tethered to the earth when his mouth and fingers sent her flying to the heavens.

And then he was with her, driving her up and over the edge so hard and fast, again and again. When they finally crashed together, flew out among the stars, she clung to him as her body went limp and all breath released in a single whoosh.

They lay silent for several long minutes, regaining their breath as their hearts slowed to a normal rhythm. Donovan lifted his head from her chest and gazed down at her with love shining in his dark eyes.

"Definitely worth the trip over here."

Letting out a short laugh that did delicious things to their still connected bodies, Mia replied, "Definitely worth it."

"Mia," he said gently, brushing a kiss along her chin. "I'm not done yet."

And before she knew his intentions, he began moving again. Slow, so tortuously slow. Building her up with a steady burn. Like the frog unknowingly being boiled alive, he pushed her closer and closer toward the wildfire he'd created.

Again, they fell, and again, he built them back up. They didn't speak. Didn't need to. Their connection felt so intimate, so intense Mia nearly forgot how to breathe on her own.

When they finally stopped moving, lying in the dark as the minutes ticked away toward midnight, she found the little bit of energy she had left and spoke. "I need to go," Mia said with a sigh. "Can't leave Alec and Ronnie hanging around too long."

"You're sure you don't want me involved with this?"

"Not yet," Mia said, brushing a kiss against his mouth. "But soon."

"Mia?" Donovan said as she stood to get dressed.

"What is it?"

He started to say something but hesitated. Instead, he said simply, "Be safe."

"Always."

Alec and Ronnie arrived just seconds after Mia entered the lobby of their meeting spot. Smoothing down the black leather jacket, she hoped her earlier activities weren't too obvious to her partner and the shy computer expert.

When Alec's eyes swept briefly down her form, she knew he could tell she'd not been sitting at home meditating. His possible delicate sensibilities weren't something to worry about right now, however.

With a finger against her lips, Mia did a sweep of their clothes and found no listening devices. Ronnie smirked at her once she'd cleared them. "I already did that."

"Just double-checking, then," Mia answered with a shrug. "But it's good practice for both of you. Yourselves, your homes. Anything you carry with you."

"This is like a movie," Ronnie said. "Kind of exciting."

Raising her eyebrows at Alec behind the younger man's back, they shared a smile of indulgence before she led them both to the doorway that would gain access to the lower levels. Ronnie geeked out over the scanning technology before being shocked silent when the wall slid open at the bottom of the steps to reveal the underground tunnels.

"Holy crap, these are real!" he said excitedly, his face bright with curiosity and questions.

Chuckling, Mia closed the wall and gestured toward the bikes Donovan had helped her bring over. "You still know how to ride?"

Alec let out a low whistle of appreciation. "Nice machine. Of course I remember. You know how?"

"Picked it up recently," she said. "Ronnie, hop on with me. Mason is waiting. And remember, he still thinks I'm Selena, so act accordingly."

They both nodded, and all three mounted, riding in mostly silence, though Ronnie pointed and yelled over the whip of wind

314

when he spotted something worthy of exclamation. With the bikes, it only took a few minutes to arrive at the destination.

They entered the same building the security team used to hold Adam. Above the cell level was Mason's domain.

Though she'd thought it strange Donovan would keep enemies in the same space as all their tech, he'd explained that it remained secure because it was the last place anyone expected their base of operations to be. The security had been heightened after the raid on the offices, so Mia waited outside the third-level door while Mason performed a scan of their persons. Her belt held several weapons, as she knew Alec would be carrying. Ronnie only had his computer equipment.

A slot opened beside the door, large enough for a briefcase to fit into. Mason's disembodied voice filled the small space. "Place your weapons in the container, Detective Woods."

Though he sent Mia an incredulous look, she gave Alec an encouraging nod, and he complied, pulling out his gun and a knife he carried in his boot. If something went down, she still had her weapons—and Mason trusted her.

Once Alec's weapons were securely placed inside the wall, the door clicked open, and Mason stood on the opposite side, sizing the newcomers up. "Hello, I'm Mason. You are?"

"Ronnie," came the reply. He sounded nervous. "Ronnie Caldwell."

"I know." Mason grinned. "Come on in. And when you leave, forget my face."

Ronnie and Alec entered with caution, staring around them in wonder. Mia had only seen Mason's work area once before, and the sheer amount of electronics still amazed her. The fact that she could only put names to about a fourth of what she saw told her how in over her head she was.

"Holy crap," Ronnie murmured, stunned speechless this time. His nervous system certainly received a workout this night. "This is incredible."

"Thanks," Mason replied off-hand. "Come on, I'll show you what I've been working on."

Alec and Mia hung back, clearly out of their league. While Ronnie and Mason talked in increasingly difficult-to-understand language, Mia glanced over at her partner. "Everything all right?"

"Yeah," he answered, running a hand through his hair. "Just tired, I guess. On a few levels. Haven't had a decent night's sleep in weeks."

"I know how you feel," Mia said. All too well. "It'll be over soon."

They watched the other two in comfortable silence for a few minutes. When Alec made sure they wouldn't be overheard, he said, "About you and Donovan."

"What about us?" Mia returned, refusing to make eye contact.

"Something going on there?"

Pressing her lips together, Mia wondered how much Alec could take. "It's...complicated."

"No kidding. He's not underground, is he?"

"No."

"Are you going to tell the chief? Agent McKenzie?"

"Not yet."

"Mia..."

"Everything will work out, Alec. I promise. Do you still trust me?" Now she met his gaze, left nothing hidden.

He blew out a breath. "I do. God help me, I do."

"Good," Mia said, taking a step forward. "Let's see what these guys came up with."

△ △ △

WHEN MIA RETURNED HOME, SHE managed a few restless hours of sleep before dressing and heading into the precinct. The two DeLuca boys had spent the night in jail; her first mission of the day would be to get them released.

Arriving well before anyone else on the day shift, Mia brewed a pot of coffee in the breakroom and took two cups down to evidence. Martin Westbrook, keeper of evidence and close to retiring, manned the desk.

"Mia!" he boomed out. "It's so good to see you."

"You too, Marty," Mia replied, handing off one of the mugs. "How are Sheila, the kids?"

"Would you believe Amy's pregnant? That'll be our fifth grandkid," he said with a wide smile.

"Congratulations," Mia said with heartfelt sincerity. "If any two people are meant to be grandparents, it's you and Sheila."

Two bright spots appeared on his cheeks as he waved her off. "Enough about me. You've been through quite the experience yourself. How are you, really?"

"To be honest, it's been strange being back. To remember who I am again. They don't tell you that part before you go undercover."

"No, and I can only imagine. Anything I can do to help?"

Perfect opening. "Actually, I was hoping to pull a couple files, review some of Alec's cases before I'm approved for active duty again. Mind?"

"Of course not," he said, gesturing her through. "Just let me know what you decide to check out."

"You got it," Mia said, walking through to the lock-up. Once inside, she found one of Alec's cases before continuing to peruse. Pausing at the most recent files, Mia glanced back to make sure Martin was otherwise preoccupied before opening the box and removing key evidence from the Moreno brothers' case.

Placing the extracted evidence carefully inside one of the closed files, Mia grabbed one more of Alec's cases and checked out with Martin.

Back at her desk, she found Alec had just come in for the day. His eyes dropped to the files in her hands, and a wordless understanding passed between them. He would find some excuse to be in the evidence lock-up this morning to help keep suspicion away from Mia. The chief would also send other officers through to help the ruse.

When Jessie's and Emilio's lawyers came in to ask for the evidence being held against them and finding none, the brothers would be let free.

And Ricky might trust Mia for just a few days. That was all she needed.

For two hours, Mia worked diligently on research before the chief called Alec and her into his office. "Woods, Gonzalez, I need to speak with you."

Alec and Mia shared a look before doing as they were told. Entering the room, they stood before Chief Alvarez and waited for him to speak. "Gonzalez, you've been cleared for fieldwork. A new case just came through; I'd like the two of you to handle it."

He passed over a file, which she took and opened, allowing Alec to read over her shoulder. "I suggest you begin with the list of witnesses. Any questions?"

"No, sir," they both answered. Alvarez nodded his dismissal, and they left the room.

"I'm driving," Alec declared as they grabbed what they needed.

"Fine with me," Mia answered. "It'll give me a chance to go over the file."

They moved in silence, through the precinct and out into the parking lot. Once they'd slid into Alec's vehicle, he held up a finger as he removed a scanner from his pocket to check for bugs. Finding none, he breathed out a sigh. "We're clear."

Bringing out the suppressor, Mia shrugged. "Just in case."

"I hate this," Alec announced. "I hate being on edge. Not being able to speak openly, in my own car or my own damn house. This is nuts."

"It'll be over soon," Mia promised. "And taking down the DeLucas will be worth it."

"Yeah," Alec said, running a hand through his hair before starting the engine. "Yeah."

As they got moving, Mia reached over and squeezed his forearm gently. "You're doing great. Thank you, by the way."

"For what?"

"For always having my back. I couldn't do this without you."

"Sure you could," he said with a grin. "But it wouldn't be nearly as much fun."

Satisfied that his moment of uncertainty had passed, Mia turned her attention to the file and listed off the address they'd hit first.

The case involved an electronic store robbery. Not typically the kind of case the chief passed on to Alec and Mia, but she understood he gave them busy work for a couple of reasons. One, they would be gone when the Moreno brothers got released. And two, it gave Alec and Mia time to talk, away from the stress of being under constant watch.

Chief Alvarez had always been a good man, and it made Mia happy to know he'd not let her down.

The rest of the day almost felt like old times. They parted ways without mentioning their late-night plans. Mia found Alec just before midnight, and together they headed through the tunnels to find Agent McKenzie. Though her face remained stoic, Mia could tell seeing the tunnels first-hand amazed the agent.

When they collected the chief, Mia watched with amusement as he spluttered expletives. "Jesus, they're real. I mean, I knew they were real, you told me, but wow."

They stood in a loose circle, not bothering to move beyond this particular off-shoot. The chief walked over to the main tunnel, looked down and back several times, just taking in the sheer amount of space.

"It's just incredible," he mumbled to himself as he re-approached.

"It is, and it explains a lot. However, we've got bigger fish to fry tonight," Mia finally said to help them focus. "Agent McKenzie, what have you got for us?"

Unzipping the backpack that she wore, Agent McKenzie handed over a thick stack of files. "This is everything the FBI has on the DeLucas."

"Perfect," Mia said, glancing through with Alec looking over her shoulder. "Yesterday, right after Jessie and Emilio were arrested, I found a note on my desk asking me to 'take care of it.' The note was left by Sam Nicolson."

"Do I want to know how you know that?" Chief Alvarez asked.

Her bland look seemed to be answer enough. "There's more. Alec?"

Pulling off his own bag, Alec took out his laptop and pulled up the file she'd given him. Information from the DeLucas. "This is a list of all public officials who are open to bribes. While not directly working for the DeLucas, we still need to watch out for them."

The chief leaned closer, sucking in a breath. "Christ. Where did this come from?"

320

"The DeLucas," Mia said, then explained how they had traded Adam for the information on that list.

"That is definitely something we need to deal with, but I think we need to focus on the DeLucas first," Agent McKenzie said. "Why don't we all go over these files tonight, meet again tomorrow?"

Agreeing to that plan, the four of them settled on the ground and prepared for a long night. As they left early the next morning, Agent McKenzie pulled Mia aside. "Can I ask you something?"

"Sure," Mia said, checking that Alec and Chief Alvarez were out of hearing distance.

"How did you know you could trust me?"

For a moment, Mia studied her face, weighed how much she should tell her. The answer was simple. "Donovan."

Agent McKenzie nodded, her mouth pressed firmly together. Mia watched her walk away, knowing the plan was fully in her hands now.

Twenty-Seven

THERE WERE ONLY A FEW hours remaining before the final piece of the plan got put into motion. Tonight, the DeLucas would go down.

But first, there was something Mia needed to do. Someone she needed to see.

Slipping through the dark, Mia made her way underground to the one place she'd felt at home in—well, ever. Donovan opened the door before she could, his face a mask of worry.

"Is everything all right?"

"We meet in two hours. But I—I had to see you."

Pulling her into his arms, Donovan circled them away from the door and simply held on. Soaking in his pure strength, Mia took deep breaths, holding his scent deep in her lungs.

"We've done everything we could, but I have no control over the plan anymore. It's terrifying."

Understanding, Donovan pulled away to look at her. "You're feeling anxious. So much is now out of your hands. You need to feel in control. Let me help you."

Taking her hand, he led Mia back through the hall. Passed by his office and into the small library. Selected a book and allowed the case to slide silently open. When the red room revealed itself, Mia sucked in a breath.

The last time she'd been in here had been by accident. In a daze of memories, she'd found the concealed room and inadvertently exposed the truth about who she was. Now, Donovan led her inside, taking both her hands in his. Kissed each knuckle gently and looked into her eyes. "Trust in me. Trust in yourself. Take the control."

Stepping away, Donovan removed his shirt and tossed it aside. Slid off his pants, his socks. Stood bare before her, no sense of self-consciousness. Before he lay on the bed, he gripped her face gently, kissing her slowly. Just as Mia began to sink into it, into him, he pulled away.

"Take control, Mia. Tell me what you want. Show me. Our pleasure is in your hands."

He lay down, waiting for her to move, to decide. With a deep breath, she stepped to the bed and rested a hand against the frame. "You trust me this much?"

"With my life."

Reaching out to stroke the strap of leather secured to the bedpost, Mia lifted it and wrapped it around Donovan's ankle. The action felt familiar, hazy. She no longer had complete control over her actions.

Selena directed Mia's movements, securing each strap as Donovan watched with hooded eyes. Though he'd introduced her to this form of intimacy on their trip to Europe, being in control now gave her an unfamiliar, powerful rush. Selena didn't attempt to take over, only hovered near the surface, supplying Mia with her memories of exploring this side of Donovan.

Mia walked to the wall, selecting a long, thin strap from the collection hanging there. Brought it over to Donovan's still form, teased along his thighs. Slapped against nerves with just a little bit of force, working her way across his skin with increasing amounts of pressure.

Watching his face, Mia remembered what it felt like to be on the receiving end. The bite of pain followed quickly by pleasure. Being worked into a fever pitch, over and over again, before allowed release.

Desire and passion filled her, fueled her. Each inward gasp, every deep moan from Donovan woke her own nerve endings, made her whole body come alive. Mia continued to tease and test until she could take it no more.

Moving onto the bed, she straddled Donovan and gazed down at him. His ruggedly handsome face, the day-old scruff she'd become rather fond of lining his jaw. His hooded eyes, dark and sensuous, watching her. Each delicious line and definition of muscle along his chest, his broad shoulders.

It was hers. He was hers. Held here, willingly, for her use. Licking her lips, Mia rose up and closed over him with an exhale of breath.

As they joined together, stars sparked behind her lids. Throwing her head back, Mia felt freer than she ever had, yet grounded at the same time. Donovan had become her world, her wings, her anchor. Everything.

She moved at her own pace, each delicious slide more frantic than the last. As Mia's body wound tight and hovered along the edge, she ripped the constraints from his wrists. She needed to feel his arms around her, holding, gripping tight.

Dropping to press against his chest, her mouth ravaged his in a desperate sort of frenzy. His hands gripped her hips, wrapped around her back. Held her so close she felt safe, protected. Her head lifted, and her eyes locked with his. And in that moment, she was no longer just Mia. Or Selena. She was both.

The two blended together so perfectly, so seamlessly. They moved with one mind, one thought. Looking deep into Donovan's eyes, they connected to him on a level Mia had never thought possible. She wasn't just one with Selena. She'd become one with Donovan.

The emotions running through her were heady, intoxicating. For a moment, they were floating, weightless. And then they were on a headlong dive of a free fall, soaring through the clouds as one. As they crashed back to earth, shattered against the ground, their limbs and hearts and minds a tangled mass, both shuddered and sighed and screamed to the heavens.

For several long moments, they panted in unison, willing their hearts to slow their frantic beat. Rising on shaky forearms, Mia looked down at Donovan, stunned. He returned her gaze with equal amounts of wonder.

With a palm, he brushed the edge of her cheek, running his thumb under her eye. For the first time, he wasn't just looking at Selena or Mia. He saw both.

"We—we're one," Mia mumbled, nearly incoherent.

"What do you mean?"

"Selena. She's—gone. But not gone. She's part of me, no longer just hovering there. I—I feel whole." Mia looked at him with dazed, shocked eyes. "Did you feel that? That moment we all connected, became one?"

"I did," he murmured, brushing her hair back. "It was incredible."

Stunned, Mia traced a thumb along Donovan's lower lip, soaking in every line of his face. "I love you. With all of my heart. You did this; you brought me together, made me whole. Your love mended everything that had broken inside me."

"You did it for yourself," he replied, brushing his lips against hers. "And I love you, all of you, with all my heart. You are my life, my breath."

Resting her forehead against his for just a moment, Mia sighed and said, "We have to do this. We have to finish it before we can truly be together."

"Then let's finish it," he said, gripping her face between his strong palms. "Let's finish it and live the rest of our lives."

With one last lingering kiss, they rose and began to dress. Each languorous movement belied their urgency. Walking into the next room, Mia watched as Donovan slipped the door closed. After tonight, there was every chance she wouldn't see that room again. Or this loft.

Donovan slid open a small arsenal, and they both loaded up with weapons. The DeLucas wouldn't go down easy, but they were prepared.

Together, Donovan and Mia left the loft and started down the stairs. Hand in hand, fully armed, they strode toward whatever this night had to offer.

Donovan and Mia split up in the tunnels with plans to meet later. She would have to check in with Agent McKenzie and the rest of the team first.

The operation had become a state-wide effort between the precincts and the FBI. With Mason and Ronnie creating a list of potential moles, Chief Alvarez and Agent McKenzie had managed to put together a team spanning every department in order to arrest all known DeLuca members in one night.

Agent McKenzie had taken the lead, and while they all gathered together in an abandoned warehouse, earpieces were passed around in order for instructions to be issued while they were all so spread out. She'd divided the team into several groups, each with their own leader that would report back to her while she would remain here to oversee all.

Each group had its own list to apprehend. Before morning, the majority—if not close to all—of the DeLucas and their lackeys would be behind bars.

While Agent McKenzie went over details with the whole group, Alec sidled up beside Mia. Leaning close, he asked, "Everything all right?"

"Yes," she said honestly. "We're taking down bad guys; why wouldn't it be?"

Quiet for a few minutes, he finally added, "You'd tell me if you had plans that didn't involve the team, wouldn't you?"

Guilt shot through her. Alec had been her closest and really only friend in the last several years. More than that, he was her partner. Their lives had depended on each other so often they'd lost track. And now, Mia had been lying to him. Unknowingly for years, but now, too, with full knowledge. "I'm in this one hundred percent, Alec. These bastards need to go down."

While she spoke the truth, Mia knew she'd left a lot out. Alec knew it too but seemed placated for the moment. She would miss him like crazy.

"Team Alpha, Beta," Agent McKenzie said, nodding toward Alec and Mia along with two members of the FBI they'd been paired with. Another four rounded out their backup. "You're good to go."

With a deep breath, Mia nodded and turned with her team. Agent Rogers took point, heading out the door followed closely by Agent Richards.

Alec gestured for Mia to go before him, and she stepped into the night. Her senses took in the cool, damp air blowing off the ocean, carrying the scent of salt and mist. The moon hung heavy above, casting its soft glow over them as they made their way to separate cars. The Beta team followed closely on their heels.

They'd gotten a tip that the four DeLuca brothers would be meeting together that night. They were the first target. Without their guidance, the rest of the association would crumble. If they started by arresting lower members, word would make its way through the ranks and allow the four brothers to hide.

They would cut the head off the snake, then quickly scrape up the pieces.

Alec drove to the meeting spot in silence. They both knew their roles, the endgame. They had nothing more to say about the mission.

In Mia's ear, Agent McKenzie spoke with Agent Rogers, waiting to send out the remaining teams until they'd completed their mission. They were only minutes away now.

"Alec, whatever happens tonight—I want you to know that I love you and appreciate everything you've ever done for me. You've been my best friend and the best partner I ever could have asked for."

"Mia, you're talking like you don't expect to make it out of this."

Mia looked directly at him, and he risked a glance over. He could see it in her eyes, the determination there to do whatever it took to take out these creeps. That thought reminded her of what they always called the DeLucas between the two of them, and it made her smile wistfully.

Crème-de-la-creeps.

"If I don't, I just thought you should know those things."

"Jesus, you're scaring me," he muttered. "But you know what? Screw it. I love you, too. Not in the romantic sense, even though for a long time I thought it could be. You're my best friend, too, and damn it, I won't lose you to these jerk-wads."

"Jeez, Alec, watch your language." Mia laughed to lighten the moment. "You might insult them to death with terms like jerk-wads."

"You're not as funny as you think you are," he said with an answering smirk.

"Funny enough. Park over here, kill the lights."

"Yes, Mom," he replied playfully, though he followed her directions.

They left the vehicle silently, not bothering to close the doors. They'd be back with the cuffs on the DeLucas—or they wouldn't be back at all.

Agent Rogers spoke in their ear, and Alec took over responding. They edged up to a door, with Rogers and Richards opposite. The Beta team had arrived, watching the windows for anyone trying to escape.

"On three," Rogers said into their earpieces. "One, two..."

They burst through the doors, calling out their identification and for all activity to cease. In the main room, they found the four brothers surrounding crates of guns, along with several of their next-highest ranked people—a veritable bad-guy convention.

"On the ground, now! Hands on the back of your heads!"

Rogers and Richards continued to call out while Ricky sought Mia out, staring through her mask as if he could shoot daggers with his gaze alone. Betrayal stamped into every feature as she trained her gun directly at his heart.

With a snarl, he turned, gripped one of his men, and flung him into Mia's path before racing toward an exit. Without thinking, she sprang after him, not bothering to waste her breath shouting for him to stop.

Instead of trying for the doors or a window, Ricky hit stairs and retreated to the basement level. Mia followed, ignoring the musky wet and darkness that instantly enveloped her. As he ran, Ricky grabbed anything available—broken chairs, empty boxes, abandoned pipes—and tossed them in her way. Running, jumping, and dodging over flying debris, Mia came within a foot and went for the tackle.

Managing to wrap her arms around his legs, Ricky and Mia tumbled and rolled, smashing against a table and sending more boxes flying. They both struggled to their feet—Ricky gripping a pipe for defense, Mia with a gun in her hands.

"Give it up, Ricky," she taunted, taking a minuscule step forward. "We've got you."

"You can arrest me all you want. I won't spend a night in jail, and you know it."

Letting out a low chuckle, she looked at him with pity. "You have no idea what's going on right now, do you? Every single one of your moles is being detained. Your brothers upstairs are being hauled into the back of cars as we speak. All throughout the city, hell, the whole state, your lackeys are being systematically rounded up. It's over, Ricky. You lost."

"You little bitch," he said with a snarl. "I should have killed you when I had the chance."

"You're right." Mia shrugged. "You should have. Pity's the fool."

"You won't take me alive."

"Maybe I won't. But you're forgetting one thing."

"Oh yeah? What's that?"

Mia smiled. "I still have a partner."

Behind him, Donovan rose up, trained a gun against his temple. "Hi there, Ricky."

"What? No! She's a cop! How are you working together?"

"Here's the thing," Donovan answered conversationally. "You're under arrest. Come willingly, or I will force you."

His eyes wild, Ricky looked between Donovan and Mia, trying for all sense and logic in the world to match what was happening. In a last-ditch effort, he turned, swung the pipe toward Donovan. Ducking effortlessly, Donovan came up to hit the butt of his gun against the base of Ricky's skull. The larger man went down but struggled to stay awake.

They were up against the wall, Mia standing several feet away with her gun trained on Ricky. His hand shot out, fought for control over a slim, silver device. For a suspended moment in time, Mia's eyes met Donovan's. A wealth of emotion passed between them as she heard shouts from above. Alec's voice, calling for her. Donovan's dark eyes filled with terror as they both realized the truth of the situation.

They'd been out-maneuvered. Ricky's thumb smashed down on the device, and the first rumble of an explosion rocked the very foundation of the building.

Locking her eyes onto Donovan's, Mia mouthed her final words to him.

I love you.

Twenty-Eight

EARS RINGING IN THE AFTERMATH of the explosion, Donovan lifted his head to find Ricky's unconscious body just feet away. The whole middle of the basement had been torn away; all that remained was an empty, blistering shell.

Blinking into the dust-filled air, Donovan caught sight of Alec. He'd been close—too close—on the stairs leading down to the basement. Struggling to his feet, Donovan stared at the destruction before him, an emptiness rising up and taking control as he realized the truth of the situation.

Mia was gone.

Rage filled him, hot and deep. Finding Ricky's prone form, Donovan straddled the unconscious man and pounded his fists against Ricky's skull.

"What have you done? You've killed her. You bastard!" Screams of rage, of grief, ripped from his very soul. Ricky's blood covered his fists, stained his arms, and splattered against his face as Donovan continued to strike, to seek vengeance. Hands attempted to pull him away, but at that point, Donovan was too far gone to respond.

"Donovan, enough! He'll pay, but he needs to be alive to do it."

Alec's voice finally cut through the red haze, tempering Donovan's rage just a fraction. Something heavy pressed against his chest, choked up through his throat. Hot tears leaked from his eyes and spread down his cheeks.

Mia was gone.

Shaking with the wash of emotions running through him, Donovan sought Alec through the bite of tears and blood and latched onto him. "He's killed her."

Thick smoke filled the lower level, leftover flames licking along the ceiling, leaving them no room for escape.

No. Death would be too easy an out for the bastard that lay bloody and broken at his feet.

"We need to get him out of here. He needs to pay," Donovan said lowly. Instead of arguing, even through his own grief, Alec nodded and bent to haul up Ricky's sorry ass. They each took a shoulder and fought through the wreckage to the stairs that remained barely intact.

Struggling through the smoke and flames to the top level, Alec and Donovan, with the unconscious Ricky between them, made their way outside. The first deep breath of the fresh air left Donovan spluttering and choking against his smoke-filled lungs.

Sinking to his knees, Donovan took a moment to catch his breath, to clear his face. Now wasn't the time for tears, for mourning. This was the time for vengeance.

Without Donovan's help to support Ricky's weight, Alec dropped him to the ground. With renewed strength Donovan stood, glaring down at the prone man. The animal inside him that had been unleashed begged to rip and tear, but something deeper kicked in, and he pulled a pair of cuffs from his back pocket. Snapping them in place over Ricky's wrists, Donovan sneered down at him and announced, "You're under arrest, asshole."

With sudden finality, Donovan's legs gave out, and he collapsed to the ground. Around him, lights and sirens sounded off, ambulance and fire surrounding the building and working to make sure everyone was clear. With dim awareness, Donovan watched Alec speaking to other officers and an FBI agent. The agent with light hair and blue eyes approached and knelt before Donovan. He spoke, though his words were hazy.

"Donovan?"

Confirming his identity, Donovan supposed. Nodding, he held out his wrists, recognizing what would happen next.

With cuffs around his own wrists, paramedics placed Donovan on a stretcher after Ricky and hauled them each into their own waiting ambulance.

△ △ △

A COMBINATION OF SMOKE INHALATION, exhaustion, and morphine knocked Donovan unconscious for several hours. When he came to again, he felt the pain in his body, but it became immediately overshadowed by a deeper, all-consuming ache.

Mia was gone.

Struggling against the restraints holding him down, fighting against the haze of his own mind, Donovan settled when he heard someone speak close to his ear.

"It's all right, you're in a hospital. Steady your breath, that's the way. Nice, slow, even breaths." The woman's voice, though unfamiliar, oozed friendliness. Attempting to follow her direction, Donovan realized he'd been fitted with oxygen and briefly wondered how much smoke he'd inhaled. When his lashes finally managed to lift, Donovan took in the kind face of the nurse tending him. "There you are. Welcome back."

"Did I die, then?" Donovan mumbled through the mask. She must have understood him because she chuckled lightly while deftly removing the breathing apparatus.

"Not dead, just unconscious. How do you feel?"

"Like I swallowed a bunch of smoke."

Smiling again, she said, "I'll notify the agent that you're awake."

When Donovan turned his head to watch her walk out the door, he saw two officers standing guard. After a few minutes, a new face appeared, but the nurse didn't return.

Agent McKenzie looked none worse for the wear. She stood beside him with a tight smile.

"Merissa."

"Donovan. You look like hell."

Wheezing out a laugh, Donovan managed to answer, "Thanks."

"What the hell, Donovan."

"Is that an official question?"

"This isn't an official conversation."

Letting out a breath, Donovan made to move his hands before remembering they remained cuffed to the bed. Raising an eyebrow, he asked, "Can you do something about this?"

"That depends."

"On what?"

"On whom I'm speaking to."

Silence reigned between them. It was time to come clean—for once and for all.

"My name is Donovan O'Shea. I'm an undercover agent for the FBI."

Agent McKenzie and Donovan locked gazes. Donovan waited, knowing she had a lot to say. "This is going to be a tough pill to swallow," Agent McKenzie finally answered. "You went off the rails, Donovan. For six years."

"I did my job."

"Your job included reporting to your superior officer. Me."

Though her tone hadn't changed, Donovan still winced at the reprimand. She certainly hadn't lost her knack for scolding.

"Selena had become suspicious. She watched my every move. If I hadn't gone deep, I would have been caught. What choice would you have had me make?"

"Telling me what you were doing before you did," Merissa replied drily. Then, letting out a sigh, she unhooked keys from her belt and loosened the cuffs from his wrists. "You're still under guard. And it won't be up to me what happens to you, but, for what it's worth, I believe you're still a good man. You've done a lot of bad things, Donovan, but underneath it all, you're still you."

Not knowing what to say, Donovan simply reached across the scant distance between them to squeeze her hand. "Thank you."

"Tell me about Selena."

Eyes dropping to his lap, Donovan said, "She's dead."

Merissa paused, and for a moment, he thought she might console him. She didn't. "Are you certain?"

"Ricky DeLuca killed her."

"And Mia Gonzalez."

The quick bite of pain couldn't be hidden quick enough. "And Mia Gonzalez."

"You nearly beat him to death, Donovan. He's still in ICU."

"He deserved worse."

"What exactly was your relationship with Selena? And Mia?"

Meeting her eyes, Donovan took a deep breath and answered. "Selena and I became intimate. She was attracted to me, and I used that to remain close to her. When Mia first came to me, and I thought she was Selena, I acted accordingly. But then her true personality came out, and I realized that even if Selena had had memory loss like Mia claimed, it wouldn't have changed who she was at the base. Selena could be mean, cruel. She enjoyed it. Mia was a good person, and I cared for her. That's all. When the truth came out, we decided to work together to bring down the real threat—the DeLucas. She paid with her life.

"Now, a question for you. Why didn't you tell Mia the truth about me before you sent her in?"

Agent McKenzie studied Donovan a long time. His explanation bordered on truth, as he'd always found the best, most believable lies were rooted in fact. Eventually, she nodded, placing a hand against his forearm. "To answer your question, it was deemed unnecessary by people far above me. They saw you as a traitor, a deserter. The fact that you started out as a cop didn't matter to the powers that be. For what it's worth, I didn't agree. But I had to follow orders." Checking her watch, Merissa squeezed her hand gently before releasing his arm. "You should rest. We'll need an official debrief once you're cleared to be released."

After she left, Donovan stared vacantly at the ceiling for a long time. He felt empty, broken. Life as he'd known it had come to a bitter, abrupt end. What did he do now?

Closing his eyes, Donovan welcomed sleep. Tomorrow would be a long day.

△ △ △

DONOVAN'S GUARDS ESCORTED HIM TO the central precinct, where Chief Alvarez, Agent McKenzie, her boss Agent Reynolds, and the Police Commissioner all waited. Once seated in interrogation, he met the solemn gaze of each in turn before settling on Merissa. Donovan had a feeling she would be leading the questions.

"Agent O'Shea, this conversation will be recorded. Please state your name for the record."

"Donovan O'Shea."

"To start, why don't you tell us in your own words what happened from the night of November tenth, 2012 to now?"

Settling in for a long conversation, Donovan recapped what he'd told Agent McKenzie in the hospital—how Selena had become suspicious, and he felt the best way to infiltrate was to cut off all communication with her and the bureau.

November tenth had been the last time he'd spoken to Merissa before yesterday. After their brief meeting that same night, Selena had almost taken a dive down an empty elevator shaft.

Saving her had been instinct and had changed their relationship irrevocably. Almost losing her had made Donovan realize how much he wanted her.

Not long after that night, Donovan admitted the truth to Selena and her to him.

Donovan, that he had been sent undercover to shut down her operation. Selena, that the reason he only saw her at night was because she only existed when Mia Gonzalez went to sleep.

At first, it had been an unbelievable story. He'd spent many weeks following Mia during the day, even interacted with her once or twice to see if there would be any flicker of recognition. Then, watching her sneak out at night as a new person, he finally believed.

And he also fell for both women. Long before he'd found Mia in that dank cell, he'd fallen for her. They were separate entities to him, yet the same. Donovan knew he would do anything for them, to be with them.

When Mia originally began investigating him—which he believed Selena had something to do with, subconsciously—and Selena's crazy plan to get Mia undercover came out, Donovan jumped in with both feet. Selfish of him, really. He wanted to be with her, with both of them, all the time. He hated watching Mia laughing with Alec. Dating losers that she felt no connection to. Some part of her, no matter how buried deep, must have known Donovan waited for her.

But now...

The four people in the room with Donovan began peppering him with questions. He went into great detail about how the business ran and how he had shut it down. Bruce and the rest of the security team had done that for him in a matter of hours. They'd also been significantly compensated, along with every person involved. They'd all known this wouldn't last forever and that one day they might need to disappear.

Selena and Donovan had made sure they would have enough money to do so.

Hours later, Agent Reynolds asked Donovan what he would like to do now. "Retire," Donovan said with the look of a man defeated. "I'm done."

Agent Reynolds and the Police Commissioner glanced at each other and shared a nod. When Agent Reynolds spoke again, Donovan felt a major weight lift off his shoulders. "You've been cleared of all charges against you. In exchange for your testimony against the DeLucas, you will be granted immunity."

This was what they'd been hoping for when Mia and Donovan had first put this plan together. The brief moment of celebration quickly dampened, thinking of her. "I'd be happy to testify."

"You're free to leave," Merissa said. "We'll provide a safe house for you to live in until the trial. After that, you'll be on your own."

Nodding, Donovan stood and shook the hands of everyone in the room before being escorted to his new home.

THE TRIAL RAN LONG AND hard. When the explosion site had been combed through, they found Mia's body had been burnt beyond recognition. The only surviving objects had been her badge and gun. Reliving the events of that night nearly did Donovan in but knowing the DeLuca family had finally been brought to justice provided a little comfort.

Ricky had recovered, though it had been touch-and-go for several days. Seeing him across the courtroom filled Donovan with hot rage, and it took all his willpower not to jump over the table and finish the job. Life in prison would have to suffice.

Once the verdict had been reached—several lifetimes in prison for the brothers and their top men—Donovan made one final trip into the central precinct. Walking into the station only served to remind him of Mia, but he fought through it in order to say his goodbyes.

The first person Donovan saw came as no surprise. Mason had opted to continue working for the police after he and Ronnie had pieced together everyone involved with the DeLucas. Though he'd been well compensated when Selena's company shut down, Donovan knew the younger man needed a structured environment to flourish. He'd now be putting his extensive talents to the good.

After saying his goodbye to Mason, Donovan stopped in to see Chief Alvarez. Deep lines etched into his face were evidence of the ordeal he'd been through the last year and a half. Donovan couldn't imagine the position he'd been in—not only finding out nearly a fifth of his department had been in the DeLucas' pocket but then losing a detective the way he'd lost Mia---Donovan felt that pain, too.

Stepping into the office, he gestured for Donovan to take a seat. The door closed; they measured each other before the chief spoke. "What will you do now?"

Donovan had had a year and a half to think of an answer to that question. "The FBI decided to compensate me for the last seven years, so I thought I'd do some traveling. I spent some time in Europe while undercover but didn't really get to play tourist."

"I can't imagine the toll this has all taken on you. I know you're set to retire from the bureau, but if you're ever in need of a job, we'd be happy to have you."

"Thank you," Donovan replied. "That means a lot."

"We've been building cases against the list of public officials you gave us. This city will have a fresh start, thanks to you."

"And Mia."

"And Mia," he agreed.

Standing, they shook hands. "The best of luck to you, Donovan."

"And to you, Chief Alvarez."

One person remained for Donovan to face. A man who had been through too much in the crazy scheme that he and Selena had put together. He'd lost his friend, his partner—and, more than that, Donovan knew how much he cared over and above those things, even when the feelings weren't returned.

As he moved through the room, Alec stepped into Donovan's line of sight. They faced off, only a foot between them. Alec's arms were crossed against his chest, his glare shooting daggers.

"Alec." Donovan nodded in greeting, not wanting this animosity between them.

"Donovan," he replied through clenched teeth.

"I'm really sorry about Mia," Donovan said, knowing that words in such a time meant nothing.

"Did you love her?" Alec asked.

Donovan winced, taking a quick look around to be sure they were alone. "More than my own life," he responded with such honesty it softened the look on Alec's face.

After another long moment, Alec nodded once and extended a hand. "Enjoy retirement."

When Donovan's hand met his, he felt the slight crunch of a folded-up piece of paper being transferred from palm to palm. Donovan's eyebrows drew together, but before he could look at what the paper said or ask Alec about it, the detective began to walk away. Donovan watched him for a moment before moving to the elevator.

Pressing the button for the ground floor, Donovan carefully unfolded the small note and read what Mia's former partner had written. His lips twitched at Alec's cleverness, and though Donovan should have been worried, he knew their secret would be safe with a man like Alec.

Take care of her, or I'll hunt you down.

Twenty-Nine

DONOVAN AND MIA SQUARED OFF in the loft. When she'd laid out the plan, she knew he'd rail against it. But what other viable choice did they have? "We have to fake my death."

"Do you have any idea how difficult that is?" he asked. "People try and fail all the time."

"Other people don't have the resources we do. We use an explosion. Fake some dental records. How hard can it be?" The incredulous look Donovan gave her was almost comical. Pushing on, she added, "You'll be able to reveal yourself when it's over. Place all the blame on me—on Selena. You can make the final arrest, give them your testimony. You know that's how it'll work."

"Agent McKenzie will see right through me."

"Maybe. But I also think she'll forgive you."

Remembering Donovan had been an undercover agent in the first place had been a shock, but the information had quickly worked itself into the plan Selena and Mia came up with.

"If—and that's a big if—*if* we consider this, we would need a body, Mason's help, and a whole lot of luck." He began pacing, working through the details in his mind. Mia watched silently, knowing this was the only way. Donovan would see that eventually. "It's too dangerous." He finally stopped the manic pace and spoke directly to her. "I can't risk losing you again."

"Donovan." One word, his name, was enough to have him stilling completely. Standing, Mia approached him, placing her hands against his crossed forearms. "It's the only way. We have to. We need to rid the world of the DeLucas."

Logic finally settled over his features as he realized the truth of the matter. If she remained alive, they could never be together. "I'll contact Mason. He can help us with the dental records and with pinpointing who's working with the DeLucas, inside the police and out. He's also infiltrated the DeLucas in the past, so it won't be odd for him to do it again."

"Why?" Mia asked sharply.

"Because we're going to have to create a controlled explosion, where one of the DeLucas will be held accountable for your death. Which means we need the DeLucas to believe setting explosives was their idea."

"It would also be helpful to know where and when they will be. To coordinate that many arrests, we'll need an inside man."

"Exactly. I'm still not one hundred percent on this, Mia. Faking your death is risky in many ways. It could go wrong, in many ways."

Reaching out, Mia clasped her hands with his. "But it'll be worth it."

Resting his forehead briefly against hers, Donovan sighed. "Yes. It will be worth it."

"You'll also need to contact Olivia Munich," Mia said, pulling away. She'd met Olivia in England—not only did Olivia control their finances, but they also helped her ship antiquities from Egypt to the States. "We'll need enough liquid to pay our employees as we shut down, and then the rest for us to live off."

"She can help you set up a new identity," he added. "She'd be willing."

"Perfect. Make the calls, start Exodus. I need to turn myself in at the station. You need to remain hidden. I'll come find you tomorrow night."

"Mia." Donovan stopped her with a hand on her arm as she turned to leave. "I love you. Be safe."

Giving in, she collapsed into his embrace and met his mouth with hers. "I love you, too."

△ △ △

DONOVAN AND MIA LAY TOGETHER, their hearts slowing their frantic beat, his ankles still secured to the bedpost. Soon, she would move, release him. Soon, they would both have to dress and face whatever this night would bring.

Selena and Mia were finally one. Finally whole.

Resting her forehead against his for just a moment, Mia sighed and said, "We have to do this. We have to finish it before we can be together."

"Then let's finish it," he said, gripping her face between his strong palms. "Let's finish it and live the rest of our lives."

Mia rolled to the side, leg and arm still wrapped around his hard form. "Mason had no trouble?"

"He's with the DeLucas as we speak. He convinced them they needed a failsafe. The brothers know about the escape route. At least one of them will run."

"Good." Mia breathed out. "That's good. And you know if Mason is caught, arrested, Alec will make sure he's cleared."

"I know. Alec is a good man. Mason marked the floor with a white X where you need to be in order for this to work. Mia." Donovan said her name sternly, framed her face with his palms. "There's still a chance it won't work. Anything and everything could go wrong. Please, please be safe."

"I will do everything in my power to be with you. Trust in that."

"I do," he murmured. "I do."

With one last lingering kiss, they rose, dressed slowly. Mia caught sight of herself in a mirror beside the door. For a moment, she barely recognized the woman reflected back. Her amber eyes were bright, steady. And the shape of her jaw looked familiar, her hair the same.

And yet, she looked at a wholly new, different person—a woman with the cocky confidence of Selena and the steadfast ambition of Mia. For just a moment, Mia studied that new person, memorized her.

And then let her go.

Walking into the next room, she watched as Donovan slipped the door closed. After tonight, she wouldn't see that room again—or this loft.

△ △ △

AFTER MEETING WITH THE GROUP who would arrest all known members of the DeLuca family, Mia found herself quietly riding with Alec. She wanted to say goodbye to him, but she didn't want to alert him to her plan. This would be hard enough as it was. But she couldn't stay silent.

"Alec, whatever happens tonight—I want you to know that I love you and appreciate everything you've ever done for me. You've been my best friend and the best partner I ever could have asked for."

"Mia, you're talking like you don't expect to make it out of this."

"If I don't, I just thought you should know those things."

"Jesus, you're scaring me," he muttered. "But you know what? Screw it. I love you, too. Not in the romantic sense, even though for a long time I thought it could be. You're my best friend, too, and damn it, I won't lose you to these jerk-wads."

"Jeez, Alec, watch your language." Mia laughed to lighten the moment. "You might insult them to death with terms like jerk-wads."

"You're not as funny as you think you are," he said with a smirk.

Her heart lightened, knowing they'd said what they needed to say, and left it on a light note. It was the only gift she could give him.

When they entered the building, Ricky took the bait and fled. After making sure Alec and the rest of the team were occupied with their own targets, Mia ran after him.

Donovan had already entered through her escape route, placed the decoy body, and waited in the shadows for her to appear. After she tackled Ricky and sent them both flying, Mia spotted Donovan approaching Ricky from behind. Though she squared off with Ricky, Mia used her peripherals to spot the white X and stood exactly center.

While Donovan and Ricky grappled for control over the detonator, Mia dropped her weapon's belt and badge. They would be found in the wreckage.

When Ricky pressed down on the button, she met Donovan's eyes, mouthed three little words.

I love you.

And the first explosion dropped her under the basement, where she immediately began to run. The second explosion sounded seconds later, Mason having built in a delay in order to give her time to get clear.

As soon as she made it into the same tunnels they'd connected all their businesses to, the third and final explosion rocked the ground, closed off all access to the escape route.

Mia sprinted forward without looking back.

△ △ △

PRESSING HER HEELS AGAINST THE sturdy Friesian horse, Mia felt his strong muscles bunch and coil beneath her legs as he gave up the easy trot and burst into a full gallop. With long blonde locks flying in the sudden wind, Mia laughed and leaned forward, urging him faster.

When they reached the top of the plateau, the breathtaking sight of deep blue waves crashing against the rocks had her slowing the eager three-year-old she'd found just a month ago.

"Whoa, Phillippe," Mia called out, worried about the uneven ground. Once he settled into a slower rhythm, she relaxed the reins and let him lead.

Together they traversed the cliff overlooking the bay of Mont Saint-Michel, the cool breeze sending mist to dew along her skin. For the first time in her life, Mia felt light, buoyant. Only one thing remained missing: Donovan.

Eighteen months ago, she'd escaped the explosion and hopped on their private plane to England, where Olivia Munich took Mia under her wing. Together they cleared out the accounts—what remained after paying out all the employees—and secured her new identification.

For the month she'd stayed with her, Mia had become attached to the horses in Olivia's stables. With nothing else to do, she helped groom and muck out the stalls, and Olivia's head trainer taught Mia to ride. He'd said she was a natural.

Leaving Olivia's home, saying goodbye to the majestic creatures Mia had come to know so well, had been almost as difficult as walking away from Donovan and Alec. If all went well, she'd see Donovan again. But Alec?

Mia knew he'd be all right. He had to be.

The cliff dipped down and back up again, and Phillippe suddenly knew the way home. The moderately-sized cottage overlooked the sea, the stonework and gorgeous gardens taking her breath away as it did each time she saw it. The yard stretched out to the barn, the stables she'd had built immediately upon moving in.

The electricity came from solar panels and the water from a well. Apart from an encrypted laptop, Mia kept no technology on the premises. Donovan and Mia wanted to live off the grid as much as possible.

Dismounting Phillippe just outside the stables, Mia walked him inside next to Belle, the beautiful Andalusian she'd acquired first. When they reached his stall, a dark figure stepped out of Belle's enclosure, and her heart stopped. As her eyes adjusted, it pounded out one hard beat before taking off at a faster gallop than even Phillippe was capable of.

"Donovan," Mia breathed out, shock holding her still.

He stepped from the shadows, took in her new look with a critical eye. "Blondes have more fun."

"So I hear. Oh my God, how are you? Tell me everything. Wait, no, I need..." Before she could finish, he marched over and his mouth crushed down on hers. They stumbled back, and Mia managed to loop Phillippe's rein around a pole before her entire world went up in flames.

Pulling back too soon, Donovan wrapped a finger around Mia's lighter hair. "I like it."

"I'm glad."

"I love you so, so much."

"I love you, too."

He smiled, and suddenly her world righted itself. When his mouth closed over hers again, Mia's heart settled, and she knew she was home.

She'd finally found someone more important to her than her work, than her life itself. She'd found her heart, her soul. Her very reason for living.

She'd found Donovan.

Dear Reader,

Thank you for reading Catching Shadows!

If you enjoyed Catching Shadows, please leave a review where you purchased this book. Reviews are the lifeblood for Indie Authors like me!

You can keep up-to-date by following me on Facebook or Instagram @AnaBanNovels or by going to the website, www.anabannovels.com

Thanks again, and happy reading!

Always,

Ana

Other Books by Ana Ban

The Parker Grey Series

Young Adult/Crime Novels recommended for ages 13+

Abstraction; A Parker Grey Novel (Book 1)

Backfire; A Parker Grey Novel (Book 2)

Coercion; A Parker Grey Novel (Book 3)

Deception; A Parker Grey Novel (Book 4)

Dubious Endeavors; A Parker Grey Novella (Book 5)

Exposed; A Parker Grey Novel (Book 6)

Firestarter; A Parker Grey Novel (Book 7)

The Gifted Series

Paranormal Romance Novels recommended for ages 18+

Allure of Home: Book 1 of The Gifted Series

Immaculate: Book 2 of The Gifted Series

Night Shift: Book 3 of The Gifted Series

Stowaway: Book 4 of The Gifted Series

Reservation: Book 5 of The Gifted Series

Shadowed Soul: Book 6 of The Gifted Series

Vows at Dusk: Book 7 of The Gifted Series (with special bonus novella *After Dusk!*)

Dark Omens: Book 8 of The Gifted Series

By the Light of the Moon: Book 9 of The Gifted Series

Seeking Redemption: Book 10 of The Gifted Series

Shelter of Smoke: Book 11 of The Gifted Series (available October 19, 2021)

Tangled Threads: Book 12 of The Gifted Series (available December 14, 2021)

Catching Shadows
Formerly:
The Mirror Trilogy

Crime/Police Procedural Novels recommended for ages 18+
Infiltration: Book 1 of The Mirror Trilogy
Split: Book 2 of The Mirror Trilogy
Wakening: Book 3 of The Mirror Trilogy

The Strangers Saga
Murder Mystery Romance Novels recommended for ages 18+
The Strangers Saga: Baton Rouge: Book One
Books Two-Five (available soon)

Made in the USA
Monee, IL
17 February 2022